BAND IN THE WIND
A NOVEL

Print 978-1-7327468-0-0
eBook 978-1-7327468-1-7

This is a work of fiction.

Printed in the USA.

Cover Design and Interior Format

© **KILLION**
THE
GROUP INC.

BAND
IN THE WIND

A NOVEL

William John Rostron

For Marilyn

(My real life Maria)

"We were living lives of passion,
Never wanting to go slow,
Never worrying 'bout tomorrow
Never knowing which way to go.

We were dancing,
We were dancing,
On the other side of the wind."

"Dancing on the Other Side of the Wind"
- Chris Delaney and the Brotherhood Blues Band

PROLOGUE

"Night Moves"
- Bob Seger

Key West, Florida – February 14, 1990

THE FULL MOON REFLECTED OFF the calm sea and illu-
minated the white coral sand beneath his feet. Daylight hours
would find this same stretch of beach crowded with vacationing
swimmers escaping the winter temperatures of the North. However, the nighttime belonged to the drunken and disenchanted.
This was where Padre did most of his business. He sought out
those that the local residents referred to simply as the "Key-
wasted." These were lost souls who had come to Key West for a
variety of reasons and stayed too long. Looking for paradise, they
had descended into hell.

Nightly, he roamed these outlying areas in search of the for-
saken. He knew that most would not listen to his message of
sobriety; he had to be satisfied with merely making sure that
they physically survived another day. He offered them a helping
hand home or some orange juice to help diminish the predictable
hangover. If he couldn't save their souls, perhaps he could keep
their bodies going long enough to be a part of their ultimate
redemption.

As he moved along the water's edge, he realized that this had been a very slow night. Was that a good thing? Did that mean on this night fewer people had destroyed their brain cells with drugs and alcohol than usual? Or were they still haunting the bars of Duval Street and would eventually find their way here to sleep off their overindulgence?

It was then he spotted his first sign of life, a single worn sandal and within a five-yard distance, its partner. He had followed this path many a night and often there was someone in need at the end. On most nights, he would find that someone within fifty yards of his initial sighting, but not tonight. He walked along the water's edge looking for clues. He knew he could not continue much longer; he had the responsibilities of his day job that needed to be taken care of very soon. He would allow himself just five more minutes. It was then he saw it.

An incoming tide was just about to drench a composition book at the water's edge. How long had it been just out of the reach of the salty waters and how much longer would it remain so? Picking it up, he noticed that he had not come a moment too soon. Some of the writing had already started to suffer the ill effects of the saltwater spray. He looked at the cover.

Journal of Johnny Cipp

Padre knew the name, and he knew this journal. He had encouraged Johnny to write it and had been by his side eight months earlier when Johnny had penned his first entry. It had helped Johnny to find his way back. At least, that was what Padre had thought until he now opened the book.

A Bic pen acted as a bookmark for the last written words in this tome. Padre began to read the partially smeared scribble that covered the page. His hands shook as he read Johnny's final thoughts. He now knew that his night could not end until he found his friend – if it was not already too late.

PART
1

"When I Was Young"

– The Animals

1

Journal of Johnny Cipp

Entry #1 – August 1989

"Where Have All the Good Times Gone"
- *The Kinks*

I SCREWED UP ... and I am screwed up. That is my motivation for writing in this damn notebook. How is that for a start?

The world as I knew it ended twenty-two years ago. All the joy and hope of my youth vanished in a matter of moments. Since then I have been consumed with guilt and fear. I haven't dealt with these feelings very well. I have not only physically hidden from the outside world, but I've also hidden from my own self-loathing in an ever-deepening shell of drugs and despair. A few months ago, there was a crack in that coating of darkness. I finally wanted to escape. I wanted to live again. I wanted to accomplish something in my life so that the sacrifices made for me over two decades ago would not have been in vain.

Padre has helped that to happen. I didn't get the message right away, but eventually, he gave me something that I had long lived without . . . hope. It might be too much for me to find happiness, but finding peace within myself might just be enough. He encouraged me to write this journal. Perhaps, if I relived those moments that had changed my life and led to my destruction, I could free myself of the guilt I have held inside.

I decided to listen to him. At this point in my life, I haven't done so well with the decisions I have made on my own. So why not listen to someone else? I know that my story will take me places I don't want to go. I know there will be a shitload of pain. Hopefully, I will survive.

The twists and turns of my life seem absurd, yet they all led me to where I am today. I know I need to start at the beginning. I need to go back to my oldest memories and work my way forward. I need to know when I became the person who made the mistakes that cost so many people their lives. Was it blind ambition? Was it love? Or was it the music? My ambition and the love of my life are now long gone. Yet, the music lives on within me. It is still a part of me. I guess that is why I've decided to give a musical title to every entry in this journal.

Somewhere along the line, I developed this tendency to think there was a song for every moment of my life. It became an inside joke between the world and me. I could find a title or a phrase to represent every event that I lived through. Recently, I heard a song that repeated the line, "Music is the doctor, makes you feel like you want to." It gave a name to this imaginary character who seemed to always be there with the right song for every occasion in my life. I call him the Music Doctor.

While it was true that music always did make me feel, it just wasn't always how I "wanted to." Music is what lifted up my hopes and gave me the feeling that all would be well. It is also what destroyed me. It has led me to places where no human being should go, and at times, it left me there to die. Yet, all these years later, music remains my only companion in the path I've taken. It is only logical then that I end this very first entry with a fitting musical reference.

"Those were the best days of my life." They really were. And just like the words in the Bryan Adams' song "The Summer of '69," I did buy my first six-string at a five-and-dime, and I did play it until my fingers bled. And we did have a band, and we did try real hard. And summer really did seem to last forever.

However, that's where my story diverges from the song. My tale occurred in the summer of 1967 instead of 1969, a small point. Furthermore, unlike the band in his song, we *were* going to go real far. Yet, in the end, even that success meant nothing.

No, the story of *my* band took a much different turn. Unlike the characters in the song, *my* Jimmy didn't quit, and *my* Joey didn't get married. In my life, they died. In fact, except for me, they all died. And I have never told the story before.

Entry #2

"The Eyes of a Child"
- The Moody Blues

I was a warrior. I was a champion. I was a hero. *I was eight!* At that young age, I lived a fantasy existence. In the lonely reaches of my attic bedroom, I vanquished evil with my imagination. I saw heroes on the big and little screens of my youth and I wanted to be them.

I became Davy Crockett valiantly defending the Alamo. I swung my toy rifle to ward off the Mexican army threatening to take over my bed. After being stabbed by their bayonets, I collapsed into melodramatic death throes. I was Errol Flynn leading *The Charge of the Light Brigade* into the Valley of Death. Due to space limitations, my valley was only eight feet long, but my charge was no less dramatic. As *Gung Din*, I saved the British army and then fell in a death swoon from the top of my headboard to my waiting bed. I died many dramatic deaths while standing up for what was right.

None of it was real. When I ventured from my seclusion, evil always seemed to win. In my real neighborhood, violence and drugs seemed to be the norm. I grew up quickly and decided very early that I needed to escape. The truth is hard to admit. Though I died those many heroic deaths within the confines of my room, I was not as brave in my real existence as the characters that I mimicked in my solitude. If I had, perhaps, my friends would still be alive.

Entry #3

"Keepin' the Faith"
-Billy Joel

If I ever meet Billy Joel, I am going to tell him to cut the crap. What the hell would a Long Island boy know about city life? Though born in the Bronx, he grew up in Hicksville in a Levitt house. You can't get any more suburban than that, yet there he was presuming to write about my life in Queens. I have to admit that he got some of the details right in his song, "Keepin' the Faith." I actually did wear Flagg Brothers shoes with the Cuban heels, a pompadour, and iridescent socks. Not to be picky, Billy, but we always matched the iridescent socks to the same color iridescent *tie*, not a shirt. I braved the wilds of South Jamaica to go to *my* Flagg Brothers, while he was probably going to some nice store in a Hicksville mall to get his Cuban heels. Then comes my real dispute with the star—the stuff that I really cared about. I'm sorry, Mr. Joel, you know squat about *spaldeens* and broomsticks. You may have written about it in the song, but I really did learn "stickball as a formal education." It was a city game. Where were you playing it? On your manicured lawns and newly paved streets of suburbia?

During the summer, I played the game from the minute the sun rose until I was called home for dinner. It helped that I lived around the corner from P.S. 147 and its ready-made stickball courts. There was not a blade of grass to be seen amid the concrete walls and blacktop floors of our "park." I would imagine that the city planners had envisioned these huge walls as handball courts when they built them, and in reality, one of the sides of the wall was used for that. However, unless you had a broomstick bat, you didn't dare step onto the other side of the wall that was painted with a rectangular strike zone.

Many of those stickball games were played against my best friend, Gio. Giovanni DeAngelis' first fastball whizzed by me when we were both eight years old. Though years later the stickball bats had been replaced by guitars, we remained close friends until a fateful night almost ten years later. Shit happens, and a hell of a lot of it happened to us in those days.

Though I loved the game, I can't remember who won or lost most of the time. Yet, I do remember that there were quite a few home runs. OK, it wasn't hard to hit a four-bagger if you had a brand new *spaldeen* and a fence that was only 150 feet away. It was on the *other side* of that home run fence that my life took so many twists and turns, good, bad . . . and deadly. There, over the vine-encrusted chain-link, lay a garden, a place that would prove to be so devastatingly crucial in my life.

Yeah, I spent a lot of time in the schoolyard. That meant that I knew everyone in my neighborhood. That also meant that another part of Billy Joel's song was also true. "The wild boys were my friends."

Entry #4

"I Saw It on TV"
- *John Fogerty*

Officially, the 1950s ended at the stroke of midnight on Dec 31, 1959. If you were alive then, you know that fact is simply not true. The thoughts, values, and culture of the fifties lived on into the sixties. To be exact, they lived on until November 22, 1963. At that time, all of us were dragged kicking and screaming into a new era. JFK did indeed bring us to a "New Frontier," but his death also brought us to the end of our innocence.

Gone were the times that John Fogerty wrote about in his song, "I Saw It on TV." Gone were the coonskin hats, Howdy Doody, and heroic death scenes in my bedroom. Gone was hiding from the real world and its real problems. When I was in grade school, we practiced huddling under our desks to shield us from a possible nuclear attack. In our youth, we bought into this false promise of safety. With age, I realized that I lived in goddamn New York City and we were target number one for the heathen commies. No ancient wooden desk was going to protect me from a direct hit by a Soviet missile. John F. Kennedy's assassination changed everything. Never again would I feel secure in this world.

I left my childhood behind at the same time that most of America did. However, that wasn't all bad. I was 14, and to paraphrase that wise seer Fogerty again, I lusted for a girl named Annette who I had only seen wearing mouse ears. To be more precise, I lusted after anything that was female. My damn hormones were raging! It was 1964. The world, with me in it, was spinning and spiraling in a way it had never done before.

Entry #5

"Love Potion Number Nine"
-The Searchers

The insanity of Beatlemania arrived in America in the late winter, early spring of 1964. That was what started it all. People would watch in awe as girls would scream, shout, and go into uncontrollable crying fits over them. It wasn't long after the British group's arrival that every male who had reached puberty knew that he had to learn to play the guitar or drums. Being a musician was the key to a girl's heart, and every boy I knew wanted to be a locksmith. Unbelievably, we talked like that in those days.

At first, Gio and I would pretend to play the latest hits on a pair of broken hockey sticks that I had gotten as souvenirs of a visit to a minor league hockey game. It was Gio who thought of trading in my broken sticks for the real thing, Sears Silvertone guitars ($20 on sale). They weren't electric, but even the Beatles had to start somewhere. We both dipped into savings accounts that dated back to our first communions at Sacred Heart Church. Initially, our parents frowned at the frivolous use of our college funds. Let's get real. No one we knew had ever actually gone to college. I think their acceptance of our musical careers had something to do with their understanding of the kind of trouble we could get into on the increasingly mean streets of our neighborhood.

It seemed so simple. You get a guitar. You practice for a few months. You form a band. You practice a few more months. By summer vacation, you're rolling in babes and money. The only drawback to our ambitions seemed to be the fact that every other guy I knew had the same plan. There was going to be a lot of competition to play the few dances that the local church sponsored.

Forming a band always followed a simple formula. The best guitar player played lead guitar. The best singer was the rhythm guitar. The bass guitar was probably some weird person because he never got to be in the spotlight. However, then you had to find a drummer. That wasn't easy. Drums were expensive. It seemed as if the guys who could afford drums couldn't play them, and the ones who could play couldn't afford them.

However, this didn't stop Gio and me from spending hours in my room practicing together. I guess we had not gotten as far as figuring out who would be lead and who would be rhythm. By default, I should've been the lead guitar, because Gio could sing. Besides, at this point, neither one of us was emerging as the next coming of George Harrison. Nevertheless, we kept on. At least, it was a step above playing hockey sticks. Our fingers often bled, and we realized soon that this rock star trip wasn't going to be as easy as we thought. Learn those basic chords, and you too can be a star. Yet, what we played was still unadulterated crap. I was beginning to think that perhaps the hockey sticks might've sounded better. Then it happened! Gio put together a few of those basic chords into a pattern that was a real song.

"Giovanni DeAngelis, you're a genius," I said before he confessed that Benny Conklin, his next-door neighbor, had shown him how to put together a C chord and an A7 chord and play The Searchers' version of "Love Potion Number Nine." Into the night, we played and sang. By 1 a.m., my parents had had enough and decided to pull the plug. This threat would have worked if we had advanced to electric guitars. As it was, we played a few additional minutes before my father threatened to make firewood out of $40 worth of acoustic guitars. The next day we were ready to form a band. We could already envision our first performance.

"Our first number will be The Searchers' 'Love Potion Number Nine.'"

Followed by . . .

"We've got a request to perform 'Love Potion Number Nine.'"

And then . . .

"We'd love to do 'Love Potion Number Nine' . . . again!"

Followed by . . .

"You can never have too much of a good song."

OK, we only knew one song, but dreams are for the young. Could you blame us? Anyone who has ever played any musical instrument knows the feeling the very first time that something you play sounds like . . . well . . . something. Excitement soared through our minds and exploded from our fingers. This was real.

We were creating music. Forget the girls! Forget the money! The music was its own reward. Well, we never actually thought, "Forget the girls!"

The hours seemed to fly away into endless nights, and more than a few times we stretched our fingers to their physical limitations. I guess it was a macho thing that neither one of us would be the first to admit we were in pain. Yet, our persistence paid off. Each day our skills grew. By spring, we realized that the more we knew, the more we needed to learn if we were going to do this damn thing right. Soon the summer would be coming, and with it more free time to practice our craft. We knew then that our original timetable was absurd, but our motives had changed. Now the summer would be a time of learning. We couldn't know that it would also be a season of friendship and love, of growing and change, and of violence, a violence that we could never have conceived of only one year before.

Entry #6

"You Really Got Me"
-*The Kinks*

With the help of our parents, Gio and I purchased electric guitars and amplifiers for our 16th birthdays. It had only been six months since we had started down this road to musical stardom and it was easy to see why we were overly ambitious. However, why did our parents buy into our fantasy? Looking back all these years later, I have come to realize what motivated them.

The neighborhood around us was growing increasingly bad. That word has meant many things to many people throughout time, and so it is impossible to describe what it meant in that place and time. *Bad* was the only word that I overheard my parents use during those hushed conversations that I wasn't supposed to hear. Were they referring to the gang violence and drugs that were working their way into the fabric of our lives with increasing regularity? On the other hand, was *bad* merely a catchphrase that whites used for the increasing integration of our area? Or was it some combination of both? I guess I'll never know for sure.

I know now that our parents would have done anything to limit our exposure to the outside world. Our brief experience with the cheap acoustic guitars had confirmed that we loved music and thought that it was our ticket to wealth and fame. They didn't believe that. However, they did know that every minute spent rehearsing was a minute not spent getting into trouble. With our fathers doing the negotiating, Gio and I were able to get a special deal on *two* Hagstrom guitars and *two* Ampeg amplifiers. Everyone wanted to own *Fender* brand everything, but our parents' dedication to our salvation had its limits. With their help and the remaining portions of our communion money, we were on our way.

With these now expensive investments in our future, a few facts became clear. We needed to practice a great deal in order to improve our skills. It was also apparent that we needed to find at least two other musicians to be in our band. Finally, we needed to expand our repertoire beyond "Love Potion Number Nine."

———◆———

It was Gio who found Jimmy and Frank. Jimmy McAvoy, or Jimmy Mac as we liked to call him, was the son of a candy store owner. Jimmy Mac's father had to work 80-hour weeks, and Jimmy Mac himself had to spend a considerable amount of his free time working there too. He stocked shelves and made egg creams for the many loyal neighborhood customers. This left no time for Jimmy Mac to achieve anything worthwhile in school, but that was OK because someday Mac and Son would provide him with all the future he needed. As a buyout for his son's time, Mr. Noel McAvoy bought him a beautiful set of Slingerland drums with Zildjian cymbals that rang with the sound of angels. He also provided lessons, though Jimmy Mac's practice was limited to precious moments stolen from his other responsibilities. He used those moments to become one of the finest drummers around. The only glitch in this deal was that Noel McAvoy didn't notice that his son was changing. Jimmy Mac loved his father and his whole family, but he felt the world closing in on him. He wanted out and saw drumming as his only alternative future.

Then there was Frank. If it was possible, he had even less skill on the guitar than either Gio or I did. He could play the requisite number of chords to pass as a "guitarist," but added no skill to the group that Gio and I couldn't perform. Yet he was Jimmy Mac's friend, and so the two of them came as a package deal. Armed with the necessary four members, we now had our band: three mediocre, half-assed guitarists, a great drummer, and a whole lot of dreams.

You'd think the first thing we'd do would be to set up a schedule to start practicing. Instead, we decided that the most important thing was to have a name. If we had a name, we could walk around the neighborhood and brag that we belonged to a band. It would give us instant street cred, as long as no one asked to see our resume. We played with some ideas, and for a few weeks, we were The Ravens. Our idea for the group name had come from our passion for a new group that had come to America on the coattails of The Beatles, The Kinks.

The Kinks, led by brothers Ray and Dave Davies reinvented music with something now called power chords. The first time I heard "You Really Got Me," I was done. The sheer strength and emotion created by the simple movement between the F and G chords drove me insane. It became the second song that we all learned. Later with the arrival of "All Day and All of the Night," we knew what direction we were going in.

The Kinks invented heavy metal music! This is a fact. Every time I listen to the first three chords of "You Really Got Me," I know this is true. And The Ravens' idea? On one of their album covers, it had been mentioned that it had been their original name. It couldn't be a more perfect name. At least, that's what we thought. A name that no one in our area had heard and it acknowledged our tribute to the style of The Kinks that we so admired. From the very beginning, I should've seen that the Ravens were doomed to failure. While Gio immediately settled into the singer/rhythm guitar position, Frank and I dueled it out for the lead guitar spot. Neither one of us was any good. We took turns pretending we could play lead while the other faked being a bass guitarist by lowering the tone on his guitar and playing some low pitch notes.

The Ravens existed on this compromise and grew our repertoire to an astounding fifteen songs for one reason only—the chemistry between Gio and Jimmy Mac. They were developing an incredible style of singing together that made us believe that we could succeed. Meanwhile, the competition between Frank and me grew into hatred.

I admit that I'm editorializing after the fact. In reality, another factor made the situation volatile. I said that Frank didn't bring anything special to our practices, and that wasn't entirely true. One thing he did have was a girlfriend, a girlfriend that I immediately fell in love with the first time I saw her.

Entry #7

"The Coming Generation"
-The Knickerbockers

To this day, no one has entranced me like Maria Romano. Her high cheekbones and prominent dimples punctuated her delicate features. Her light green eyes sparkled against her mocha colored skin. That perfect tan was a result of both her Italian heritage and her frequent trips to the beach that summer. Indeed, her entire slender body looked healthy, vibrant, and yes, sexy. When she spoke, her shy smile had the effect of making you think that she had a special place in her heart for you and only you.

I don't think I thought like that at sixteen. I know that I wouldn't have written something like that all those years ago. I do know that I just couldn't stop thinking about Maria. I found out later that Maria and Frank had been set up by their parents and that explained a lot. He was her first boyfriend. I'd had a few girlfriends, but they hadn't meant much to me. I know with certainty that I had never felt about them the way I felt about Maria. However, she was Frank's, and there was enough tension in the band already. After practice one day, Gio confronted me.

"You were practically undressing Maria with your eyes. What were you thinking?"

"I'm thinking that I really like her. I mean really, really like her."

"And I'm thinking that you're fuckin' nuts."

"I won't do anything about it because of the band."

"Fuck, Johnny! Either you're lying to me, or you're more fuckin' stupid than I thought. I know that you sure as hell *are* going to do something."

"Why?"

"Because, you idiot, she was looking at you the same way!"

———◆———

Still, I held in my feelings, and the band progressed nicely despite our lack of musical talent. The harmony created by Gio and Jimmy Mac made the audience go wild. The "audience" consisted mainly of Maria, Jimmy's little sisters, and some neighborhood kids who watched through the open basement window. However, at the time, we thought highly of ourselves and continued to develop a growing list of songs. We were no longer limited to doing Kinks' songs. Moving away from our inspiration led us to have a band meeting about changing our name. No one in the band said it, but we also realized that *Ravens* was not being received well by our friends. A raven is a *black* bird.

Ideas for new names were thrown around. Every time that I suggested a name, Frank mocked me. To be honest, I did the same to him. Frustrated with our progress at both playing and picking a name, we took a break to listen to some music from Jimmy Mac's extensive collection of 45s. It was then that Gio lifted The Knickerbockers' "Lies" record and for some reason flipped it over to the B-side. The song he found there was titled, "The Coming Generation."

"That's it . . . 'The Coming Generation.' The name says we're young and we're on the way up, we're modern!"

I think that I was the first one to laugh, but it wasn't long before Jimmy Mac and Frank were hysterical. Gio's facial expression betrayed his confusion. No one ever accused him of being the sharpest tack, but even as he was saying it, he picked up on our attitude.

"Hey, dickwad, *coming* . . . really?" said Jimmy Mac. There wasn't a teenage boy that I knew who didn't think that the word "coming" had a sexual connotation. While all four of us were trying to calm ourselves, Gio put the record on the spindle, and we listened to the song lyrics.

"That's it! The song is about us being young, and about the future ahead of us," said Gio, doubling down on his choice. For my part, I started to feel a bit more positive about the way my life was going. OK, maybe something would happen with the band to improve our situation, or perhaps I'd find another way out of this violent, screwed up neighborhood.

Even as I tried not to see it, it was all around me. Danny Capio had died of a drug overdose. Davy Macy walked the streets with an obviously broken nose. He told anyone who would listen, "You should see the other guy." We all knew that wouldn't happen because the other guy was black and lived on the other side of the line. These are just the two stories that I knew to be true. If I believed all the rumors that were around, the situation was much worse. Yet, I blocked most of it out. I didn't want to know how bad it was. At that singular moment in time, I was happy. We were young, and we were laughing and having a good time. And that might just be enough.

We continued to calm down until the line, "We hold the future in our hands." The soda that Jimmy Mac had been drinking exited his nose in a fit of uncontrollable laughter. I mean didn't that line describe our sex lives? Minutes later, we voted unanimously to change the name of the band to The Coming Generation. It wasn't our finest moment.

Entry #8

"We Gotta Get Out of This Place"
- *The Animals*

After the laughter was over, I left practice that day with my mind spinning. Where was I going with my life? I was about to enter my third year of high school, and I was confused. However, my confusion was fueled by an overwhelming desire to get away from the world in which I lived. I needed a hook to pull myself out of this place. Yes, I had a great family and great friends, but their lives were hard, and I didn't know if I had the strength to face a future as dismal as theirs seemed to be. I felt suffocated. If I had no choice but to continue down the path to which I appeared destined, I might have gone insane.

Looking back with the wisdom of hindsight, I guess that I may have gone in many directions. I honestly was a jack of many trades and a master of none. I knew that I *needed* to get out of this place. I thought of playing every angle. Could I get out with a good education? Could I do it through music? Could I do it through sports? Life was so perplexing, and there wasn't anyone to guide me. Not that there wasn't anyone who cared, it was just that no one had ever been there before, not in my circle of friends, not in my family, not in the Heights.

When I graduated from elementary school, my parents made the decision that I would go to a Catholic high school. Being Italian-Catholics, that seemed like a no-brainer. However, there was more to it. The local public school was in decline. That once proud institution now reflected the violence that was gradually overtaking the neighborhood. Most of its teachers were too busy trying to stay alive to give a damn about anything other than surviving each day. Like the communities that fed it, the school was the home of white gangs, black gangs, and a whole lot of screwed up people. This didn't mean that there weren't great people there in both the student and teacher categories, but their ability to function was affected by the problems surrounding them. There were enough of my friends there that I could have physically survived the experience of the school. The question was: Would I have learned anything?

By the time I was two months into my first year of high school, I had my answer. Most of the people that I knew were changing. I could see them slowly slipping into the acceptance that their parents' lower class blue-collar existence would soon also be theirs. Moreover, this realization didn't bother them. No, I knew I had to get out, and my family supported that idea.

My father had taken a second job cleaning up after the gamblers at Belmont Race Track. He would go there after driving a truck for eight hours. From 6 a.m. to 2 p.m. each day, he made sure that all the stores in the area had their quota of Wonder Bread. At that time, this product claimed, "to help build bodies eight ways," but I know that the strain of the heavy lifting broke *his* body in at least that many locations. My mother waited until he came home from the second of his two jobs, then she would drive our eight-year-old Mercury Comet up to an ice cream parlor in ritzy Nassau County. There she'd serve shakes and sundaes to rich kids and their parents who were more interested in the finer things in life. They had nothing in common with the waitress who was working so that her son could break her family's endless cycle of poverty.

For my part, I saw the sacrifice and thought of it as a gift. Nevertheless, I was hedging my bets. What if I couldn't get into a public college? Where would the money come to pay for a private school? I couldn't ask them to continue with their heavy workloads. Yes, I would work my way through college, but could I make enough? Not in my mind. There had to be a plan B and even a plan C.

I remember those days of confusion so well, and I relive them now in this journal. I must. It was this obsessive desire for escape that led to my ultimate downfall and the deaths of so many people.

———◆———

I had a friend named DJ Spinelli who sat next to me in most classes. Together, we dealt with our boredom in different ways. We would daydream and doodle separately, and then compare notes. I remember one day in particular that symbolized all that was going on in my life. As if reading my mind, D.J. had scribbled a little poem that he'd been working on called "Words of Doubt." I don't know what his *words of doubt* were, but he couldn't have summarized my life any better than that. We were close, and we talked about all our problems.

I was torn. I wanted a real shot at financial success, yet I wanted to be like D.J. I wanted to forget the real world and create *something* out of nothing. I was fascinated by the acts of creativity that were taking place at the desk next to mine. I fantasized a life as a writer or maybe a songwriter. I decided that I should work even harder to get good grades, and then see where that education would take me.

Ironically, that inner desire to create is finally coming out in this journal. Better late than never?

———◆———

There remained a third option. I had grown up with a passion for sports. It was all I thought about in my younger years. Like many young boys, I had delusions that I could be a professional athlete. I realize now, that was a long shot. But could my talent at least help me pay for college? There were scholarships out there. However, to my knowledge, no one from my area had ever received one. Boys from Florida and California were playing baseball twelve months a year in warmer climates than New York. The reality was that real baseball played on real grass was hard to come by in my part of town. Could a city kid compete for the rewards that baseball offered to the worthy?

Boy, was I an ass! If I had seen reality in 1965, these delusional thoughts would never have crossed my mind. However, reality was the furthest thing from my mind, and I believed that baseball was a third path that I could follow. As my junior year approached, I had hope and determination. After my hour bus and train ride home from school, I would schedule time to study, to practice the guitar, and to work on a fitness program to help me become a baseball superstar. Little did I know that before the next summer vacation, fate would steer me down a path I could never have envisioned during those hopeful days of the fall of 1965.

Entry #9

"Changes"
- Moby Grape

The obsessive work schedule I set up for myself didn't lend itself to doing anything else in life. I had no social life. In a world where everyone seemed to find his or her niche, I was a bit of a weird duck . . . niche-less. Most people I knew were too shallow to see deeply into a person's being. Everyone seemed to fall into cliques. People dressed, talked, and lived life according to their chosen allegiance. Whether you were a jock, greaser, hippie, or "quif" (a word we invented to mean something like geek or nerd today), "in crowd," a madras wearing collegiate, or an outcast, everyone fit nicely into a box. Maybe, this is true today. I don't know because I still don't get out much.

I was an exception. Maybe I wasn't the only one, but I was the only one I knew. No one in those days talked about finding himself. I played sports, so I was a jock. I came from a neighborhood where everyone was a greaser, and I did have those Flagg Brothers' boots with the Cuban heels. Greaser – check. I played music, which automatically classified me as a hippie (at least to everyone in an older generation). I went to a private school and studied at night. So, which box did I fit in?

Returning to school for the fall of 1965 brought many changes in my life. My junior year meant tryouts for the varsity baseball team. My high school team had a city and state reputation for quality. Players from my high school were noticed across the country by major league teams and college programs. The bad news was that every prospective ballplayer in New York wanted to go to my high school and so the competition for a spot on the roster was going to be tight. Even with my over .400 batting average on the JV squad, I was one of the borderline players.

Practice was required during the off-seasons of both the fall and winter and started the very first day of school. For a long-distance commuter like me, this meant catching my first bus at 6:57 a.m. and getting home well after 7 p.m. After my twelve-hour day of commuting, classes, and practice, I faced a warmed-up dinner and hours of homework and guitar practice. Sometime after midnight, I would roll into bed. The next day, the whole process would begin again. After Saturday morning baseball practices, there would be band rehearsals all Saturday and Sunday afternoon. Exhaustion rapidly became a way of life. Decades later, I can't help but think back to the youthful naïveté that made me assume I could have it all. I've often wondered how long I could have lasted at that breakneck pace. I'll never know. Less than two months later, it was all over.

Entry #10

"Wonderful Tonight"
-Eric Clapton

All I can remember of that first week of school was that I was exhausted. The moment I finished dinner that first Saturday night, I passed out for fourteen hours of uninterrupted sleep. Though television wasn't even an option most days of my life, I did have a compulsive love of old cheesy science fiction movies. I knew that I was physically beat when I slept right through the *Saturday Night Creature Features*. I'd been looking forward to the broadcast of a double feature of two of my favorite movies: *The Amazing Colossal Man* and *The Incredible Shrinking Man*. Here they were offering a theme-based juxtaposition of height mutations, and I'd slept through it! Now this exhaustion thing was cutting into my science fiction interests, not to mention my non-existent social life. I have to admit that the catch-up sleep was not only necessary but also a great escape from the self-imposed pressure that consumed me.

Band practice hadn't gone well on Saturday. Besides the usual arguments over who would play lead and bass, Frank caught me gazing at Maria just a little too long. He sarcastically commented on everything that I said and did that day. I held my temper and bit my tongue as Gio saw what was happening and reminded me to stay calm. Of course, that wasn't the real me, and I couldn't maintain my composure for long. While reaching for the volume control on my amp, my guitar "accidentally" hit Frank in the butt and I offered a very insincere "sorry."

"Kiss my ass," was his heartfelt response.

"My guitar already did," I said letting him know that hitting him in the ass had not been an accident. I obviously was not the slightest bit sorry. Maria fought to hold back a giggle at my put down of her boyfriend.

How long could the band exist with the tension that was building at every practice? Gio and Jimmy Mac were producing something special with their harmonies, but to be honest, I didn't see where either Frank or I fit in. Throughout Sunday's practice, I remember thinking to myself that maybe this is what I should give up. Then Monday morning arrived, and there was no time for thinking. My exhausting weekday life cycle had begun again.

At baseball practice, I had hit some good shots to the outfield gaps that would've fallen for doubles at any field. I was proud of my accomplishment until Bob Schmidt, a six-foot muscle-bound competitor for one of the five outfield slots, drove one over the fence. A few minutes later, he repeated this accomplishment. My gappers were looking pretty insignificant. Was this God telling me where I was going to find free time? Was this worth it? On my way home the next day, it became abundantly clear why I was going to keep going to practice.

I will never forget getting off the subway and working my way to the Q3A bus only to find myself face to face with Maria. I was tongue-tied. She gave me a shy smile and moved into one of the few remaining seats on the bus. I stood near her but said nothing.

It occurred to me that maybe her presence at the bus stop was a one-time only occurrence. Perhaps I shouldn't get too excited. She went to an all-girls Catholic school not too far from where we caught the bus in Jamaica and her usual dismissal time was a good three hours earlier. I still decided to rush my shower after practice the next day in hopes of getting to the bus in time to see her. However, there was no Maria. Then, just as the driver was just about to close the doors, I noticed her rushing towards the slowly accelerating vehicle. I shouted for the driver to hold up because *someone* was trying to catch the bus. As she entered, there were no seats available. However, a certain gallant young man gave her his spot.

I am forty years old now, and I can't remember what I had for breakfast. However, I remember those days as if they were yesterday. I frequently find myself imagining what our life *could* have been together. Through the years, I have created an alternative scenario to my existence that does *not* result in me being a broken man. In these flights of fancy, my life has worked out great instead of the shithole the real world brought to me. In my dreams, I'm married to Maria. We live out on Long Island with a few kids.

Gio and I are in our middle ages, and we are still close friends. Gio and his imaginary wife come over for a barbeque at our decidedly suburban home. After we grill burgers to perfection and put down a few beers, the acoustic guitars come out of their cases. These are not the old $20 Sears Silvertones on which we learned, but nice Gibsons with a sweet sound to die for.

Our kids play together, and our wives chat happily over the cleanup chores. Maria is stunning. Though she is no longer the young girl that sat beside me on that Q3A bus, the years have only enhanced her beauty. She turns for a moment and smiles that heart-melting smile. She mouths the words, "I love you." I answer her with a similar sentiment.

Gio and I play Clapton's, "Wonderful Tonight," and every word is dedicated to Maria and Gio's wife. A warm feeling con sumes me as I sit with guitar in my hand, friend at my side, and the love of my life in my gaze. Yes, everything is perfect. But it's not real. Gio is dead.

Entry #11

"Bus Stop"
-The Hollies

By the third week of school, Maria and I had worked out a way of meeting at the bus stop every day. I knew how I felt about her. But what was she thinking? After all, she had a boyfriend – the hated Frank. Sitting together every day, we got to know each other as friends (at least that's what I told myself for the sake of band unity). Eventually, she told me her story, and in today's liberated times, it seems almost antiquated.

Born into a very traditional Italian family, she was expected to follow a very traditional pattern in her life. She attended a commercial school to be trained as a secretary. After that, she would work for three or four years until she met the right man to marry. Then she would have a houseful of *bambini*. She would stay at home the rest of her life while her husband went on to earn a living so they could afford to have a house big enough for the brood. Her life had been planned down to the very last detail. However, somewhere along the line, the tradition train went off the tracks.

Whether it was the changing society of the mid-sixties or Maria's own independent streak, I guess I'll never know. She had decided that she wanted to go to college. This created a bit of a problem on many fronts. First, Anthony Romano was pissed off that his little girl was going to risk spinsterhood by putting off marriage for a career. If she ever did get married, it might not be until her mid to late twenties, an embarrassing family scandal in the eyes of Papa Romano. You really had to be there in the 1960's to believe this shit. The second problem was that Maria was in a school that had no college track courses. This fact pretty much eliminated any possibility of admittance into a public college.

Sister Mary Beatrice had listened to her plight and had come up with a solution. Every day when regular classes ended, the middle-aged nun would spend three hours instructing Maria in what she would need to get an academic diploma worthy of college consideration. It was a hard and tedious task that the two of them had committed themselves to accomplishing. I thanked God and His dedicated servant because this situation landed Maria at the bus stop at the very same time as me every day. We only talked about school once, and it just made me love her more.

"I want to be something, Johnny. I want to achieve something."

"And you will, Maria. I can see all you are going through."

"I want to be my own person so that when I find the right man to love, I will come to him as an equal. It won't be a relationship based on me needing someone to support my kids and me."

I thought I'd be witty and say something like, "You have kids?" However, I realized she was being serious, pouring her heart out to me.

"You said *when*."

"Yeah, *when*, so what?"

"You said, 'When I find the right man to love.'"

"Yeah, so?"

"I guess that leaves Frank up shit's creek."

"Johnny, you're terrible." But her broad smile and playful love tap to my arm told me she thought otherwise.

Our friendship developed on all those afternoon bus rides, and like The Hollies' song, we even shared an umbrella at that bus stop. I began to wonder what would happen when my fall baseball practices ended. Could I somehow find another reason to stay after school?

I was still puzzled by the question, *What about Frank*? I knew I was gaining ground on him when Maria's hand brushed mine one day on the bus and she held it in place long enough for me to hold it. This all might seem too sweet and innocent considering the post-Woodstock realities of free love. However, it was what it was. Before there ever was a time for passion, we grew to be very, very close friends, possibly beginning a relationship that would have lasted forever. It's now two decades later, and I've never cared for anyone like I cared for Maria. I miss her.

Entry #12

"The Eve of Destruction"
- *Barry McGuire*

OK, time to cut the crap. The purpose of this journal is to deal with all the shit that I lived through. Yet, I have been avoiding all the things I didn't want to face. They tell me avoidance is not the way to help myself. I didn't do too well making decisions on my own, so maybe I should listen to them and try to figure out where it all went down the crapper. I've been writing about puppy love, music, and sports. In reality, even when those things were bad, they were good. It was the world that I lived in that wasn't good, and that is where the whole damn story gets confusing. This is why today I am twenty years and thousands of miles removed from everyone I cared about or who cared about me. Time to write about the ugly stuff. I know that I must do this to be truthful.

———◆———

October of 1965 began with hope. I felt that I had a chance with Maria. I even thought I had a decent chance to make the team. And surprisingly, the band was still together. However, by the end of the month, my world would come crashing down around me.

It was only when I stopped viewing the world through the eyes of a child that I began to see the monumental changes taking place outside my door. My childhood world was in its death throes, yet all I was concerned with (in Gio's words) were "baseball, the band, and the broad." He liked and respected Maria, but couldn't pass up the use of alliteration.

The end began quite innocently at band practice. I remember distinctly that it was Columbus Day, a day off from school and an opportunity for an extra session. And so, for the third day of the week, we met on a beautiful Indian summer afternoon to practice in a dank basement. Perhaps that was the problem. Frank and I barely held it together for two practices a week, and I guess that three visits with each other was pushing it.

Ever the diplomat, Gio suggested songs he knew would go smoothly. We started with a few grinders. I haven't used that term in decades, and it makes me chuckle a bit to think back to our unique band lingo. Grinders were songs that were played slow and sexy. This was to let the guys out there dance just close enough to a girl to get excited. I'm not proud of this admission, but we did have to live up to our Coming Generation name if we wanted to be popular.

When we played a church dance, we had to be careful not to do too many of these. We would infuriate the priests and nuns who circulated the dance floor making sure there was "room for the Holy Ghost" in between each couple. In turn, these moral interruptions would frustrate the guys who didn't place the Holy Ghost above their natural lustful urges. We knew it required a delicate balance to satisfy both the *horny* and the *holy*.

Still, we reached back for some real 50's doo-wop like "Daddy's Home" and "You Belong to Me." These songs highlighted the great harmonies that Gio and Jimmy Mac were developing. I hated to admit it, but Frank was coming along very well in adding a third part to those harmonies. This increasingly made me the odd man out.

Decades later, with some help from other friends, I would realize that I had a passable singing voice. However, in those days, I was horrible. Because Gio and Jimmy Mac did what they did naturally, they really couldn't teach me how to be a fourth part to some harmonies. I was relegated to non-singing vocals. This included my one and only "singing-like" performance on "Louie, Louie." My solo was the result of two factors. First, it was a raspy non-melodic lead singer's song, and second, I was the only one (probably in the world next to its composer) who knew the words. The obvious vocal difference between Frank and me made me realize that I was expendable. Maybe, that was what led to the events of that day.

By doing slow songs, the music took second place to the harmonies, and the practice moved along. We then decided to go over some of the garage band standards like "Hang on Sloopy" and (for my sake) "Louie, Louie." That was when the problem arose. In "Louie, Louie," I had learned the lead guitar break by merely mimicking the extremely easy solo on the record. (I guess that guy wasn't Eric Clapton either.) However, before we started the three-chord song, Frank announced that he too could play the solo. He reasoned that because I was singing the song he should be lead guitar. I think he added something to the effect, "If what you do can even be called singing."

"Screw you," was my eloquent response.

"You just fuckin' want everything for yourself." His facial grimaces were all out of proportion to the argument. I realized this was not about "Louie, Louie," the band, or music at all. He was talking about Maria.

"You're a fuckin' asshole," was my only response, and I didn't care which topic we were discussing. With that, Frank took a swing at me, which was somewhat ridiculous when you think about it. We both had guitars hanging on our bodies and cords intertwined on the floor in the confined space of Jimmy Mac's basement.

Jimmy Mac, thinking we would blow off steam and then return to practice, suggested we take it outside. I guess he was also wondering where we would ever have practice again if his mother came down the basement to find an all-out brawl. In reality, I was very calm. In the brief period of time it took us to work our way out of the basement and a safe distance from the house, I'd already decided that it was over. The band was going nowhere with me, and even without me, stardom was probably not an option. I had nothing to lose. Maybe I would just feel good about kicking Frank's ass and leaving on that note. But then, how would Maria feel about that?

It wasn't much of a fight. If you were male and grew up in the Heights, you knew how to fight, and since both of us hated each other, it could have been an ugly scene. Though he was filled with rage and came at me with fists waving wildly, his accuracy left a great deal to be desired. Upon one of his missteps, I threw him into a bear hug and his attempt to escape caused us both to fall into a neatly arranged flower bed on a neighborhood lawn. We rolled around destroying petunias until a little old lady came out with a broom and proceeded to swat us until we got up and broke clenches. Soon Gio and Jimmy Mac arrived and held us apart.

"The Rumble in the Flowers," as Gio called it for months

afterward, was over. I proceeded to the basement, unplugged my guitar, put it in its case, and left. As I walked up the stairs, I announced that I was done with The Coming Generation. As I look back, that wasn't as depressing as it seemed. In actuality, it would have been a moot point had I not quit the band that day. Three weeks later, I would make a mistake that would end my guitar playing and change my whole life. My world was on the eve of its destruction.

2

"The Other Side of Life"
-The Moody Blues

The World of Johnny Cipp

JOHN CIPPITELLI WAS SIXTEEN IN 1965, the year that his world began to unravel. His jet-black hair was cut short because of the strict regulations of his Catholic high school. His skin retained the swarthy permanently tanned complexion that made evident his Italian heritage, and his Roman nose seemed just a bit too large for his liking. His light green eyes often attracted the attention of girls he came in contact with, but an extreme case of shyness seemed to hamper his response on most occasions. However, his broad shoulders and an endearing smile kept the opposite sex interested in competing to break through his timid exterior. Occasionally, they were successful.

"Johnny Cipp" was known to all of the guys who made up his neighborhood. He had grown up with them, and it bothered him that some had left their childhoods behind at far too young an age. By 1965, many had drifted away into different lifestyles. They had become like The Standells' song proclaimed, "Lovers, muggers, and thieves." The harsh reality of their blue-collar world had taken its toll. Some had dropped out of school to go to work. Some had experimented with alcohol and drugs. Others had already found their way into violence and crime. And a few had even "done the right thing" and married their pregnant teenage girlfriends.

While the friends of his youth had drifted into different directions, they all remained physically trapped in the same neighborhood. A bittersweet wave of the hand by Johnny while passing in the street hinted at their shared pasts. However, Johnny found it sad. They had seemed so much more vibrant in their younger days. What had happened? More importantly, would it happen to him if he did not escape from the boundaries of the Heights? Johnny understood little of what was going on around him. He had loved his childhood and all that it had entailed. However, the world around him was changing, and he had to be ready for those changes.

"Out in the Streets"
-The Shangri-Las

The town of Cambria Heights first came into being in the late 1920's. Up until that time the area had been mostly farmland. The blue-collar area's name had fittingly come from the Cambria Construction Company which had been instrumental in the construction of many of the buildings. The "Heights" designation was laughable to most people who had traveled outside the five boroughs of New York City. Cambria challenged such the illustrious "mountain" villages of Jackson *Heights* and Richmond *Hill* for the honor of being the highest point in the county of Queens with an oxygen-threatening elevation of 49 feet.

People had lived in the area for decades before the city of New York saw fit to extend gas lines to the hamlet. It had been commonly referred to as "Kerosene Hill" well into the twentieth century. This condescending nickname referred to its only source of power until the advent of World War II.

From the very beginning, the area had been populated almost exclusively by Irish, Italian, German, and Jewish families who could not afford to live in either the more established neighborhoods of Brooklyn or Queens, or the affluent suburbs of adjoining Nassau County. At the extreme outer fringes of New York City, it received services only after most of the city's budget had been spent on the upscale sections of Manhattan. When there was a power failure, it might get fixed in the Heights, eventually. When a water main broke, it might get fixed, eventually. Moreover, if there was a heavy snowstorm, it was only hoped that the city plows would somehow locate Linden Boulevard sometime before the spring thaw.

The post-World War II period brought the influx of returning veterans who wanted homes in which to raise their baby boomer families. Unfortunately, their finances relegated them to this tiny corner of the city where resources and transportation were almost non-existent. They then witnessed the construction of the Cross Island Parkway which succeeded in permanently cutting off Cambria Heights from the wealthy suburbs of neighboring Nassau County.

Still, the area grew into a thriving community with its own identity. Its bustling economic and cultural life flourished around the main street of Linden Boulevard. With an overwhelming percentage of the residents being Roman Catholic, Sacred Heart Church and its large adult membership and Catholic school population generated many of the social activities of the community. The adults attended church-sponsored dances and communion breakfasts, or simply sat outside on their *stoops* with the neighbors on hot summer nights. Though Mr. Softee and the Good Humor Man made their annual attempts at drumming up business, "Joe, The Ice Cream Man" owned the Heights and buying from anyone else was considered nothing short of a mortal sin.

The CYO baseball team from Sacred Heart won the championship of all of Brooklyn and Queens in 1963. This meant that of all the teams created in an area of over three million people, the fourteen players from the Heights were the best. This pinnacle of success fueled the already evident community spirit of 1950's and early 1960's, creating an atmosphere that would never be forgotten. It seemed as if this lower-middle-class neighborhood had become a place that no one would ever want to leave.

By the end of the 1960's, over 90% of the white population of Cambria Heights had moved away. The years of the mass exodus were a time of change throughout the city, indeed, throughout the country. However, it was nowhere more violent or convulsive than it was in this tiny hamlet. An astute real estate investor might have seen the fall of the neighborhood coming and sold very early in 1964 when the prices were at their highest. This area was "pretty" but poor by the standards of its surrounding areas of Queens Village and Laurelton. The residents of the neighborhood did not have much material wealth. Though they worked hard, they frequently held jobs at the lowest pay levels in a city.

However, they did have their homes, and they did have their neighborhood. Right or wrong, the source of this pride often revolved around the fact that their turf was exclusively white. Later years would judge these people harshly regarding their racist beliefs; however, the decade of the 1960's was a different time. People in poor white areas knew almost nothing about those who were in any way different from them. The late twentieth-century concept of diversity had not yet made it to the Heights. Socializing or even speaking to anyone "too different" was almost non-existent, and most people rarely married outside their nationality or religion. A "mixed marriage" usually meant that someone of Irish ethnicity had somehow found common ground with an equally open-minded Italian. Manhattan may have moved way beyond this kind of thinking, but the outer boroughs remained steeped in the past. Real estate agents looking to make exorbitant commissions incited some of these feelings. Residents were constantly bombarded with the idea that once their neighborhood started to become integrated, the value of their houses would be gone.

In 1964, just as the Beatles were triumphantly conquering the hearts of American teens, Cambria Heights was poised for the dissolution of its way of life. Located between the overwhelming black areas of Hollis, St. Albans, and Jamaica and the solid brick wall of the extremely expensive neighborhoods of Nassau County, the residents developed a siege mentality about their turf. Pressed from all sides, they found themselves with very few options. All it would take was one loose brick, and their fortress would crumble.

"Remember the Days at the Old Schoolyard"
- *Cat Stevens*

Officially, it was just a road called Springfield Boulevard. However, there was no one on either side of the two-lane blacktop highway who did not know that it was "the line." With a few rare exceptions, everyone west of the line was black, and everyone east of the line was white. There were genuine racists on both sides of the line. However, what made this place different from other hotbeds of racial conflict was just how many people felt nothing but fear of the unknown. Therefore, blacks and whites kept to themselves, without ever venturing to the other side of the line except at their own risk. That was until the change.

In those politically incorrect days of racism, "black" or even "colored" would have been preferable to what most of the white Americans called African-Americans behind their backs or even to their faces. To white boys in white neighborhoods in the segregated boroughs of New York City, this was not an issue that came to their minds. When they used the phrase "eeny- meeny – miney – mo," it was not a *tiger* that they imagined catching by the toe! Even the racial slurs that lingered in their daily speech did not always reflect any deep-felt belief system to most of the pre-teen and teen boys who spouted them. They very often were merely mimicking what they had heard their elders say. They knew nothing about and cared less about the affairs of the world. This all changed when the world came knocking on their door.

———◆———

The schoolyard that adjoined P.S. 147 was the center of white teenage social life in the Heights. Whether it was stickball, handball, or goof balls, it was going on there. The very young with their innocent athletic pursuits mingled unnoticed with gang-related and vastly horny mid-teens, and the burnt-out, strung-out late teens. It was all happening at the yard.

The City of New York, in its infinite wisdom, had finally decided to spend some of its tax dollars to re-do the schoolyard of P.S. 147. New blacktop, new softball fields, and the construction of basketball courts were an effort to improve the lives of the young people of the area. The politicians failed to realize that blue-collar white kids did not play basketball in the Heights. They had no practical use for these new courts. In fact, they resented the loss of space from the handball and stickball courts sacrificed for these unwanted hoops. That reasoning paled in comparison to the other adverse result of the changes that infuriated the overtly racist in the area.

The newly constructed courts served only as a beacon of temptation for "the line" to be breached by the influx of young boys of color from the other side. It would not be long before the invisible barrier of Springfield Boulevard was obliterated. Many adults reacted to the influx of "others" by putting their houses up for sale. However, the young hormone-engorged males viewed this challenge to their turf as a call to arms. Unaware that their parents were in the process of pulling up stakes and heading to distant white suburbs on Long Island, they prepared to fight to the death against the encroachment of "them."

"Bad to the Bone"
- *George Thorogood*

Gypsy Rose, Twister, Gallo Port. Name your cheap poison, and Dominick Provenzano knew all about it. While most of the white people were getting ready to use their fight-or-flight instinct when it came to the integration of the neighborhood, Provenzano continued to build a small empire in this little section of Queens. He cared little about affairs that did not affect him.

He ran his mini-empire out of his liquor store on Springfield Blvd. Because of its location "on the line," he made enormous profits by overcharging both the black and white youth for the high that cheap wines administered. Race or age did not matter if it brought cash into the Provenzano coffers. It did not matter if it was illegal to sell to those underage when the owner of that store was connected. Indeed, half of the police precinct serving Cambria Heights knew to stay clear of the trouble created by harassing the Provenzanos; the other half simply knew the Provenzano family just a little *too* well. Besides making money on wines, Dom Provenzano also produced stuff a bit stronger than alcohol if you simply knew how to ask in the right way. With a little bookmaking and prostitution added in, the Gambino crime family considered "Dom the Pro" a real moneymaker, and he had hopes that this would help him to move up in the organized crime hierarchy.

Dom's only soft spot was his family, particularly his two sons. He had no moral objections to what he was doing to others as long as *his* sons did not use the crap he sold. The money from the liquor store and its satellite businesses supported his children in a manner far above the level of the area. Let those trashy kids of both races fall deeper into misery, this boss was going to take care of his own. "The King of Cambria Heights," a nickname that the elder Provenzano encouraged, groomed his sons to be the heir-apparent princes of his empire. The finest clothes and cars were at their disposal. Eventually, they would rule his kingdom and possibly something more in the future. He needed them to be prepared. They attended the best private schools, not because of the education, but rather because they were all white. Dom Provenzano was an equal opportunity dirtbag when it came to his business enterprises, but he would be damned if his boys were going to come in personal contact with those "coloreds," or "mulanyans," as he liked to call them.

For their part, the Provenzano boys had picked up handily on this feeling of privilege. They roamed the streets of the Heights with an attitude of superiority that manifested itself both in verbal abuse and physical violence. Most teens made themselves scarce when the two brothers walked the neighborhood together.

Gaetano Provenzano was the older of the two and by any definitive measure, the meaner brother. Though his family just called him Guy, the neighborhood boys called him "Mad Guy," and looked twice to make sure they were not saying it in front of anyone who would relay the slur to Provenzano. He had beaten kids mercilessly for offenses much less severe than name-calling. At 21 years old, he was being readied for a major leadership role in his father's empire. His father hoped that the capos in the "The Family" would take notice of all three Provenzano men and they would rise together in the organization.

With his curly black hair combed in a pompadour, hazel eyes and olive complexion, Guy was the heartthrob of every girl who could look past his mean nature and see only his outer beauty as well as his wealth and power. It was known but never discussed, that more than one young girl had left town to visit a distant relative for a nine-month period. Guy laughed the incidents off by just saying that the girl was a "whoo-a," the uniquely Queens' version of the word that the rest of the English-speaking world pronounced, "whore."

Tony Provenzano was only 18 and idolized his older brother.

Though as good looking as his sibling, Tony's meanness just mimicked his brother's attitude. At heart, Tony was a kinder and gentler person than Guy. However, in his ambition to impress Guy, Tony willingly participated in all of his brother's sadism and bullying. Nevertheless, it did not sit well in Tony's heart. Though he wore a smile outwardly, he grew more troubled with each passing day. He could never be Guy and would always pale in comparison with both his family and his brother's gang. He also could not find friendship and companionship with "the ordinary people." A relationship with anyone outside the circle of his family and his brother's friends was out of the question.

With each passing day, Tony became more isolated. As his anger and frustration grew, he indeed became more like Mad Guy. He might have become his brother's equal in cruel behavior had not the events of October 1965 occurred. It was at that moment in time that the lives of Tony Provenzano and Johnny Cipp became unexpectedly and permanently linked.

———◆———

As the last vestiges of sunlight were disappearing from view on October 15, 1965, the schoolyard went through its daily transformation. A younger generation interested only in athletic pursuits began to give way to the drinkers, the drug-addled, and the dregs of the Heights. They came out each night following a schedule not too different from that of vampires. It was in this world that the Provenzano brothers ruled and there was almost no one who did not take notice of their entrance into the yard. The only exception was a pair of twelve-year-old boys too busy finishing their stickball game to see the changing of the guard.

Jay Accardi threw the rubber ball toward the painted rectangular strike zone. His opponent and best friend Tommy McCarthy's eyes lit up as he swung with all his might at a pitch that was right in his wheelhouse. A *spaldeen* was just a high-quality rubber ball. Because of this fact, no matter how hard it was hit, it could not seriously injure anyone. This did not matter to Tony Provenzano when the ball ricocheted off the back of his head.

"What the fuck?" howled Tony as he turned and advanced on the frightened younger boy. He had no plan.

"Knock the shit out of him," screamed his brother, and his

lackeys echoed that sentiment.

"I asked you what the fuck do you think you were doing?"

"I . . . I didn't mean to . . ." answered McCarthy as Tony grabbed him by his shirt and pushed him into the wall. All the while he heard the chorus of *knock the shit out of him* coming from behind. On his own, Tony might have just been content to shove the kid around and scare the hell out of him.

"Knock the shit out of him! Knock the shit out of him!" chanted the gathering crowd of Provenzano followers.

"Please . . . please don't hurt me," begged McCarthy, and Tony hesitated as he saw the terror in the young boy's eyes. This was not him. However, faced with his need to please his brother, he continued to pin his terrified victim to the wall. Guy approached his brother, leaving the crowd behind.

"Hey, pussy-ass, do something," yelled Guy for all to hear, but then whispered in a voice only Tony could hear, "You're making us look bad. Are you a fucking wimp?"

Tony's first strike sent Tommy McCarthy's head into the concrete wall and blood gushed from both his mouth and the cut that opened in the back of his skull. He slid down the wall. Tony's mind went blank as he proceeded to kick the wounded boy incessantly until Guy's minion, Joey Pasco, pulled him off the barely conscious victim.

"Now that's what I'm talking about," laughed Guy, as he put his arm around his brother's shoulder and walked him away from the scene.

Tommy endured months in the hospital with a wired jaw and broken ribs. Even after he returned home, the boy lived with mental and physical scars that would never heal. There were at least twenty witnesses to the assault, and any one of them could have sent Tony away for many, many years if they had chosen to testify. The truth was that no one would ever talk. It was the rule of the yard that no one ever snitched about what happened there. Moreover, if anyone had considered the acts of Tony Provenzano vicious enough to break that deep-seated rule, overwhelming fear would have negated that option.

Tony took a swig of beer. This was the only "drug" not strictly controlled by his father because it could be purchased in supermarkets. He gave a smile to his friends, and then without explanation, turned to leave the yard. As he walked out, he passed one of those silent witnesses, a sixteen-year-old boy named Johnny Cipp. Johnny had seen what everyone else had seen, as well as one more sight that was his and his alone: tears running down Tony's face.

———◆———

Most of the time, Tony Provenzano did not show any signs of the guilt that percolated inside of him. He had been depressed long before this particular wanton act of cruelty. The fact that he despised everything about his life would have to remain inside of him. No one knew about his inner turmoil. He was a Provenzano. He was a prince. Nevertheless, there had to be relief. To most of the Heights, any form of escape would usually lead to a purchase of some substance that would directly profit the Provenzanos. Whether it was cheap wine, marijuana, or heroin, those seeking escape always found themselves at some door of the Provenzano Empire. However, if you actually *were* a Provenzano and you needed an escape, where did you go? The products so readily available to everyone else in the neighborhood were out of Tony's reach unless he wanted to risk his father's wrath.

Even the occasional beer by Tony was still a risk. Though he could easily purchase a six-pack, it remained a gamble due to his father's ability to smell alcohol a mile away. Tony saw another way. Though he knew the path he would choose was more dangerous than using any of the options that his father offered to the public, his guilt over the beating of Tommy McCarthy rid him of any inhibitions. He reasoned that as long as he stayed out of sight while under the influence, there would be no proof that he had indulged in getting high.

And Tony really needed to get high.

3

Journal of Johnny Cipp

Entry #13

"Strange Days"
-*The Doors*

I have lived almost four decades on this planet, and it has been a wild and crazy ride. . . and that's just the parts I can remember. I will always look back on a handful of days in October of 1965 and wonder how it was possible that so much could happen to me in such a short time span. Nothing can explain how events would change everything I *thought* would happen in my life. It started innocently with that stupid fight and my subsequent quitting The Coming Generation and escalated through the next weekend. It was strange, so strange. Never was it easier for the Music Doctor to pick a title for an entry in my journal.

———◆———

It had been six days since I had walked out on the band and I still hadn't talked to Gio. I had no gripe with him, but I knew that I'd left him on the spot. This first Saturday after the blow-out, the group would probably be meeting to practice. However, would they? Or would they be sitting down trying to figure out what direction to go in the post-Johnny Cipp era?

Following Saturday morning baseball practice, it was a strange feeling having my afternoon free. After putting away my mitt and spikes and throwing my dirty sweats in the wash, I usually would've just had time to throw my guitar and amp on an old wagon and make my way to Jimmy Mac's house. However, that day I had nothing to do. I looked over at my guitar and wondered if I would ever again play it anywhere but in my basement.

I decided I would call Gio later in the day and suggest a late stickball game followed by watching Creature Features with some ice cream floats my mom always made available. It had been less than a week before that I had felt smothered by my busy schedule, and now I had an open time slot on a Saturday afternoon. Time to reclaim the ability to relax once again.

When I was six years old, I had started making plastic models. I had continued this hobby until my schedule hadn't allowed it. Though my friends probably would have laughed at me for this childish pastime, I loved to spend a few fleeting moments now and then with the monsters. Carefully I would assemble the pieces of one of my favorite movie creatures with glue. I would then paint every detail of the villain's costume down to the rivulets of blood on Frankenstein's hands, Dracula's teeth, and all over the Wolfman's body. Eventually, the finished product would find its way to my Hall of Monsters, as I classified a particular shelf of my room.

Lately, this relaxing distraction had been put on hold. Months before, I had finished the Big Three monsters of my collection, and they had sat waiting for a new arrival to their domain. With my newly found leisure time, I decided to make a trip to the Men at Arms hobby store to pick up my next project. I would have to travel the entire length of Linden Boulevard, and then cross the bridge into Elmont. I reasoned that this was a good thing because the distant location of the shop would help me go unnoticed while on my errand. Being seen in a model shop could hurt my cool factor.

I wasn't there long when I came upon a new product in the aisle and decided that the Creature from the Black Lagoon would make an excellent addition to my collection. After grabbing a couple of tubes of Duco cement glue and some red paint, I proceeded to the counter to pay for my items. There I came upon an older boy in the midst of purchasing a rather large model of *Old Ironsides*. I could only see his back as I caught the end of his conversation with Harry.

"Do you want the paint kit with the required colors for that beauty?"

"Uh —no. I'm good. But I could use about six tubes of glue to put this baby together."

"I like to make money, but you really shouldn't need more than four tubes to do this job."

"Uh . . . yeah, but I've got a few smaller projects to finish up too."

Even I knew he was getting way too much glue. Suddenly, the stranger turned to leave and ran into me. He knocked my purchases to the floor, and I stood face to face with Tony Provenzano. What surprised me most was that Tony seemed to know me. With that recognition, came a glare that said by its mere expression, *you never saw me here.*

After the initial shock, I looked down to see my two tubes of glue and the broken bottle of red paint I had been buying to gorify my latest monster. Harry and I both rushed to clean the mess. In the process, I smeared red paint from the broken bottle all over my right hand. Under other circumstances, I might have found it funny to see my hand in the same state I had painted all of my pet monsters.

"Don't worry about it kid," said Harry trying to make me less nervous, but it didn't work. As I picked up the glue, I found I had also covered the tubes with a coating of red.

"Here let me take those, and I'll give you some clean ones," said Harry.

"No, I messed them up; I'm not going to stick you with them," I replied, and the owner appreciated it. He was about to say something else when the forgotten Tony entered the conversation.

"I've done that model. You need three, maybe three and a half tubes to finish that. Hey, mister, give the kid two more tubes on me." With that, Tony threw two dollars on the counter and finished, "It's on me. Us Heights guys take care of each other." Both Harry and I knew that two tubes were more than enough, but Tony had a way of discouraging any disagreement with him. Was this a bribe for my silence? Harry wrapped up the purchase (including four tubes of glue, two covered in red paint) and gave them to me while neither of us noticed that Tony had left. When

I walked out of the store, Tony was waiting for me. He wasn't there to exchange pleasantries.

"I'll take that bag, dipshit," was all that Tony said and I meekly handed over my purchase to him. Tony quickly dumped the contents onto the sidewalk, only hanging onto the paper bag. He scooped up the four tubes of glue, including the two covered in red paint. *The Creature from the Black Lagoon* lay alone at my feet.

"You can have that," Tony said pointing to the model. "In fact, you can have this too," he said as he emptied the contents of *his* bag on the sidewalk and only scooped up the six tubes of glue. He left the massive battleship model where it had fallen and walked away.

He had cut off my balls. No one in the Heights would ever dare defy Tony, even if they thought they stood a chance of getting out of the situation alive. If (a big IF) somehow a person could win a confrontation with one of the Provenzano brothers, his life expectancy was about as long as it would take that information to make its way to the rest of his gang. No, I did the sane thing when I allowed Tony to leave with my glue. However, that didn't decrease my sense of shame. Sixteen-year-old boys don't back down from fights even if the bully is older, taller, heavier, and one of the meanest motherfuckers on the planet. I rationalized that one fight a week was my limit.

A true child of the Heights, I knew exactly what Tony was going to do with the glue and the paper bags. You didn't have to be a huffer to understand how it was done. I'd seen too many of them roaming the streets with a glazed look in their eyes. There were too many glue-encrusted bags strewn on the stickball fields and in the hidden recesses of the yard not to know that Tony had never made a model in his life. Yeah, I knew exactly what he was going to do with the massive amounts of glue in his possession.

When Tony was out of sight, I found my way home. When I left, both models remained outside the Men at Arms store. Model making would never be a relaxing escape again.

Entry #14

"The End of the Innocence"
- *Don Henley*

For most of my life, I had played the city games all hours of the day. When there were not enough players for softball, I would effortlessly convert to stickball. I loved the one-on-one competition. I pitch to you against a wall, and then you pitch to me. All that was needed was a *spaldeen,* a cut off broomstick, and a wall with a strike zone rectangle painted on it. There were rules, and anyone who played in our yard would know them. Any batted ball not caught by the fielder was a hit. Hitting it over the fence into the garden was a home run. The climbing of that fence between the stickball fields and the garden was where I took my first detour toward hell, a journey that would occupy the next two decades of my life.

Gio and I had settled into a competitive stickball game, continuing a tradition we had observed for the last eight years. When life threw you curves, then you went out and threw curves. Whenever we had conflicts, we always settled them with a friendly game of stickball. Rather than proving the right or wrong of either side, the game merely served to make us both forget that there had even been a dispute. The game that we played in the early evening of October 16, 1965 ended whatever awkwardness had developed between Gio and me. We didn't speak about it. We were friends, and nothing that had happened between Frank and me or with the band was going to change that fact.

There wasn't much sunlight remaining in that autumn evening. With the fading light of dusk, my fastball became almost invisible. Repeatedly, I hurled it against the concrete wall of the schoolyard and Gio's flailing bat barely even tipped the ball. Nevertheless, it was fun to be with Gio doing one of the things that we liked to do. And then, I good-naturedly began to trash talk.

"I'm going to take a little something off the next pitch. If you can't do something with it, you hang up your spikes." Usually, I never talked like that. However, the heat of the moment had taken over. I would soon regret it. I actually did take everything off the next pitch. Perhaps, I meant it as a peace offering to make up for my uncharacteristic boasting, or maybe it was a friendly challenge for my friend to show what he could do. I just don't know. I've thought about this small point many times in the years that followed. As that final pitch came in, Gio's eyes lit up in anticipation of the distance the ball would travel when he connected. He could hit a little bit, but he never had power, and he almost never reached the fence against me. All that changed with my final pitch.

Entry #15

"Sympathy for the Devil"
- *The Rolling Stones*

Of all days, there didn't seem to be any hole in the fence facing the schoolyard. This made my journey to retrieve Gio's home run ball even more humiliating. As I walked out to begin the climb of shame, I heard Gio yelling something like, "Open your mouth and change feet." I guess I deserved every bit of his ribbing.

I had to climb the fence on the outer edge of a garden located in one corner of the schoolyard. Some misguided principal had convinced the New York City Board of Education that if an area roughly 40 feet by 60 feet were set aside, students would cultivate it into gardens and therefore learn about agriculture. Why he thought students in a lower class second-generation immigrant neighborhood would care about farming remains a mystery. Soon the weed-infested area, with a ten-foot chain link fence around its exterior, fell into disuse. Now only two groups of people, the athletic and the addicted, noticed its existence. It had become a no man's land on the other side of the home run fence for those who played stickball; it became a promised land for the glue sniffers and drunks.

Somewhere along the line, the place took on the ironic name of the "Garden of Eden, " and it stuck. Years later, I discovered that Iron Butterfly's "In-A-Gadda-Da-Vida" was actually written as "In a Garden of Eden." Because this sounded so much like the way most of the huffers slurred their pronunciation of the place, I often wondered if somehow this California band had its roots in my area. By then, however, I knew that my garden could never, would never, lead anyone to fame and fortune.

It was at the top of the fence I heard an unusual sound. At first, I thought that it wasn't worth the cost of a *spaldeen* to go into the garden with the huffers. Yet, what I heard didn't sound like the distinct noises that every kid who frequented the park knew them to make. No paper crinkling or heavy breathing. No incoherent conversations. Instead, I heard a sound I knew very well. The rapid motion of fingers on the fretboard of a guitar made a distinctive screech usually lost in the power of the amplified sound. Occasionally, I had wanted to play after my parents had gone to bed and I had gone "unplugged." Now I descended into the garden to not only retrieve the ball but also to find the source of the music that I heard. Most people in the outside world wouldn't recognize this barely audible tone; however, it was sweet music to my ears. I felt compelled to find its source.

As I descended to the ground, I quickly spotted the errant home run ball and picked it up. I then continued in search of the faint guitar strains. I dragged myself deeper into the dense undergrowth of the garden. This was risky. There were just too many chances of running into someone you didn't want to run into or seeing something you didn't want to see. Still, I pressed forward in the direction of the tinny sound. As I emerged from a final set of overgrown bushes, I found that *someone* and that *something*, and it had nothing to do with my now-forgotten quest for unamplified guitar music. There I spied Tony Provenzano, his face engulfed in a brown paper bag. I immediately knew what was going on. I'd pictured this very scene since I'd seen him in the Men at Arms earlier that afternoon.

Just as I thought that Tony would rise up and punish me for violating his privacy, I saw the pupils of his eyes roll to the top of their sockets and his entire body go limp. I vaguely heard Gio's voice hailing me from outside the garden and yelled at the top of my lungs for him to get over the fence. I immediately jumped on Tony's body and ripped the bag from his face. I quickly realized he wasn't breathing. I didn't know first aid and was lost about what to do next. I tried shaking him and pounding his chest in futile attempt to wake him, and somehow save him from his impending death.

"Let me," I heard a deep voice from behind me say. I knew it wasn't Gio speaking. However, Gio was there. He stood open-mouthed next to a taller boy who now strode toward Tony. "I learned something in health class that might work." The stranger knelt next to Tony and placed his hands on Tony's chest. He started to pump in a timed method. I looked at Gio and realized there was a way we could also help.

"Go to the Provenzano house and tell them what happened. I'll get the police or an ambulance or something," I yelled to Gio. We had only taken a few steps toward the fence when the stranger briefly interrupted his rescue efforts and spoke.

"Go that way," he said as he pointed to the direction he had come from only moments before. "Cut out in the fence, hidden by overhanging bushes. It'll get you out to the street."

"Sonofabitch," was all that I responded. We didn't know that any opening could ever stay hidden. As we both ran on our separate missions, I couldn't help but notice that in a small clearing by exit lay an electric guitar. I would try to solve that mystery later. First, I had to try to save the life of the bastard who had bullied me only a few hours earlier.

I ran across 115th Road and banged on the first door that I came to, all the while shouting like a lunatic for the use of a phone. My violent knocks must have served only to terrify the people from coming anywhere near their door. I gave up on the first house, ran the short stretch to next home and received the same silent response.

As I was about to approach the third house, I saw a police car coming up the perpendicular street that intersected 115th Road. I ran with all the speed that I could muster to intercept the cruiser. As I explained the problem, they didn't seem to care about Tony's plight until I mentioned the name. Everyone understood that many of the patrol officers received Christmas gratuities from the Provenzano family. It was clear that I had stumbled upon two who hadn't had coal in their stockings. As one cop called in the information to emergency services, the other ran to climb the fence only to see me pointing to the hidden entrance. As I led help to Tony, the sirens continued to wail in the distance. Within minutes, powerful bolt cutters were expanding the opening to allow what seemed like the entire medical staff of Mary Immaculate Hospital to enter the garden. They were followed very closely by Gio, who was leading Dominick and Guy Provenzano onto the scene.

With the professionals now firmly in control of the situation, Gio and I faded into the background. We noticed that the big kid soon slowly drifted out of the garden and down the street. Gio motioned that perhaps it was time that we hit the road too. We had done nothing wrong. In fact, in our eyes, we were heroes who might have given Tony a chance to live. However, events in the Heights were always colored by how the Provenzano family perceived them. Who knew how they would react to all this, and so it was better to leave than to find out how our actions were to be evaluated. Eventually, we would discover exactly how Mad Guy felt.

Gio left the garden first as I lingered a few seconds more. I couldn't shake the thought of my run-in with Tony that very afternoon. I then looked down at the paper bag that I had thrown off Tony's face during my initial excitement. I had unconsciously hurled it away into a bush far from the main scene. A thorn had impaled the bag about three feet in the air. The contents of the bag lay on the ground beneath. There lay the glue, the very same tubes that I hadn't had the balls to keep from Tony outside the store. I knew this as soon as I saw the red paint that covered their exterior, the very same blood-red paint that I still found hiding in the crevices of my hands.

Entry #16

"Last Chance"
- *John Mellencamp*

I naively resolved not to allow that night in the Garden of Eden to affect my life. Though it never really left my mind, I fooled myself into believing I could go on with my daily routine. Outwardly, I succeeded in this deception. The next morning, I proceeded to live my life as if that previous evening had ended with the stickball game with Gio.

I probably could've gotten out of school the next Monday. I'd been up late Sunday giving the police my statement about what had happened. They had caught up with Gio and me before we'd been able to slip quietly into the night. However, I was still in denial, so I prepared for school as if nothing had happened. I had compelling reasons to catch the bus that Monday morning. It didn't matter how little sleep I'd gotten. The days were growing shorter. Fall baseball season was ending in five days. By that time, the fringe players like me needed to make an impression on Coach Callan. He would have all winter to ponder our performances.

Of equal importance, the days that I could see Maria on the bus were getting very limited. Five days, that was it. We now had been taking that trip home for almost five weeks, and we'd grown closer as the days passed. Frank be damned. I believed I had a shot with her. The Monday bus trip had encouraged me, but left me confused.

"Maria, this is my last week of practice," I had said, trying to get a feel for what was going on in her head.

"Oh," was her muted reply. I had caught her by surprise, and her response was just an attempt to stall while she carefully thought of what to say. I knew I had put her on the spot and I quickly tried to move the conversation along.

"I guess that we'll do this again in the spring . . . if I make the team."

"You'll make it. I know it," Maria said continuing a conversation about which neither one of us cared. We were feeling each other out.

"I'm not so sure," I continued the charade.

"You will," were her words, but it was her actions that spoke to the real issue. She gently caressed my right hand with her left. She then clenched it tightly. She turned to me and raised her right hand and placed it on my cheek, all the while staring into my eyes.

"You will," she repeated.

I wanted to say so much. I wanted to ask Maria what this all meant? I wanted to ask her about Frank. I didn't give a damn about him, but did she? In the end, I said nothing. Still looking into her eyes, l let go of her hand and tenderly put my arm around her shoulder. She moved her body toward mine and softly placed her head on my chest. We stayed that way all the way home on the bus. Not another word was spoken.

I thought about her all day at school on Tuesday, and I continued to think only of her at practice. I'll never know if it was my lack of concentration that caused what happened that day. Maybe it would have been the same even if I hadn't been thinking about Frank . . . and Maria . . . and Tony . . . and red-stained glue tubes. Maybe it had nothing to do with me at all. Perhaps it was just that damn asshole, Tom McLaughlin, and his goddam inability to control his fastball.

It was a known fact that if you played for the Bishop McCarthy varsity baseball team, even as a sub, you had a good chance of a scholarship. This is what I had fought for all these years, and it became especially important since I'd recently shortened my future opportunities list the week before. It had come down to three of us for the last two open spots on the roster. My chances had improved when the coach had approached me and asked me to spend some time with his assistant coach that winter. He wanted me to become a catcher. I had tried that position a few times in CYO ball and hated it, but if that is what it took to secure a spot on the team, just call me "Yogi" Cipp.

Things were starting to look up. Yet, in my life, every time things seemed to be working out, I'd get the shit kicked out me (sometimes quite literally). During the last week of autumn practices, that's exactly what happened. We'd been working out about an hour when my turn at bat came up. My competition remained Bob Schmidt, and he had stroked a few long balls, but they were catchable. Ever the conniving opportunist, I made a point of letting the coaches see me trying on catcher mitts. Oh, what a phony piece of shit I was that day. You really shouldn't deceive a Catholic school coach. God will punish you. And he did.

My first few swings were nice line drives over shortstop, easily hits in a game. I then lined the next pitch right through the middle, barely missing batting practice pitcher McLaughlin's head. I could see that he was a bit angered by his narrow escape. I really could have messed up his pretty face.

I decided I would drive the next pitch to right field, demonstrating I could place the ball anywhere I chose to hit it. The next pitch should have been a slow lob as was expected in batting practice. This is where I made a severe miscalculation of how much I'd pissed off my teammate with my last swing. I only realized this fact as the ball came rushing toward my head.

My forward momentum didn't allow me many options. Not expecting the velocity of the ball to be McLaughlin's fastest and the location he had chosen to be my face, I reacted defensively and threw my arms and hands up to block a direct hit to my head. Locked into a forward motion, moving away was out of the question. I braced for the hit.

Entry #17

"I Want to Hold Your Hand"
-The Beatles

I never let anybody know how badly I had injured my left hand that day. I know now that was a mistake. In protecting my face, my hand had taken the full force of the fastball square in the flat area below my knuckles. As I reeled away from the plate, I heard a soft, "I'm sorry," from McLaughlin. At that point, I neither believed nor cared what he said or did. *Fuck you, McLaughlin. You changed my life.*

The pain was intense, but I tried to convince Coach Callan that it was nothing. Great programs aren't built on wimps. Being the responsible and caring coach, he sent me back to the school to put ice on the injury. He had plenty more players where I came from.

At the time, I was thankful to go back alone. I didn't want the coach to see how badly I was hurt. Our practice field was quite a distance from our school. With every step of my long walk back, my hand got worse. By the time I put it in icy water, my hand already looked like I was wearing my baseball glove (hell, maybe even a catcher's mitt). It's all a little blurry now, but I remember somehow showering and dressing before the team returned to the locker room. I again submerged my hand in the water so that no one would see how swollen it had become. The coaches took my word for it when I told them I was okay, and I exited the locker room and the school before anyone asked to look at it firsthand.

I met Maria on the bus, and I think she was the first to suspect something was wrong. I was doing everything with my right hand while my left hand stayed in my pocket. However, she didn't say a word. It was a rarity, but we found a pair of seats together on the bus. She sat by the window while I hugged the aisle, all the while my left hand safely held out of view in my pocket. We talked about unimportant stuff while both of us seemed to be hiding something.

"About you and Frank . . . and the band," she started to say, breaking an awkward pause in the conversation. It had been about ten days since our brawl, and I had never mentioned it to her. Coward! However, Frank had been babbling to her over this past weekend. While I was busy saving a life, Frank was attempting to destroy mine by informing her of "what an asshole Johnny had been with the band." In his version of events, he had taught me a lesson with his fists, and I had quit the group because of my shame. I thought that Maria was asking for my side of it until she explained that Gio had told her what had happened. The whole affair had backfired on the jerk, and she now seemed to warm up to me a bit more.

The moment was interrupted when the bus hit a pothole, and I practically fell into the person standing in the aisle next to my seat. As I felt myself careening downward, I had no choice but to reach out my left hand to break my fall. Thanks to my quick reflexes, I didn't leave my seat. However, you would have thought I had fallen off the Empire State Building by the volume of my involuntary scream as my injured hand took the full force of my weight.

Maria looked at me as if I was crazy. Secret martyr time was over. As soon as I had my ass safely back in my seat, I raised my left hand in front of her eyes. When she saw my purplish-blue swollen hand, her expression revealed a little shock and quite a bit of tenderness. She carefully took my injured hand and softly caressed it, and I could swear that I saw the beginnings of a tear form in her eye. I wasn't going to give up that feeling for any reason, but as my hand started to throb, I needed to rest it on my lap. She let go of my left hand, but in one motion took my right hand in hers and held it tightly. These were the actions of a *girlfriend,* not a *girl friend.* I knew that something had changed the day before, but I still couldn't get a read on what was happening.

"I guess that you were wrong about being sure I would make the team. This is a whole new ballgame."

"I don't care about that," she answered and started to cry.

"Hey, you didn't get my *whole new ballgame* pun," I said trying to lighten the mood. It didn't help.

We rode in silence for a short while, and I enjoyed the moment, not wanting to ruin the mood by opening my mouth. Occasionally, we would turn to face each other, and she would give me a beautiful, loving smile. The last time this happened, she placed her head on my shoulder. I was in heaven.

When we came to Maria's stop, I decided to get off with her instead of staying on the two additional blocks that would take me closer to mine. With regret, our hands separated. Of course, I had to use my right hand to carry my books and balance myself, but this was offset by the beaming smile on her face when she realized I was exiting with her. OK, it wasn't as if I was going to walk miles out of my way, but I think that she understood what that gesture meant. As we walked toward her house, we were silent for a while until finally, she spilled her guts.

She told me how she and Frank had an argument about me, and she had broken up with him. Everything made sense to me then. Maria was not the type to cheat on anyone, even an asshole like Frank. However, now she was free, and I was loving it. As we approached her house, she had one final revelation for me.

"Frank had been playing me for a fool," she began. We were near her door but strategically out of view of her parents' eyes. "After I told him we were done, he hit me with the news that he was moving and that he had just been stringing me along until his family relocated to Levittown soon."

Everything changed in that moment. Our eyes met and not a word was spoken. We both knew that it was time. There was nothing now to keep us apart. It was a tender moment that foretold a deep relationship rather than short-lived puppy love. Our kiss was not anything that would ever be considered hot and steamy, but it was much more than I'd ever hoped for when I woke up that morning. Overall, it had been a strange day. I now had seen my second path out of Heights blocked. Two weeks, two dreams lost. And yet I had finally won the heart of Maria. "Strange Days" had found me.

In all that happened that day, an important detail would be lost in my confusion, pain, and joy. Frank Campo and his family had sold their house and would be moving to Levittown during Christmas vacation. Frank's parents, fearing that the "Colored" invasion was going to destroy the value of their cute little semi-attached house on 218th Street, had become one of the first of the white flight families out of the Heights. It was not long before everyone I knew would be gone. This exodus would include the Romano family (with Maria) who would leave amid the violence and heat of the next summer.

Entry #18

"Tear Drops Will Fall"
-John Mellencamp

It has been awhile since I have opened this book to write. I'm embarrassed to face myself. I've again fallen (plummeted?) off the wagon. Though I believe that this journal is good therapy, sometimes it hurts just a little too much to remember. Is it more painful to dwell on the good times or the bad? Writing my last entry brought back so many feelings, wonderful feelings. However, knowing how the story ends completely negates what could've been a good memory. And so I gave up and gave in to temptation. Now I'm back. Relive it, remember it, and rescue it from the dung heap of my mind. Did I sound profound there? Or did I sound like some self-help guru trying to sell someone my get-well program?

As I reread this saga, it has often read like a story of teenage puppy love and silly adolescent antics. Maybe I have unconsciously been thinking that way. Perhaps that is my way of recapturing the feelings and the mood of the way it really was. Or maybe I am running away from reality. Who the hell knows? Maybe if this journal does its job and I recover my sobriety, I will think about sending it to Maria. In the real world, Maria and I became much more than puppy love. But, that was almost two decades ago. To my everlasting shame, I never told her why I left. I need to forgive myself for that before I ever think of asking her or anyone else for forgiveness. I deserted her to save my life . . . and hers. How could I tell her that?

Entry #19

"Centerfield"
-John Fogerty

I awoke Wednesday morning thinking to myself, *What the hell do I do now?* No matter how much ice I put on my hand, the swelling only marginally went down. I should've told my parents, but I didn't. If they saw my hand, there would be a doctor visit and a strong recommendation that I not use the hand. Goodbye, varsity baseball team. More importantly, that meant no late bus with Maria. I wasn't giving that up. Not now!

So, I shut my mouth, kept my hand in my pocket, and went through my day at school in quite a bit of pain. At practice, I kept my mitt on as much as possible. I stayed out of the range of the coaches and hoped that I had built up enough brownie points so far to get me through the final cut. Could I fake it for just three more days?

Because the coaches were so focused on the batting cage, they never really noticed that any ball hit my way was allowed to slow down so that I could handle it with my bare right hand. Sometimes, I just let it roll until it stopped. When it came time to shag fly balls at outfield practice, I adapted various methods of slowing down so that I didn't reach the ball on a fly. If I couldn't avoid catching it, every play became a two-handed affair, with an emphasis on the right hand.

Batting was another challenge. I held my left hand close enough to appear to hold the bat, all the while only using my right hand to power the wood through the strike zone. The result was an awful lot of weak grounders to the right side of the infield. If I could make it through this week, I would show them what I could really do in the spring. My deceit *almost* worked.

On the Thursday of that final week, Coach Callan announced that the next day we would be playing an exhibition game against a team his younger brother coached, a bit of sibling rivalry.

The game started rather innocuously with our team scoring first on a two-run homer by Steve Donato, our senior stud first baseman. All seemed well with *our* Callan brother. Then, St. Joseph's scored three times in the fifth inning off some very sloppy pitching by Tom McLaughlin, and the mood changed rapidly. Though I don't think that God answers prayers for revenge, I did give a little look skyward and mouth something like "thank you" for the decline and fall of the hated McLaughlin. On the other hand, did his two walks and a hit batsman prove he really had no control over his pitches? Was I just another victim of his acute wildness?

When we regained the lead in the last inning, our coach decided to let some of us fringe players get in the game. Most of my life, I would have been the first one chanting John Fogerty's words from his classic song "Centerfield," "Put me in, Coach, I'm ready to play . . . today." Since centerfield was my position of choice, this would've been very fitting. However, in my present condition, I was trying to find a dark hole to hide in. Still, the last inning found me in centerfield, praying the ball would not be hit to me. My prayers were not answered! With the game at stake, a sinking line drive came in my direction.

If I had played it safe and let it fall, the tying runs would surely have scored. But that's not me. I chose to go for all or nothing. I was fast, and there was nothing wrong with my legs. In fact, if I had slowed down, it would have been obvious. And so, I ran full speed. As I neared the rapidly dropping sphere, I could envision nothing else but what a spectacular catch would do for my chances. I knew that I'd be locking up a position on the team.

With the adrenaline flowing, I fully extended my left arm and caught the ball without regard for my injured hand. Even as it was hitting the pocket of my glove, sensations of pain coursed through my arm and my involuntary reaction was to flinch, allowing the ball to come free. With two outs, all the runners, including the fast runner on first, scored. I tried to recover the ball in time to make a play that would salvage my error, but it was too late.

As we walked off the field with a 6-5 loss, I dreaded facing Coach Callan. As I passed him, all he said to me was, "If you touch it, you should catch it." With those words, I knew that my time with the team was over. I would never play another baseball game in my life.

4

The Other Side of Life:

"Dancing in the Dark"
- Bruce Springsteen

"FUCKING RETARD, THAT'S WHAT HE is," screamed Guy Provenzano.

"Don't use language like that in front of your mother," his father said as he raised his hand with thoughts of physically enforcing punishment on his older son. Implicit in his reaction was the fact that he did *not* disagree with Guy's analysis, only his language. Carmela Provenzano still grieved for her living younger son and as usual, came to his defense.

"He's lucky to be alive."

"Is he?" Guy reacted with a pent-up rage that often spilled out in these family discussions. After these outbursts, the family once again fell back into a quiet dinner of Carmela's homemade pasta highlighted by a side dish of sweet sausage that was a favorite with the men of the family.

Tony Provenzano had not been seen in public since his near demise in the Garden of Eden. Due to his inexperience in the fine art of huffing, Tony had inhaled an exorbitant amount of glue fumes. A lesser quantity would have produced a buzz that would have relieved his mind from all of its woes, if only for a few fleeting moments. However, he had taken in too much, and the results had been traumatic. Just barely clutched away from this sweet relief of death, Tony had suffered irreparable brain damage that had led to severe mental impairment. He had the thoughts and emotions of a young child, and much to the embarrassment of his brother and father, he would never develop beyond that point. Dominick had been furious with the turn of events that had left him with only one heir to his criminal empire. How could this boy be so stupid after all that he had done to show him the right way?

Carmela had the opposite reaction to that of her husband and son. She was just grateful his life had been spared, that she still had some part of him. The family arguments were frequent and loud about the question of Tony. In the end, Dominick had felt some uncustomary softness in his heart and had given in to his wife's wishes. Tony would stay in the sanctuary of the Provenzano home instead of being sent away. The question of whether he would ever be allowed on the streets again would be discussed at some later date.

Outside of the confines of his house, Guy could be more open about his feelings. He had a small cadre of friends working on uncovering the true story behind his brother's tragedy. Time had passed and he had grown impatient. Now he was ready for some answers.

"What have you got?"

"According to the official report," started Sal Timpani before Guy interrupted quickly.

"Who's the contact?"

"Richie Shea slipped us out a copy from the precinct," answered Timpani.

"Cousin or not, it's about time Richie earned that grease we've been giving him for years. Go ahead."

"Tony bought six tubes of glue in a place up in Elmont that afternoon. The police found a total of ten near him in the garden that seemed fresh, so they think he got some more from someone else."

"Are you fuckin' kidding' me? Most huffers use one, maybe two. You're telling me my brother used six or more?"

"The store owner said he had sold tubes to a kid right after your brother. He figured the two of them were in on it together and shared."

"How'd he come to that brilliant conclusion?"

"He found the models that your brother and the other kid bought laying in the street in front of the store."

"And why was this guy so eager to help the cops?"

"He was threatened with some kind of drug charges for selling the stuff. The fuckin' rat was afraid of losing his business license."

"Losing his license is the least of his problems." Guy thought for a few moments.

"So, tell me more about those shitheads who saved my brother's life in the Garden of Eden? What do we know about these so-called heroes?" The sarcasm was evident in Guy's tone. Even to his closest followers, the words "shitheads" and "saved my brother's life" seemed a bit incongruous in the same sentence. However, they almost instinctively knew what he meant. Guy had more than once gone on about an all or nothing scenario. Either he should have his brother like he always had been, or Tony should have had the good sense to just die. Only now had he stated it so bluntly for all to hear.

"It's funny you should say that because the police were a little sloppy about getting info. There were either two or three of them. You know that one is Gio DeAngelis because he knocked on your door. And the one who ran and got the cops is Johnny Cipp," reported Timpani. "We are working on the third kid because he disappeared in the middle of all the action. The other two didn't know him at all according to the police report."

"Maybe this other kid was Tony's partner in buying the glue, and he got my brother into that shit. I'm gonna kill that motherfucker!" Guy's face grew redder with rage.

"Not the same kid, Guy. The kid at the store was average height. The unknown kid in the garden was big. We're tracking down some people who think they know him from high school. They think it's something like Bran . . . Bratow . . . I don't know, something fuckin' Polack that begins with a 'B' and ends in a 'ski.' You know what I mean."

The wheels turned in Guy's mind. If any of these three kids had anything to do with what happened to Tony, they were dead. But, what if they really were heroes? They still had screwed up his life by leaving him with a mere shell of a brother. Even if he did want to let these guys know that they had not done him any favors, it would have to be subtle. His mother already wanted her son's saviors declared saints by the Roman Catholic Church. It would be hard for him to do anything other than go with the flow, at least for now.

What to do with Tony would never be simple for Guy. Ever the self-centered egotist, he looked at his brother's misfortune only as it affected him. A handicapped brother lowered the tough image that he had worked hard to cultivate. Moreover, what would happen when his parents passed away? Would he be saddled with this loser for the rest of his life? No fucking way. The minute both his parents' caskets were lowered into the ground, Tony had a one-way ticket on the loony tunes express to whichever upstate facility cost the least amount of money.

He would put up with Tony and have patience about the two or three heroes. However, there was one detail that he could take care of without delay.

"Playing with Fire"
- *The Rolling Stones*

The Elmont Fire Department was a volunteer organization. While one member always operated the phones and sirens in case of an emergency, most of its members slept well each night in their middle-class suburban homes. Only the Cross Island Parkway separated this area of neatly kept single-family dwellings from the chaos and crime of adjacent New York City. For that difference in lifestyle and safety, its residents paid handsomely for the homes. Moreover, it did not matter that some services, like fire protection, had to be provided by volunteers rather than paid professionals.

It would matter to Harry Rothstein, proprietor of the Men at Arms Shop. One late night as he prepared for the Christmas 1965 rush, he was too busy to hear the distant noises at the front of his shop. Before he knew what was happening, two masked men had overwhelmed him, and a single blow to the head had left him unconscious in the rear room of his store. After the strategic placement of Harry near some flammable chemicals, a single match was sufficient to create an inferno of immense proportions.

By the time a passerby noticed the first flames and notified the single communications person at the volunteer fire station, the fire had already created impenetrable walls of heat at both the front and rear entrances of the building. By the time the sirens had sounded, and the first volunteers arrived at the scene, their only hope was to save as many of the adjoining shops as possible. By the time the fire was extinguished over six hours later, there were almost no recognizable remains of either the Men at Arms Shop or Harry Rothstein.

With the Nassau County Police Department in its relatively new phase, an experienced arson squad was merely a dream of the future. The whole affair was chalked up to the careless handling of flammable materials by the now deceased store owner. There was no need to proceed any further with the case.

Mad Guy Provenzano had tasted the blood of his first kill.

"While My Guitar Gently Weeps"
- *George Harrison*

It was always worse this time of year. The Christmas spirit should have made it a bit easier to live with the old man, but it was just the opposite. The short daylight hours of winter meant fewer hours that Stan Brackowski could work in construction. Fewer work hours meant less money, which made the always-angry drunk even more belligerent. A workday that ended around 4 p.m. allowed him more time to drink after work before he came home to the only person who would ever be waiting for him, his son Rocco. Unfortunately, Rocco knew that the combination of less work and more alcohol meant only one thing – more beatings. It was not because the boy had done anything wrong, and it was not because he had failed his father in any way. No, the beatings were the result of him having been born. In that one act, Rocco Brackowski had changed the life of his father forever.

Rocco was the offspring of an infrequent event in southeast Queens, a "mixed" marriage. His deeply religious Italian mother Josephine had somehow fallen in love with a young third generation Polish boy, Stanley Brackowski. Her family, at first dismissive of the outsider, grew to accept him because Josie had fallen in love with him. It also helped that "at least those Polish kids are Catholic." The family was even more accepting when

Josie announced on her first wedding anniversary that she was pregnant. However, Josephine Brackowski had died giving birth to her only child. She only lived long enough to hold her son once and proudly name him after her father, Rocco. Josephine soon succumbed to unstoppable hemorrhaging.

On that fateful day, her newborn son had been tainted with guilt by his initial act of life. It was not that Stan overtly understood what he was doing when he treated his son with cruel and abusive behavior. In a time before grief counseling, his sorrow festered into an uncontrollable rage that manifested itself mostly in the small ramshackle attached home on 219th Street in the town of Cambria Heights. In the confines of that home, there was only one victim available. And so, Rocco took the beatings, somehow feeling that he deserved them for the "murder" of his mother.

Now sixteen and standing over six feet in height, Rocco could easily have resisted his father's attacks. Indeed, he could have administered them in return. Yet, he never did. Instead, he made sure that the punches landed everywhere but on his hands. Bloody lips, blackened eyes, and welts on his body were acceptable, as long as his hands were left untouched. Rocco Brackowski's hands were his only escape. When he was sure that a beating was over and that his father had passed out on the couch, Rocco retreated to his world.

Quietly he would descend the basement stairs toward his salvation. Tiptoeing across the painted concrete floor, he would approach the storage section of the lower level. The drunken sadist who inhabited all the other stories of this house very seldom descended the stairs to Rocco's kingdom. The young man would lift old and forgotten boxes to retrieve his treasure, a Fender Stratocaster. His fingers quickly would warm up to the six strings that were the center of his universe.

For a few years, he had honed his craft on a broken down acoustic guitar that an old man had given him. However, lately, he had upgraded to a Strat. It had not been easy to skim money off the small paycheck that he earned for the three hours of work he did each day at the local A&P Supermarket. His father had gotten him the job after doing some of the masonry work on the front of the store. Stan required that the younger Brackowski turn over his entire check promptly on each bi-weekly payday. However, sometimes people tipped Rocco for the bagging services that he would provide. Because *he* would never pay some kid "to do his job right," it never occurred to the father that tipping ever occurred. Rocco also learned very quickly how to skim a certain percentage off the top of his check when he was allowed to cash it himself. If the paycheck cashing happened to coincide with his father already being drunk, he had hit the jackpot. Rocco soon had enough to buy his salvation.

Most boys his age would have probably thought an electric guitar would be useless without an amplifier. Most boys were not Rocco. Not only would it take a while to save for such a luxury, but also it would serve no purpose. Rocco could never have his playing heard. He lived in fear that even his non-amplified practice down in his basement would be discovered. He could only smile at the thought of hooking up to a powerful Fender Bandmaster amp and letting it crank. The sound would be glorious for one brief, shining moment before all hell was unleashed and his musical journey would come to an abrupt end.

With amplification unaffordable, unsafe, and impossible, Rocco labored alone in his basement with his guitar. For Rocco, however, playing meant bending his head low to barely hear the sounds he created strumming the unplugged instrument. Sometimes when Rocco could not judge whether his father was alert enough to catch on to his hidden place, he would sneak out of the house with his guitar in hand. He knew a secret place in a school garden where he could play in solitude without fear of repercussions. Until recently, that had been a good place for him. Maybe he could return in the spring.

Whether he was safely tucked away in his basement hideaway or on a road trip to the Garden of Eden, he played for hours each and every day. He played every moment his miserable existence allowed. The mere act of playing took him far away to a place where his mind escaped the hell that was his life. His father's cruelty had left him with no friends, no interests, and no life. And so, he played for everything he was missing.

He played chords, and he played riffs. He played sounds that he copied from the music he heard others listening to at school lunch, and he played original variations that flowed from his tortured spirit. He played until his fingers bled and his wrists went into spasms from overuse. Sometimes he thought of nothing, and sometimes he thought of the mother he never knew and the friends he never had. And he played. If he had lived long enough, he would have loved to have heard and played George Harrison's "While My Guitar Gently Weeps." Though Rocco Brackowski himself never shed a tear because his father had beaten into him that men never showed emotion, his tears came out in his true soul . . . his guitar. His guitar wept often during those lonely nights and days of the mid-sixties.

5

Journal of Johnny Cipp

Entry #20

"My Hometown"
-Bruce Springsteen

ALL DURING THE AUTUMN OF 1965, white kids had been verbally harassing the black kids who dared to come across "the line." It hadn't reached the point that Springsteen sang about in his song "My Hometown." His words, "There were lots of fights between blacks and whites," hadn't become a reality in *my* hometown, at least not yet. There had been pushing and name-calling through the summer of 1965, but that was about the extent of it. The renovation of the schoolyard had taken longer than expected, and so the expected influx of the basketball crowd had been delayed. This subdued what could have been a long hot summer.

It was on a sunny Saturday during November of 1965 when Mad Guy Provenzano raised the stakes. The stream of black kids who were showing their faces on the white side of the town had become much more noticeable with the completion of the basketball courts. Most people waited anxiously to see what would happen next. For years, Tino's Pizza Palace had housed a gang of young men who had prided themselves on being something of a border guard against the racial invasion. "The Tinos" had more significance around the Heights as the name of the gang than as a pizza place. They had a reputation that struck fear into all of the black *and* white kids who crossed their path. However, not much had been heard from them lately.

I guess they had just gotten too old for that shit. When their members started to think about jobs, marriage, and the real world, these gangs just faded away. We used to call that growing up. With The Tinos' abdication of power, a void needed to be filled. They had left the border unguarded. The basketball courts in the yard drew the newcomers, and for a while, there had been no formal answer. The white kids kept waiting for a response that would never come. The one person who did notice was Guy Provenzano and it was my unfortunate luck to have been witness to his violent reaction to the situation.

Wrapped up in my own traumas of the previous month, I wasn't thinking about the coming conflict that the new yard was creating. I was feeling depressed about both the state of my musical and baseball careers. I needed a break, and so I decided to take my mind off my problems by catching up with some old friends at the yard.

My friends told me that Mad Guy had been spending more time around the yard since his brother's accident. He just didn't want to be around that "retarded fool," as he was heard calling Tony. No one knew how it happened, but Guy and his buddy, Jack "Leo" Leonardo, had gotten involved in a handball match with two kids from across the line. Who challenged who got lost in the details of the eventual story that passed through the Heights. Guy had entered the match because his partner Leo was beyond doubt the best handball player around. Provenzano could hold his own as a player, but Leo was unbelievable.

Guy had expected to crush his opponents and was shocked when this wasn't the case. The match had become extremely tight, and the smile that had perpetually been on Guy's face seemed to fade as the outcome remained in doubt. While his partner played the best he ever had, Guy increasingly resorted to his cheap tricks of tripping and holding his opponents. It wouldn't be enough. As the match ended in a loss for Leo and Guy, the white audience didn't have to wait long to see how their local lunatic would react to defeat.

Before the black kids even finished collecting their ball to leave, Guy had grabbed a stickball bat from someone. He caught the first of his targets with a surprise blow to the back of his head which sent him plummeting to the asphalt. As blood oozed from a gash opened behind the boy's left ear, his friend seemed indecisive about whether to run or help his downed partner. Guy's friends grabbed him by both arms. The first blow landed in the midsection and cracked two ribs, doubling him over in pain. As both boys lay on the floor, Guy encouraged his comrades to kick them numerous times. They all willingly did so. The notable exception to this attack was Guy's partner, Leo. As he looked at the savagery that Guy and his gang were inflicting on the hapless victims, Leo couldn't control his outrage.

"Stop it! Leave them alone!" bellowed Leo. A shocked Guy turned to his partner.

"Who the fuck are you talking to in that tone of voice?" replied Guy as all eyes turned to Leo. This allowed the two victims to escape the park. Leo then mumbled something apologetic to Guy that I couldn't hear from my location. The moment was over. Provenzano seethed with anger, but he did nothing that day.

Entry #21

"I Can't Keep from Crying Sometimes"
- *Ten Years After*

Most of us there that day had watched the older Provenzano son grow from a young bully into an all-out thug. We knew that Leo hadn't heard the last of him. When given the time to plan his cruelty, Guy had proven to be a first-class sadist.

By that time, I had made the connection of Harry Rothstein's shop burning down mysteriously just after Tony had bullied me out of my glue supply. I was pretty sure that the older Provenzano had something to do with the fire and the murder. I mean he fucking killed Harry Rothstein, the nicest old man you'd ever want to meet. I didn't tell anyone this, because I didn't have any proof. Yet, I knew from watching the treatment of his friend Leo, that Provenzano was nuts. I had seen Leo disrespect Guy, and so had most of the neighborhood. Therefore, his humiliation would also have to be a public affair. Even Guy's mother couldn't get away with raising her voice to Guy the way that Leo had. And he loved her!

Guy had planned well. Knowing that Leo wouldn't voluntarily show his face in the yard, he sent the innocuous Joey Pasco to his house to tell him that all was forgiven and that a big match had been set up. As Joey would relate to everyone later, Leo didn't buy the story for a second. Still, he didn't dare refuse to meet Guy when commanded to be there. It wasn't as if he could avoid him forever. While he headed to the yard, word spread to anyone within shouting distance. By the time the sacrificial lamb arrived for his slaughter, the yard was filled with those who had a morbid curiosity about what was going to happen. It was not going to be pretty, but no one wanted to miss it.

At first, it appeared as if Guy was looking to forgive and forget. He slowly bounced a *spaldeen* and welcomed his once and seemingly future partner. As Leo took a position a few feet away from Guy, they readied themselves to warm up. Leo suspected this was not going to end well when he noticed no other team in sight. The look of confusion turned to pain as Guy turned to Leo, and hurled the ball right into his partner's family jewels.

"You ball-less prick," screamed Guy. There was a mixture of gasps and quite a few giggles from the crowd. The nervous laughs were reflective of *I'm glad it's not me.* As I think back now, I can't believe that I had become so callous to the violence that I looked on with only slight surprise at what was happening. I remember immaturely thinking *Ball-less prick? Does that qualify as an oxymoron?* My internal grammar discussion got no further as the action escalated.

"Are you a nigger-lover? Is the asshole that I shared this fucking handball court with so many times a cocksucking, nigger-lover?"

Whether it was the pain emanating from his groin, or the realization that there was no correct answer, Leo suffered his humiliation without response.

"I said are you a fuckin' nigger-lover?" Within a split second, Guy pulled out a gun that he had tucked in his rear waistband underneath his baggy shirt. An ominous silence fell over the crowd. Before Leo even had a chance to see the weapon, the black, shiny pistol was half an inch from his forehead. Perhaps out of fear, or maybe even shock, Leo finally spoke.

"But, Guy, they won fair and square. You didn't need to beat .

. ." He never finished the sentence. All hope seemed gone. Leo Leonardo, formerly a member of Guy's circle of friends, started to cry.

"Wrong answer," said Guy. He made sure that Leo stared at his index finger as he slowly proceeded to pull the trigger. Out came a stream of water that covered the tears that rolled down Leo's face. However, nothing covered the stream of liquid that flowed down from his crotch to his inner thighs and stained both legs of his jeans for all to see.

Entry #22

"True Love Ways"
-*Buddy Holly*

Since the end of baseball, I had intermittently found various excuses to stay and meet Maria at the bus stop. Occasionally, we would sneak back into the subway station and grab a few stolen kisses. At other times, we would just hold each other tightly for a few minutes. It was all we had. Yet, it was so real.

Now that the band and baseball were gone, she was all I had going on in my life. Then, as quickly as we had warmed up to each other the month before, the chill of November seemed to cool down our relationship. She seemed reluctant to find the time for our rendezvous. When we did meet, she seemed distracted. Yet, when we held each other, it was as if she never wanted to let me go. I was confused. About two weeks after Halloween, we decided to take a walk after we got off the bus. As we strolled around the neighborhood, she explained to me that her parents had been doing a great deal of talking to Frank's parents.

"Johnny, my parents are selling our house." The tears now started to roll down her face. "We just got started a few weeks ago, and now . . . "

"Now what? Maria, are you breaking up with me?"

"No . . . I just don't know what this all means for us?"

"Maria, this just makes our lives and our . . ."

"Our what?" She knew the word I left hanging in the air. Damn.

"Love. This makes our love more difficult. Maria Romano, I

love you." I didn't take those words lightly. I had never said them to anyone before, and neither had she. We had talked about it on the bus at some moment in time when there seemed to be no pressure on our relationship.

Her crying increased but even as her watery eyes looked up at mine, she smiled. She pulled me close and whispered in my ear, "Johnny, I love you." We embraced, and the outside world faded away. That is until a passing school bus full of pre-pubescent school kids let out a chorus of whistles and *woo-hoos*.

We started to walk hand in hand toward where she lived. We soon arrived at our special place, a place as close to her house as we could get without being seen. We always stopped there for our goodbye kiss.

"Johnny, I didn't force you to say . . . you know. I mean we haven't been going out that long."

"Maria, I've loved you for 124 days, since the first time you walked down the stairs of a Ravens' practice. And for more than a hundred of those days I had to put up with watching you with that asshole Frank. If I can survive that I can survive anything."

We kissed.

Entry #23

"Street Fightin' Man"
-*The Rolling Stones*

To some extent, my words were a fraud. The façade was not how I felt about her, but rather about my confidence that we could make it work from a distance? I could think of nothing else but her moving away. I was so angry and upset that I decided not to go directly home, but rather to walk off my frustrations. The more I walked, the more my situation gnawed at my gut, and I wallowed in self-pity. Band gone, baseball gone, and Maria going. Now every part of my life was in the crapper.

Lost in thought, it was already too late when I realized that my rambling path had taken me across the line. I knew that I was in trouble when I found myself surrounded by five young gentlemen who were not giving me friendly looks. Almost immediately I found myself trapped with my back to a fence and five sets of piercing eyes staring at me. I guessed that these angry young men probably had been the victims of similar actions on the other side of the line and now was the time for a little payback. I don't know if even they knew how far they were going to take this intimidation. In reality, very seldom did "we" ever venture to their side. I certainly didn't mean to be there. When I recognized that one of my assailants carried bruises inflicted by Guy Provenzano only days before, I knew that I was in deep shit. First, there were threatening comments, but I wasn't listening.

"What the fuck is your white face doing here?"

How could I answer that? There was no right answer. I said nothing. I was busy looking for a way out. Next, the leader feigned a slap for the sole purpose of making me flinch. This was a typical maneuver among teenage boys. See how scared the other guy is before you take action. See how far you can push him so you know if he will push back. Embarrass the enemy. I'd seen these pre-beating rituals before as a witness, but never as a victim. I did my best to calculate how long it would be before the real beating would begin. Though it was dusk, there was too much light for this to happen out in the open. If I could just hold out long enough, I was sure someone would come by and chase them away. I mean, we were on a main street, and a white boy like me was obviously not stopping to visit with old friends.

Then came the shoves, and like my reaction to the verbal abuse, I just stared ahead and ignored them. I didn't respond. I didn't show fear. It wasn't that I didn't have fear, but I knew that this wasn't going to end well no matter what I did. (Thank you, Mr. Guy Provenzano, for putting these fine young men in the mood to beat the shit out of the first available white kid). In fact, I wasn't even acting tough like I'm sure most of my friends would have done. In reality, I was numb.

There was already so much going through my mind when one thought came to the forefront; I was being bullied. I only then realized that the last time this happened to me, it had been by Tony Provenzano. I had done nothing to stop him from taking the glue I had bought from the Men at Arms store. He had humiliated me. It was only this imminent beating that made me realize how much this had been bothering me. Years of reflection have led me to understand that Tony had destroyed my self-image. He had made a fool of me and then fate had intervened to destroy his brain before I could ever regain my place in the world. I don't know what I could have done besides get myself pummeled by Tony. And now I'll never know. These thoughts ran through my mind as I silently absorbed the barbs, threats, and pushes of my assailants.

Anger grew in me. Anger at Tony. Anger at Maria's parents. Anger at Frank. Anger at Coach Callan. And most of all, anger at myself. Never again would I allow myself to be at the mercy of others. The next action of the ringleader was the final straw. With a smug smile that he turned to share with his friends, he asked, "Ya got any cash, honkie?" Not that I held a vast fortune on my entire body ($1.25 and subway token), but I had just sworn to myself *never again*.

"No, motherfucker, I don't," I responded extraordinarily loud and clear, depositing a fine mist of spittle on his face. This didn't go over well with him. He then decided he was going to find out for himself whether or not there was any financial gain to be had while exacting revenge on this random white boy. He reached out his left hand and attempted to check the contents of my front right pants' pocket.

The anger growing in me was going to make me act eventually. In the end, it was the one singular act of this stranger's hand moving toward my crotch that caused my immediate irrational response to this final humiliation. With everything I had, I grabbed his extended hand with my right hand and held it with an iron grip, inches from my lower body. Almost simultaneously, and in one sweeping motion, my left hand connected with and bloodied his nose. Caught by surprise, he staggered backward. His four friends were not amused, and they decided to show me exactly how unhappy they were.

No matter how hard I try, I remember very little between the time I landed my only punch and when I woke up in the hospital hours later.

Entry #24

"Accidentally Like a Martyr"
- *Warren Zevon*

It was the beginning. It was the end. I now had become a first-hand participant in the violence. I'd gotten my ass kicked, and had become a hero because of it. You know like in the movies when they were always saying, "Remember the Alamo." Well, in my neighborhood they were saying, "Remember Johnny Cipp." I guess I should be glad because I didn't have to die like Davy Crockett. That was the good part. The bad part was that it took a long time for those not-so-fatal wounds to heal. You can do extensive damage to your hand when you land a punch . . . and then find out that you *already* had broken bones in that hand. Yes, my self-diagnosis of a sprain had proven to be completely bogus. With two already cracked bones unable to support the force of my ill-thought-out punch, much of the damage was concentrated in the remaining hand bones. I won't even mention the injuries from the punches and kicks that I *received* as I lay on the ground.

I don't remember many details of my medical care except there were metal pins, a plaster cast, and my first experience with extreme doses of painkillers. I should've learned then that I didn't have much willpower in the drug dependency area. But that comes later.

What I didn't see while I was in the hospital was the violence that was now beginning in earnest on the streets of the Heights. Of course, I only heard one side of the story. Many of the people who visited me (and amazingly this included some girls who wouldn't even look at me before "the incident") couldn't stop talking about how the neighborhood had united to get revenge for what had been done to me. Who knew this is what it would take to become popular?

Apparently, there was the understanding very quickly that there would need to be a little gang recruitment if the Heights was to stay safe for white people. Almost overnight a new crop of "young guns" came together in various forms. The first of these was "Young Tinos" who tried to cash in on the older, now defunct gang's reputation. "The Heights Heathens" drew their name from the ironic fact most of them attended Catholic high schools and the name contradicted their backgrounds. Other groups came and went on an almost daily basis. Many "gangs" consisted of small groups of friends who were styling for the girls because *not* being in a gang meant that you were somehow not a man.

This was the world that I returned to upon my release from the hospital. Every one of the real and pseudo-gangs of the era actively recruited me. I had no interest. It seemed as if that one destructive punch had driven all the rage from my body. Could it have been the potent painkillers that made me so mellow? As the stories of the violence in the Heights drifted back to me, I paid little attention to the details. I was done.

Looking back now, my beating *should* have been the one over-riding event that solidified my turning to the dark side of racism. Evidently, it had been for the rest of my neighborhood. For me, my attackers were merely continuing the cycle that Mad Guy had initiated. That epiphany and the little-known fact of how I survived that day was a game changer for me.

Lost in all the commotion was the fact that one John Barlow, a black kid who had been walking by, had been my savior. Upon seeing my plight, he yelled to a nearby store owner to call the police. He then ran headlong into the scrum of attackers and drew their attention away from me long enough for help to arrive in the form of an ambulance and half of the NYPD assigned to southeast Queens. It is with great remorse that I never sought out John Barlow after the police told me about what he'd done for me. I really should have thanked him for my continuing exis-tence. I would never follow the path to racism that so many of my friends and neighbors did.

This time was also the beginning of the end. While my beating incited the young males of the Heights to rally to defend their turf, their parents rapidly were concluding something entirely different. Spurred on by blockbuster real estate agents who called daily to encourage the sale of homes, white flight escalated at a breakneck speed. The end of the Heights, as I knew it, was coming.

In the midst of the panic to escape the violence, Maria's parents officially put their house up for sale.

6

The Other Side of Life:

"All Along the Watchtower"
- Bob Dylan

THE RESPONSE TO JOHNNY CIPP'S beating was not long in coming. Communications in the fall of 1965 were solely dependent on word of mouth. With bad news always traveling faster than any other kind of news, the white neighborhood became aware of the situation much sooner than the areas west of the line. If this had not been true, the six black teenagers involved in a friendly game of basketball in yard might have been just a bit more alert to their surroundings.

Due to an errant pass, the ball bounced out of bounds towards a group of white boys. If the basketball players had not been so intent on the game at hand, they might have noticed that these white boys had been watching them for quite a while. Seeing the ball scooped up by one of them, Davis Jones, Jr. approached the hostile crowd with great trepidation.

"This your ball?" Owen O'Neill's voice seemed neutral in tone. He repeated his question this time belatedly adding a final word, "This your ball, nigger?" He quickly produced a knife from his back pocket. He waited a few seconds for some response from Jones. When he received none, an evil smirk crossed his face as he plunged the sharpened weapon into the basketball. The hissing sound seemed to be louder than life in the now silent schoolyard.

"C'mon Davis," said one of his friends and the six black boys silently agreed that the presence of a knife had raised the stakes just enough for them to ignore the insults and the damaged ball. Just as Davis had turned to leave, Owen lunged at him with the knife. The white boy's actions were meant to cause the retreating boy to show fear, and at the same time earn the knife-wielder points for style. However, his actions were not seen by the youth who was already walking away.

"Going so soon, coon?" Owen called after the boy.

Davis Jones, Sr., the father of the now imperiled boy, had returned from Vietnam six months earlier. During his ten years in the Marines, he had become an expert in hand-to-hand combat with a particular emphasis on a Japanese form of karate that was quite effective in disarming weapon-threatening opponents. Jones, Sr. had been working quite regularly with his son to make him capable of taking care of himself in tight situations. This was one such situation. With lightning speed, Jones' right foot swept from the ground in an arched motion that quickly landed on the hand that held the weapon. The knife spiraled through the air and fell to the ground. Before Owen could even acknowledge his loss, his attacker administered a series of punching and kicking moves that sent the white boy staggering backward to the hard macadam ground. Torrents of blood streamed from his nose.

Davis' friends cackled with laughter. They knew that he had been taking lessons from his father, but had no idea how far he had progressed. In truth, Davis knew he had not progressed as far as it now seemed. His father had only been home a short time, and his lessons had not been that extensive. However, the first skill that he had studied had been defensive moves against a person attacking with a knife. This seemed to have been a very timely choice until Owen's older brother Sean emerged from the cluster of white kids.

"Now, let's see you try that fuckin' shit with me." Sean carried no weapon of any sort. His hands were all that he needed. This was especially true because those enormous hands were attached to an equally enormous body. Jones had not yet progressed to the lesson on dealing with much bigger and stronger opponents, and so he did next best thing – he faked it. Going through a series of *katas* ("karate ballet" as Davis called them to his father), he tried to appear more skilled than he actually was. As he primed and posed with his arms making menacing but meaningless movements, the older O'Neill merely looked at him quizzically and showed no signs of fear.

"Hey, prick, you want to fight me . . . or dance with me?" The white boys laughed, though the stunned Owen O'Neill did not join in from his front row seat on the ground. Still, Davis Jones twirled and spun with his arms spinning wildly. Perhaps he could retreat now and come back after he had taken a few more lessons from dear old dad. Davis figured they would allow him to go because they had seen what he *could* do. At the urging of his friends, he turned his back to leave for the second time that day.

"Hey, nigger, you forgot your ball," goaded Sean O'Neill, as he hurled the now deflated basketball directly at the black boy's back. Humiliated and angered by this huge mindless jackass, Jones turned and ran toward the white boy, stopping a few feet away from him. Unfortunately, he got too close to O'Neill who quickly removed his hands from his hips, and unlike his rival, gave no warning of what was to come. His right fist connected with all the force of a jackhammer with Jones' mouth and at least two teeth found their way to the schoolyard asphalt in the wake of the white boy's only punch.

Sean's friends laughed heartily at the stark contrast between the energetic movements of the black boy and the one-punch knockout by the brute that they called a friend. They did not care if the six frightened black boys slipped out of the park and back to their side of the line. In all the action, neither side seemed to take note of the significance of what had just happened. For the first time, but not the last, a lethal weapon had been brought into play.

"Takin' Care of Business"
- *Bachman – Turner Overdrive*

The black van waited on the corner of 219th Street and 115th Avenue. Its windowless back doors opened on a signal from the driver, and two of the Provenzano family's most trusted employees emerged with their hands resting firmly in their pockets. They did not expect any problems from these customers, but you could never be too careful when dealing with weapons. Anyone who would harm them would deal with the wrath of their boss.

However, realizing that the stakes were now higher, the dealers decided that it was better to be safe than sorry. They took every precaution that they had been instructed to follow and took no chances with the valuable cargo they carried.

"What'll it be?" As ordered, there would be no idle chitchat. This was one venture that the local police had not sanctioned. No amount of Provenzano bribes would ever be enough to allow the sale of weapons.

"How much for that blade?" said the slim teenager whose affiliation with Young Tinos had begun only the previous week. He pointed to a smooth-handled switchblade that he would be able to carry inconspicuously around school.

"That's a sawbuck," replied the young weapons dealer.

"Shit, man, that's a lot. Can you throw in some brass knuckles for that price?"

"That's another fin. You think you're in fuckin' Chinktown negotiating for a better deal? You want it or not?"

"Yeah, I'll take it," answered the younger boy begrudgingly. His friend purchased the knuckles for $5, and they quickly slithered away into the night.

"Come back when you want some real firepower like this," said the dealer holding up a shiny gun. The doors of the black van closed and the salesmen moved on to their next appointment. This process would be repeated almost nightly along the streets of the Heights, on both sides of the line.

———◆———

"You don't shit where you eat," offered Dom Provenzano with his son Guy at his side. He was dressed in his most impressive suit and attempted to exude the aura of a very powerful and intelligent man. He needed to impress the *capos* with the importance of the proposition he laid before them. However, his choice of vocabulary belied any façade of class. Misreading his boss's quizzical look as misunderstanding instead of disgust at the crassness of the speaker, Dom tried to elaborate. "I mean . . . that's why you have a toilet and the stove in two different rooms." He only made matters worse.

Guy watched his father alienate the mob bosses. He debated whether he should interrupt his father before he embarrassed them any further. When the older man hesitated, his son jumped on the opportunity to inject his wisdom.

"What he is trying to say is that we want to move our operations across the county line into Nassau. We would like permission to bring our traditional businesses into the extreme western areas of Nassau County. The Heights has become a sewer that I wouldn't bring my kids up in."

"But if I understand correctly, it is your family that created this sewer . . . as you call it," replied Queens Capo Gus Travante. "I'll use your father's analogy – you're the ones who shit on your kitchen floor, and now you're complaining about the smell."

"Yes and no," responded Guy not wishing to contradict a boss. "We live there, and we see with our own two eyes what's going on. We may have accelerated the process, but the *jigs* were coming in no matter what." Travante merely nodded, and Guy saw this as a sign that perhaps there was some room for negotiations in this meeting.

"That may be true, but you may have cost us a whole lot of money with your actions." Both Guy and Dom could see where this conversation was going. It was always about the money. It was then that Dom explained how they had strong-armed their way into the real estate business and were making massive amounts of money by aggressively using blockbuster techniques to accelerate the sale of houses.

"We fucking provide the motivation by cracking a few *mulanyan* skulls. When they retaliate, the white kids fight back. Here's the genius of the plan. The white parents don't want that. They wanna run to someplace safe so that their precious little kids wouldn't get hurt. So, what do they do? They put their houses up for sale. And who controls all the real estate offices that sell those houses? Yours truly. As you can see, your cut from the Heights will be higher than ever," finished Dom.

Guy interrupted his father to prevent him from accidentally giving too many details about their side business. The extra profit made from dealing weapons to both whites and blacks was not something that they should discuss with the bosses. Any action that could hamper their working relationship with the law could affect all the operations in that borough, maybe even the entire city. As a bonus, the Provenzanos reasoned that that money from weapons sales did not have to be shared.

"I'm impressed with your innovation," remarked the now more cordial Travante as Dom handed him an exceptionally thick envelope. He timed the payment to have an impact on the approval of where their new business was going. As Travante placed the envelope in his jacket, a bit of a scowl came across his face. "You do realize that we will be stepping on the toes of the Long Island bosses if we let you go on to their turf?"

"They are no match for your power," said Dom. His answer was both a statement of fact and an attempt to massage the ego of Gus Travante.

"Yes, but even with friends there is a certain protocol."

" If we give 'em a little slice of the action, we could smooth things over. That area is earning almost nothing for them now. And of course, you get 100% of the Queens side of the business cut."

"I will make some inquiries with our country cousins out there and get back to you. But, remember this is virgin territory. You need to get your police connections in line and respect the Long Island bosses."

They shook on it, and the Provenzanos left the meeting assured their empire was now expanding. The plan was good, but the details needed to be worked out. Unfortunately, neither one of the Provenzanos was a master of taking care of details.

"A Different Drum"
- *The Stone Poneys*

In January of 1966, stores began to open in the virgin areas of Elmont, Franklin Square, and Valley Stream. Ostensibly, these Provenzano Fine Wine and Liquor Stores would be the typical run of the mill spirit retailers. Before long, they would become hubs for a wide variety of illegal means to get high. Realizing that their clientele was a bit more upscale than the Heights, these *"purveyors of fine wines and liquors"* changed their inventory from *Twister* and *Gypsy Rose* to the classier *Gallo Port*.

Also in the works was the opening of a variety of clubs to take advantage of the growing dance scene. Moreover, if the attendees at these clubs needed more lubrication than legal alcohol could provide, illegal stimulation was available behind the scenes. If the gentlemen were unable to secure the company of ladies to fulfill their dreams, the Provenzanos could take care of that problem too – for a price. Yes, all was moving along well in the Provenzano world.

Back in the Heights, the upsurge in violence was evident but tempered by the onset of colder weather. Forced indoors, both sides of the conflict found fewer opportunities to display their growing rage. The next spring and summer would produce unparalleled bloodletting, and in every sense of the word, it would be a hot summer in this part of the city.

In the interim, life went on in the schools, houses, and occasional social dances. Each person went on with life in his or her own way, each planning for the future. To some, the future meant how and where they would escape from the Heights. To some, it meant how they would get in shape for the next sports season or the next round of fights. To some, it meant thinking about the next assignment due in school. To some, it meant planning who would be the next girl they would screw. To some, the future was only as distant as what was for lunch that day. Time passed for all these people in the Heights with very few of them realizing that behind the scenes, one family determined the direction of their futures.

Increasing numbers of people would be drawn into the swirling kaleidoscope of life that became the Heights. They were all moving to the beat of different drums and trying to travel along on their own paths. For some, those paths would lead to destruction.

"The Loner"
- *Neil Young*

A lone figure shuffled along 116th Avenue. With his right leg less agile than his left, he walked with a lumbering gait reminiscent of the character of Quasimodo in *The Hunchback of Notre Dame*. Occasionally, he lifted his left arm to his mouth and removed the drool that had accumulated there on an all too frequent basis. The vacant stare in his eyes seemed to probe an overwhelming world. The pedestrians who passed by him on the street often looked away. Occasionally a short gasp of horror would seep into the whispers. The lone walker could hear but not understand what was being said about him. In his mind, he had a destination, yet his limited capacities would not allow him to understand the motives behind his quest.

Tony Provenzano was on the streets again. With both her husband and son busy with work, Carmela Provenzano had become his sole caregiver. Dom and Guy chose to ignore his very existence. It had now been almost two months since the unfortunate event in the Garden of Eden, and Carmela was Tony's only contact with the human race besides the occasional physical therapist who attempted to restore, or at least improve, the movement of his limbs. No amount of therapy could restore his mind.

Carmela had decided that even a young child needed to get out in the world. Tony's brother and father had argued vehemently it could be dangerous out there for him. Their ruse had not worked on the determined Carmela who accurately gauged their motive as embarrassment. For one of the few times in her life, she had won a battle, and Tony's reemergence into the world had commenced. A rare winter heat wave that had brought temperatures into the mid 60's had allowed Tony's mother to pick this day for her son's new freedom to begin.

He moved on a path that seemed to have some direction, though the doctors had determined complex thinking was beyond his capabilities. Still, he consciously made decisions as he approached each intersection. Though it appeared as if he did not consider whether it would be safe or not to cross the street, he did muse whether he should turn or go straight at each junction of the road. He continued this process until he finally reached 219th Street. After much indecision, he turned right and headed along the street that held the block-long complex of Public School 147 on its western side. About a quarter of the way down the asphalt path, the school building disappeared and gave way to the massive yard. Tony had once been one of the feared and brutal princes of this turf.

On the last used quadrant of the park lay the Garden of Eden. The overgrowth of trees and bushes created areas where any sight of the fence had been obliterated. It was behind one such growth area that Tony stopped. Possibly by some buried memory or by some animal instinct, he knew that he had reached his destination. Tony moved to a location that held a hidden break in the chain link fence. He crawled through it and staggered into the empty garden. Though he tripped on the vines, Tony continued until he finally stopped and sat in the weeds. He rested after his arduous walk from home. It was beyond reason and logic that Tony would end up in this location, but he had. He had found the exact spot he had been carried from only months before.

———◆———

Rocco Brackowski opened the outside metal doorway from the basement and mounted the concrete steps leading to his backyard. Inspired by the second day of unusually warm temperatures, he had decided to take his music on the road. During the spring, summer, and fall, he often escaped from his moldy, basement bedroom. Though the basement offered a hideaway from the tirades of his abusive father, sometimes he just needed to get away. The Garden of Eden provided such relief.

Humble by nature, Rocco had no concept of how good he was at his craft. Cold weather could have done damage to his prized tool. This caused him instead to bring his cheap acoustic guitar. Today, he would hear with some clarity the notes that his fingers picked across the frets of the worn-out Gibson guitar. Still, he kept the noise down for fear of attracting the attention of any passing pedestrian. As soft as his controlled strums were, they would still be too loud for his home. Someday he would buy that Fender Bandmaster amplifier and blast his hidden talent in front of all who would listen. Someday, all his secrecy would not be necessary. Someday.

Rocco sat in the tiny alcove of forsythia bushes that created his own enclosed mini-amphitheater. The yellow flowers of the spring and the green leaves of the summer were long gone from the surrounding shrubs, but the intertwining mass of the branches provided more than enough cover from the outside world. Here Rocco played on with visions in his head of a much brighter future.

His silent thoughts were disturbed by the sudden sound of an intruder. In the warmer months, an occasional stickball player retrieving an errant home run ball, or desperate huffer might invade the fringes of the garden. Hidden in his little hideaway, they had never stumbled upon Rocco's little corner of the world. However, in the winter, no one ever came anywhere near this pit of weeds. So, who had changed this pattern?

Rocco looked up and gazed at Tony Provenzano. This was not the same person that he had saved, but rather a shell of that former being. The eternal loner, Rocco Brackowski had not even followed the local gossip about Tony's fate. He was caught totally by surprise at what he saw before him and was at a loss for words when the interloper spoke.

"You play good. I listen to you," mumbled Tony. Still trying to take in all that was before him, Rocco just stared at this intruder. "You play; I listen," continued Tony. In his former life, these words from Tony would have amounted to something of a command performance. Rocco quickly assessed the Tony before him and realized that it was merely a request wrapped in a compliment.

He played on, and Tony sat across from him and listened. When he went into his version of The Beatles' "Act Naturally," complete with a country-tinged guitar solo, Tony's face broke into a broad smile that was so infectious that even Rocco allowed himself a small grin, a breakthrough for the usually stoic Brackowski. After he had finished the song, Tony started to break into long applause to which Rocco quickly reacted.

"Shh, this is my . . . err *our* secret place," whispered Rocco.

"Why?"

"If people knew that we were here, it wouldn't be a good place to be, so let's keep it just between you and me."

"Yeah, between Tony and . . . What's your name?" questioned Tony.

"Rocco Brackowski"

"Rocbat . . . Braw . . . Roki," struggled Tony before finally saying with a smile, "Bracko!"

"You know what? That's just fine. Bracko it is."

Every time that Rocco got a chance that winter and spring, he went to the Garden of Eden to play. On every occasion, he had an audience of one.

"Roll Over Beethoven"
- *Chuck Berry*

Joseph Tinley Jr. was tired of being good. He always did exactly what his overly ambitious, social climbing, anal-retentive father wanted. He did not know any other way to live his life. Sometimes Joey just wanted to break loose and tell that asshole where to go. Of course, he would use all the proper words his father continually reminded him were a sign of education and class. Instead of asshole, Joey might use something like *gluteus maximus void* or *derriere aperture* so as not to disturb his father's unique sense of vocabulary. He would get the point.

Even his name was pretentious. To his friends he was Joey, but this disturbed his father's sense of the universe. Therefore, his father always corrected his acquaintances and told them to call him Joseph. (*Someday, I am going to be a psychologist's trip to Europe,* thought Joey). Yet, he put up with this crap (*That is feces to you, Mr. Tinley*) because if he showed the slightest rebel streak, the screaming would become insane. Joey (*That is Joseph, Mr. Tinley*) could handle it. What he could not handle was the abuse that his mother would take if she tried to intervene. It would not be physical abuse, but rather a verbal barrage of such devastating intensity that it would rip the very core of his mother's spirit from her frail body. Therefore, Joseph Tinley Jr. usually did what Joseph Tinley Sr. said.

The main conflict between the two centered on how much time the young boy should spend practicing the piano. Tinley Sr. was obsessed with seeing his son becoming the greatest pianist who ever walked the Earth. Anything less would be failure and he let his son know that fact quite frequently.

Joseph Tinley, Sr. was one of the few college-educated and trained music professionals in the entire Heights area. Teaching general music and chorus to the college-bound and snobby girls of Mother Seton Academy upset him all day long. He had been asked by one young student, "Will knowing the notes of a scale help me meet a rich husband?" On most afternoons, he then rode his ancient Ford Fairlane throughout the affluent areas of Great Neck to give private piano lessons to the equally spoiled children of those areas. He would have loved to open a studio in his basement, but that was an absurd idea. None of the lowlifes in his neighborhood cared about music. They did not even know *real* music. They listened to the trash that some deejay calling himself Cousin Brucie was ceaselessly playing over the airwaves. No, he could not fill one afternoon with scheduled lessons from this town that had no idea who Bach, Chopin, or Mozart were. They might know the name Beethoven, but they thought his first two names were "Roll Over."

The first real musician to come out of the Heights would be none other than Joseph Tinley Jr. His father would make sure of that. He would use every spare moment that he could squeeze out of his busy schedule to instruct his only child about the skills and nuances of being an accomplished pianist. Most children faced with Mr. Tinley's overbearing methods of instruction would rebel against not only him but also the instrument itself. Joey, however, not only loved to play the piano but also genuinely excelled at it.

By the age of seven, he could play "Für Elise" and many other staples of classical music to perfection with both style and skill. By sixteen, acceptance into Julliard was a foregone conclusion. Yes, Joseph Tinley Jr. was from the Heights, and he could play the classics with accuracy and skill. However, he kept hidden from the world the fact that he also could play the latest rock songs with equal skill and a great deal more passion. He told no one his musical secret. Besides being able to play Bach, Chopin, and Mozart, he could also play Beethoven, both Ludwig and "Roll Over."

7

Journal of Johnny Cipp

Entry #25

"Crossroads"
- Eric Clapton

BY THE BEGINNING OF DECEMBER 1965, I was pissed off and depressed. Less than two months before I'd had this great checklist of daily tasks to help make my life better. Now I had a list of a different kind. Baseball and band gone – check. Big freaking cast on my left arm – check. Future screwed up – check.

Maria's house was about to be sold, and her parents had a binder on a place in Valley Stream, about seven miles away. The writing was on the wall. I'd been lost since getting out of the hospital and returning to what passed as my normal life. I mean, what was normal about it now?

I did have some good moments. Maria visited me quite often while I was recuperating. My parents were cool about that. I lived in a secluded finished attic. The creaky wooden staircase that led to my refuge was usually an obstacle course of my possessions for anyone who wished to visit me. On the days when Maria was that visitor, my junk was more abundant. This was not to keep her out, but rather to make it next to impossible for either of my parents to surprise us while we were busy making out.

Gio also visited frequently. On those days, the obstacle course was relatively light. This was to encourage my parents to offer snacks to us while we bullshitted. I often think that my mother had figured out the pattern of my *stair junk*. After a few weeks of visits by Maria there were almost no attempts to storm the Bastille. Meanwhile, Gio and I grew fat on Hostess Sno-balls and chocolate milk.

Though our friendship was as tight as ever, our musical connection had ended. Gio didn't want to talk about it and neither did I. I figured out that The Coming Generation no longer existed. Frank had moved. Gio and Jimmy Mac still practiced their harmonies and fooled around with the music, but one guitarist and a drummer do not make a band. Only once did the topic come up.

"Giovanni, the doctors told me that there is a good chance I might never regain the fine motor coordination in my left hand. That would mean I won't be able to place my fingers on the frets of a guitar."

"What do those fuckers know?" was his supportive but stupid answer.

"Hey, watch the language. You know how my parents feel about, you know."

"You mean the word 'fuck'?"

"Yeah, that's exactly what I mean."

"OK, I'll make you a deal. You don't call me *Giovanni* anymore, and I won't say *Fuckers*, at least not in your house."

"It's a deal, Giovanni. Hey, you got in one more f-bomb, so I got in one more Giovanni."

I knew what he was doing. He was sharper than he let people know. The whole conversation had been to get my mind thinking of something else. Gio was a people person, and he always knew what to say. My musical future didn't look bright, and Gio knew it.

On one of my better days, I asked him what was going on with Jimmy Mac and him since Frank had moved. They were planning for the future but had no prospects about how to recruit good musicians to join them. They agreed they wouldn't settle for crap. They had to be great. Jimmy Mac's drumming had always been exceptional, and now Gio had committed himself to being the best damn rhythm guitar around. He had developed great timing and a wrist strum that perfectly syncopated with Jimmy Mac's drums. But, it was their harmony that was the single most mind-blowing part of their collaboration. The sound they produced was so smooth and unique it seemed as if it had come right off the radio. I found this out when Jimmy Mac came along with Gio on one of his visits. After hearing less than one song, I was overwhelmed. At the same time, it broke my heart that I'd never be a part of that world. Seeing my apparent despair, they cheered me up by telling me a story about auditioning a musician to join them.

An old classmate had called Jimmy Mac. He wanted to show them what he could do on keyboards. Though Jimmy Mac and Gio had been concentrating on filling the bass and lead guitar slots first, they figured maybe they might have lucked out by getting this call. Keyboard players were rare in the Heights. The scene looked promising when Carmine Guardino showed up with a brand new Farfisa organ and a Fender amp. Asked what he would like to start with, Carmine excitedly said, "96 Tears." This classic garage band staple by the one-hit wonders, Question Mark and the Mysterians, relied heavily on a single dominating organ riff throughout the song. Though not very difficult, it did require a bit of endurance on the part of the musician.

Jimmy Mac and Gio ran through the song with Carmine adequately handling the organ work. They both had high hopes that perhaps their duo had become a trio until they asked the keyboardist if he wanted to try one of The Rascals' tunes. Carmine replied that he didn't know any of them.

"How about 'House of the Rising Sun?'" asked Gio.

"Nope," answered Carmine.

"Blues Project's 'Where There's Smoke' or 'Gimme Some Lovin' by Spencer Davis," pushed Gio further.

"Nope and nope," answered Carmine.

"Well, what *do* you know how to play?" blurted out Jimmy Mac who had lost patience with this whole process.

Carmine responded by going into a chorus of "96 Tears," and said, "That's it." He had rented the organ, practiced the one song, and hoped to fake the rest of his musical career. He had heard that band guys met girls and he had been suffering through an excruciatingly long losing streak in that area. We never stopped laughing at this story.

A few days after their visit, the cast came off my left hand. I didn't speak much to my parents on the way home from the doctor's office. I guess that they knew that I was anxious about how well my hand had healed, and how well I would be able to perform the tasks of daily life. Screw daily life, I only cared about whether I could play the guitar.

My stomach knotted as I anticipated trying to play some simple chords. Could four fingers of my left-hand move in the coordinated motion needed to hold the strings down on the frets of the guitar? I didn't sit still for a second during the ride. What song would I try? "Love Potion Number Nine" just for the sentimental value? Easy or complicated chord creation? Acoustic or electric guitar? In the end, it didn't matter. The doctors had been right. I wasn't able to play.

Entry #26

I tried to think of a witty song title, but nothing came to me. Music Doctor, have you deserted me? I was in the midst of one of those frequent bouts of depression that Padre has warned me I would have. I want so much to drink something, to take something – anything. I want to forget. My hand seemed permanently damaged. No baseball. No guitar. No way out. I think that I will try and write again tomorrow.

Entry #27

"Lost in a Lost World"
- *The Moody Blues*

It was time to turn to the boring *Plan C* of my life. College. Recent events had made this the only viable option to escape the Heights. I was getting decent grades that might get me into one of the free city colleges. If my grades were not on a level that would get me into Queens College, there was always the community college route. Whatever I did, it would be a start, more than anyone else in my family had ever done. I guessed it was time to take this whole life choice thing more seriously. However, that led to the eternal question: *what would I be when I grew up?*

It was then that I turned to my old friend DJ. Dennis James Spinelli had sat next to me for almost three years of high school, and we had developed a friendship based on our mutual hatred of all math and science classes. We had shared laughs and, at times, some deep thoughts. Now, however, since my world had been turned upside down, DJ and I became even closer friends. In the end, he affected my life more than I could ever have envisioned when I first met him.

DJ turned me onto the world of words. In the twenty years since I last saw him, more than once I have picked up a *Rolling Stone* magazine and seen the byline, DJ Spinelli. Even back then, I could tell he would make it. His devotion to the written word was almost at a religious level. When the rest of us were struggling to produce two-page essays, he was producing masterful tomes on whatever topic he tackled. But his real gift was poetry. His work was colorful and inspiring, with a hidden layer of meaning that was waiting to be found much like a Christmas present waiting to be unwrapped. I envied his ability to use words in a way that I could only dream of doing. This was especially true when I realized that his poetry was so similar to the writing of song lyrics that he could have easily gone in that direction if he wanted, and I told him so.

During every chemistry and Trig class, we would drift off into our separate dream worlds. He encouraged me to keep a journal as he always did. We shared our writings and thoughts about music and life. We pushed each other to understand the meaning of words that increasingly lay hidden in 1960's music. Great thoughts were there for those who cared enough to unlock the secrets of those songs. This brought me back full circle to the music. If only I could play again, I would write songs that had lyrics that would match the quality of the notes that embraced them. If only, I thought.

DJ and I tried out our ideas on each other, and our creations grew from the feedback we received. Sometimes we even collaborated to create lyrics for songs, which at that point in my life could never or would never have music put to them. Little did I know that many of them would have been on my band's first album.

Entry #28

"Saved by the Music"
- Justin Hayward and John Lodge

My story could have ended at this point. I could have been one of the masses of young men who found themselves eking out an existence while waiting for my draft notice to arrive. That letter would include an all-expenses-paid trip to Vietnam, offered on a can't-refuse basis. Perhaps I would have found my way into college and made something of myself. I guess I'll never know. On a cold December morning in 1965, my life took another turn, only this time for the better.

It was DJ's idea. Without giving me a reason why he convinced me to cut out of lunch and follow him on what he called a secret mission. No matter how many times I asked for clues to our destination, he remained mute. However, once I got within shouting distance of the auditorium, I began to put the pieces together. It was then that I heard the notes of a piano wafting through the hallway. Because my high school had no formal music program, the tinkling sound of the keys aroused my curiosity.

"Well, what do you think?" said DJ.

"What do I think of what?" I answered.

"You . . . me, holiday concert chorus."

"Yeah, right," OK, I did miss music, but my experience with it had revolved around playing it, never singing it.

"On my way to the office one day, I heard this kid playing in there, and I was blown away. Not our type of music, but unbelievably good stuff."

"So?"

"We get to know him. And then he puts some music to our words. Simple, huh?"

"Yeah, simple? How do we do that, genius?"

"We join the winter concert group."

"Now I know that you're nuts! You know that I sing like some fucking dead frog."

"Make that a *live* frog. A *dead* frog would sing better than you because he would be dead . . . and silent!" shot back DJ. He then explained that the concert consisted of about a hundred guys singing corny Christmas songs in unison. There were no tryouts, and there was even a place for live croakers like me. The quantity of voices seemed to be more important than quality.

He had hatched this half-assed scheme while hanging out in the office doing a part-time job filing papers. Always the snoop, DJ was privy to the gossip. He had been following this whole scenario from the beginning. Apparently, a student Christmas pageant was a tradition in other Catholic high schools, and our new principal didn't want to be outdone by anyone. DJ's info was that he was being encouraged by some of the younger faculty, mainly a certain Brother Christian who was both musical and mysterious.

When the whole project seemed to be falling apart, this young Turk pressured his boss with *it's-time-to-shit-or-get-off-the-pot*. (Though I'm sure that the religious side of these particular brothers would have prevented using those exact words). Brother Christian had found that Mother Seton Girls High School couldn't afford their full-time music teacher any longer. As a solution, our school agreed to pay part of his income in return for this teacher offering some afternoon music electives and the supervision of two shows per year. Thus Mr. Joseph Tinley joined the staff of Bishop McCarthy High School. This deal had one other stipulation that radically altered the course of *my* life. Ever the shrewd negotiator, the music teacher insisted that part of his compensation include a full scholarship for his son. And this was how Joey Tinley found his way into the auditorium of Bishop McCarthy High, and eventually into a band with me. Not knowing any of this at the time, I still balked at DJ's plan until he threw in the clincher.

"Rehearsal runs until four. And then you can catch the train to meet . . ."

"Maria," I blurted out when it dawned on me just where his sales pitch was leading.

"You got it," he said with a smirk on his face.

"You should have just led with that. I'm in."

———◆———

Life went on as the Christmas holidays approached. My time

with Maria was wonderful but tempered with the reality that she would be gone before the next summer ended. Houses in the Heights were selling at a breakneck pace. White flight had blossomed into a full-scale Caucasian stampede.

At those moments when I wasn't around Maria, I seemed to be going through the motions of life. DJ called this malaise. Only he could use a word like that at sixteen and get away with it. I should've known then that he'd go far. The winter concert was a joke to us, but we continued to show up at the rehearsals. I did it to kill time before meeting Maria, and DJ did it to try and strike up a friendship with the keyboard player. He eventually got his wish.

One day, DJ and I were busy *not* paying attention to our chemistry teacher. While he was rambling on, DJ was busy writing some song lyrics for an imaginary band that he somehow would front one day. Meanwhile, I was listening to music through an earphone stuck in a small AM radio that I had hidden in my jacket pocket. Because we were both preoccupied, we didn't hear our teacher read a series of announcements that typically would be broadcast over a now non-functioning PA system. As a result, we showed up for a chorus practice that had been canceled earlier in the day.

Entry #29

"The House of the Rising Sun"
- *The Animals*

We knew that something was wrong when we realized that we were the only ones headed to the auditorium. We might have bolted to the subway quickly if we hadn't heard the sound of a keyboard playing The Animals' "House of the Rising Sun." As we carefully opened the door, we saw the young pianist who accompanied Mr. Tinley at our daily rehearsals. Though we didn't know him, we did know *of* him. Despite DJ's best efforts, we still hadn't found a way to make the first-hand contact with him. He wasn't in any of our classes, and he never seemed to be just hanging around. This was strange. He was from the Heights. Many factors could have contributed to our lack of knowledge of him and his total absence from both the Heights and high school cultures. He was new to the school, and because his father worked there, he never took the bus or train in either direction. It was evident he spent much of his time practicing his craft, and we eventually found out he never left his house.

The one thing we did know about him was that he sure could play. He backed up his organ solo with a driving beat on the lower keys of the instrument. It was the constant chord changes made with his left hand that made the song so irresistible to us as listeners. To hear this music played by someone sitting in front of us was a mind-blowing experience. We were motionless until he completed his serenade. Only then did he become aware of our presence.

I remember very little of the actual conversation that would begin my friendship with Joey. He was embarrassed and shy when confronted with an audience. As confident as he was as a musician, he lacked that same quality as a person. It didn't take a genius to figure out he never left his damn house. How the hell was he going to learn how to interact with people?

We talked about the Heights (not that he had a lot to contribute). We talked about him (don't ever call him Joey in front of his father—it had to be Joseph). We talked about school (he loved it, except for the shorter haircut required). Most of all, the three of us talked about music. *Don't tell my father what you had heard me playing.* There were quite a few rules in his life so he enjoyed running wild when his father wasn't around. To most people (and especially in the Heights) playing an Animals' song on an organ didn't qualify as "running wild," but I guess it was all a question of perspective. Not allowed to play what he liked at home, these were golden moments for him. He loved all the same music as DJ and me but didn't own a single record that reflected that preference. It was forbidden. As he looked at the clock, we realized that he was already anticipating the end of the faculty meeting that had given him this brief moment of joy.

Joey Tinley was on the fast track to a great life, but it was not *his* life. It would be his father's dreams and ambitions that would guide every decision in Joey's life. Therefore, he played the concert tunes correctly and vigorously, but with no heart. He loathed his life. To him, getting out was not everything it was to me. He wanted to get out on his terms.

Entry #30

"Teacher"
– Jethro Tull

It was a crime punishable by detention, but DJ and I decided to cut out of lunch every day after that first visit to the auditorium. We knew that Mr. Tinley didn't arrive at the school until just after the first lunch period. This scheduling fluke allowed Joey the freedom to play for his entire lunch period as per another deal with the administration. However, our principal was a stickler for rules, and therefore Joey required faculty supervision. And this is where Brother Christian entered the story of my life.

Extremely young, both chronologically and attitudinally, he often found himself in conflict with his much older and more conservative colleagues. He had come to religion after a very sordid teenage and young adult life. Brother Christian never gave us all the details because then he would have to use the phrase that we all hated so much, "Do as I say, not as I do." His own choice of hairstyle and extreme political views made him a pariah among his peers. Yet, strangely, he did belong there. He was a profoundly religious man, and he loved to instruct kids, always presenting exciting history lessons with enthusiasm not often found in any classroom in any school.

The administration thought they were punishing him for his actions. They couldn't give him detention for his hairstyle. Instead, they believed they were making him suffer by forcing him to sit in an empty auditorium every day babysitting some musical prodigy. Little did they know that much of Brother Christian's debauchery between college and his religious life had involved music. This much he told us. He loved the time spent listening to Joey play and even encouraged his more diverse musical choices.

Brother Christian looked to be about twenty years old, but the fact that he had gone to college, gone astray, and then found God, told me that he was probably in his late twenties. His jet-black hair, blue eyes, and pale skin hinted at the fact that he was probably Irish. Brothers, however, didn't use last names in those days and so I never really knew what his background was. Years later, I would try to locate him, but with no last name to work with, this would prove impossible.

He was about six feet tall and skinny, but I never knew if this was the result of an effort toward fitness or the residual effects of a life of drugs. He had a laid-back attitude and found it easy to smile at almost any circumstance. He would turn out to be both my guardian angel and my savior, and I never got to thank him for it.

Our lunchtime visits to the auditorium continued every day even though DJ and I didn't have permission to be there. The first time I understood that Brother Christian was different than most of my teachers was when he uttered the words, "I won't tell if you won't."

———◆———

Those stolen moments spent with DJ and Joey remain some the fondest memories of my high school years. At first, we simply listened to Joey go through his "secret" repertoire of songs. However, as time passed, DJ and I would pull out some lyrics that we had scribbled on pieces of paper. We would mesh our words with a tune Joey would create. This was our initiation into the world of songwriting. One of those songs, "Words of Doubt," would have been recorded. In June of 1967, the contracts were there to be signed. It never happened. However, none of that tragedy could be foreseen. We didn't know what lay ahead; we were just having fun.

It was about mid-January when I got a stupid idea. The instruments that had been used by the concert band still lay on the stage almost a month after the performance. The students who had played them cared so little about music that their instruments were now gathering dust. In a moment of immense stupidity, I picked up the guitar. It had been a while since my last attempt to play. Perhaps, I had healed.

My right hand fell right into a rhythm as it struck the strings in a beat that was jubilant and upbeat. However, the sound was reminiscent of a dying cat. No matter how hard I tried, the fingers of my left hand couldn't move close enough on the frets to produce the notes and chords that had once been almost second nature to me. Aware of my visible struggle, DJ and Joey tried not to look at me for fear that I would be self-conscious.

I walked away from them to the seclusion of an off-stage area and tried to run through some simple riffs. Slowly, very slowly, I attempted to form a bar chord found in any of a dozen songs that, until a few months ago, I played with ease. It was of no use. I felt as if there were tiny walls in between each of my fingers that restricted the ability of each to come in contact with the others. With this impediment, the chord formation proved to be an impossible task. It hit me all at once that I would never be able to do this again.

Though my stomach churned and I desperately wanted to scream, I did nothing. After a few moments, I returned to the room and calmly replaced the guitar on the stand. I turned without a word to either Joey or DJ and walked away. At that moment, I wanted to strike out at someone, anyone. Such was my depression, I might have sought solace in any number of destructive ways if there had not been one other person in the room for all this drama, Brother Christian.

In typical adult language, he said, "Do you want to talk about it?"

"No, I'm good," I quickly responded. But I did want to talk about it. I had for a long time. It couldn't be with Gio or DJ because they just didn't get it. And God knows, it couldn't be with my parents. They were great about doing things for me and caring about me. However, they had gone through the Depression and World War II, and what was bothering me wouldn't be a big deal to them. Right now, I had no one and nowhere to turn. And so, I sat down with Brother Christian.

My tears may not have come out, but all my pent-up feelings and thoughts did. Everything that had piled on me for the last three months was out there. Maria and her moving, the band fiasco, the fight, the broken hand, the loss of my baseball career – it all came out. I laid my inner feelings bare for this stranger to hear. I don't know if I thought that this was like going to confession and he was bound to silence. I didn't care. My words flowed like water and didn't stop until the story was complete. I hadn't looked him in the eyes as I told my story, but I was acutely aware that he was staring at me.

When I finished, I waited for some words of wisdom about what I should do, and all I got was, "So what are you going to do?"

What am I going to do? I thought. *You're the adult, and adults are always telling me what to do and now when I really need some advice, nothing!*

"Do you think anybody but you is going to solve your problems?" It was then that he uttered the words that I would hear so many, many times later in my life.

"God grant me the serenity to change the things that I can change,
The courage to accept the things that I cannot,
And the wisdom to know the difference between them."

I remember looking at him as if he was crazy. Though I thought the words were very insightful, I recognized them as the Serenity Prayer from Alcoholics Anonymous (knowledge given to me in 11th-grade health class). I reacted strongly.

"Of all my problems, drugs and alcohol are not on the list," I shouted at him.

"They were on my list. My answer was a life of sobriety, serenity, prayer, and teaching. I am extremely happy with my choice. However, my choice *is not* your choice. A different set of problems means different solutions. What are *you* going to do?"

I don't know what changed that day, but I did know that I would find a solution to my problems and that Brother Christian would be there to help me.

Entry #31

"Something Better Beginning"
- *The Kinks*

The next day I dawdled and didn't get down to the auditorium until much later than usual. I could hear music coming from inside. Another faculty meeting meant Joey was forced to stay and wait for his father. This also meant he could play whatever he wanted for about an hour or so.

As the music drifted to my ears, I noticed something was different. It wasn't just the keyboards that could be heard, but rather the sounds of a band, and *they* were playing one of my favorite songs of the time, "Gimme Some Lovin'" by the Spencer Davis Group. The bass guitar pounded its now legendary riff that was soon joined by a joyous organ and an exuberant tambourine.

As I opened the door, it was DJ as the whirling and twirling "Mr. Tambourine Man" that first caught my attention. My eyes quickly moved to Joey playing the two-chord shuffle with his left hand on the piano, while simultaneously playing the immortal organ introduction with his right hand on his Farfisa organ. The final puzzle piece became apparent as I watched Brother Christian enthusiastically thumping the integral bass notes to the tune.

What are you going to do? Brother Christian had asked me yesterday, and now it seemed that I had my answer. I wanted so much to be a part of this musical event that it hurt. If only I could pick up the guitar lying there and join in with the simplistic G and C chords. However, the lunchtime fiasco the day before had proven that it was not an option.

I've often wondered if what happened next was fate, or if Brother Christian had planned the course of events with the cunning of Machiavelli. The glint in his eye made me think to this day that the latter was the case. The PA system blared at a volume that drowned out even the raucous music of the makeshift band. Its message was clear, as if explicitly directed at Brother Christian, "*All* faculty will report to the library at this time for a meeting." On cue, the brother rose to leave with a remark that again seemed staged.

"That's me they're calling," and with that, he unmistakably changed my life by handing me the bass guitar. In seconds, he showed me the powerful yet simplistic note changes that were involved in the song. He was then out the door with what I swear was a little wink of his eye. I then hit the first note in my new musical career.

At first, I struggled with the pain that coursed through my left hand. Very soon, I realized that I could bear it. I also realized that the physical restrictions placed on my damaged hand while playing the guitar didn't apply to the strings and frets of the bass. Rather than having difficulty in maneuvering my fingers into the tight spaces of the guitar, the bass ironically spread my fingers to their limits in a way that was not outside the realm of my abilities. I found this feeling overwhelming. I was no Jack Bruce that first time, as I simplistically played the single bass notes that corresponded to the chords I would have played on the guitar. But, shit, the fact that I could play anything amazed me.

Yes, Brother Christian, *what will I do now*? I had no answers, but at least I had questions. How could I build on this skill? Could my hand physically hold up to the stress of the practice schedule I was already planning in my mind? And more importantly how the hell was I going to get a bass of my own? You might say I was a bit impulsive after a mere fifteen minutes of playing. You might have made a case to a rational sixteen-year-old, but you wouldn't have won that case. I was desperate, and there was absolutely nothing rational about me. More than that, I really, really knew what I wanted.

What had started some years before as a passion for the guitar, had now almost instantaneously morphed into a specific desire to play the bass. It was unexplainable. Some people are meant to wail solos out on guitars and be out front in the spotlight, but that wasn't me. I had always liked to be in the background, enjoying the creation of sound from a close but separate distance. I don't know what mind set put me here in this place, but I immediately took to laying down the backbeat of sound that others could shine in. To this day, I swear that this should have always been my path. Why had I never thought of it before?

The next day during our half hour lunch escape, I again felt the sensation of pure bliss as Joey and I repeated the "Gimme Some Lovin'" performance of the day before. I knew this was an act of charity on the part of Joey because he very seldom used his few precious moments of musical freedom to do repeat songs. He was doing it for me, and I appreciated that fact. However, Brother Christian wasn't there, and that bothered me. Had he been called away? Had he gotten into trouble for our lunchtime concerts?

I now started to work some rudimentary riffs into our duets. Joey would play a basic chord progression on the piano. In turn, I would experiment with hitting the notes of those chords in a pattern that would go along with what Joey was playing on the keyboards. After many tries, I developed something that was reasonably good, at least I thought it was. I never knew in those early days whether Joey was just nice or if I was actually doing OK. This went on for three days, and Brother Christian was still missing.

After only a half hour of playing each day, I would tiptoe into the kitchen at night and relieve the freezer of all its available ice. I found an old bucket in the garage and each night filled it with ice and water. I then submerged my hand into this mixture for as long as I could physically stand it. I was enjoying my bass experience, but I was paying the price.

Entry #32

"No Time Like the Right Time"
- *The Blues Project*

On the fourth day, Brother Christian returned to our lunchtime meetings. In his hand, he held a clipboard much like an executive who would be instituting numerous changes in his company's policies. However, the only changes that he had in mind would involve me. I found out very soon that he had been very busy. From his notes, he read his manifesto. I don't remember all the details except I felt a whole lot better when he finished talking to me.

First, he had called my parents and gotten permission to speak to my family physician, Dr. Neumeyer. What he proposed to my doc was the use of the bass as a therapy to facilitate my rehabilitation from the hand injury. The doctor warned that if I practiced too much, too soon, I would suffer a significant amount of pain. However, when I heard I wouldn't do any damage to myself, I chose to ignore the pain part of the equation.

Second, he had gotten permission from the principal to have me stay after school every day so he could work with me on my rehabilitation (translation: instruction and practice on the bass guitar). To the conservative leadership of the school, he sold my rehab as an act of mercy. They could now loudly tout at prospective students' open houses how caring they were. They were going to milk this act of kindness for every ounce of goodwill they could. What the hell did Brother Christian and I care? As an added benefit, my new savior noted that the lessons would end at 4 p.m., exactly the time I needed to meet Maria every day for the bus ride home. Too much of a coincidence? When I grinned, Brother Christian looked over at DJ and Joey. They both let go with knowing smiles. My losing streak was officially over.

His serious face couldn't disguise his pleasure as he got to the last item on his clipboard, which he now laid gently on the piano. He walked over to the bass, picked it up, and then placed it in my hands.

"Won't the owner mind?" I said looking up at him.

"You *are* the owner."

"I don't have the money to pay for this,"

"It's taken care of. Some of my ill-gotten gains are now being used for good. I stashed away money in another lifetime."

"But?" I tried to think of a way to thank him, or at least say something. I drew blanks.

"Do something great with it . . . or just have fun."

I didn't know what to say to that either so I silently caressed the black Hagstrom bass. I would come to know and love this instrument. For the next year and a half, I would spend more time with it than any person or thing on this planet. In the end, I had to leave it behind like everything and everyone else in this world that I had loved.

The ensuing months were filled with pain – a great deal of it. I never told anyone just how acutely my fingers fought every moment of their forced labor. I carried that bass everywhere. I didn't practice only after school like Dr. Neumeyer and Brother Christian had prescribed. Every waking moment available was spent in my attic room in the painful rapture of my newfound love.

After hours of practice each night, my left hand would convulse with spasms, as each muscle would rebel against its grueling overuse. Relief came only in the nightly ritual of the ice bucket. This curtailed the pain to some extent, and I still use this method decades later when I have a reoccurrence of the soreness. My left hand has still never had a day without some pain coursing through its injured members. It was a tradeoff.

The days of that winter passed quickly. I remember little about them besides the moments I held either the bass or Maria in my arms. Brother Christian was a master, I a willing pupil. He taught me technique and theory. He made me listen to the masters of jazz, pop, and rock so that I would develop a mindset for my own style. When I was alone, and pain prevented me from playing even a single note more, I'd just listen. I'd spend secretive hours past midnight with my ear to my radio. I had permanently adjusted the tone on the machine to maximum bass. It was only the backbeat that mattered. How could I duplicate what I heard? How could I change it and make it my own? Many would have thought I was mad. To most people, playing the bass without any other instrument to accompany it would prove a difficult and unrewarding task. I'd never been happier.

8

The Other Side of Life:

"In the City"
- Joe Walsh

Winter 1966

MANY A YOUNG MAN THROUGHOUT America lusted for Mary Weiss, the lead singer of The Shangri-Las. The long blonde hair and pouty grimace that appeared on album covers only served to increase the sales of these girl group phenoms. In an era of The Shirelles, The Supremes, and what seemed like a thousand other groups singing about their devotions to the opposite sex, The Shangri-Las were marketed as the musical version of *The Great White Hope*. Not lost in this image was the fact that these girls sang about a life they knew about first-hand from growing up in the Heights.

Press releases referred to the fact that they came from "a rough section of Queens, New York." Unlike most images fabricated for the record-buying public, this statement was true. The people of Cambria Heights listened to these hometown stars sing about a rough life they shared in common.

Before stardom, the girls had hung out at Ted's Luncheonette on Linden Boulevard. Though the real "Leader of the Pack" did not die as in the song, "Jimmy" was actually one of their boyfriends. However, even as The Shangri-Las were singing about the gang life in southeast Queens, the scenery was rapidly changing to something they would not recognize when they came back from touring. Their life had been a story of white on white violence, a fifties scenario rapidly fading away. The stories they sang about had been fights between the guys from Ted's and the guys from Tino's. Their battles had been legendary in the eyes of all the young boys growing up in the Heights. But these two gangs no longer existed.

From the ashes of these two groups rose a new type of gang in the Heights. Gone was hanging out in a dinette replete with milkshakes and girls. Gone was any social aspect of membership. This group would have its origins in the schoolyards and basements throughout the entire neighborhood. It would include those who attended the local public school as well as any of the dozens of Catholic high schools in the area. It would not be exclusive, but rather inclusive of any guy who wanted to defend his turf from its imminent destruction. It dwarfed the fledgling groups of the Heights Heathens and Young Tinos and eventually drew them into their fold. If there were any doubt about who were their enemies, it was dispelled by their name: The White Devils.

Not everyone thought of The Shangri-Las in terms of the gang lifestyle. Some Heights' teens emulated another side of their story. They saw a group of kids who had made it out of the neighborhood through music. These were role models for quite a few musicians struggling to find their own way out.

"Knock on Wood"
- Eddie Floyd

Everything changed for Rocco Brackowski when his father, Stan, got transferred to the night shift. While he was at school, his father would be sleeping. While his father was working, he would be free to do whatever he wanted in the home. He now bought an amp and blasted away the notes that previously he had only performed in hushed tones. Hour after hour, Bracko played and never cared that he had no accompanying band backing his solos. Someday he would follow that path when he was away from the sadist that he called a father. Until that day, his audience would consist of the mildew encrusted curtains and moldy furniture that inhabited his basement realm.

Occasionally, his audience would consist of a certain Tony Provenzano. Though the Garden of Eden was no longer necessary for his practice sessions, he still felt like a superstar when he played for the limited (in every sense of the word) audience of one. Though he preferred to practice on his Fender, sometimes he made a point of bringing his acoustic guitar to their secret hiding place. The old hollow-bodied guitar lifted Tony's spirit. The smile on the former bully's face was the highlight of Bracko's days, and he knew just how to elicit the broadest of these smiles from his friend.

Every time the two met, Tony required Eddie Floyd's "Knock on Wood." A great dance tune, Bracko had fooled around with it just to warm up his bar chord functions. However, when he reached the part of the song where the vocalist sang, "I think I better knock . . . on wood," the pause between the words "knock" and "on wood" was filled with an actual knocking sound three times. In the studio, this sound effect was replicated by the banging of a drum simultaneously with a wooden door brought into the recording area. In the Garden of Eden, Bracko effortlessly turned the guitar on its reverse side and knocked on the lacquered wood before swiftly returning to the serious side of the instrument to hit the next chord. It never got old for Tony, and so Bracko staged the same show each day.

It would be hard to find a more unusual friendship than that of Bracko and Tony. One was the suave, handsome son of a crime lord who had turned into a sad, lumbering spectacle with a mental impairment. The other a tall, handsome, and talented young musician who had suffered a life of abuse that had stunted his ability to form a relationship with anyone – besides Tony. Yet, they stayed faithful to each other until the end of their lives.

"You Can't Always Get What You Want"
- The Rolling Stones

Noel and Adele McAvoy had long since fallen into an exhaustive sleep. The twelve-hour days at their candy shop had worn them out to the point where no human noise could awaken them. Meanwhile, their loving son chose to practice his drum skills. Long into the night, Jimmy Mac beat his well-worn drumsticks onto the hard rubber pads that acted as a quiet substitute for the beckoning drum set that lay only a few feet from him. So as not to disturb his parents, he quietly practiced each night when he too should have been asleep. Jimmy Mac wanted out of the business. He wanted out of the neighborhood. He wanted success on his terms, playing and singing in a band.

Jimmy Mac's parents saw their son's ambitions and did not discourage him. They always felt that when this silly childhood fling was over, he would appreciate the substantial business they had built for him. Little could they know that the changing neighborhood and burgeoning multiplex movie complexes would hasten the demise of the Cambria Theater. The death of this local venue would doom the local candy shop to failure. The McAvoy family would have been bankrupt if they had lived to see that day.

In those late hours of the winter of 1966, Jimmy Mac only had thoughts of glory. With money from his first album, he would buy his parents a house in the suburbs and perhaps set up in a less strenuous business. For his sisters there would be new dresses and anything else the three wanted.

The worn sticks hit the pads in ever more complex syncopated combinations of rhythm. Jimmy Mac was going to be the best damn drummer the world had ever seen. He may well have been if things had not gone wrong.

———◆———

Giovanni DeAngelis' life was in chaos. He knew what he wanted, but he felt lost in a maze. It was evident to him that he was not an exceptional musician. He was a master of chords and rhythms but just did not have the creative juices to pull off a solo performance. What he did have was a voice. He could sing lead, or he could harmonize with all the natural smoothness that he frequently heard on hit records.

Fate had brought him together with Jimmy Mac, and the two of them almost instinctively knew where the other's voice registered in the harmonies they perfected. When both of them could get away from the daily grind, they ditched the instruments and used their precious time together to develop their singing. They frequently vocalized on their walk home from school each day. However, they knew they needed at least two more musicians.

Gio still spent many hours of the day racked with guilt. It had not been his fault that Johnny and Frank had fought and that Johnny had quit the band. It had not been his fault that Johnny shattered his hand and was now suffering through a long rehabilitation. Still, he felt as if he had let his friend down. They had started this whole thing together. Gio and Johnny—musicians. Gio and Johnny—stars. Now only Gio was moving ahead with their dream.

When the two friends met, they avoided talk of music. Gio's hopes for the future would only shine a light on the terrible failure of his friend. He could not know of Johnny's own newfound hope, a hope that his friend needed to nurture in private before telling him. Each night, the two friends went their separate ways, to different houses and different dreams. They would come together eventually. However, they could not know that during those cold winter nights.

———◆———

Joey Tinley had changed in the last few months. His formerly secret repertoire had suddenly and irrevocably become a public pleasure. Joey lived for the moments rocking out with his friends DJ and Johnny. He did not have any illusions. There could not be any future in an endeavor that included one kid on tambourine and the other a musical novice on the bass. Oh, but how he enjoyed it.

Each day Johnny seemed to improve in leaps and bounds, and occasionally, Brother Christian would join in on guitar. Joey enveloped himself in the pulsating beat of the music. His fingers found new life as they alternately tickled and pounded the keyboard. Playing this music was an act of his heart and soul rather than his mind.

However, was this enough to quell the passion he was developing? It was now spring. When the school year ended Johnny, DJ, and Brother Christian would go their own ways. What then? He could not bear the thought of spending the summer under the thumb of his overly focused father. He could not go back. At some point, he would have to confront his father.

Because of the Easter break from school, he had not had his fix of good music in days. He had no idea he would miss it so much.

When his father left the house for a few errands, he saw it as an opportunity to regain his sanity with a few bars of The Animals' "House of the Rising Sun." He loved to break out into the Alan Price organ solo he found only on the album version of the song. He could not foresee his father forgetting his shopping list and returning home suddenly. With his mother doing a load of wash down the basement, Joey was prepared to take the expected verbal abuse when his father discovered his secret practice.

"What are you doing playing that primitive animal music?" came the opening salvo of his attack. His ironic choice of word "animal" had led his son to first smile, and then outright laugh in his face. He didn't know about it being primitive, but it indeed was *Animal* music.

"You're laughing at me, you ingrate," bellowed Joseph Tinley, Sr. as he crossed the room in a pace unnatural for a man his age. It seemed as if he would tear his son to shreds with his bare hands.

"Don't you dare lay a hand on him, you asshole," screamed Margaret Tinley in a voice that neither father nor son had ever heard. Their jaws dropped not only at the volume and intensity of her outburst but also at her choice of words. No one in the Tinley household ever used off-color words. Those kinds of phrases were for the riff-raff who did not have the vocabulary to use in situations of this nature. However, Margaret knew exactly what she was saying and had specifically chosen *asshole* not only for its shock value but also because she thought it was very descriptive of her husband at this moment, and perhaps most of the time.

"Your son is going to be seventeen in a few months. Don't you think he has earned the right to enjoy his life just a little bit?"

"But I won't have him engaging in the kind of behavior that will inhibit his talents and lead him down the road to failure."

"That may work now, but what do you think is going happen when he goes out in the real world, and he doesn't know how to make choices for himself? He's less than two years away from going to college. Are you going to share a dorm room with him?" Joey cringed at that thought.

"But there are so many mistakes he can make."

"And in the general scheme of things, playing 'House of the Rising Sun' on his organ doesn't rank up there with drug use or violence."

Again, Joey's jaw dropped. Not only had his mother been listening to him play outlawed music, but she knew the song he was playing. It seemed someone in the Tinley house had stashed a contraband AM radio down by the washing machine.

"But those songs will lead to aberrant behavior."

"Bullshit!" Momma Tinley had now crossed the vocabulary line twice in five minutes. Joey had always hoped to see his mother stand up to his father, but the two of them screaming at each other was not what he had pictured. It saddened him, and he felt he had to join the fray.

"Mom, Dad, stop!" A hushed silence came over the room. "I promise that I won't play my . . . ah . . . that music ever again. Just stop fighting."

"You sure as hell will play it if you want to," answered Mrs. Tinley and turned to stare at her husband. She dared him to say anything. It was Joey who again intervened.

"Have I ever done anything wrong? I mean legally or even morally? I love music, all kinds. That's all I'm saying. Why can't you see that?"

"*I* see it," his mother said, "and I'm sorry I never spoke up before." Gone were the harsh tones. Joey recognized the tender side of his mother. There had been times when he had seen her brought to tears by his father, yet she had always been submissive to her husband's dictates.

"I just want him to be happy and successful," was his father's reply as he now also spoke in a softer, gentler voice.

"Well which one is it, Dad? Happy or successful? They're not always the same thing. Haven't you always told me musicians through the ages have suffered for their creative desires? Right now, I am a successful musician by your standard. But I'm not happy."

The three of them talked into the night. The tones of their voices became respectful and their attitudes conciliatory. Each member of the Tinley family spoke and, more importantly, each listened. In the end, Joey was permitted to play whatever music he chose. He could follow his dreams with the proviso that if those dreams fell through he would then accede to his father's wishes.

"The *gnocchi* taste great as usual, Ma." It was a lie and Guy felt a twinge of guilt even as he complimented his mother. He lied to just about everyone concerning just about everything. However, his mother was the one person in this world that Guy felt the slightest bit of remorse about doing so. He hated *gnocchi*.

Who was the first schmuck to take a good idea like pasta and mess it up with the stupid mick food of potatoes? This just made a heavier version of the food that went so well with his mother's Bolognese sauce.

Guy knew why his mother continued to produce this meal week after week. Tony, his fucking retard of a brother, loved the stupid shit. If only the asshole had died from that huffing crap, his life would be much better. No, he had to go and live, and thereby burden the entire Provenzano family with the embarrassment of his sniveling baby act. Now to Guy's dismay, his mother had bought into the whole handicap routine. Tony got every fucking thing his little heart desired. For the sake of his mother, Guy often suffered through long stints as nursemaid and babysitter.

If he ever had the chance to take care of those two (or three) morons who saved his brother from death, he would not hesitate a second. Unfortunately, Carmela held a special place in her heart for those two kids (or three) who had saved her baby. For now, they were untouchable. However, Carmela would not live forever, and Guy had a long memory. Therefore, he ate the damned *gnocchi* and complimented his mother and smiled at his father, all the while suppressing the seething anger he felt toward his brother and the world in general. He hid his feelings well in front of his family. None of them could see the explosion that would occur one day very soon when all his planning and scheming went awry and his ability to hide his feelings completely abandoned him.

Tony Provenzano's world was simple. He rose from bed when he felt the urge. His expanding girth attested to the fact that his mother fed him massive doses of whatever he wanted for breakfast, lunch, and dinner. He often spent the remainder of the day watching mindless soap operas whose plotlines baffled his limited comprehension.

Much to the embarrassment of his brother and father, he spent the early afternoons roaming the streets of the Heights. It was as if he was searching for something he could not comprehend. Every person, place, and thing looked familiar to him, but a foggy presence over his mind prevented him from understanding why. And so he walked as if perpetually looking for answers that would never come. Little children feared this apparition of a disheveled, overweight monster. Some laughed at the local moron, and still others felt pity for the intelligence that had once graced his Adonis body.

The late afternoons inevitably led him to the Garden of Eden. There he hoped to find his friend Bracko. If he were there, Tony's day would be complete. He would listen quietly as his friend played a variety of intricate and entertaining guitar riffs and songs. He seldom commented, but sat in the overgrown weeds, content merely to listen to the sounds made by the guitar strings. He knew that at some point, Bracko would perform *his* song, "Knock on Wood."

One afternoon in early April, Bracko surprised Tony. He played the first eight chords of the classic and then abruptly stopped. Any break in routine was extremely upsetting to Tony, and he looked bewildered. However, it was Bracko's turn to smile, a rare occurrence in the musician's life. Almost magically, he retrieved an object that he had hidden in the overgrown bush behind his back. Most people would have laughed at the gift that Bracko presented to Tony. The guitarist had retrieved a string-less, faded ukulele only minutes before it was to be hauled away by a garbage truck. Despite its decrepit condition, Tony reacted as if he had been given a gift of gold.

"My guitar?" questioned Tony.

"Your guitar," answered Bracko and placed it in the correct position in Tony's arms.

"My guitar!" Tony screeched excitedly as a broad smile lit up his face.

"We can play together."

"Yes, on my guitar," was the only response from Tony. Bracko began to play "Knock on Wood." Tony, in turn, mimicked the motions of his friend without any hope of making a sound. He was content merely to play at being a guitar hero. The highlight of their "duet" occurred when the song reached its signature *knock* section. Tony's face brightened with a smile that could light up the skies as he took his instrument and pounded (perhaps a bit too briskly for the ancient instrument) the requisite knocks on the backside of the wood. They shared a hearty laugh and continued with the verses of the song, each relishing the knocking on wood.

Yes, many felt pity for the former bully who had once shared the rule of their neighborhood. Perhaps only Bracko understood the tragedy had made Tony a happier person.

"Summer in the City"
- Lovin' Spoonful

As the warm spring weather trumpeted the upcoming summer in the city, the pieces had all fallen into place. The greedy machinations of adults had assured there would be blood on the asphalt battlefields of the Heights. The maneuverings of the old had set in motion events with only one obvious conclusion: violence.

As the real estate vultures promoted the fears of homeowners, their venom stirred the seeds of racial hatred. To make untold wealth off the buying and selling of homes, they instigated violence. In doing so, the fears and anger engendered in the parents found its expression in the fists of their children. Those children sought an advantage in the coming war. The Provenzanos eagerly jumped at the financial opportunity that arming the youth of both sides provided. Drugs would help those who needed some artificial courage to face their oncoming trials. Again, there were profits to be made by those who would not suffer any of the negative aspects of the impending conflagration.

The misguided officials, who dined at their political fundraisers and bragged about their tireless efforts to upgrade the poor unfortunate souls of their voting precincts, never cared about the real-life consequences of their planning. If the restructured park in the Heights resulted in the violent clash of two groups of hoodlums, it was probably because their parents had not brought their kids up the right way. Nobody could ever argue *their* good intentions.

Inspired by a panicked older generation and fueled by the testosterone that coursed through their youthful bodies, the White Devils prepared for war. They would make their stand on the street corners and parks they called home. This summer in the city was going to be exciting, like no other they had ever experienced.

PART
2

"Come Together"
– The Beatles

9

Journal of Johnny Cipp

Entry #33

"How Much I Lied"
-Gram Parsons

I STRUGGLE TO REMEMBER THE FACES of the White Devils. It's not because I didn't know them, but rather because I knew them too well. These had been my childhood friends, yet I didn't understand what they'd become. Disenchanted by a neighborhood that had nurtured them and now seemed to abandon them, they couldn't comprehend the world around them. Many of my closest friends had shared a championship baseball season in a CYO league. Now those same wooden baseball bats were thought of only as weapons. But why? What had changed?

The White Devils first approached me while I was in the very throes of depression after the surgery. In reality, that was why I was so aggressively recruited by my friends and acquaintances alike. How could they know that my belligerence was not the result of courage or rational thought? I didn't do it in defense of my race or neighborhood. I was merely a screwed up boy, lashing out in frustration and anger. This journal has forced introspection upon me.

I know now I hated the five individuals who pummeled me with their fists until my face was unrecognizable. However, I hated only them and not an entire race. How I had gotten to that point is a work in progress in my mind. Some of my feelings may have had to do with the one individual who stepped up to save me. If he could do that for me, how could I condemn all black men and think that the "color of their skin was the color of their soul." That had been the sarcastic message I had picked up from the song "Better Man Than I" so long ago on a contraband radio in chemistry class. The White Devils were not better men than I. Their beliefs were wrong. I had seen the best and worst of it all in the same violent afternoon.

Because I had already proven otherwise, no one questioned my courage in turning down the frequent requests to join in their onslaught. I did give lame excuses about the use of only one hand, but as the rehab took hold, I needed to move in another direction. I admit now I was a coward. Not about wanting to fight, but rather about confronting them with my real feelings about that fight itself. At first, I walked around the Heights with my hand wrapped in an Ace bandage, and sometimes even a sling. As that story grew old, I dedicated myself to a schedule that left me no time to be out and about. As I think back now, I wonder if I would have found something else to occupy me had not Brother Christian's salvation led to my obsession with the bass.

I'm ashamed to say I faked racism. When they told their racist jokes or bragged about some head they cracked open, I sheepishly stood there with a shit-eating grin as if I agreed with them. I will do my penance for this non-action someday. I understand now I wasn't part of the solution, therefore I was part of the problem.

All of these thoughts and feelings were the furthest thing from my mind during the winter, spring, and summer of 1966. When I looked in the mirror, I saw only the face of a person with an overwhelming obsession to learn the bass. I never saw the face of the coward denying the world around him.

The long nights with my hand in the ice bucket were agonizing, but I never stopped smiling. Blood blisters formed on the tips of four fingers. While I was impatient for the calluses to form in their natural time, I abused my already ailing hand. My mind seemed to spin with the combinations of riffs that could be played to melodically provide a bass line for any chord combination played on the guitar. I learned standard backbeats that were Brother Christian's expertise, and I experimented with note combinations to create my style of bass playing. Under the watchful eye of my teacher, I grew in ability in insane strides I'd never achieved on the guitar.

By the time the first day of spring arrived, I was able to adequately and professionally accompany Joey on his piano performances. Thoughts of starting a band with him tickled my imagination. If his father would ever allow him the freedom to play, he could carry a band all on his own.

Entry #34

"Bungle in the Jungle"
- Jethro Tull

It was on a Friday afternoon in April when all the pieces of my life finally started to come together. I had a plan. I took an alternate bus route that led to the front door of the local library branch on Linden Boulevard. Because I decided to take the Q4 bus, my life changed. I probably should have gone home first and dumped off my stuff. It wasn't very logical to get off that bus and lug all my school books plus the bass guitar around. I not only had to go to the library itself but then all the way home. I wasn't thinking with a logical mind, but rather with a scheming one. By carrying the bass around half of the Heights, I was announcing to the world that I was just too busy to be involved in any other activities (translation: gangs). That had been my purpose when I left the library, but little did I know that it would develop into so much more.

Directly across the street from the library was Mac's Candy Shop. I had realized that my growing proficiency on the bass had opened up the possibility of a reunion with Jimmy Mac and Gio. Because Gio and I talked about everything *besides* music, I didn't know how to approach him. If the duo had someone else on bass, I didn't want to seem needy by asking to join them and then being rejected. My only solution was to have Jimmy Mac see me with the bass and break the news to Gio. I walked by the front door of the store four times to draw his attention before I sucked it up and went into the damn place.

We talked about many things while I slowly enjoyed a choco-late egg cream. However, the elephant in the room disguised as my bass guitar never came up in the discussion, even as we talked about the Yankees and latest Beatles' album. I knew he saw my bass, and he knew *I* knew he had seen it, but not a word was spoken.

I left Mac's very proud of my cunning. I would probably have patted my own back many times if it weren't for what happened next. My accumulated books from both school and the library weighed heavy in my arms. I created a makeshift sling from my tie and hung the bass in its hard-molded case from my shoulder. Still, my heavy load forced me to stop every half block to read-just all the objects in my juggling act. It was during one of these stops that I heard it. I knew the sound immediately, yet my brain refused to accept my seemingly illogical conclusion – it was an electric guitar without amplification!

My ear had become attuned to this distinctive sound during the many nights that I had remained unplugged out of respect for my parents' need to sleep. But why did I hear it on the street? I took a long listen and faced the Garden of Eden. As I approached, the faint sound grew stronger. I knew where the secret entrance was located from my experience six months prior. I awkwardly attempted to enter the opening fully loaded. That didn't work so I slowly unburdened myself with a few short trips into the gap. As I placed my books on the ground within the confines of the garden, I carried the bass alone. Books in dirt–bass in hand. Was there any question what my priorities were at this point in life?

It wasn't long before I came upon the source of the muffled guitar playing. It was the strangest sight I had ever seen. Tony Provenzano sat cross-legged on the weeded ground holding an old ukulele. This was the first time I had seen him since I was part of the threesome that had supposedly saved his life. I wondered if we had really done the guy a favor. The Tony in front of me had gained a massive amount of weight. This made his face almost unrecognizable. His eyes displayed a permanently confused expression, and his head and neck hung at an awkward angle. His hair, which had always been meticulously combed into a pompadour, now had been shaved down to his scalp in an attempt by his caregivers to make him more low-maintenance. Yet what surprised me most was the smiling expression that lit up his face.

Facing Tony was a familiar face, the third member of Tony's rescue team. That night, I had seen a guitar lying in the grass but had never made the connection to this stranger. Apparently, this person had been a regular at the Garden of Eden. I didn't know whether he had known Tony before he saved his life with something called CPR or if this friendship had developed afterward. Some primeval instinct had drawn Tony back to the scene of his tragedy, and somehow the two of them had bonded.

Though he too was still sitting cross-legged in the weeds, I could tell that this mystery guitarist was tall, at least six feet. His light brown, almost blonde hair was straight and long enough to cover his ears. This was a sign that he went to public school because no Catholic high school would have allowed hair that length. His pale complexion and blue eyes told me (incorrectly, it turns out) that he wasn't someone with Italian blood in his veins. However, of all my first observations that late afternoon in April, it is the image of his fingers that still haunts me. Though he had stopped strumming with his right hand the minute I came into view, the fingers of his left continued to move effortlessly and swiftly over the strings of his Fender Stratocaster guitar.

"Who are you?" asked Tony. He didn't remember me from his previous life.

"I'm Johnny, Johnny Cipp."

"I'm Tony, Tony Pro ... Provi . . . Provino. I'm Tony." Sadly, he was overwhelmed with the concept of remembering his surname.

"Pleased to meet you, Tony," I answered. I honestly was pleased to meet *this* Tony because it meant that the other Tony, the one who had bullied me, was gone forever.

"He's Bracko," Tony replied as he pointed to the boy across from him. I don't know why I did it, but I remember instantly unclasping the latches on the case that held my bass and taking it out. It was almost like I was proclaiming to this Bracko character, *look at me!* It was absurd. An unamplified bass made even less sound than a guitar of the same status. But we faced each other and began to play in what I like to think of as dueling mimes. I started first by breaking into the classic bass line of The Yardbirds' "I'm a Man." Bracko immediately recognized the very distinct note pattern. Looking back at it now, I realize Bracko probably could have played anything I might have played. We played on, and I enjoyed the almost silent jamming created by our duet. Tony, while straining to hear us over the outside street noise, seemed to be rocking out. I smiled at my first opportunity to test my new bass skills with a guitarist and was really into following his finger movements until we came to the solo break. As a diehard fan of The Yardbirds, I expected certain riffs to be played. Yet what he performed was so raw and bluesy I merely looked on in awe. Sensing my confusion, he spoke (without ever missing a note in his performance).

"The original . . . Bo Diddley."

As I gazed at his fingers moving over the strings and frets of his Strat, I knew I needed to hear him play more. I mean *hear* him play more. This mime music was great, but we needed to do some serious playing. I saw my opportunity when suddenly Tony rose from his seated position and started to walk away. I was stunned by the suddenness of his actions and stopped playing. I realized almost immediately my partner had also abruptly halted his part of our duet.

"He does that every day," said Bracko, "As soon the sun hits the top of the handball wall, he knows it's time to go home for dinner."

"Wow, sort of like the *Eloi* did when they heard the sirens go off and automatically went to be fed on by the *Morlocks*." The expression on his face made it clear Bracko thought I was insane. I guessed he wasn't a science fiction fan. My reference to the movie *The Time Machine* went right over his head. Didn't every guy know this movie? Hadn't we all lusted for the stunning Eloi maiden played by the gorgeous Yvette Mimieux?

Please save her from being eaten by the Morlocks!

In the time it took us to have this brief conversation, Tony was gone from sight. It was getting darker very quickly, and this was a deterrent to the music, which we were playing by sight rather than sound. An idea occurred to me. I asked Bracko if he wanted to come back to my house to continue our jam with actual sounds. He thought long and hard before answering me. I thought perhaps he just wanted to get rid of me. Or maybe he had better things to do with his time. The look on his face was one of confusion. Then I figured it out. Here's this guy I'd never seen hanging around with anyone in the Heights. I find him in a patch of weeds. He has no friends. My invitation is a new experience for him, and he doesn't know how to react.

"Stay a few minutes or stay a while. It's Friday. I've got nothing else going on, but maybe you do." I guess that pushed him over the edge because he agreed to come in his very own verbose way.

"Yeah, OK."

It only was a silent block and a half walk to my house. In all the time I knew Bracko conversations with him were almost non-existent. He spoke through his guitar. And when he spoke in *his* language, he was the master.

Entry #35

"Mr. Downchild"
- *Savoy Brown*

It's been said that to play the blues you must have suffered in your life. Living a hard life made the music come up through your soul and into your instrument. Teenage white boys usually didn't have those kinds of experiences so blues was a style of music that we played *at* rather than just played. Bracko was the exception. After we had run through some easy rock songs we both knew, he educated me on some lesser known groups and songs that bordered on jazz and blues.

He would play a bass line for me to copy, and once I could mimic his actions sufficiently, we attempted to play the song together. At least, I would try. He could play anything, and I mean anything. We did some Ten Years After, and I had never seen the skills I witnessed when he went into "I May Be Wrong, But I Won't Be Wrong Always." My fingers felt like they'd been put in a grinder as I played eight-note bass riffs for almost every one of the many chord's changes that Bracko made. He mixed chords and notes with interchangeable ease that made me think that I was playing with both a rhythm and lead guitarist at the same time. When he went into solo breaks, I was forced to new levels of skill by the sheer necessity of filling in for an entire band that wasn't there. It didn't matter how much pain I felt, I wasn't stopping. There would be plenty of time later for a midnight ice bucket. For now, the music made the pain secondary.

Bracko smiled a bit, though it was hard to tell because the very act of moving the sides of his mouth in an upward motion seemed foreign to him. I didn't know his story then, and I'm not sure if I wanted to. He couldn't have had a happy life, and his expressions led me to believe that our duets may very well have been the highlight of his existence so far.

He looked over at me after just a few too many songs that had strained the very makeup of my left hand. Involuntarily, my fingers seemed to go into spasm. Bracko saw I was in pain. He had no formal knowledge of music but had an ear for the natural flow of tunes that would shame the finest music teacher. He heard my sixteenth note misses, and realized I just wasn't keeping up any more. When we finished "A Train Kept a' Rollin'" (The Yardbirds' version), I tried to shake off the knots that made my hand incapable of movement. He looked quizzically at me and without thinking I told him how I was recovering from surgery. I hadn't meant to tell him. I didn't want him to see any faults in me as a musical partner. I was pretty good, but I knew that he was great.

Bracko had a heart. He suggested certain songs that were simple for the bass guitar. Many of them required only two notes, and if I was careful and smart, I could rotate my fingers to hit those two notes. This method allowed us to continue playing despite the fact that I had been limited to light duty. It also let me sit back and wonder at his playing.

"Do you know 'Mr. Downchild' by Savoy Brown?" Bracko asked me.

"Don't think so."

"An up and coming British blues band. Here. I'll show you the bass line," Bracko said running through some very simplistic bass riffs. I would play the A–G–A notes on the top string of the bass to match his very softly strummed A-minor chord. When he switched to a D-minor chord, my part required a D–C–D pattern. It was an uncomplicated and slow blues pattern. I could handle it. What I wasn't prepared to handle were the emotions created by his rendition of the song.

He hadn't sung many of the songs up until that point. The music had been the priority, and when he did sing, his vocals merely gave clues to where the song was going and at what intensity I should play. "Mr. Downchild" was something else altogether. I knew why. This song was Bracko's anthem, his life. On his cue, we started to play soft and slow. Soon his rich baritone voice filled the room. As he sang about being a "down child" and being down since the day he was born, the lyrics struck me as personal—real.

His voice boomed with intensity and feeling. The words poured out from his inner soul in a manner I had never experienced first-hand. If I hadn't known better, I could have sworn I saw tears as he sang verse after verse. Progressively, his voice and chord volume keyed me to more strength and conviction in my two measly notes. I wondered how he could make a few simple minor chords sound so very good. And then he worked more magic.

The solo he took in the middle of the song has never been matched in my eyes. I am now twenty years removed from that evening, and I have spent most of my waking and conscious (not always the same thing) moments involved with music and I still can't compare anything to what I heard during that one song. Each note he hit was chosen for its dramatic effect and created a mood of both despair and hopelessness. His facial expressions reflected these feelings. He was lost in the moment. The notes were reflections of real pain that this guy had lived through, a pain that I wouldn't understand until later in my life.

The notes rose in crescendos of feeling tempered by soft moments of reflective contemplation. When he finished the solo, I was happy not to have been distracted away from my very simple duties. He returned from his playing to sing one final line of the song that seemed prophetic in its simplicity.

"Won't somebody, please, help the down child?"

I guess at least one white boy had earned the right to sing the blues. The moment was over. I wondered how we would ever follow up that song when my mom intervened by yelling down the basement to me. She said something about dinner, and I saw Bracko immediately flinch and make rapid moves to pack up his guitar. Before he could, my mom was already down the stairs.

"Pasta, OK with you two?" asked Mom, skipping right over the invitation and assuming that Bracko would be joining me. The guitarist looked stunned. This was obviously another social situation that he had never experienced. But my mother always knew how to break the ice.

"Hi, I'm Mrs. Cippitelli." She held out her hand and waited for a response.

"Bracko."

My mother gave a questioning look which meant she was asking herself, *first name or last?*

As if reading her mind, he responded, "Rocco Brackowski, but my friends call me 'Bracko.'"

Mom put out some hot baked ziti with a side order of my personal favorite *braciole*. Bracko, at first looked at it in confusion, but quickly dug in with a passion for eating second only to his love of music. After he had consumed three very large forkfuls of the ziti, he looked up and said to me, "I thought we were having *paster?*"

"We are. This is pasta." I didn't know how to answer his question because I didn't realize he had never heard the word. But that was only the beginning of my confusion. His next question floored me.

"What brand is this? It's great."

He had never had Italian food that had not come out of a can.

"I guess your mother's not Italian." I said casually, intended as a throwaway remark.

"No, she was. But she died giving birth to me." He went back to eating and didn't say another word except to thank my mother when he was finished.

I understood so much about him now. I knew where the guarded personality had its beginnings. It explained why he was playing alone in the Garden of Eden with only the company of a disabled friend. I understood where all the heart and soul in the notes he played had their origins. *I've been down since I was born.*

Entry #36

"In the Midnight Hour"
–Young Rascals' version

I've noticed that I've been writing in this journal more frequently in the last few days. It now seems obvious to me why. I've been thinking about how Bracko had no one in his life and nothing to care about. I can't bullshit myself. That is me now!

Tonight is Christmas Eve. I can't help thinking back to all the wonderful times I had with my family during the holidays. The meals we had with over two dozen of my closest relatives. The homemade pasta. The decorated tree (complete with arguments each year as to whether we should stay real or get artificial). The decorations. The presents. The music (whether it was about Frosty or Jesus). Unless you count the Music Doctor who gives a title to each of my journal entries, I have no one. His title inspirations are great, but I realize he is imaginary and I am alone, all alone. I know that kind of thinking is dangerous to my recovery. Keep writing, if only not to . . .

——◆——

The rest of our first band practice (as I then thought of it) was mostly uneventful. We worked on connecting with the standard songs every band performed in those days. We never spoke the words, but the feeling was growing that we were into this for more than one night. The little conversation we engaged in between songs led me to understand he had never been in a band and therefore was depending upon my vast experience to take the lead in this matter. The hunger in his eyes and his fingers told me this was something he had wanted for a very long time, but had never had an opportunity to pursue his dream.

From my point of view, I hadn't just found gold but had found the mother lode. This was the guitarist that every band in the Heights had been searching for. I had found him in the weeds. After six months of seeing my dreams crushed one by one, my life seemed to now be working out just fine. Maybe my Mom's novenas had done the trick. Alternatively, on the secular side, perhaps I was finally on the receiving end of some plain old dumb luck. Whatever it was, I was halfway to a damn good band. I also knew where I could find the other half.

Though I had never seen Bracko at any of the church dances, he seemed to know the score as far as what kind of music a band had to play to get jobs. Perhaps it was just that he knew every damn song ever recorded. I sometimes wondered if he had a life outside of music. However, I'd already asked one stupid question, and I'd almost crushed the kid's ego. I wasn't making that mistake again. When in doubt, ask nothing. If he wanted me to know anything, he would tell me. Eventually, I did find out his story. But that night was about the music. A little Stones, a little Beatles, a lot of songs by one hit wonders.

I don't know how, but Bracko even understood the concept of the *grinder* song. Hell, if a band played the "Star-Spangled Banner" very slowly with a C-Am-F-G chord progression, they were golden. How could Bracko know about this without ever attending a dance? There were so many of these songs that a band could do a very long medley of them without ever changing the beat or the chord structure. I tried to stump Bracko in the area by daring him to change songs every two minutes while not missing a beat. Real musicians hated these kinds of songs. It went against all their instincts to pander to the sexual requirements of hormonal teen males. In the never-ending legend of Bracko and his miracle guitar, he played for almost a half hour without ever changing from the same four chords. He sang with all his heart as if he loved the songs that I knew must have stuck in his gut. I was amazed as he worked his way through "Angel Baby," "Daddy's Home," "That's My Desire," "Earth Angel," "Donna," "Good-night Sweetheart," "Tonight, Tonight," and even "Surfer Girl." Most of these songs belonged to an era when I was still playing with trucks and watching cartoons. However, while some teens of the sixties only knew of them vaguely from the scratchy 45-rpm records of older siblings, musicians knew of them for their arousal potential. Bracko's knowledge of these songs was inhuman. He sang and played, and at times seemed in a zone of euphoria that would go on and on.

I then saw him look at the gaudy Rheingold beer clock that my father, in a total lapse of taste, had placed on the basement wall. At first, I thought it was the clock itself that had drawn his attention, but I was wrong. He stopped right in between the words "Surfer" and "Girl" and quickly unplugged the wire that connected his Stratocaster to my amp. As he threw the guitar in its case, I could swear that his face registered a look of fear. He glanced up at the clock again as he jerked his possessions into his arms and made for the stairs that led to the side door of my house. I tried to assure him my parents didn't mind how late we played in the basement, but I soon realized my house wasn't the problem. The clock read 11:46 pm, and I knew there was someone he feared coming in the midnight hour.

Entry #37

"Liar, Liar"
- *The Castaways*

Writing this Christmas morning 1989 . . . alone. Tough time to get through. Keep writing about 1960's . . .

He'd left so abruptly I worried I'd never see Bracko again. We had exchanged phone numbers after dinner so I hoped that I would get a call. Exchange isn't the right word because Bracko took my number but steadfastly refused to give me his information. He wouldn't explain why, but like everything else about Bracko, time would make things clear.

His call came at noon the next day. He whispered into the phone as if afraid someone would hear. We arranged for a 6 p.m. session that night. I offered to start earlier, but I think he felt funny being there for dinner again. After he hung up, I went down to the basement and started warming up for our session. It then occurred to me I had double-booked my Saturday night. Gio and I had arranged to watch the Creature Features on WPIX with Zacherly. Tonight was *The Blob*. We just couldn't get enough of the red goopy stuff consuming the fictional movie theater. Loved it. Gio was supposed to be over at eight.

OK, that's a lie. What good is it to tell a story to try to ease my demons if I'm only going to lie to myself? I knew Gio was coming when I committed to Bracko. I was trying to let Gio hear Bracko play, and maybe just as importantly, let him listen to me play the bass. I wanted him to hear us before I even discussed Jimmy Mac and him joining with Bracko and me. If I had the conversation before he ever heard Bracko, or even knew I'd learned the bass, I would've put him on the spot. I knew that after seconds of listening, the quality of our playing would convince him. No discussion would be necessary.

Nevertheless, I still admit that I was a liar. Bracko and Gio never knew for sure how conniving and deceptive I was that night. Gio was suspicious of what I called "my lucky mistake," and Bracko couldn't care less. Knowing Gio always showed up exactly at the time agreed on, I continued my plotting by making sure my mother would answer the door, and that Bracko and I would be in the middle of just the right song to show off our talents.

———◆———

It seems almost inconceivable that one single British Invasion band served as the proving ground for three of the greatest guitar players of all time. Eric Clapton, Jeff Beck, and Jimmy Page had all put in time with the seminal band, The Yardbirds. Even more amazing was the fact that a few unique songs featured both Beck and Page. It was a version of one of those songs, "The Train Kept a-Rollin'," that I just happened to suggest to Bracko as I watched Gio's legs walk by my basement window. Knowing that my mother was in the kitchen and would send him down the stairs, I cued Bracko to begin.

On the record, this classic starts with a guitar sound that is eerily reminiscent of the train mentioned in the title. It then proceeds to move forward at a frantic pace that kept time by a bass run that throbs and moves with all the speed and power of a locomotive. At one point, the recorded song features dueling solos by Beck and Page, which makes it one of the greatest guitar songs of all time. Bracko played with abandon, as he never lost a beat in trying to recreate both parts of those epic guitar solos. With no drummer (or any other instrument for that matter), I was responsible for keeping a backbeat and rhythm that would fill all the voids created by the missing instruments.

Reality check here. Bracko could not ever be Beck and Page at the same time. However, he was doing a damn good job of being the best guitarist that I, or the now approaching Gio, had ever heard. This was a long way from Frank and I competing for lead guitar by playing a few rehearsed notes copied from a scratchy 45-rpm record. And with no humility at all, I must say I was extremely impressed with myself on the bass.

Gio heard every note as he made his way down the basement stairs with a look of confusion on his face. He said nothing. He did nothing. Was he angry I had not been waiting for him for our movie night? Did he think I was showing off? Happy? Sad? Pissed off? We were midway through our instrumental version of this song when I got my answer. A microphone stood vacantly on its stand in the middle of the room for the occasions when Bracko would sing. On this song, however, he was silent. Gio suddenly pranced (yes, pranced. He'd been watching too much of the Stones on their TV performances) over to the microphone. Very dramatically, he pulled the Shure unidirectional from the clasp that held it on the stand and started to sing.

"We made a stop at Albuquerque,
She must've thought I had real good jerky,
But she looked like a hood, Mack,
I just couldn't let go.
The train kept a-rollin' all night long . . ."

Looking back, I knew that he was singing all the wrong words but I didn't care. He wasn't even close. However, Gio sang with a soulful voice that showed the full volume and range of his vocal talent. It very quickly occurred to me exactly what was going on. I had set out to impress Gio with what Bracko and I had to offer, and it had worked. It was now Gio's turn to try to impress us with the need to consider both him and Jimmy Mac. And why would he do that? He was thinking the same thing I was thinking, two plus two not only equals four, but it also equals a band.

Entry #38

"All Day and All of the Night"
- *The Kinks*

Still Christmas. Second journal of the day, and third in the last two. Higher Power, help me through the holidays.

When the song was over, I introduced Gio and Bracko to each other. Bracko didn't say much, but I knew in my gut that he understood where this was going. It wasn't long before Gio held my Hagstrom guitar in his hands. He noticed it was already perfectly tuned to our instruments. As he found a spare cord and plugged into my amp, Gio gave me that son-of-a-bitch look that told me he suspected my scheming. He also gave me a smile that said, *but I don't care*. I gave him no response because, at this point, I began to worry that perhaps three instruments plugged into my one amp were a bit too much.

All that faded away when Gio hit the first power chords to The Kinks' classic, "All Day and All of the Night." Compared to every song I'd played with Bracko, this was an uncomplicated bass line. Bracko played along with the chord progression while Gio sang the lead. I could see Bracko's ability to throw in a little harmony impressed Gio. This was overshadowed when Bracko knocked his socks off with a perfect replication of Dave Davies' guitar solo in the middle of the song. After only one song, it was Gio who came up with the obvious conclusion this would sound even better with a drummer.

"Gee, do you know any?" I said with extreme sarcasm. We both knew where this whole thing was going. "The phone's in the same place it's always been." After he climbed the stairs, I could hear him dialing and then speaking.

"Jimmy Mac, get your . . . ass. . . -ah . . . behind over here to Johnny's." He remembered a bit too late that my Mom was only inches away from him.

"Giovanni DeAngelis!" My mother always used his full name when she was acting with authority invested in her by *Gio's* mother. "I don't care how darn good the music sounds; there's no call for that kind of language in my house."

Knowing Gio, he must have turned red before my mother reassured him she'd let this one slip be forgotten. And then I heard *her* say loud enough to be heard on the other side of the line, "Jimmy Mac, get over here. There's a group in my basement that really could use a drummer."

Jimmy Mac arrived about a half hour later. An attitude of skepticism reeked from every pore of his body as he walked down the stairs. He carried a snare drum in an army surplus bag in his left hand and twirled his ever-present drumsticks in his right. Though neither one of us had any bitterness over the old band, he still pictured me as that guy who didn't have enough talent to play anything other than rhythm guitar, and not enough voice to justify just being that kind of musician. Yet, after he came down the stairs, he took one look at me and smiled. I guess he was thinking what I was thinking. We may not have been good, but we sure had good times.

"Is this the location of The Coming Generation Reunion Tour?" We laughed, and it was as if a weight was lifted from all of our shoulders. Jimmy Mac and Gio had been looking for two players to complement what they brought to the table, and if Gio hadn't been pulling his leg, the search was over. He set up his one single drum on a stand and looked at Bracko.

"I'm Jimmy Mac, and I do own more than this one drum. And according to my buddy here, you are the greatest guitarist the Heights has ever seen." How the hell does a guy answer that statement? Bracko chose to respond in his language – guitar.

Bracko took only seconds to move the switches on his Strat to the settings he thought were just right for his next move. He then immediately broke into the opening of The Yardbirds' "Heart Full of Soul." Though not the most difficult of guitar riffs, he had imitated the reverb, echo, and fuzz settings of the original. This immediately drew the attention of Jimmy Mac who quickly caught up with the beat on his snare drum. Gio and I added our parts when the time came. Gio started to sing.

After the first verse, a chorus followed that Gio and Jimmy always nailed perfectly . . . "She's got a hea-r- r- rt full of soul." They had probably harmonized on this line hundreds of times both with The Coming Generation and later while practicing together. What they had never experienced was a third voice. Bracko now added a new facet to the harmony that was pitch perfect and full bodied. After the word "soul," Bracko didn't miss a beat as the song called for a reiteration of the opening guitar riff. He did it perfectly, but I hardly heard it over Jimmy Mac's amplified scream of "Holy shit." He had been duly impressed not only by the harmony but also his perfectly timed guitar play-ing. Add in an incredible solo that mimicked Jeff Beck's, and the drummer's second "Holy shit" (into a mic) was soon uttered. As soon as the music ended, however, there was no time for praise because from the top of the stairs I heard my mother yell,"Hey, Jimmy Mac, watch the mouth on you!"

We all started to laugh, and I quickly remembered how much fun I'd had with Jimmy Mac and Gio. However, Bracko still looked serious, and I knew why. This was an audition. Jimmy Mac was still the greatest drummer, and possibly lead singer around, and *we* were still auditioning to prove ourselves worthy to join *him*. Though not even presenting half his talent on that one Yardbirds' song, Bracko had easily proven himself to the drummer. But Bracko knew that I still hadn't shown much, and so he nodded at me and at that very same moment hit the opening train sound of the "Train Kept a-Rollin'," knowing this song would be the final stroke to wipe away any doubts that Jimmy Mac might have.

My fingers rolled along the bass strings with a speed that reflected the months of practice (not to mention enough ice on my hands to rival the iceberg that sank the Titanic). Bracko and I played with even more intensity as we now had a drum beat to tighten the sound and a rhythm guitar to fill in the void. When Bracko spun effortlessly through solo after solo, our fate was sealed. Gio sang. This was extremely fortunate because it meant the drummer's microphone was turned off for numerous *Holy Shits* he couldn't suppress while Bracko played. When the song was over, there was a moment of silence before Jimmy Mac understated the feelings of us all.

"I think we have ourselves a band. And I'm going to kick the ass of anyone who starts talking names for the band before we get some serious work done."

And Mom said from upstairs, "Amen, Jimmy Mac, but that mouth on you."

Entry # 39

"Something in the Air"
- Thunderclap Newman

Tonight, I choose to continue writing in this journal long after I should be sleeping.

Unexpectedly, the writing has brought me great joy. I know this joy will be short-lived because soon the best time of my life will turn ugly. I know when I get to that part of the story, my insides will be torn to shreds and there will be pain. However, it's hard to imagine I've now come to the greatest time during my entire stay on this planet.

The only factor that kept us from having a full-scale practice the next day was the fact that it was Easter Sunday. I didn't sleep that entire night. This wasn't unusual though because I often didn't sleep the night before a holiday.

My parents were real holiday people. Though I was almost seventeen years old, my parents still filled a basket with an impressive haul of candy. Easter afternoon would mean a big family dinner at least five courses long – Grandma's homemade soup, followed by the antipasto salad, and then the homemade ravioli. To most human beings, the amount of food served would have been enough to satisfy a week's worth of meals. However, to Italians, these courses would only be a prelude to the American food portion of the meal that consisted of ham, turkey, potatoes, stuffing, and vegetables, and . . . I know I am leaving something out. Then there were the desserts, which filled the table with fruits, nuts, and ten thousand varieties of Italian pastries and cookies. We always felt the average non-Italian-American would die of an overinflated stomach had they not been trained from childbirth to consume these massive quantities of food.

However, on this one particular Easter Sunday, my mind couldn't stop swirling with the possibilities the next day would bring. We had all agreed to meet on Monday for our first official practice. I never went to sleep that night. At 4 a.m., I finally accepted sleep would never come. I descended from my attic room to the kitchen two stories below. As expected, my mom was already there preparing for the feast.

While surprised to see me at this early hour of the morning, my mom had already set out my basket and took a break from cooking to present me with this year's collection of sugary delights. Uncharacteristically, I merely picked at the marshmallow peeps and jelly beans at the feet of a large chocolate bunny. I wasn't thinking of candy. Mom asked if something was wrong. I explained to her that it was just the opposite. Everything in my life was so fantastically right.

Mom was more of a Frank Sinatra kind of person ("If Frank didn't sing it, I don't know it!"). However, she had picked up on the harmonies and musical potential of what she had heard the night before. She knew all the struggles I'd been through in the past year and had always been nothing but encouraging. Those had been hard times, and I wasn't the type to open up and discuss things with anyone. I guess she'd always known more than I thought she had.

She carefully stirred the sauce that would smother her contribution to the day's festivities. She then washed her hands and went to the cabinet that held her largest pots. Thinking she was ready to move on to some other course of preparation, I paid little attention as she walked to the refrigerator and opened the door to the freezer. She withdrew the two ice trays and filled the pot with a combination of ice and cold water. She then walked over to the table where I was sitting and placed it in front of me.

"You think I didn't know? Just don't push too hard," she chided me.

"Alright," I answered sheepishly. We both knew I was lying.

I spent some time stirring sauce and making one misshapen ravioli before deciding to take my shower and dress for the day at 5:30 a.m. With absolutely nothing to do, I decided to go for a walk. Coming out of my house, I could have chosen many directions in which to walk. Usually walking west was not an option because, in one block, I would be across the line, I still could have gone in three other directions. What made me choose east, I will never know. I was heading toward Sacred Heart Church, and I knew that the first mass would be at 6:30 a.m. However, I never had any intention of attending *that* mass because I'd be meeting Maria to go to church at nine. This was just another example of how great my life was going at that point. Maria and I had gotten very close. I would be so proud to walk into church with the most beautiful girl in the Heights on my arm. I could picture her in the green dress I'd reluctantly helped her shop for one Saturday afternoon. Her long brown hair hung over the shoulder of the dress, and her eyes sparkled an effervescent shade of green. We'd been seeing a great deal of each other, and had sworn undying love and devotion to each other. These vows would be tested when Maria moved in August.

Gio had already talked to Jimmy Mac, and every plan had been made for our first get together that next day. We were all off from school for the Easter spring break. We had agreed to meet at the McAvoy house at 4 p.m. for our first official practice. Bracko, Gio, and I would find ways to get all our equipment there. I could think of nothing else that Easter Sunday morning of 1966.

I was within a block of the church when I began to hear the distinct sounds of the church's massive organ. Music always lured me to its source, and that morning would be no different. What was that song? Was it something classical? I needed to know more, and like a rat drawn to the Pied Piper, I found myself uncontrollably drawn toward the church doors. Usually, they were locked for the night, but not this time.

Upon entering the nave, I remembered the balcony held the large organ. As if I were performing a criminal act by being there uninvited, I slowly and quietly took each step as if any minute the church police would arrive and arrest me for unscheduled worshipping. As I hit the top platform and peered into the empty chairs of the uninhabited choir space, I saw the back of a figure hunched over the organ. I was amazed by the deep emotion created by the incredible quality of the organ playing. At that very moment, I recognized both the singer and the song.

". . . turned a whiter shade of pale," was belted out by Joey Tinley. I had heard this song on the radio only once or twice and been blown away by the keyboard work and surrealistic lyrics. I'd been playing at lunch and after school with Joey for months now, and hadn't appreciated the capabilities of this guy. I still always thought of him as a mere kid because of his baby face and shy behavior. However, listening to him play, I realized that his musical maturity was light years ahead of me.

I stood by the doorway and listened. The song had only been released recently in America, and so I wasn't familiar with all the lyrics. I was caught by surprise when he wailed at the top of his lungs, "one of sixteen vestal virgins who were leaving for the coast." I lost it, and let out a tremendous belly laugh that quickly alerted Joey that he wasn't alone. I don't know if it was the line itself, or the fact that I somehow didn't think that singing about vestal virgins in a church was an acceptable concept. I mean this was good for at least half of eternity in Purgatory, right?

Joey's playing abruptly ceased, and he turned to see who had intruded on his makeshift concert. I thought perhaps he would be angry with me for eavesdropping, but instead, he turned with a smile and said, "Hey, Johnny! Happy Easter."

"I'm sorry I interrupted," I answered, but he just looked at me and smiled.

"Oh, no. I've got to stop anyway." Joey nodded at the door. "He's coming back soon." I knew exactly who *he* was. Joey explained that his father arranged all the music that would be used at each of the services that day. Some masses had an adult choir, some a children's choir, and some just had Joey Tinley on the organ. Joseph Tinley, Sr. organized all of this for the parish on a volunteer basis.

"Yeah, I imagine he wouldn't be thrilled with you playing that song. I've heard it on the radio, but can't place it."

"It's 'A Whiter Shade of Pale' by Procul Harum." He turned and played the opening introduction on the organ one more time and then dramatically stopped. "I only can get that sound on this organ, and so when my father left me off here at five, I figured I would get in a few licks."

I remembered how his father felt about him playing anything but approved songs. I remember thinking to myself *if only he were allowed to follow his musical choices.* As if he had read my mind, he looked at me and told me the situation between his father and him had gotten much better in the last week. We spoke like we had been close friends all our lives and he explained about a family blowout between the two of them and how his mother had intervened. They had come to some understanding about music and life.

"As long as I still practice all that he teaches me, I'm allowed to play the music I like in my free time," he said with a little chuckle. "But, singing about sixteen vestal virgins *in a church* might be pushing the issue."

It was at that moment, as the founder of the four-man no-name band, that I made a command decision. I asked Joey to join our group. I knew Gio and Jimmy Mac had auditioned keyboard players before our reunion and therefore would be up for a fifth man. Bracko was just so thrilled to be playing with other human beings that he wouldn't care. As far as auditioning, give me a break! There was no one better perhaps in all of New York City, and if there were any doubt, Gio and Jimmy Mac would both hear him at the nine o'clock mass we would all be attending. The reality of the situation was that Joey's father would be the toughest obstacle to overcome. Playing his music and playing in a band were two entirely different matters to Mr. Tinley.

I don't know if I had been emboldened by my recent streak of good luck because what happened next astounded even me. As Joey's father entered the choir loft, I blurted out, "Mr. Tinley, can Joseph join my band and play rock music?" Apparently, either the Easter Spirit or the new Tinley family values were in effect. He didn't reject my offer outright. We talked about what kind of commitment his son was in for and why he should do this. Divine intervention! This was the right kind of place for that question!

By the time the crowd started to shuffle in for the 6:30 mass, Joey was a member of our group. Besides promising to continue with his father's prescribed program, he also made his father a promise that haunts me to this day.

Joey knew his father considered rock music as a gateway to drugs and alcohol. In reality, later years would bear out this philosophy. Many superstars died early deaths from overindulgence. To subdue his father's fears, he solemnly swore he wouldn't even sample a single substance until after his 21st birthday. Of all of Joey's good character traits, perhaps the most stunning was that he was incredibly honest. He kept his promises, and he never lied or cheated. Therefore, this pledge was as valid as if a hundred New York lawyers had drawn up a contract and had him sign it with his blood. And so Joey Tinley became the fifth and final piece in my handpicked band.

I know to this day that Joey would never break his promise to his father. That is why I am confident the reason given for his death a year later was a lie.

Entry #40

"Louie, Louie"
- *The Kingsmen*

I can't say I wasn't terrified when it all came together. I knew all of the pieces were there. But would it work? There were so many questions. Could I keep up with the abilities of the other four guys? Could the brooding Bracko with his lack of social skills fit in with the rowdy behavior of Jimmy Mac and Gio? Could the polish and intellect of Joey Tinley, with his classical training, endure the four of us and our streetwise attitudes? As we waited in the cramped basement, Joey carefully brought his equipment down the stairs. We still hadn't played a single note together, and I could feel the tension building. I thought about how I had brought the naïve keyboardist into a den of uncouth street kids, and I worried. That feeling didn't last long. It was Gio who spoke first in an awkward attempt to welcome the newest member of the group.

"So you're the famous Tinman that Johnny has been raving about," blurted out Gio.

"Tinman? Why would you call me that? You think that I don't have a heart?" shot back Joey defensively.

"I'll vouch for him having a heart and a whole lot of soul," I quickly countered. I hoped there wasn't any friction developing between my two friends.

"Relax, Johnny, I was just doing a takeoff on his last name. It could get confusing here, you know, Johnny, Jimmy, Joey. Why can't you guys have unique names like Bracko and me?" asked Gio.

"It's OK. I can deal with being Tinman . . . but does that make you Dorothy?" snidely countered Joey.

"Touché," I yelled.

"Wow, Johnny, I like this kid. He's got balls," Gio said laughing out loud and pointing his index finger at Joey.

"Yes, he does . . . *Dorothy*," I said, winking at Joey.

"Does that make me Scarecrow or Lion?" chimed in Jimmy Mac.

"More like Toto," I answered. Bracko started to play "Somewhere Over the Rainbow." The ice was broken, and our keyboardist forever became Joey "Tinman" Tinley.

I knew from experience that Jimmy Mac and Gio's voices were excellent, but I had also heard Bracko knock the socks off of a blues song and the newly christened Tinman was no slouch. Would egos clash? Had I assembled too many chiefs with no vocal Indians (besides me)? These thoughts ran through my mind as we individually set up our instruments. There were short individual conversations as each of us tried to feel each other out. Gio and Joey laughed together about something I couldn't hear while Jimmy Mac and Bracko talked about harmony. Bracko then approached Tinman and started to tune his Strat to a note Joey hit on his Farfisa organ. The impatient Jimmy Mac threw a drumstick and hit Gio in the ass. We then all joined together for one final tune-up to a single harmonious C note played on the organ.

Gio positioned himself dead center in the group with Bracko to his left and me to his right. Joey placed himself back towards Jimmy Mac's drums but not far from the three of us in front. There was no more small talk.

What song to start it all? Who would sing first? Who would be offended? I looked over at Gio as if he had the answers, and to my lasting surprise, he did. He gave me a smile that reminded me of the first time Mary Lou Simmons flirted with him in seventh grade. When the usually straight-laced Bracko cracked the first inklings of a grin, and Jimmy Mac and Joey couldn't help laughing out loud, I knew something was up. The four of them had apparently talked at some point and had devised some kind of plan without telling me.

As if on cue, Gio spoke, "You brought us together, and there is no room for egos here."

With that Bracko hit the first notes he had ever played as a member of a band. The choice of song apparently had been decided while I was distracted and it was symbolic of something I'll never forget – their loyalty to each other and me. When he played the A, D, and E minor chords in a rhythm I knew so well, I wasn't surprised to feel the microphone thrust under my chin. I would sing the first song that we would ever play together. After all, I was still the only one who knew the words to "Louie, Louie."

10

The Other Side of Life:

"I Can't Get No Satisfaction"
- *The Rolling Stones*

TONY PROVENZANO'S WORLD EXISTED IN a fog, reality clouded by a cloaking haze. Considering how depressed he had been before his life-altering brain damage, Tony might have looked at the situation differently. His new world might be considered sugar-coated rather than fogged. He no longer understood the violence he and his family had been perpetrating on innocent people.

His brother Guy was now just a man who did not smile much and always yelled at people. Still, he was his brother, and he occasionally allowed Tony to follow him around during the day. Guy met with many equally unhappy and loud people. They talked about things Tony no longer understood. Tony did not care. His Mother gave him big meals followed by many kisses. She kept Tony's favorite – black raspberry ice cream – always around. His father did not give him food or kisses, but he always talked to him in a soft voice.

In between the periods of food, kisses, ice cream, and following Guy around, Tony was allowed to roam the Heights. She made the soft-spoken father and the loud, mean brother let him go out. Tony liked to be out. He could not understand the funny looks people gave him when he walked down the street. It was a different look than when he had his brother by his side. He did not understand the vast difference between pity and fear. Either way, he liked to be out in the streets, breathing fresh air. *Inside* his house he breathed air polluted by two-pack-a-day smokers. Outside, he liked seeing people. He loved watching little kids play on swings and older kids play stickball.

Though he did not understand what they were saying, he liked watching the guys hang out on the corner *bullshitting*. He didn't know why his brother Guy called it that because he did not see any male cows, and he certainly did not see them using the toilet! However, he liked seeing how they moved their hands with every word spoken. That was fun to watch. His brother told him that's just what Italians do. Tony didn't know what an Italian was, except that he was supposed to be one. He did not move his hands when he talked. Still, it was fun to watch.

Most of all Tony liked music. Not all music, just music played by his friend Bracko. The best part of his whole day, maybe his whole life, was coming to the Garden of Eden to see and hear his friend play the guitar. Then he had met another friend called Johnny who also played the guitar, and now he had two friends. But for a long, long time, maybe even five days, he had not seen either one of them. He had gone to the Garden of Eating. He didn't know why they called it that because no one ever ate there. No one had been there. He was not happy. Where could his friends be?

Money
- The Beatles version

Business was booming for the Provenzano clan. If people drank, they made money. If people used drugs, they made money. If people moved out of the neighborhood, they made money. If people fought, they made money. However, for every penny earned by the family, there were real human casualties. It was *other* people who paid the price. This was of no consequence to Dom and Guy Provenzano. The more they proved they could be moneymakers, the more influence they would be able to wield with the upper echelon bosses. This would give them opportunities to expand their business even further and make more money. The spring of 1966 was a beautiful time to be a bastard in the non-literal sense of the word. Even with all the success, Guy grew impatient. He wanted the whole process to move along more swiftly, and he would do anything necessary to make that happen. Often his father was not even aware of his son's misguided enthusiasm.

The black Dodge Charger with heavily tinted windows edged its way down Colfax Street. Just slightly over the borderline between racial areas, this was often an area of confrontation, and therefore proved an ideal location for their mission. On this isolated side street, the car slowed to stop. A lone teen emerged. His red hair would not be as apparent to any random witnesses who might spot him at a distance only because the light of dawn was still at least an hour away.

Red, as his fellow gang members knew him, was a skinny, pimple-faced 17-year old. He was too young to drive within the confines of New York City. However, one of the perks of working for a crime boss was that minuscule matters like being unlicensed were overlooked. One of the reasons Red Licasi wanted this mission was the chance to drive the Black Beauty Car. Being Italian with red hair led him to be the butt of an obscene amount of jokes that ranged from his parentage to his masculinity. Red was always trying to prove himself to the rest of the guys, and this seemed like a real opportunity.

Locating a white cinder block wall, Red withdrew the can of red spray paint from his jacket pocket. He'd thought of many messages to leave on the wall. However, he had been given precise instructions by Guy to limit his work to one three-letter inscription. His boss could have ordered a variety of racial epithets telling the damn *mulanyans* where the hell to go. However, fearing that Red's limited intelligence would lead to a spelling mistake that might make the whole gesture humorous, his instructions were to write something very simple.

He had just finished forming the third "K" in a row when Jonas Beech noticed him. Jonas was also seventeen, but his coffee-colored skin encased muscles, the result of three years of gym training. His goal was to be the best damn running back Jackson High School had ever seen. He hoped that would lead him to a better life via a college scholarship and education. He did not run with the gangs, and he usually was too busy working out and practicing to have anything to do with the chaos around him. Trouble was the last thought on his mind as he made his way to the school. However, he had pride in his race, and he knew the history of hate that the "KKK" on the wall represented.

"What the fuck do you think you're doing, punk?" barked Jonas as he caught Red by surprise.

"None of your business," answered Licasi.

Within seconds, Jonas Beech had Red Licasi in a headlock. He was still deciding what to do next when reinforcements emerged from the black car. Jonas barely noticed before a blow from a tire iron sent him plummeting to the ground. Quickly, all four of the assailants were upon him.

Jonas Beech's football career ended that day. The skull fracture and contusions to his body and head would eventually heal. However, the damage to his lower body—mainly his left knee—would forever rob him of his speed. Minutes after his assailants had departed, some of his teammates found him lying unconscious directly under the ominous "KKK" message.

As an ambulance arrived, Jonas regained consciousness just long enough to describe one of his attackers as a "skinny red-haired white kid with a black tee shirt." This description spread through the area west of Springfield Boulevard with speed born on the wings of anger. Someone would pay for the carnage inflicted on Jonas Beech.

"Hero"
- David Crosby

Neil Connaughton was not a dead ringer for Red Licasi. He was, however, skinny with red hair. When he had gone to his dresser that morning, he had made the unfortunate decision to wear a black shirt to school. That had sealed his fate. A vengeful trio of Jonas Beech's friends happened upon Connaughton and assumed this was the villain who had attacked their friend. Skinny, red-hair, black shirt. how could this not be the one?

The unsuspecting white boy soon found himself surrounded and vilified with accusations that he could not understand. At first, he was merely taunted and pushed while his assailants tried to get him to admit to his crimes. When they quickly became frustrated with this tactic, Neil Connaughton took the first of many punches to his stomach. He soon fell to the ground where the real beating began. For the second time in one day, it looked as if a good, peace-loving kid was going to have his life shattered. Instead, a voice yelled for fighting to stop.

The three black boys knew that it was a calculated risk to venture into the white turf in search of revenge. They knew they had to strike and leave quickly. But visions of Jonas being raised into the ambulance emboldened them far beyond logic. As they looked toward the voice that had admonished them, they saw a lone white boy. True, he was large, but still only one person. The white stranger approached the trio who surrounded Neil Connaughton. The victim was conscious and moaned in pain. The three looked at the oncoming stranger in bewilderment. Was he crazy? His facial expression seemed void of either fear or hate.

As the stranger approached, Marcel Wilson, the erstwhile leader of the raiding party, stepped forward to meet him. Though he stood three inches shorter than the white boy, he had an advantage, a switchblade from his rear pocket. He efficiently twisted the six-inch blade between the thumb and index fingers of his right hand. He made short lunges at his opponent with the express purpose of creating fear in the larger boy's mind. The white boy showed no fear. As the two circled each other, Marcel Wilson's two friends did as instructed and backed off to allow a "fair" fight. This stranger deserved some respect. He was trying to be a hero. A stupid hero, but a hero nonetheless.

However, before the two combatants could even engage each other, shouts rang through the air from a half block away. Reinforcements had arrived in the form of six White Devils. They too had heard of the morning events and had geared up for inevitable retaliation. As they got closer to the scene, they slowed down to try and understand all the factors that faced them. They could not comprehend why the two other bastards had not jumped all over this white guy when they had their chance. The most puzzling question was why was Neil Connaughton laying on the floor?

As Marcel Wilson looked at his impending attackers, he signaled his friends to cover his back. Inexplicably, the white boy held up his hand as a sign that they should back off. They looked at him incredulously. *Yeah, like we're going to desert our friend.* But then, in almost the same motion, he turned to the White Devils and told them to stay back.

"All I want is to get this kid out of here," said the white stranger.

"No fuckin' way after what he did to Jonas." A loud round of laughter from the White Devils greeted this statement by Wilson.

"You think that Neil the Squeal beat up your boy this morning? He couldn't fight his way out of a locker. And I should know because I've put him in enough of them," said Bobby Mason, leader of this small contingent of White Devils. All of his followers dissolved into raucous laughter at the humorous but true statement.

Marcel did not laugh but did seem confused. This might be true, but these fucking pricks had to know they could not just come into their part of town and hurt a good kid. His knife waving grew in intensity, and no one watching doubted the abilities of this kid to do some serious damage. He spun the blade like a whirlwind and created a breeze that buffered the face of his opponent. Finally, he moved the knife in a sweeping motion with the express intent of inflicting injury. At first, the weapon did not appear to do any damage. However, when the white boy looked down, he noticed his shirt had suffered a three-inch gash and the skin below had begun to bleed. Still, the silent giant remained calm and focused.

When a second jab lunged at his stomach, his left hand moved with lightning speed and knocked the blade out of Wilson's possession. He then grabbed his attacker's right arm and twisted it behind his back. Applying pressure, he pushed Marcel Wilson to the ground. This resulted in both of Marcel's friends jumping to his side in preparation for the expected advancement of the White Devils. However, both sides were halted by the victor. When he leaned down on his opponent, Wilson's friends anticipated another hit-him-while-he-is down beating similar to that given to Jonas Beech earlier. That was not to be.

"Go home," said the white boy into Marcel's ear. He then let go of his arm and extended his hand to help his opponent from the floor. It was not an order, but rather a sympathetic warning that this would be the best way to avoid the looming white gang becoming involved. With a small, weary smile the white stranger repeated in an even softer voice, "Please . . . just go."

Someone in the advancing white mob yelled, "Get them," but

the white boy stood upright and glared at them while Marcel Wilson and his friends made a quick exit.

"No, it's over," roared Bracko with a tone and volume he seldom used. He stood tall and defied any of them to disobey him. When it became apparent he had intimidated them into inaction, he turned back to the fallen and forgotten Neil Connaughton. He gently picked up the skinny centerpiece of the day's actions. He carried Neil Connaughton home.

———◆———

Bracko made a brief appearance at school that day. He cut out after about an hour and spent the day roaming the streets of the Heights. When his father had left for work, he slipped into his house and bandaged the cut. After changing his shirt, he picked up his equipment and went to band practice. Though all the members of the group knew what had happened, they waited for Bracko to talk about it. He never did, and practice took on a very business-like demeanor.

Bracko returned home that night well before his father's usual midnight arrival. With the end of the brief spring break, this had been the first time practice had taken place on a school night. After the events of that day, Bracko had been extremely glad to find refuge with the band. However, it had still been one of the most exhausting days of his life. He looked forward to the sweet release of a good night's sleep. He was already wrapped in his blankets when he heard the front door open. As usual, he soon heard the familiar sound made by the opening of the refrigerator. He knew that his father had begun his nightly beer binge. Each night, Bracko made it his goal to be safely tucked away in bed before the can opener punctured the top of the first Rheingold can.

If tradition held, Stan Brackowski would probably down a six-pack in less than an hour. A few shooters of Rye would follow those beers. Stan Brackowski would then pass out on the couch. When all sounds ceased emanating from the floor above, Bracko knew he could finally rest in peace. However, tonight was different. Bracko heard the dreaded footsteps of his father descending the stairs to his basement room. The monster now stood over Bracko who could do nothing other than fake sleep. He hoped that this would discourage his father from any further actions. He was wrong. The bellowing voice of his decidedly inebriated father demanded his attention immediately.

"I got a call from a Mr. Connaughton today while I was at work. He wanted to thank me for raising such a wonderful kid. I told him he must be wrong because I only had you." Bracko took the insult in stride. Perhaps his father was going to get to the point that he was finally proud of him. He rose from his bed thinking his father might shake his hand or maybe pat him on the back. It had been an excellent week for him, so maybe this was the topper.

"So you knocked down the nigger, huh? Just like your dad would have done. Right?"

"No, I just pushed him down."

"Then you beat the living shit out him, right?"

"Well, no. I let him go so I could help Neil," replied Bracko. He really could not figure where this whole thing was going. But then again whenever his father finished his six-pack, conversations never went in any positive direction.

"You let the fuckin' nigger go? What are you, a fuckin' nigger-lovin' pussy?" With that, his right fist hammered his unsuspecting son's right cheek. While the boy was still staggering, his father followed with an equally powerful left hook. The combination of the two blows sent Bracko spinning toward the floor. The elder Brackowski then kicked his son in the stomach. Bracko had not even felt the last blow. He was already unconscious.

"That's what you should have done, you little prick." Stan Brackowski exited the basement.

<hr />

The next afternoon, Tony sat in the Garden of Eden. He had been there every afternoon for more than a week, waiting to see his friend Bracko and to play his ukulele. But since the day that his new friend Johnny had shown up, Bracko had never once come back. He was confused. They had met in this place so often during the last few months. Maybe Bracko was never coming back. Tony thought about this for a long time, and then he cried. Tony now had no friends. He was alone.

11

Journal of Johnny Cipp

Entry #41

"Summertime Blues"
- *Eddie Cochran (or Blue Cheer)*

IT'S A NEW YEAR, 1990. I hear the celebrating on Duval Street. I have no desire to participate in the joyous times taking place outside my window. I'm not strong enough to resist the temptations that come with the celebrations. I'm lying again. Of course, I want to be out there on the streets and in the bars. For the first time in two decades, I'm resisting. Perhaps, it's the writing in this book. Or, maybe I've finally matured. In my heart, I know it is fear. If I ever go down that path again, there'll be no coming back, ever. I have an overwhelming need to tell my story. Whatever is driving me, I know that I'm sitting in my lonely room instead of doing what I've done every New Year's Eve since 1968, destroying my body with any and every form of chemical escape possible.

———◆———

Why couldn't life be simple? We had met for that very first week of practice and every minute had been golden. Our instruments clicked, and the singing voices meshed perfectly. It was so easy to run through the essential songs required of any group that wanted to do the local dances and parties. Whether it was Beatles, Stones, Cream or one-hit wonders, each of us had been learning these songs separately for at least a year, and now we were putting it all together.

We were golden. The key was a mature professionalism that none of us had ever had the patience to display before. Somehow we all knew it would work in the long run. No need to rush. No need for competition. If either Bracko or Tinman's voice more suited a lead, our two lead singers would willingly give up the limelight for the good of the sound. If a song went better with an organ solo in the middle or a guitar break, the five of us decided without regard to our egos.

In many cases, I developed into the musical arranger. That is not to brag and say that I could hold a candle to Tinman's musical skills. This responsibility came from the fact that I was neutral in the whole equation. I wasn't the one vying for an instrumental solo, and I certainly wasn't the one looking for a lead singer position. Overall, in those first five practices, I was beginning to develop into a role I had never anticipated. I was the only one in the group who knew everyone, and I had brought the whole gang together. After that first week, we had created a repertoire of songs that would be the envy of any group that had been together for months. But then, it seemed to all come crashing down.

Following Easter Sunday, we had scheduled practice at 4 p.m. each day. But Friday night came, and Bracko didn't show. Saturday brought the same. By the time I returned to school Monday, I had visions of the whole group collapsing. Once we had heard Bracko play, no one could ever take his place. One of the many truths about band development is that you never want to take a step back. Losing Bracko would be one gigantic step back.

When Joey and I met for lunch, we tried to figure out our next move. Truth be told, none of us even knew where Bracko lived and he had refused to give out his phone number to anyone. Though Jimmy Mac and Gio went to school with him, Bracko hadn't been there since the previous week. I became determined to do something. It had been eight days since that magical moment when we had played together the very first time, and I wasn't about to let that feeling, or that sound, die. Tuesday, I rushed out of school to catch the first train and bus home. I had an idea where I might find Bracko.

I would say that great minds think alike, but I didn't believe that

I had a great mind and I knew that Tony unfortunately barely had a mind at all. Even so, Tuesday afternoon found us both sitting in the Garden of Eden hoping for the arrival of our mutual friend. I was no Bracko, but Tony seemed thrilled to see a familiar face. He told me how he had been waiting for Bracko. I realized, that in my enthusiasm to form the band, I had stolen away from him the only bright spot in his life. It was so sad to think of him waiting there each afternoon, only to be disappointed. I made up my mind to try making it up to him. I had brought my acoustic guitar in hopes that if Bracko would show up, music would again be the icebreaker. I now turned this musical strategy into a way to pass the time with Tony. I started to play a little tune I'd been working on up in my room.

My songwriting had begun after the first band had died and before I'd hurt my hand. It was a very private expression of my feelings. I never meant to share my songs with anyone. I had always been so impressed with the way DJ had used words to paint pictures and create emotions. I had watched him toil in the back of a notebook. I had gotten so inspired by DJ's way with words that each night I would sit in the solitude of my attic room and create my fabric of music and lyrics. I wanted so much to express my deepest thoughts in songs that I was always writing. When eventually I was able to play a little bit of guitar, I started to put music to my words. It was uncomplicated music because my damaged hand allowed nothing else.

In the end, I discarded much of what I'd created as crap, with only the best making the final cut of my life's songs. I don't know if I lacked confidence in my ability to write a good tune, but I did know that I lacked confidence in my ability to *sing* that tune in front of anyone. And so, even the best of my creations stayed in my bedroom "studio" with little expectation of ever seeing the light of day. That was true until I looked into Tony's eyes. He couldn't judge my poor singing. He just smiled at the first strum of my strings and continued to smile as I ran through some silly songs. It was condescending of me. Bracko had played everything for Tony from Cream to Mississippi-based blues. Meanwhile, I'd play songs that I deemed suitable for a young child. In truth, I'd only recently become able to strum basic chords on a guitar. Therefore, I didn't have much to offer Tony. He particularly liked Sam the Sham and the Pharaohs' "Wooly Bully" and "Little Red Riding Hood." Eventually, my fingers started to strum a little tune that I had created.

It was a very uncomplicated song that only possessed three chords, but its message was serious. I had written the song about Tony. In a broader sense, it was a socially relevant ode to all those I had known who had overindulged in mood-altering drugs.

If only I had listened to my own lyrics.

As I sat looking into Tony's eyes, I didn't have the nerve to sing the lyrics out loud. He would never understand what I was singing about, but I still found it impossible to respond to his rapt attention by slapping him in the face with reality. I played the chords and hummed the tune. The words ran only through my mind.

Blew my mind,
On a bottle of Gypsy Rose,
And now I don't need no more.

Blew my mind,
With some lazy grass,
And now I don't need no more.

Blew my mind
In a white powder haze,
And now I don't need no more.

Blew my mind,
In a brown paper bag,
And now I don't need no more.

I blew my mind,
I blew my mind,
And now it ain't there no more.

◆

Wednesday went by and still no Bracko. Again, I had rushed home and found my way to the Garden of Eden to find only

Tony. I had again blown off Joey and Brother Christian after school. I had missed out on another bus ride home with Maria. However, the smile on Tony's face when I started playing for him made up for all the disappointment I felt. Tony asked me to play "that song" again. I didn't know what he meant until I realized I had hummed the whole performance, so he had no idea what to call the damn thing.

I played "Blew My Mind" again for him and this time made up some nonsensical words about maple trees and green grass that followed the same syllable structure as my original lyrics. Tony began to call it the "The Maple Tree" song. I guess that would have to do. It occurred to me that even if I didn't hurt Tony's feelings with the real words, there could be other problems. What if he went around singing my verses in front of his brother or father? I'd be up shit's creek then. So "Maple Tree" it was.

As Tony was about to leave, I told him not to be upset if I wasn't there every day at the usual time. I had a long trip home from school and many other obligations. He didn't understand what I meant, but I knew I would try to be there as much as possible. I meant it. I don't know to this day if it was all pity on my part, or if I merely enjoyed making Tony smile. Or maybe it was just nice to have someone actually like my singing!

On Thursday, I got there much later but still arrived in time to play a few tunes for Tony. Friday, I knew, would be even tougher. I had an after-school meeting with Brother Christian to fine-tune my bass skills. I rushed to catch the bus with Maria. I had neglected her too much in the last two weeks. She had been great about all the time I had spent away from her for the sake of music, however, that didn't stop me from feeling guilty.

"I'll buy you a Ford Mustang. I'll buy you a Ford Mustang, if you . . ." I started to sing to Maria on the bus that Friday. It was a line from a favorite song of mine that was a running joke between us. It was code for I'll make it up to you. She didn't even let me finish the first verse when she interrupted me.

"Sorry, not good enough."

"What?"

"I think a Ford Mustang is not gonna make up for taking me for granted," teased Maria. "Maserati. Yeah, it's gonna take a Maserati, or maybe a Porsche, or maybe both. Yeah, that's it,

Maserati and a Porsche, yeah, both in red," she said, keeping a straight face as long as she could. Then she smiled the biggest smile I had ever seen.

"You're OK? I mean you're not mad at me for not being here enough?"

"Johnny, I love you because of who you are. You are kind and considerate. I know that you are going to see Tony every day instead of being with me. You're a good person."

"I guess I am pretty great."

"OK, Mr. Bigshot, I said 'good' not 'great,' I also know that you are doing it in hopes of running into Bracko."

"You know me too well."

"Yes, Johnny, you are ambitious too. You want big things and so, Maserati and Porsche . . . in red . . . when you are rich and famous."

"I'm only ambitious because I want us to get out of here and have a good life."

"Johnny, don't you understand that I don't need a whole lot besides you?"

I had no answer to her last comment. It was so Maria. So perfect.

"And Johnny, if you do love me . . . eh, don't sing anymore."

<hr>

Traveling on Fridays in New York City is always a bitch. As my commute seemed to linger for an eternity, I lowered my expectations to merely being able to catch Tony for five minutes before his strict sunset deadline. I gave Maria a quick kiss goodbye as we exited the bus and sprinted home. I flew in and out of my house in a matter of seconds and estimated I would arrive at the Garden of Eden with about eight minutes to spare. As it turned out, Tony was not there alone. As I ducked through the cut-out section of fence, I heard the sounds that could only mean one thing . . . Bracko was back!

Entry #42

"Born Under a Bad Sign"
- Albert King/Cream

Bracko looked surprised to see me there. It didn't occur to Tony
to tell him I had been coming there almost every day that week.
Would that knowledge have made him stay away? I still had no
idea what had happened to him to make him disappear from not
just our group, but also the world in general. He looked at me but
continued to play for Tony a very long version of Cream's "Born
Under a Bad Sign." Bracko hadn't written the words to this song,
but its meaning told the story of his life. As I quickly took out my
guitar and played an acoustic bass riff that mimicked what Bracko
was fingering on his guitar, I realized he was very specific in his
choice of this song. He was telling me about the problem. He was
reaching out as well as he could in his own way.

I could see the remnants of severe bruises on his face as he sang
"Born Under a Bad Sign." I agreed with the words of the song. If
it weren't for bad luck, he really didn't have no luck at all.

As we finished the song, Bracko merely held his head down. I
could tell he was embarrassed by the way he had treated me and
didn't have any idea what to say. It was Tony who broke the tension by asking me to play the "Maple Tree Song." Incredibly, a
mind that retained almost no memory on a day-to-day basis had
remembered the name of my song. Bracko looked confused, or
perhaps even amused by the request. I gave him a little smirk and
broke into the chords and humming version of the song.

"Where are the words?" muttered a bewildered Tony.

"Yeah, we want words." chimed in Bracko who let a slight
smile form on his mouth. He caught on that I had probably sung
for Tony. However, he knew that I had never sung in front of
anyone else.

"We want words. We want words," chanted the two of them
in unison.

Trapped, I began my silly song about maple trees. To my surprise Bracko not only didn't laugh, but he proceeded to join in
with harmony on top of my singing. This wasn't an easy task
since my pitch was all over the place. He added some guitar riffs

at strategic pauses in the chords that made the song almost sound like something ragtime, thus further emphasizing the silliness of the whole event. I had barely hit the last note when Tony stood up signaling it was his time to leave. He was gone from the garden in seconds, departing with a simple, "Bye, bye, my two best friends."

Now alone in the Garden of Eden with me, Bracko tried to pack up and leave too. He didn't want to face me. I knew that asking him outright what was wrong would only drive him away faster and so I didn't. Instead, I said to him, "Do you want to hear the real words to that song?"

"No, I think I've heard just about enough of your singing as I can stand." I was destroyed by the comment until I looked up at him to see him with a big grin. "Just kidding, go ahead sing it." A joke? Had Bracko attempted humor? I couldn't believe it. And how did I reward him for his breakthrough behavior? I sang my real version of "Blew My Mind."

"It's Tony. No wonder you don't sing the words to him. I like it. It means something." He hesitated for a second as if he was contemplating the mystery of the universe and then spoke again. "Songs should always mean something."

I guess I couldn't bring myself to ask him what was wrong, and Bracko couldn't bring himself to tell me.

"I write songs too. I wrote one this week. I'd like you to hear it." He had taken all the pain and all the horror that was his life and put it to words and music. Like any good song, he never stated the real events that inspired the dramatic lyrics that followed. Almost anyone could have taken the words and interpreted them to fit his or her circumstances. But I knew from the first verse that it was Bracko's story.

> He keeps taking things away from me,
> A little more each year,
> And with my mind and body,
> So grows my fear.

It was the first time Bracko had ever played and sang the words aloud. It was the beginning of my understanding of Bracko, the person. It would be more than three months before anyone else would hear the song that he had created. Eventually, the song would speak for all of us in the band. It would've been a spectacular hit song if we had ever made it to a recording studio. As the two of us played on into that late spring night, I came to understand Bracko. When it became too dark to play at all, we stayed and just talked. That night I learned the details of Bracko's life. After all we had shared in the dark recesses of the Garden of Eden, any discussion of the band seemed almost trivial. Still, as we parted, I couldn't help but ask, "Are you coming back?"

"Yeah," was his simple response. Then almost as an afterthought, he continued, "I wouldn't want you to perform either one of our songs without me." He grinned with a gusto that I would seldom if ever, see again. For better or worse, I'd become his first real friend. Sure, there was Tony, but he couldn't understand the inner feelings Bracko had shared with me. I now knew and understood Bracko more than anyone else ever had or ever would. We would be friends for life. I just couldn't know how short his life would be.

Entry #43

"We Ain't Got Nothing Yet"
- *The Blues Magoos*

The months that followed were times of happiness mixed with an overabundance of chaos. If we'd been able to achieve the destiny that seemed assured to us, those days would have warmed the heart of any viewer watching the documentary movie of our rise to fame. As I try to pinpoint the details of what happened, it all seems to melt together into a collage of memories that bring a smile to my face even now.

We practiced whenever our schedules allowed which is really a way of avoiding the truth. We practiced whenever Bracko's father worked. At first, I covered for him when the others tried to schedule our work sessions for times that I knew he'd have a problem. Eventually, Bracko let the others in on some of his life. He never gave them details, but by then they knew that his father was a real prick. They just didn't know how much of a prick. Only I knew of the beatings.

It's easy to lose sight of the fact that this was the 1960's. People didn't just butt into other families' problems. You didn't call Child Protective Services or the police. It was a more "spare the rod, spoil the child" type of times. Those days revolved exclusively around the band, and no outside distractions were allowed to enter that private realm.

I still can envision the five of us playing for endless hours. When we decided we could achieve nothing else at a session, we'd sit and bullshit. We might talk about some new song we had heard or some fight that had taken place in the streets. Or we might talk about sex. I mean, did Angela Filgato stuff her bra with tissues or not? Was George Sapienza actually getting hand jobs from Jane Mackenzie *every* night? We were five teenage boys. What did you expect? Some of the conversations were as asinine as which poster was better to jerk off to. Raquel Welch in her cave girl outfit or Brigit Bardot in black leather on a motorcycle? I guess we hadn't matured that far from our days in The Coming Generation. At least, we didn't let our immaturity seep into our song list as it did with that band.

"Remember how we did Wild Thing?" Gio said to Jimmy Mac. I laughed, and Bracko and Tinman just gave us strange looks.

Bracko knew the song and proceeded to play and sing the chorus, "Wild Thing, you make my heart sing." Gio just shook his head.

"Nope," said Jimmy Mac and pointed to Gio to play.

"Wild Thing, you make *my thing ping*," sang Jimmy Mac and Gio in perfect harmony.

"You didn't?" responded a stunned Tinman.

"They did," I said, "What did you expect from a group that was stupid enough to pick a name as a sex joke? Oh, and that's not all. When we did 'Well-Respected Man,' Gio used to make a little swishy move, when he sang, 'He likes his fags the best.'"

"Yeah, but, in England, fags means cigarettes, not homosexuals," questioned Tinman.

"You think that these two numbnuts knew that?" I said pointing to Gio and Jimmy Mac who hung their heads in mock shame.

We had enough sense not to engage in this raunchier stuff when we had an audience. Yes, we let others into our private world. The most surprising of these visitors was Tony. It was an unspoken commitment of Bracko and me to give him a little joy in his life. It seemed only fair because Tony had brought us together on three occasions, each of them in the Garden of Eden. It was Tony's near death that had first introduced the two of us. It was my chance encounter with Bracko and Tony that led to the formation of the band. It was my daily serenading of Tony that led to our reunion after Bracko had quit. It seemed as if we owed him something, perhaps, everything.

All of our practices took place in Jimmy Mac's basement. Mr. and Mrs. McAvoy enjoyed the commotion and the music in a way that few of their generation ever did. The added benefit of this arrangement was that it provided Noel and Adele McAvoy with five built-in babysitters.

Jimmy Mac's three sisters couldn't get enough of sitting on the stairs listening to us play and became the first official members of our entourage. I don't know if they even listened to our performances because most of their time was spent giggling. During one of our breaks, Jimmy Mac told us that they were busy deciding exactly which of them would someday become "Mrs. Gio," "Mrs. Bracko," and "Mrs. Tinman." I wasn't upset that none of them fought to become "Mrs. Johnny." The girls really liked Maria, and she too attended our practices. Girlfriends usually were a no-no at band practices. In this case, however, the guys made an exception because they knew she'd soon be gone. I hadn't let that upset me (yet) because she was still so much a part of my life for most of that summer.

I still remember my amplifier and bass being tied to an old red wagon that served as transportation. Sometimes we walked hand-in-hand with my free hand deftly pulling the wagon along the sidewalk. On one trip, Maria feigned exhaustion and climbed upon the wagon and rode my amp the entire three-block journey to Jimmy Mac's. The white shorts and a pale green tank top that she wore accentuated her tanned body. Her brilliant white smile held back the giggles as I pretended to struggle with the extra weight her slender body added to my load. In truth, I would have pulled that wagon to the gates of hell and back if Maria had asked. This was possible because I pulled the weight of the two things most precious to me in the world--my musical equipment and my girl. What I wouldn't give to have those moments back again.

"Johnny, you're so strong," said Maria with feigned admiration and a fake flutter in her voice.

"Anything for you," I answered with a slight smile.

"Really? Anything?"

"Anything."

"Kiss me. Right here, right now," Maria countered with a look that told me she wasn't joking.

"But, you know, we're in the middle of the street," I was confused. I generally would kiss her anywhere, anytime. However, Maria was much more discreet than me about public displays of affection.

In one motion, Maria threw herself off the wagon and wrapped her arms around me. She lifted herself on her tiptoes so that she faced me eye to eye. I leaned in and softly kissed her lips with a gentleness that belied the passion that I felt for her that moment. Maria briefly returned my kiss with an intensity that we usually reserved for our very few moments of privacy. I felt the tears running down her face and reluctantly pulled away from our embrace.

"What's wrong," I asked.

"What's going to happen to us? I'll be too far away until you can drive. And you know how my parents feel about you."

"We'll find a way. You know like they sang in West Side Story, you know the song, 'There's a Place for Us.' Maria, we'll find that place."

"Johnny, you do know that that the character Tony in that movie died?" said Maria finally smiling.

"Oh, yeah," I responded as I wiped the tears from her cheek with my index finger and smiled back at her. "Well, that ain't gonna happen to us. I promise we'll be together forever. Nothing is going to make me leave you. Nothing will ever tear us apart."

I took her hand in mine, and we walked the rest of the way to practice.

Dammit! What a bastard I was to her. Why did I leave? I wonder what she is doing now?

———◆———

Some of the time at practice was spent in serious discussion about which style of music we should play. Interestingly, whatever minor conflicts developed with the group had to do with music versus money. Many groups had these problems. Just how much of a sell-out would we be? Playing creative, exciting music that we loved was weighed against playing the commercial trash that dance audiences wanted. Whereas Bracko and Joey always leaned more heavily toward blues, jazz, and long-running jam sessions, Jimmy Mac and Gio would have played whole sets of "Happy Birthday" if it brought them fame and fortune. I lay in the middle because I liked all kinds of music, even "Happy Birthday."

The discussions were never really confrontational, but each of us knew where the others stood. What developed was our style. We played all the basics that the crowds would clamor for at a dance. Yet, we not only played some edgy music that was on the fringes of popularity, but we also put our personal spin on every song. A rasping Bob Dylan song might end up with three-part harmony. A basic dance number might feature some amazing guitar and organ solos that the original group couldn't have performed. We were focused and determined, and we were damn good.

There was a commercial somewhere along the line that used the catchphrase, "We will sell no wine before its time." Well, that was our unspoken attitude. We would not play anywhere or for anyone before we were ready. Hell, we still hadn't picked a name!

Often at practice, Gio would try out his song introductions and audience byplay. We laughed because the sisters McAvoy had no idea what he was doing when he went into his shtick. They sat confused but amused as he went through his repertoire of phrases.

"Glad you all could come out here tonight." The sisters hadn't come anywhere. They were in their basement.

"We'd like you to grab your favorite girl and dance to this one." The sisters looked around for who was going to ask them to dance.

"This next song is from our album." That caused a flat-out laugh.

"You are listening to the sounds of. . ." OK, it was our turn to laugh. He still couldn't finish that sentence. We had agreed that there would be no silly name-picking meetings until we were ready to step out on the stage. Eventually, Gio practiced his intro by calling us "The No Name Quintet." When we finally did pick a name, it would have a meaning for both Gio and me.

Entry #44

"Under the Boardwalk"
-*The Drifters*

Summer offered the most job opportunities for any band looking to make some bucks. Most of the dances and parties took place during June, July, and August. This was a tradition that had come down indirectly from God. It was almost as if all the Catholic, Protestant, and Jewish clergy had a meeting one night and decided that the majority of their dances would occur on those hot summer nights.

Outwardly, the rationale was that during the school year they didn't want to take away valuable time that could be used for studying. In reality, the teenage pregnancy rate during hot summer nights soared, and the religious leaders were trying to cut into the time spent in *other* activities. Still, sex was happening "Under the Boardwalk," and "Up on the Roof," and a thousand other places that the religious leaders had never imagined, or had been sung about by Motown groups. They weren't going to stop the urges of both sexes that seemed to be magnified by the violence of their surroundings. It was almost as if the neighborhood kids had taken on an attitude usually ascribed to soldiers going off to war. I heard more than one White Devil tell a girl, "We better do it tonight. Who knows what is going to happen to me tomorrow on the streets?" Worse yet, I'm pretty sure she fell for it.

The clergy and the parents would have been much better off if they had thrown in some birth control education. Ha, yeah right. This was the 1960's, and that wasn't going to happen. Hell, the pill had just barely been invented. All this is my way of saying that the summer magnified everything in our lives. There was just so much more time for good times and bad.

Unfortunately for our band, our timing was off. Not musically, but logistically. We had found each other just a little too late in the season to get hired for most of these jobs. By the time we got up and going, it was already mid-June. We knew we could have rushed into the fray by learning enough songs at a just-good-enough quality to support ourselves through a whole night's work. We could have done some "Wooly Bully," "96 Tears," and grinder progressions to make everyone think that we were good. But we didn't want everyone to think we were good; we wanted them to know we were great. We didn't want to play a dance here or there for a few dollars and a little adulation. Well, yeah, we could have used a few bucks and praise, especially if it was coming from females!

In the end, we held off. Better to give no impression at all than to give one that did not knock the people dead. Besides, we had another problem. We had decent enough instruments and amplifiers for the audience to hear us. However, to go far, we needed a sound system for our singing voices. Well, not mine. Most bands got away with plugging a microphone into one of the inputs of a guitarist's amplifier. The audience could, therefore, hear the singer to some extent. The trouble with that was that the guitar sounds coming out of the same amp sometimes drowned out the singer. Considering the quality of most lead singers, this was not a bad thing.

At this point, we knew that we could have three to four-part harmonies on every song and we wanted people to hear the voices loud and clear. This required a separate and distinct sound system of reasonably high quality. In turn, this required money!

Entry #45

"Money"
- *Pink Floyd*

Share #1: Jimmy Mac conned his father into paying him just a bit more for his work in the family store. In return for a few more hours a week, Mr. McAvoy slipped his son some extra bucks. The son volunteered for the after-dinner shift. He'd rather sell candy

to the women who frequented the shop at night than the daytime
brats who fingered all the penny candy before deciding between
the Red-Hot Dollars and the Mary Janes. The local homemakers
were much nicer and occasionally tipped him if he made their
egg creams just right before they caught the latest Rock Hudson
or Tony Curtis flick.

Share #2: Joey "Tinman" Tinley had some money saved from
gifts given to him for his first communion, confirmation, and
birthdays. He convinced his father to allow him to use it.

Share #3: Bracko had saved some money from jobs he'd had
through the years. He'd spent most of it on his guitar and amp,
but after a few weeks of doing grunt labor for an old Italian
bricklayer, he had more than enough. Giacomo Latini had promised to teach his helper all of the skills necessary to follow in his
lucrative footsteps. Bracko had explained all of this to me with
mixed feelings. He loved the old guy, and he loved the money he
made. However, the thought of working with bricks the rest of
his life did not seem appealing. For the time being, he would do
it to kick in his share of the sound system.

Gio and I still needed to come up with our parts. We were both
tapped out from buying our guitars and amps the year before.
Our only option was to hit the summer job circuit. Because
Bracko's father had switched to the day shift for the summer,
that's when practices would be scheduled. Now Gio and I had to
find nighttime employment, not an easy task.

Gio landed his job at the Carvel on Springfield Boulevard. This
meant that he had access to all the shakes and cones that he could
devour when his boss wasn't there. This also meant, however,
that he spent every night on the line between the warring racial
areas. He encountered both black and white customers. This
in and of itself didn't bother Gio in the slightest. The problem
arose when the customers themselves got into conflicts outside
his serving window. With the way tensions were growing that
summer, it didn't take much for a real or perceived misstep on the
line to become a fight.

Gio was safely locked behind the enclosed glass of the walk-up
window and could've ignored the violence outside. That just
wasn't Gio's style. On more than one occasion, he had ventured
out into the melee to soothe tempers. Sometimes, he even gave

away some free product to soothe the combatants' nerves. I had to tell him that he'd been watching too many Western movies. He was the bartender who stopped the gunslingers from drawing their weapons by offering drinks on the house. He smiled and said, "You know me too well." I would find out later that I didn't know him well enough to know what else had happened while he was working those late nights.

My experience working in a grocery store wasn't nearly as exciting as Gio's job. However, this was more than made up for by my adventures on my nightly trips home *after* work.

Entry #46

"Miracles"
- Jefferson Starship

All good things come to those who wait. I don't know where I heard that before, but it seems to fit what happened next to the five of us. We were committed to perfection, and that meant not performing until we had a quality sound system. We were OK with this decision, but it didn't make us happy. And then a miracle happened.

When we showed up at practice one morning in late July, we had an unexpected visitor. Joseph Tinley, Sr. sat in Jimmy Mac's basement waiting for the rest of us to arrive. We didn't know the man at all. We politely said hello each time he happened to drive Joey to practice. While helping his son lug equipment from his old Ford, there might be a passing wave. However, none of us had ever had a conversation with him that had lasted longer than, "Hello, nice weather, isn't it?" Of all the band members, I probably knew him best because of his job at my high school. From the neighborhood, I knew nothing more than the others.

That morning, while we all sat waiting for him to leave so that we could get started, Joey got our attention. I thought perhaps he was going to tell us that his father was making him quit the band.

"My dad would like to hear us play a few songs before . . ." *Before what, damn it?* Joey never did finish the sentence and simply began to hit the first notes of "Whiter Shade of Pale." The organ introduction was impressive, but Mr. Tinley already knew that *his son* could play well. It was when the rest of us joined in at just the right moment that the music teacher seemed to take notice. He nodded as Gio professionally sang the parts about "the sixteen vestal virgins leaving for the coast." The final shock to his musical senses came when he heard our original arrangement. The third time we hit the chorus, all the music stopped, and Gio, Jimmy Mac, Bracko, and Joey sang that part of the song in perfect a cappella four-part harmony.

Our instruments joined back in without one of us missing a beat, and the song soon concluded. The tightness of our sound and the blending of their voices blew away the dumbstruck music teacher. When the last note had finished resounding in the basement, we all stood silently looking not at the father, but rather at the son. I remember being the first to open my mouth and asking him to finish the sentence he had started before the song. Before he could answer, his father spoke.

"So how much more money do you need for the sound system?" You could hear a pin drop. "I have been teaching music and coaching choral groups for twenty years, and I have never seen anyone as excited about music as I've seen my son for the last two months. I just had to see what it was that made him finally show the enthusiasm I have been trying to build in him his whole life. And you played something classical."

"It's Procul Harum. It just sounds like Bach or one of those guys," said Jimmy Mac.

"Procularum? Never mind. And that harmony! I have been trying to get that from groups for years. Who trained you?"

I figured that if I answered, they would all laugh. First, because Mr. Tinley was my music teacher and second, I was the only one who couldn't sing. It might go beyond ironic to the brink of insulting. Therefore, it was Jimmy Mac, always the extrovert, who answered that we had no formal training. I think that Mr. Tinley either didn't believe us, or the reality of it shook the very foundations of his universe. The question and answer period officially ended.

He took a moment to regain his composure. "As I have told Joseph, I am prepared to front the rest of the money for the sound system that the group needs." We were so surprised by his offer that we were left speechless. Gio looked at me and mouthed,

"Who's Joseph?" I nodded my head toward Joey and silently mouthed, "Tinman."

"It would be a loan that would be paid off with the proceeds of your first paying jobs. I will help you with some of my musical contacts to get some breaks on equipment and such. And I'll even help line up some jigs." We all looked at him like he was crazy. Had he just made a racist comment? Joey corrected his father.

"It's gigs, Dad, gigs!" Not flustered at all, the elder Tinley fluffed off the correction and continued.

"I'll help out until you can get a real manager. No fee, of course. Family discount," he said with a little giggle. Rather than embarrass him, we all faked being amused. After all, this guy had just moved up our timetable quite a bit. It was Bracko who tried to bring reality into the conversation as he spoke for the first time since we had arrived in the basement.

"But we don't have any jobs yet to pay you back with," mumbled a shy and embarrassed Bracko.

"Oh, I didn't tell you the best part." He withdrew a little pocket calendar from his crisply tailored suit jacket. Who the hell wore a suit jacket in the summer?

"All day music festival at the Wollman Skating Rink in Central Park on August 17. You go on at 1:15 p.m. Then on the 24th, you play at the Café Wha in Greenwich Village. Then it is the 'Back to School Dance' at McCarthy High. If you have three hours' worth of material and you are as good as that one song I heard, you'll end up the house band at the McCarthy High monthly dances."

There wasn't a sound in the basement until we heard a stick hit the floor. Until we noticed Jimmy Mac picking up a lost drumstick, we all had thought that stick had dropped out of our savior's ass.

Entry #47

"Summer Song"
- Chad and Jeremy

Holy shit! I remember thinking. *This was real.* We would have a sound system, and more importantly, some real money. I could quit my shitty summer job.

That summer was a time where every waking moment was either filled with joy or the anticipation of joy. I find it hard in this part of the story to even think of where I know the story will inevitably conclude. I've had to work through the events of my immaturity, my naïveté, and my devastating depression to get to this point. What form of therapy would this journal be if I didn't face the reality that this indeed was the last summer of my youth? No, it was probably the last summer of my life. I don't mean that I didn't physically live for many afterward, but rather the enthusiasm that children of all ages hold for those months of endless sun and spectacular nights would never again be a part of my life.

It was a summer when Maria and I would bond in a way that would commit us to a life together. No words were spoken or act committed that made our love a done deal. It was instead a commitment of our souls to each other that merely required our gazing into each other's eyes to be as solid as any band of gold could ever be.

Sometimes we would meet at Rockaway Beach and find a nice secluded section under the boardwalk. Other times we would situate ourselves in the back row of the Valencia Theater in Jamaica. However, most of the time we would just meet in the neighborhood when she could sneak away from her parents' excessive watchfulness. We didn't have much privacy then. It was the reason we would eventually need to get out.

Every waking moment that wasn't dedicated to Maria was spent with the band. It had taken a convoluted chain of events to bring us to this place and time together. We knew it was right. It was so right that every practice produced new wonders. The future was ours. Songs were learned with a fluidity that amazed even us. Original pieces were created with a quality that surprised us all. Our abilities combined were far above the level of any of us individually possessed.

Yes, it was the best time of our lives. It was all ahead of us until it wasn't. Yes, the summer of 1966 was my last "Summer Song." By the summer of 1967, it was all gone.

Entry #48

"Hard Day's Night"
- The Beatles

A Hard Day's Night. Yeah, I know, *I've been working like a dog.* My despised job had been the only way that I could contribute my share of the money to the group's sound system. Now Joey's father had saved me from that fate. Yet, the experience lingered in my mind.

Through my father's truck route, I had made some connections. I was given the very prestigious title of stock boy at the local Associated Food Store. I had no problem with the minimum wage pay or the mind numbing task of putting cans on shelves. There was only one thing that made the job difficult – the location. The store was on the other side of the line. I was working very deeply in enemy territory. Either Dad didn't have any friends on the white side of Springfield Boulevard, or this was a lesson in racial tolerance. It didn't bother me that I was working "over the border." However, tensions had escalated so badly that summer that anyone caught on the wrong side of the line by either side was fair game. I didn't want to be that game.

Thanks to Mr. Tinley's generosity, I could finally quit. However, I decided to work one more week to have some money to buy something for Maria. After my last night of work, I was especially vigilant on my way home. I stayed out of the streetlights and made no sounds. I wasn't going to run into anyone accidentally. I would see them coming before they saw me and I would hide. I only had three to four more blocks on Murdock Avenue when I heard the voices.

I couldn't make out the muffled conversation, but it seemed to be no more than two people. Could I handle two? It was better than five, but I didn't want to find out. As I tried to figure out how to get to the other side of the street without being seen, I realized these two people wanted to be heard less than I wanted to be seen.

Was it because they were waiting to catch someone by surprise?

No, the tone was somehow non-threatening. My mind finally focused, and I realized one of the speakers was female. Now I'm thinking one on one at worst, and I think I would be okay with that. He might fight more fiercely to show off in front of his girl-friend, but it would still be better than two on one. Or maybe he's a lover, not a fighter, more interested in getting in her pants than he is in knocking me out of mine. The voices I heard were romantic in tone. I was now close enough to know that they had other things on their mind. Good! I was going to make it. I was close enough to tell that they only had eyes for each other. I was also close enough to tell that I knew one of the voices.

Entry #49

"Society's Child"
- *Janis Ian*

Gio! I couldn't hold myself back. I quickly crossed the few feet that separated us and was face to face with my best friend and a beautiful black girl. Her hair hung to her shoulders and encased her high-cheekboned face. Her mocha-colored skin had only a faint touch of makeup, and to be honest, it didn't even need that. Though her eyes were brown, even in the dim lights of a street lamp, they seemed flecked with lighter colors that made them sparkle with brightness. Her natural beauty was stunning. I had suspected that Gio had met someone, though he hadn't said a word about it. This was unheard of for Gio, and now I knew why. We stood a few feet apart, both of us dumbstruck. He had kept this secret so well that I wondered if he thought that he would keep it forever.

"This is Riet," he said softly to me. It seemed that the shock of seeing me there was gone. I offered a meek, "Hello." I'd never known any interracial couples, no less one including my best buddy.

"Riet, this is Johnny." I remember that he pronounced her name like the word "riot" which for some reason set off warning signals in my mind. This was trouble.

"Come in the light so I can see just how white you are." Like I said, trouble.

With that comment, I realized that the red blush of my face had made her statement no longer true. She had meant to put me off guard, to frazzle me, to put me down a peg. God, what had Gio gotten himself into? We stood silently for a while until I saw a small smirk start to come over Gio's face and then Riet's. Soon they were both laughing uncontrollably.

"You should see the look on your face," said Gio as I stood speechless.

"He really does have a stick up his ass," said Riet and I remember being offended that I was being described the same way that we had all described Mr. Tinley. This made what happened next even more of a surprise to me. She put both arms around me and gave me a warm, lingering hug.

"Any friend of my guy is a friend of mine." Gio smiled and just looked at me. This was real.

The closest I'd ever come to interracial love was listening to Janis Ian's "Society Child." You know, "Come to my door, baby. Face is clean and shining black as night."

As I gazed at them holding hands, smiling, I knew two different worlds couldn't keep them apart. It was the whole Romeo and Juliet deal. We talked longer, and we laughed together. I forgot where I was, and who I was talking to. And out of the blue, I stopped the conversation dead with one line that wasn't well thought out.

"You should come to one of our practices," slipped out from my never-guarded mouth.

"Oh yeah, where are they held?"

"Jimmy Mac's house." This brought silence. Reality intruded.

"Sorry, we all know that I can't do that. Little black girls stay on this side of the line." Her voice sounded sarcastically like Prissy in *Gone with the Wind.* "You all know that the other side of the line is for people like you . . . you know, *those born free!"*

Holy shit, I thought, *witty and beautiful.* I just stared, at a loss for words.

It was time to go. Though Gio continued to see her until the very end, I never saw Riet again. With my job done for the summer, I stayed on my side of the line, you know, with the rest of *those born free.*

Entry #50

"The Name Game"
- *Shirley Ellis*

Gio was also glad to be done with his job, but he would miss his time at Carvel. In one of the few conversations we had about Riet, he explained they had met while they were both working there. Carvel was one of the few equal opportunity employers in the area. While serving floats, sundaes, and cones, Riet and Gio had developed an unlikely friendship that eventually developed into a romantic relationship. No one had any idea, except for me.

Yes, Gio would miss seeing her during his work shifts, but we both knew it was time to devote our full energies to the band and the upcoming unveiling of our talents to the public. We now had a solid repertoire of songs that would prove more than sufficient to play all the gigs.

Individually, or together in harmony, Gio and Jimmy Mac sang about two-thirds of our list. Bracko and Joey shared the rest, except of course, for my one starring role in "Louie, Louie." Many of the songs found them singing in three and four-part harmony that blew the socks off of any other garage band around. Sure, we were no Beatles or Kinks, but some groups out in the Top 40 markets were getting by with much less than we could produce. Of course, we knew of groups like Question Mark and the Mysterians who created the hugely successful "96 Tears" in their garage in one take. I had the feeling that much of that was luck since the organist played a catchy but repetitive riff that required no keyboard talent at all. The rest of that group's musical contributions were unimpressive at best, and I could have done the singing. But it was a hit, which only goes to show that the song sometimes trumped the group.

To that end, we had already started creating originals. Some of the early attempts were brutally bad. By the beginning of August, we had worked on three tunes that showed promise. With the three-dozen cover songs we had down pat and a handful of originals, we were ready to pick a name. This is one of life's great idiotic experiences. I'd already gone through the whole Ravens and Coming Generation lunacy. Those rituals were conducted with an immense amount of immaturity. This time it would be better.

Wrong! For all our extensive work in producing our sound, we reverted to immature teenage boys when the name game began. Each of us had been thinking of this separately, and therefore each of us thought we had the ultimate name. In retrospect, most of the choices, including mine, were absurd. Some were so bad, that if the Beatles had chosen any of them, they would still be playing to empty venues in Liverpool.

There were the fad names. Some current groups around at the time were the Electric Prunes and the Strawberry Alarm Clock. I don't think any of us was pushing for something like the Chevrolet Bathtub or Chevron Sundaes. That brought us back to the basics and by that, I mean THE basics. You know names that began with "THE." Let's face it; this concept had been beaten to death in all the major kingdoms. I mean, there were The Beatles (insect), The Seeds (plant), The Rolling Stones (mineral), The Animals, (duh, animal). When all the phylum of the biology book had been used up, you had The Zombies (undead) and The Who (?). What was left?

I remember us sitting around in silence for a very long time. This was becoming harder than actually making the music. Finally, I'd had it. I started venting what we all were feeling in the form of a screaming rant about the situation. I don't remember much of what I said except for the very last part.

"The Fuckoffs, The Shitheads, The Asswipes, The Turdbuckets!" I was losing it. Of course, this set off a contest of who could come up with the most absurd variation on my theme: The Diarrhea Dudes, The Hole Asses, and The Piss Ants. Now we were all laughing, yet I was still angry. "The, The, The . . . everyone uses "the." Those groups have no imagination. Those groups . . . Those . . ."

I remember stopping mid-sentence. It had come to me. We were entering the late 1960's, and young people all around were claiming to be unencumbered by the restraints of the older generations. It was a time when drugs, sex, and rock and roll would know no boundaries, no limitations. As I turned to Gio and mouthed my idea, a big smile came across his face. The name had had its birth in sarcasm, and that would remain our secret until the end. I turned to the others. "No more The's. How about Those . . . Those Born Free?"

Entry #51

"Just Like Romeo and Juliet"
- The Reflections

As I tell my story, I think perhaps I've focused too greatly on the music and a life that was so totally absorbed by it. At times, I neglect the other story that dominated my life at that point–Maria. It might seem like my story is about a musical group and what it meant to me. However, those experiences were for the sake of Maria. Life with her was still the end game. The music was a passion, but it was still only a path to my ultimate goal, a happy and full life with Maria. That is the reason why I still can't write about her moving away from the Heights without feeling intense anger. As her moving date of August 10 approached rapidly, I felt a fury rising in me. I tried hard to control those feelings, especially around her. With the band's upcoming big break bookings, my life should've been beautiful. It wasn't.

I was torn between spending every waking moment either with the band or with Maria. There weren't enough minutes in each day for both. Looking back, it's strange to think that this devastating move was only seven miles away. To those of us who lived in that place and that time, those few miles had a real distance equivalent to living on the two different sides of the Berlin Wall, so close, yet so far. To get from Cambria Heights to Nassau County was an absurdity. To travel even seven miles east, I would need to go ten miles farther westward *into* Queens to then catch a bus back *out* to Nassau. My journey would total over two hours of time and twenty-five miles of distance each way!

This situation was exasperated by the fact that while the rest of New York State allowed seventeen-year-olds to drive with driver's education, New York City didn't allow anyone under eighteen to drive under any circumstances. Maria's parents, white flight, the transportation system, and the DMV were just some of the enemies that made me seethe with anger as her move grew closer.

Entry #52

"Pretty Flamingo"
- *Manfred Mann*

"Pretty Flamingo" was a catchy tune by Manfred Mann that seemed to be in my head that day, August 9, 1966. Maria was moving the next morning. Though there was sadness in me that day, all-consuming anger was my most dominant emotion. The band saw this and knew that I needed a break.

We'd all given up our summer jobs to practice almost eight hours a day. Most of the summer Maria and I had found ways to be together before, after, and sometimes even during practices. However, in the last week, her parents had demanded she stay home and pack. The band all liked Maria, and so on that last day, we broke early so I could be with her.

I ran over there only to find she was next door at her friend Diane's house. When I knocked on the door, they both came to answer it. I told them about my short break, and Maria made an effort to come outside and see me. Incredibly, Diane was adamant about the fact that this was *her* time, her last time with her lifelong buddy. I had always liked Diane, but I was furious. Maria just gave me a sheepish look that told me that she wanted to be with me, but she didn't want to hurt her friend's feelings. Whereas we were in love, we had only known each other a little more than a year. Diane and Maria had been friends since their cradles were placed side by side seventeen years before.

As I stood outside Diane's house, my rage grew, and I wanted to strike out at someone or something. Not being violent by nature, I wouldn't hurt a living person with my temper. The same could not be said for inanimate objects. They were fair game. I don't know if singing the song made me aware of the flamingo, or the flamingo made me sing the song. But there it was on her front lawn, and I was angry.

Like so many other lawns in the Heights, the amount of grass was so minuscule that it could be "mowed" in fifteen minutes using only a pair of scissors. This made it doubly confusing that people chose to decorate these small patches of green with really cheap ornaments. The most common of these ornaments were plastic pink flamingos. I still don't understand the reason for an ugly tropical bird being placed on a lawn in New York City. However, they were in abundance in our neighborhood, including the one that I had symbolically chosen to strangle in frustration that very afternoon.

In the midst of my attempted murder of the plastic flamingo on Diane's lawn, her mother came out. As a feeble explanation, I blurted out, "The flamingo started it." Diane's mother was not amused and asked me to leave. At that moment, I hated both Diane and her mother. However, I knew that cursing them out would only cause me trouble with Maria, Maria's parents, and eventually my parents. And so, I stared into the black paint of the flamingo's eyes and softly uttered, "This isn't over."

When finally I looked back, Maria held her hand up to her ear and mouthed the words, "Call me after practice." I returned to the group at least satisfied we would meet up later in the night.

When practice ended, Bracko and Joey bolted quickly from the basement rehearsal area. Jimmy Mac and Gio were both still there when I called Maria's home to arrange our final rendez-vous. They could see my frustration grow as her father refused to let her come to the phone. He said all kinds of things: they were going out for dinner, they still had packing to do, and they had to get up early the next day. It was all bullshit. They never really liked me and were trying to end it right there and then. I could hear Maria begging her father to let her out, but it was to no avail.

Jimmy Mac and Gio had picked up the gist of the conversation and knew that I was livid. Both of them signaled me to calm down. They were right. I couldn't show my anger to Maria's father, or I'd never see her again. I politely hung up the phone and then started to rant. Jimmy Mac cautioned me that to do it in his house would mean problems finding a new rehearsal location. And so, I held it in again.

Once out in the street and a safe distance from Jimmy Mac's block, I let loose with a stream of obscenities that didn't end until we had traveled to the eastern border of the Heights. Knowing my pain, they just let me go on. When I finally stopped speaking, Gio's humor finally cooled me down a bit.

"I didn't know that you knew half the words you just yelled out. You've come a long way in the obscene vocabulary development. I'm proud of you, young man." This got me at least to smile. Ironically, I found myself standing next to, of all things, a plastic flamingo.

"Screw you, and your smiley pink face too," I remember saying to the flamingo that was taunting me. Apparently, in my mind, this pink guy had spoken with Diane's plastic bird on the flamingo hot line. Gio laughed and then broke into a chorus of "Pretty Flamingo," and Jimmy Mac was soon harmonizing with him. My anger came down a notch or two, and I began to breathe normally again. I had a plan.

We each made excuses to our parents about where we were going to be, and they all mistakenly trusted us. We were up to no good. In the Great Flamingo Round-up of 1966, the three of us found and freed from lawn captivity every flamingo that had been bought by the evil flamingo slaveholders of Cambria Heights.

After requisitioning three shopping carts from the Bohack Supermarket, we systematically scoured the streets of the Heights for our prey. Early in the evening, we were afraid of being noticed by nosy dog walkers and random pedestrians. We covered our wagons with sheets and other materials that we found in our travels. By midnight, only the miscreants and thugs roamed the streets. It is important here to remember that these were my people. They loved me because of my unique experience of getting beat up. Upon running into some of these guys, their reaction was to help us.

By four in the morning, we'd herded all the stray flamingos into our wagon train. We then had the first and only flamingo drive in recorded history. They arrived at their final destination--Diane's house--a little before sunrise. We carefully and quietly placed the more than three-dozen plastic birds on her lawn. When every inch of the grass was covered with our pink friends, we filled every inch of concrete, railing, and exterior walls of the house with the overflow birds. We would have liked to have stayed and watched their reaction, but we were afraid of getting caught *pink-handed.*

Each of us snuck into our own homes a little before dawn so we could be found sleeping there by our parents. We each explained we had changed our minds about a sleepover and had returned home a bit after midnight to get a good night's sleep.

In my anger, I had only hurt myself. I couldn't go and say goodbye to Maria as her family prepared to leave the next day. What a jerk I had been. In my fury, I had lost any chance of seeing Maria one final time before she moved.

Even so, there was great satisfaction in knowing we had reunited an entire tribe of birds that had so long been separated by man's inhumanity to ugly but innocent plastic birds.

12

The Other Side of Life:

"Heroes (and Villains) in the Night"
- "There were villains in the night,
One black and one white."
- Chris Delaney and the Brotherhood Blues Band

WILLIE CALDER DIDN'T KNOW JONAS Beech, but he knew what had happened to him. Did they think they could get away with screwing with a brother? He didn't know about anyone else, but he was going to do something, and he was going to do it right now. The hate he felt inside grew with each passing moment. He heard all the big talk from his friends, but he wasn't waiting to find out what everyone else was going to do.

He slipped into his brother's room unnoticed. There was no one there to notice because Lucien had spent the night at some hot number's crib. He always did. Willie worked his way over to the bed, lifted the mattress, and removed the 9mm Smith and Wesson. He checked that it was loaded, and then stuffed it under his belt behind his back. With the weapon hidden underneath a bulky shirt, Calder took a basketball from the floor and headed to the street. Once he crossed the line, he started dribbling his way to revenge. *Some shithead is going to think that he has a fool like Beech to pick on and then bang-bang, one dead white motherfucker!*

◄──────►

Freddy Resch had snuck out of Mary Lou Casali's house at approximately the same time that Willie Calder had crossed the line. Because both of her parents were oblivious to what she did in her basement bedroom, Freddy often found it easy to stay the whole night without anyone noticing. He could do it to the *skank* without having to worry about messing up the insides of his car. It was the only reason he kept seeing this sixteen-year-old he considered way below his standards. In reality, they never went *out*. He wouldn't run the risk of any of his friends seeing him in public with this piece of shit. She was good for a few more weeks of *fuck'em and forget'em* sex then he was leaving her for someone with a little better body. That was the plan until that morning.

Just as Freddy was about to walk out the door, Mary Lou told him she was pretty sure that she was knocked up. *Fuck*, he thought, *I ain't marrying this piece of shit.* Even visiting Sally the Solution, and her basement treatment room was going to set him back the money he was going to use for brand new rims for his 1962 candy apple red Impala. *She's talking like she thinks he's going to marry her. Marry that whoo-a, no way. But then she brings up that he can get arrested because she's only sixteen and he's twenty. What the fuck?*

All this was going through Freddy's mind as he exited quietly out of Mary Lou's house. However, once out the door, his anger erupted. He had grabbed a baseball bat that Mary Lou's brother Tommy had left by the door, and once safely away from the house, he started hitting every garbage can that lay in his path.

"Fuckin' skank *whoo-a*. Probably some other prick did it," Freddy muttered under his breath though he had never used any form of protection. He seethed with anger as he approached the corner of 217th Street. Distracted, he did not look up as he approached the end of the block where the view of incoming pedestrian traffic was obscured by six-foot high, untrimmed hedges. Willie Calder approached the same corner. Concentrating on dribbling with his left hand, he kept his right hand poised behind his back ready to retrieve the 9mm. Unfortunately, he didn't have any warning as the overgrown hedge also obscured his view of the impending confrontation with the already insane Freddy Resch.

The collision of their bodies pushed Willie back into hedges with the basketball resting in his midsection and his right hand (and gun) trapped behind his back. Meanwhile, Freddy fell to one knee as the bat he carried pushed into his stomach and knocked the breath out of him. He quickly recovered and soon saw his assailant. In one motion, he was on his feet and had the bat poised over Willie's head, ready to pummel the helplessly trapped boy. As he staggered toward him, all of the anger he had felt since Mary Lou's announcement rose in his body.

Willie struggled to free his pinned right arm as Freddy approached with the bat in hand. Unable to move left or right because of the confining action of the hedges, he reacted with the only option open to him. He drew the basketball into his stomach with his left hand and then propelled it outward in a slingshot motion toward his attacker.

Excruciating pain racked Freddy as the ball powered into his family jewels. He looked up thinking that the punk would now run away. Instead, he witnessed the shining outline of what he knew to be a gun. If he tried to flee, he probably would take a couple of slugs before he even made it a few yards. With no choice, Freddy raised the bat and tried to race the draw of Willie Calder.

The crack of the bat and discharge of the gun were almost simultaneous. When the sounds ended, the gun lay on the floor, and the bat remained in Freddy's hand. Finding himself disarmed, Willie chose to flee back to the safety of the line.

"You fuckin' nigger. You're dead," said Freddy as he rose to his feet to follow the younger, smaller black boy who now had a half a block lead. Willie ran for his life down 115th Road, a sloping thoroughfare that emptied into Springfield Boulevard. He looked back and saw the enraged Freddy Resch with the bat in one hand and the gun in the other. All he could think of was the damage this maniac would inflict if he caught him.

If Willie had taken another look, he would have seen Freddy had fallen to the ground after a few steps, blood freely flowing from the bullet lodged in his stomach. Instead, his mind blindly focused on the safety that lay on the other side of Springfield Boulevard. He had to make it. He sprinted across the road, never noticing the Duggan's Cake truck whose path he crossed.

Willie Calder died before the ambulance ever arrived. Freddy Resch, covering his wound under his jacket, lost himself in the crowd of startled onlookers. He was never identified as the alleged pursuer.

———◆———

A new militancy rocketed through the youth of both sides. Immediately, violent clashes on the streets of the Heights grew in intensity. Skirmishes in the halls of the high school would be unstoppable once school reconvened in a few weeks. Though no more deaths occurred, the emergency rooms of Queens General Hospital swelled with the results of beatings and stabbings.

———◆———

To the five members of the newly named *Those Born Free* band, the world outside seemed the last thing on their mind. They saw their way out of this hellhole. They had heard about Willie Calder, but they tried not to dwell on it. They knew that they were on the right track to escape. Just don't screw up. And so, even as violence increasingly spiraled out of control, it was never mentioned at practice.

"So You Want to be a Rock n' Roll Star"
- *The Byrds*

All of the members of Those Born Free had been born in 1949. That same year, Kate Wollman donated the money for the skating rink named in her honor in Central Park. Throughout the winter this venue drew tens of thousands of skaters to share in its frozen wonderland. In summer, this flat paved expanse at the southern end of Manhattan's largest park became a music venue.

The daylong event was a showcase for a few dozen groups who had somehow worked their way onto the playbill. In some cases, powerful agents had used their extensive networking abilities to procure a slot. In other situations, groups were the winners of very competitive battles of the bands held throughout the metropolitan area. In one case, however, a group made the cut because its manager, Mr. Joseph Tinley, had attended college with the talent director.

The members of Those Born Free never questioned how they got booked for this huge event. The small appearance fee would barely cover the cost of renting a van to get their equipment to the location. Any money left over would be used as the part of the loan repayment to Joey's father. The money was not enough to change any aspect of their lives. It was the opportunity that created excitement in their hearts. The Wollman was a place to show what all their hard work had created. It was to be the beginning of everything.

The rental van driven by Mr. Tinley picked up the boys and their equipment at the McAvoy house just a little after 9 a.m. This departure hour allowed the group to skirt the massive jam of cars entering the daily rush hour gridlock of the city. However, this time was still extremely early for a group that was not scheduled to perform until the early afternoon. Mr. Tinley had always been an observer of musical performances. Getting there and ready hours in advance would give him the opportunity to scope out the other acts and judge the mood of the audience. He needed to know what kind of songs were going over well and what kind of showmanship was striking a chord with the crowd.

After surveying the situation, he explained that the band would be playing in front of thousands of young kids and teenagers who would be young and silly. The band's popularity would probably be based more upon how the preteen and teen girls analyzed their looks. This was a slap in the face to most serious musicians, but they had to start somewhere.

13

Journal of Johnny Cipp

Entry #53

"Blinded by the Light"
- Manfred Mann version

OUR FIRST PERFORMANCE BEFORE AN audience is something I will never forget. I mean who the hell chooses to make their first public appearance in front of four thousand people? We were young, brash, and mostly stupid. Given a chance to perform because of who we knew, we had entrusted our careers to Joey's father, and he was even more naïve than us about the music world.

Observing the sea of youthful onlookers, we decided to play some covers of popular hits.

This particular audience would dance and scream and appreciate the performance given to them. But after the applause had ended, they would forget who we were and what we had done. Our name would leave their minds as quickly as the sugar in the sweet snacks that they seemed to devour throughout the day's activities. That was our mistake. We were good but bland. We played to the four thousand teenyboppers rather than the handful of truly musically knowledgeable fans.

We opened with The Kinks' classic "All Day and All of the Night." Though by now it was already two years old, ancient in musical terms, we felt it would be a crowd favorite. It did get them on their feet and dancing. Therefore, it seemed only fitting to continue the performance with "Keep on Dancing," a prime example of a hit song that would soon be forgotten by the masses.

Looking back, I can't shake the impression we were just performing not to make a mistake. We didn't even succeed at that limited goal. We royally screwed up our last song, "Gloria."

Why did the American public buy into a Shadows of the Knight version of Van Morrison's classic song? And why did we choose to play this cover? Who knows why anything happened in my life to make it turn out as it did? The song was a three-chord repetitive E-D-A progression. I mean how can five great musicians mess up three chords? After singing of his devotion in the first verse, the lead singer (in this case Jimmy Mac) reveals the object of his affection is indeed named Gloria. However, for some reason, Van Morrison felt that he needed to spell the damn girl's name before proclaiming his undying love for her. I mean the name was not Esmeralda or Scheherazade. If he had just sung to Gloria, I'm pretty sure that even those who had not scored passing grades on their last spelling test would have figured out the six letters necessary to spell G-L-O-R-I-A.

In all fairness, we had done this song so many times that each vocal and instrumental note could be repeated with little thought. Unfortunately, we had never done it on a giant raised stage in front of thousands of listeners. It wasn't stage fright that was our undoing, but rather our inexperience. Just before beginning our final song, we were informed that the far distant reaches of the audience couldn't hear us very well. To be crowd pleasers, we then moved our speakers from behind us to a more forward section of the stage. Mistake! We didn't realize we couldn't hear our own voices. Most of the other groups were experienced enough to realize this venue required sound adjustment. But with no sound check between each group and no prior jobs, we fell right into the trap of not being able to hear ourselves.

I don't know if it would have been better or worse if we had chosen any other song under those circumstances. "Gloria" never changed a single beat or chord pattern from beginning to end. When Gio started with his first notes, we all fell right into line. Panic almost immediately overcame us as I turned to see that Jimmy Mac had begun singing, but we couldn't hear him. I looked at the crowd and noticed that there was a sea of rhythmically swaying heads that were enjoying the drummer's vocals. It was only the four of us on stage with him who were not privy to his golden voice.

If we had done a less ambitious version of the song, the terror in our eyes would have been less obvious. Whereas Jimmy Mac could sing along with a chord progression that would not change, Gio, Bracko, and Tinman had vocal parts that needed to be precise. When Jimmy Mac arrived at the location in the song where he began to spell the lovely Gloria's name, the three of them were supposed to echo his spelling in three-part harmony. This task would prove difficult if they had no idea where he was in the song.

The result was an unmitigated disaster. Nobody heard his first "G" which was bad enough. However, when they attempted to do their responding harmony, they couldn't hear each other's voices. The result was that Jimmy Mac's "G" received no response while a "G" answered his "L" from Gio and "L" from the observant Joey, and an "O" from Bracko who was merely guessing where they were at that point.

As the only one not tied to a microphone at that point, I edged my way up to the speakers and became aware of the disaster. I'd like to say we resolved the problem immediately, but that would be a lie. Gloria's name became an unrecognizable alphabetical mess that only came to an end when each singing member of the group thought they had spelled the name in its entirety. The expression on my face told them of the disaster and begged them to find a solution before the next arrival of the now hated name. It was then that Jimmy Mac ever so slightly changed the method of his drum style before each verse he sang. Though we couldn't hear his voice, we knew the second stanza was soon coming to an end, and a nod of heads signaled that we all understood that no one but Jimmy Mac was to sing again. Too much damage had already been done. It was then that Bracko saved the day.

No longer anchored to his mike, Bracko faced our drummer and proceeded to read his lips and locate the upcoming spelling test. When Jimmy Mac proffered the first letter "G," Bracko responded with a synchronized blues note that sounded remarkably like a vocal response. He proceeded to play his responses to each of Jimmy Mac's vocal cues. When the final "A" had been called, Bracko gave a head motion to all of us that meant he was going into an unplanned solo. His strings rang with an incredible combination of notes that couldn't have fit better into the structure of the song if we had practiced the performance day and night for a year. As he ended his solo, he gave a nod to Tinman who then proceeded to improvise an equally creative organ break that drew even more of the crowd to its feet.

But how the hell were we to get out of this mess now that we were making it up as we went along. I looked at Bracko, Gio, and Joey, and signaled for them to stop playing. I, however, continued. Jimmy Mac caught the hint and limited his drum playing to the slightest tingle of his high-hat symbol. What resulted was the sound of the bass and drum softly playing as the final verse was sung. Now, however, every word was heard and understood by the entire band, and remarkably the harmonized responses to Jimmy Mac's leads were restored. We finished with four dramatic chord changes and a drum roll. The song was over. Our day was done.

Had our alphabetical disaster destroyed our performance and our reputation? The audience responded with heartwarming applause.. However, every band had received this kind of response. After all, it was a free concert, and the listeners were not the most musically aware kids in the world. We had learned a lesson in humility. But how expensive would that lesson be?

Entry #54

"The Year of the Cat"
- *Al Stewart*

As we packed up our equipment and left the stage, our heads were hung low. Up until this point, we had always been assured of our ultimate success. Now, we had flubbed our first performance. We weren't invincible. Joey's father tried to cheer us up with some generic compliments. However, we were not to be consoled. That is until we met the "The Cat."

We had no interest in staying to hear other bands play, and so with the van packed and ready to go, we took one final look at the stage. Abruptly, Gio bolted our group and ran up the stairs to the stage. There waited the next performers. A young, fresh-faced group around our age awaited its introduction. We looked on as Gio spoke to a guitarist who appeared to be giving instructions to the rest of his band. Gio then bounded down the stairs and returned to us. Jimmy Mac started to question what he had done. However, before he could answer, we noticed the movement of a speaker away from the direction of the audience and toward the band. We understood.

"You know, unbelievable as it is, some groups don't realize that they can't hear themselves sing with all the speakers facing out," Gio said. We all had a good laugh and felt a bit less depressed. That was Gio at his best.

It was then we noticed a stranger leaning on the van. His jet-black hair was longish though retained a bit of a greaser air about him. He probably was in his mid-twenties, and his swarthy good looks relayed to us he did not have much trouble landing any woman he desired. I remember vaguely the conversation that ensued.

"Boy, was that version of 'Gloria' . . ." He paused as if looking for the right word and then suddenly seeming to find it, continued, " . . . unique."

"Crappy, I think is what you meant to say," responded Jimmy Mac.

"No, it was ballsy the way you guys saved it after. . ."

"Our spelling disaster," chimed in Gio.

I didn't speak. I was too interested in hearing what the stranger had to say.

"My name is Vinnie Catalano, Vinnie the Cat, or just The Cat. I came to see the music and look at the talent."

"You some agent or something?" asked Jimmy Mac with excitement.

"Well, not exactly, but I am looking for a few good groups for my boss who is opening some clubs in the next year."

"And you are talking to the boys . . . why?" said Mr. Tinley asserting his pseudo-manager status into the situation.

"Well, mostly because they are from my old stomping grounds. I still have a fondness for the place and for good music."

It was then I realized why his name sounded familiar. Vinnie had had some part in bringing The Shangri-Las from the obscurity of the Heights into national stardom as the sexiest white singing group of our generation. His name never appeared on any contract or album cover, but his involvement was a legend in our area. He had helped bring someone from the Heights to stardom. Now he was talking to us.

"Just some friendly advice from one hometown boy to some others," he began. "You're not ready, but neither are the people that I represent. Take your time, polish your act."

"Learn to spell," chimed in Gio.

"I wouldn't be talking to you if you hadn't screwed up that song," said Vinnie losing his original train of thought. "If you had played those three songs as perfect covers, I would have filed your name away with about ten other proficient groups. The way the band recovered and . . . those solos. They blew me away. Real potential there."

"So…" said Jimmy Mac, always the outgoing one.

"No promises, but you keep improving, and I'll look you up next spring."

You could have knocked us over with a feather. Vinnie, the legendary fucking Cat, had noticed and liked us.

"Oh, and one more thing. I'm not looking for a straight cover band. I want you guys to come up with some original songs, ideally enough for an album. The quality of those songs can make or break you guys." He winked at us and walked away. Holy shit! Club dates, albums! None of us would sleep that night.

The Music Doctor winks at me as I write this. That one brief meeting with Vinnie Catalano changed our lives. We rededicated ourselves to a year of hard work on cover songs, and more importantly the creation of original works. The song had not been written yet or surely one of those cover songs would have been "The Year of the Cat."

Entry #55

"Love Minus Zero"
- *Bob Dylan*

I needed to see Maria and tell her we were one step closer to making it . . . and to tell her I missed her. Her parents were still making it hard for me to get through on the phone so we had only talked once since her move. I took a bold step and waited patiently for Diane to leave her house on a sunny August morning. I then "accidentally" ran into her. The conversation was awkward at first.

"Johnny, you're an asshole, always have been."

"Yeah, I know. Sorry about the flamingos."

"Ha, that was actually funny. I couldn't believe the look on my parents' faces. But you're still an asshole. Maria couldn't see you that morning because of your prank."

"I screwed that up."

"Yeah, but Johnny, that was what made me realize you and Maria had something special."

"Diane, I need to see her," I said softly.

"Johnny, her parents are doing everything possible to end it between you two. They want her to move on with a nice boy from the suburbs."

"Oh," was all I could say.

"Hey, asshole, that's what *they* want. Maria's not buying into it. I talk to her every day, and all she can talk about is you . . . asshole."

"Thanks, Diane."

"For what? Calling you an asshole?" She laughed. "Johnny, I'd do anything for Maria and apparently, that means I've got to tolerate you." Her words were a bit sarcastic, but she softened the tone and touched my arm. "Johnny, she's suffering."

"I know. I am too."

"I know you are, Johnny, but not like her. You miss her, but your time is occupied with the band. She has nothing."

"What do you mean?"

"She's seventeen in a new neighborhood filled with strangers. Her one unbelievably wonderful friend . . . me . . . is still here in the Heights. Oh yeah, and so is her mediocre boyfriend. It's still summer, so she doesn't even have school to distract her. Who has it worse?"

"Diane, I need to be with her."

"I'll see what I can cook up, asshole. Remember you are not a big favorite in my house either. My parents call you the Flamingo Kid."

"Wow."

"It's not a compliment, jerk."

"So I've been demoted from asshole to jerk?" She finally let out a faint smile.

"Give me your phone number, you fucking asshole. There, you feel better?"

———◆———

Three days later, Maria and I met at Green Acres Mall in Valley Stream. I hitched to the shopping center near her home, and she convinced her parents to leave her off to do some shopping. I had saved some money from my summer job, and I had decided that I would buy Maria a token of my feelings. It was nothing expensive, just a simple silver ring with some hearts carved into the surface. When we walked into the Sam Goody music store and one of my favorite songs, "Catch the Wind" was playing over the loudspeaker.

"Me and you, Maria, we're going to catch that wind right out of this place,"

"But, Johnny, there may be no getting out."

"When the band makes it big, we'll get married right away."

"Johnny, you're such a dreamer," she replied. Sure, things were looking great for the band after talking to The Cat, but that kind of success might not be permanent, (at least that was what her father always told her). I *was* a dreamer. I never denied that.

"We will get out of here . . . no matter what it takes." It was then I surprised her with the news I was going to apply to Queens College. She had already decided that was where she wanted to go.

"If it ever looks like the band is not going to make it, and I do mean *if*, I'll be right there beside you at school and we'll make that future together, one way or another."

"Do you mean it, Johnny?" she asked me. "What about the music?"

"I love the music more than anything in this world except you." With that, I took out a little silver band and placed it on her finger. "I promise you a future together. I'll do whatever it takes." Then she surprised me by taking the ring off.

"I don't ever want you to compromise what you want in life."

She placed the ring in the palm of my hand. "When you get where *you* want to go, whether it's with the band or with school – whatever – then give me the ring. When you know what you are doing with your life, then I will take it. When your journey is over, then come to me. That is the only way I want it . . . or you."

I took the ring from her hand and placed it on my pinkie. She couldn't know it would stay there for decades.

Entry #56

"Break on Through"
- *The Doors*

We noted the Cat's comments and decided that we'd make that real effort to create our own songbook. Though first we had to get up the courage to face our second live performance. Despite the positive feedback from Vinnie, we still had to regain our confidence after the events of our Central Park debut. This next venue would be different.

The Café Wha was an intimate setting by any standard, but especially so compared to our Wollman Festival experience. The audience, which might reach triple digits on a busy night, consisted of much more discerning musical critics. They didn't want to hear the same old crap that they could listen to on the radio. They wanted originality whether that took the form of an original song or the arrangement of a classic with a different twist on its presentation.

Could we survive another failure? Was our friendship strong enough to weather the pressure placed upon us? We argued more than we ever had about who should play or sing every note of the songs we had chosen to perform. How original would it be to change a tempo here and there? Or add some harmony where there normally would be none? How many guitar or keyboard solos would impress the crowd without seeming pretentious? I recall us being at each other's throats and our smiles were few and far between.

Events hit rock bottom when we tried to re-create the magic of the "Gloria" solos at Central Park. It just wasn't working out. In a rare moment of emotion, Tinman stopped playing, frowned and shook his head. Professionally and classically trained, his sense of what sounded good was impeccable. I struggle to remember all the details of what happened next, but I do know that it changed the direction of that day and perhaps the future of the band. Gio and Jimmy Mac began to raise their voices in disagreement. It was more frustration than anger, but to anyone unfamiliar with our ways, it would sure seem like a fight.

To our permanent guest, Tony, it was terrifying. He sat so quietly at almost every practice that we often forgot he was there. He placed himself in the same rickety old rocking chair that lay in a corner of Jimmy Mac's basement. He listened to every note we played, smiling and sometimes even applauding, no matter how badly we sucked on some occasions.

I have no idea what his home life was like. I guessed there was probably a great deal of violent screaming. I assumed we were Tony's shelter from the storm. Whenever *we* got loud and confrontational, Tony would cover his ears. If we continued this for any length of time, Tony would leave. He had left many times that week before our performance at the Café Wha. Tony's exit that day abruptly ended the skirmish between us, and we all acknowledged it was time for a break. Little did we know it would also be time for a breakthrough.

Entry #57

"Gypsy Rose"
- *Those Born Free*

Though all members of the group reacted to Tony's emotional escape, Bracko and I took it particularly hard. He had touched our hearts in a way that had never seemed possible when he had haunted the streets in his former life. We hated to see him in pain. We all sat silently after his departure. His leaving punctuated the frustration we had mistakenly allowed to explode into hostility. Now we sat individually and collected our thoughts.

The quiet was broken by the sound of Bracko's guitar. I immediately knew what he was playing. I had written it. It was the simple two-chord strum about maple trees I had sung to Tony months before as we sat in the weeds hoping for the return of

Bracko. After the first two times that he strummed the two chords and sang the "Blew my mind" phrase, he embellished the riff by adding a G chord followed by the sarcastic reply that I had written, "And now I don't need no more." It was not only grammatically incorrect but also factually wrong. (Brother Christian would have corrected me to say *anymore*.) But more importantly was the fact that in the real world, *they always needed more.*

Bracko and I had forgotten about it until Tony's rapid departure had stirred the feelings that Bracko had kept inside for so long. He strummed the chords and sang the words both he and I had unceremoniously discarded after that day in the Garden of Eden. As I recognized the ode to Tony, I joined in with the bass runs I had used to accompany the simple chord pattern. Soon Gio was softly mimicking the chords, and Jimmy Mac was keeping a simple beat of the drums. With such a simple little tune, the tense emotions that had filled the room only moments before disappeared. From that point on, the song became so much more.

When Tinman joined in with the Farfisa organ, the tune became almost comical. After the words, "and now I don't need no more," he added a few notes that sounded as if we belonged in a carnival. Though it's hard to explain musical notes in words, it was as if he was punctuating the end of each line with a "la-di, da, da!" It worked. The silliness of the music was juxtaposed with the seriousness of the message.

We worked on it the rest of that day. It brought us back together with each member contributing something to the song. What we would do with the song was a mystery. It was so "un-rock n' roll" that we doubted we would ever perform it in public. Nevertheless, it was fun, and at that time, that's all that mattered. While we had at first had referred to it as "Blew My Mind: An Ode to Tony," we realized that was not a very good idea. Because we had made the little addition that included Tony's name, we soon couldn't change it back to "Blew My Mind." We couldn't get the full title out of our heads.

Imagine if we slipped and called it that in public. Tony might not get the reference, but it wouldn't pass inspection with the other Provenzanos. Therefore we referred to it as "Gypsy Rose," naming it after the cheap wine that had become the drink of choice among our peers.

Entry #58

"On the Road Again"
- *Canned Heat*

The vast hordes of snowbirds have begun their migration season. All around me are drunken northerners trying to forget that eventually, they would have to return to their colder climates. This influx at the beginning of January is unbearable for most residents of the area. For a recovering drunk and addict who is in the struggle of his life, it is even more challenging. I must keep saying to myself that I will take their money in tips but not join them in their celebrations. Tough week.

We again boarded the same rented van we'd used to go to Central Park the week before. We'd worked hard and prepared for our second job. The word "job" is a bit of an exaggeration though. Bands weren't paid at the Café Wha. It was considered an opportunity to be seen, and indeed, I don't doubt that many groups actually *paid* the club for a spot on the bill. Luckily for us, Mr. Tinley again had some musical connection that allowed us to have the opportunity of a lifetime.

A mere six weeks before our arrival, Chas Chandler, The Animals' bassist turned music executive, had discovered Jimi Hendrix in this very location. He had played on the very same stage that we would perform on that day. Of course, we had no way of knowing this, or perhaps it would have made us even more nervous than we already were. Gone was the brash attitude that we had displayed before the G-l-o-r-i-a debacle. Now, we were confident but careful with our approach. We had no hopes of being whisked away to England and selling millions of records like Hendrix. We, instead, would be happy just to play our music and eventually be paid to do so. Looking back, perhaps Jimi Hendrix should have hung around to listen to our "Gypsy Rose" song. Then he might not have died of a drug overdose less than four years later.

We set up on the snug little stage and were so tightly configured that we could have easily played each other's instruments. The Wha was known for its quality of the music rather than for the accommodations provided for the performers or the audience. It had been a centerpiece of Greenwich Village dating back to the folk music era of the 1950's. The popularity of rock music since The Beatles' arrival had necessitated the change away from the folk music that had made this little club the center of everything new and different. It wasn't long before beatniks became hippies in the Village. It also wasn't long before Peter, Paul, and Mary and the folk god Bob Dylan gave way to Hendrix and the *rock* god Bob Dylan. Now it was our turn.

We started with "Gimme Some Lovin." I again enjoyed being the first one of the night to hit a note. We had practiced spicing it up a bit with four-part harmony in many strategic parts of the song with extensive solos by both Bracko and Tinman. It was different, and we hoped it was just different enough to please the savage beasts who thirsted for more than a run of the mill band could give.

We followed the opening song with a cover of "I May Be Wrong, But I Won't Be Wrong Always." Most of America hadn't been privy to the work of Alvin Lee and his group Ten Years After. We hoped that most of the audience wouldn't recognize this largely ignored British group. Failing to trick them into thinking that this was an original song, we hoped to dazzle them with our musicianship even if they had heard the original on the "Undead" album produced by the British rockers.

As I sit here writing in this journal more than a thousand miles and twenty years removed from that dingy club in lower Manhattan, I can still smile. That performance is one of my many wonderful memories. We played our hearts out. There were guitar solos. There were organ solos. There were drum solos. And even yours truly on a bass solo. Bracko played jazzy chords I didn't even know existed. Jimmy Mac, Gio, and Joey, sang harmonies that did not appear on the original recording. When the fifteen-minute performance came to an end, the crowd showered us with applause. They couldn't help but appreciate the skill and soul that we had offered on that day. I can't speak for the others, but that one song had ultimately thrown every muscle of my left hand into spasm. For fifteen minutes, I had plucked my way through scores of notes to provide a backbeat for this fast-paced number. After we had completed it, I could feel the pulsating pain and yearned for an ice bucket.

Mr. Tinley caught our eyes, flashed us a huge smile, and then held up the five fingers of his right hand to signify time remaining. I don't remember what song we had planned to perform as our closer, but I do remember what song we finished with. As I looked out into the crowd, I was struck by a familiar face that stared back at me from the rear of the club. The Cat had come to see us again. Getting the guys' attention wasn't hard because we were standing on top of each other. I motioned out to the crowd and said only, "The Cat." I then pointed to Bracko and said, "Gypsy Rose." They understood. The Cat wanted original, and we would give him original.

We had enjoyed our day-long trip of creation with "Gypsy Rose," but would anyone else even like it? Would they get it? We had refined it. We had thrown all kinds of harmonies into the singing and amazing riffs into our playing. In the end, we liked what we had produced, but would anyone else?

We had just finished the first verse when we realized that the audience was singing along with us. True, it didn't have very complicated lyrics, but give me a break. The crowd was singing along with a song that we were performing for the very first time in public. Then I realized why. They were *not* getting the meaning of the song at all. They joined in each time we sang, "Blew my mind," reveling in the ramifications of doing just that. They didn't get the sarcasm or the anti-drug message. They not only were buying *into* the concept of a blown mind but also cheering for it to occur.

When we finished the last note, we again received applause, which we graciously accepted. We walked off the stage and just shook our heads in amusement. They didn't get it, but they did like it. It was then that The Cat walked up to us. He congratulated us on a good performance and reiterated the fact that he would keep track of us for the coming year. I'll never forget his parting words.

"Original song, huh? It was pretty good." As we thanked him for his comments, we all wondered whether he was just like the mindless stoners of the audience who didn't get the meaning. Or was he different? Did he truly understand what we were singing? We got our answer almost immediately. As he turned to leave, he put on an all-knowing smirk and said out of the side of his mouth, "I wouldn't sing that in the Heights any time soon. The Provenzanos like their private business . . . well . . . private."

Entry #59

"Forever Autumn"
- Justin Hayward

With that performance at the Café Wha, our summer had ended. It was time for us to prepare ourselves for all the changes that would take place with our return to school schedules. We all accepted that the clock was ticking on our futures. If we hadn't succeeded by this time next year, the real world would intrude on our dreams. Each of us would have to accept failure and find a new path in the world.

I would have to decide if I would go to college. I'd made a vow to Maria that if all else failed, I would join her at Queens College. I knew Gio's plans were a bit sketchier. Perhaps, he would take off with Riet to find somewhere in the world where they would be accepted.

Joey wouldn't have a choice in his destiny. He had made a deal with his father and he understood that failure meant he would submit to whatever his father desired. His life as "Tinman" would come to an end, and he would be Joseph forever.

Jimmy Mac knew that by Labor Day of the following year he either would be a rock musician or forever tied to the ball and chain of the family business which he hated.

Bracko counted the minutes until he was free of his father. He was waiting for his eighteenth birthday and his high school graduation to leave the man who beat him unmercifully. What he would do after graduation depended on the band. If successful, he would stick around and find a place of his own to live. If Those Born Free failed, he would leave for destinations unknown.

Labor Day set the clock ticking. We had agreed we would have our final year of high school and the summer that followed to make it. If not, our lives would permanently veer apart. The winds of change would blow us in five very different directions.

And so, life for each one of us settled into the pattern that the onset of the school year imposed. Though enthusiasm for the group and its goals did not diminish in the slightest, we molded our daily lives around school. The weekends brought intense practice time as we worked hard perfecting our song list. The dream was there, and nothing was going to get in our way.

Entry #60

"On the Threshold of a Dream"
-*The Moody Blues*

We did have our share of paying jobs throughout the 1966-1967 school year, though we never did play in the Heights. It was a conscious decision to avoid our stomping grounds. Of course, we felt that natural desire to show off to all of our friends. However, we fought that tendency for many reasons, but mostly because of Vinnie the Cat. We considered him our hook to making a breakthrough to the big time but the group decided to avoid him until we could knock him dead with our live performances as well as with the quantity and quality of our original work. It was a daring choice, but we had all agreed to it.

In the end, what matters is that Those Born Free never performed in Cambria Heights. Upon reflection, that's why I'm still alive today.

———◆———

The time and place of our performances that fall and winter never seem to find focus in my thoughts. I can't put them in chronological, or any other kind of logical order, at all. Even when and where we wrote each of our original songs remains fuzzy. It is the "how" of each of these moments, however, that I remember with a clarity that cannot be explained on any biological level.

The comments of The Cat launched us on a yearlong quest to write original material. The results were inconsistent. Some of our efforts were dogs, worthy only of laughter. However, in various combinations of collaboration, Those Born Free produced almost a dozen quality works. They were songs with lyrics that spoke to the raw realities of our lives, accompanied by the best musical arrangements our young minds and hearts could produce.

Those songs only exist in *my* mind now. Occasionally one of them will find its way to my fingers as they caress the six strings of my guitar. I will play one or two, and then it will all come back. We learned a great deal about each other from those songs. Now it is just me they haunt.

It was a time of creation. It was a time of growth. It was a time of hope. I do know that through that ten-month period we lived a fantasy existence that denied the real world entry. It was a time when we had the inexplicable feeling that everything was going our way. To borrow the title of a Moody Blues' album, we were standing together on "The Threshold of a Dream."

Entry #61

"See My Friends"
- *The Kinks*

As the year progressed, we grew closer and closer to each other not only as musicians but also as friends. We could finish each other's sentences in conversation equally as well as we could know what note each of us would be playing at any moment in a song. We knew each other's personal lives outside of the band and accepted each other for who we were. We were so different in many ways, yet so focused on what we did share.

The others knew of my love for Maria and cut me slack when my frustrations about seeing her made me grumpy. They lived with my moods and frustrations. They knew when to console me and when to tell me I was acting like an ass. They were all there in their own way whenever I needed them. . . pretty flamingos and more. I did occasionally find ways to see Maria. Sometimes it would be my sympathetic father who drove me over to her house. At other times, I just stuck a thumb out and hoped for the generosity of passing motorists. Still other times, we both took buses to the equally accessible shopping areas of Jamaica.

Eventually, the rest of the guys caught on that Gio had someone special. He took lots of ribbing from the guys about when and if we would meet his mystery date. Of course, the more that time flew by, the more he received teasing about what he must be hiding. Jimmy Mac gave it to him most. The comments ranged from how fat she must be, to questioning if he indeed was even dating a girl at all. Bracko even chimed in once by regaling us with an instrumental version of "If You Want to Be Happy for the Rest of Your Life, Never Make a Pretty Woman Your Wife." They never guessed the truth. No one even hinted at playing "Society's Child," a song which had been on the record charts throughout that entire year. I guess to the rest of them this was so far out of the realm of reality that they didn't even think to joke about the topic. And so, Gio's love for Riet remains my secret to this very day.

Everyone knew of Jimmy Mac's many romantic conquests. How could we not? He amused us with so many stories that featured him as the Irish-American version of Don Juan that Gio dubbed him Don McJuan.

Joey and Bracko never discussed their social lives. Let me rephrase that. Joey and Bracko didn't have social lives. Between the strict code of conduct enforced by his father and the number of hours that the old man required him to practice his piano, Joey lived the life of a caged animal. What would he be like once he was freed from that cage and went away to college? I will always wonder about that. He never tired of telling us that the band was his only outlet. We knew.

Then there was Bracko. Beaten and bruised both outwardly and inwardly, an eternal sadness surrounded him. I don't doubt the only smiles that ever crossed his lips were when he was with us. It was that very sadness which made him the guitarist he had become. Again, the band was the outlet for the pent-up emotions of one of its members. Every note that Bracko played seethed with the anger that he could and would never show outwardly in any other form than music.

It was on one such occasion he brought the kernel of a song to us. It was from the deepest reaches of his depression that our best creation had its birth. From it, we learned of Bracko's soul and attempted to share his pain.

Entry #62

"The Thief of My Forever"
- *Those Born Free*

"He keeps taking things away from me,
A little more each year,
And with my mind and body,
So grows my fear."

I'd heard the song long ago in the Garden of Eden, but this was the first time that Bracko had performed it for the full band. At the time, we'd been embroiled in another of our petty disagreements, which resulted in a period of quiet and reflective sulking. As we all sat in Jimmy Mac's basement that day, brooding and scowling at each other, I heard the muffled vibration of guitar strings. I immediately recognized what Bracko was playing. I was transported back to that night in the Garden of Eden. This song had entrusted me with a dark secret. Now he brought his tale into the light of day for all to hear.

The guitar chords were so haunting we all sat in awe, our petty disagreements laid aside. We knew what direction the rest of this practice would take. We would be working on this song.

First, I joined in with a bass line that enhanced the musical progression. Gio almost simultaneously mimicked the chords that he saw the lead guitarist laying down. The three of us were soon joined by a smooth backbeat provided by Jimmy Mac on drums. Finally, the genius of Tinman on his keyboard magically gave depth to the song. With Gio holding down the rhythm, Bracko broke into a guitar riff that stunned us with its simplicity and its beauty. The recurring six-note formation rivaled the memorable work on many of Eric Clapton's classic tunes. We found ourselves enthusiastically following Bracko's lead for an endless amount of time. Without ever bothering to return to the lyrics that had drawn us into the web of his song, we embellished on Bracko's original tune with a myriad of our own ideas. Without missing a beat, each of us experimented with different styles of performing our individual parts. We played endlessly to refine and perfect the flow of the song. There were no breaks. We lost all track of the world around us. Once we had the instrumental part down, we decided (with Bracko's enthusiastic permission) to work on expanding the lyrics.

I try so hard to remember who contributed which verses. I don't know why it is important to me, but it is. A song that had started out in the hidden recesses of Bracko's mind had now become all of ours. Following the meter and the phrasing of Bracko's three-stanza outline, we combined to create a much longer piece of work. By the time we finished, our song had a message. Indeed, it had multiple messages. The song was about each of us separately *and* all of us together. Collectively, we came up with the title of "The Thief of My Forever."

To each of us, the thief was someone or something different, and each of our verses spoke to that truth. But we needed a universal thief, one who could be seen to steal everyone's forevers. We agreed that the song needed to cloak reality a bit. Not as much as a maple tree replacing a huffer's bag, but just enough that people would argue about the interpretation. Astute listeners could see the thief as any villain in their own reality.

In the end, it is *time* that takes away our hopes and dreams and robs us of our youthful desires and ambitions. The universal concept of time became the mask that Tinman, Bracko, and Jimmy Mac could hide behind.

Tinman's verse was a subtle attack on his father. We hoped this would be lost on that very man when the "time" interpretation was emphasized at the end.

He pushes me too far too fast,
Before I feel I'm ready,
Sometimes I walk a confident path,
Other times, doubt leaves me unsteady.

Bracko's lines lashed out at the evil monster who was his father – the man who destroyed both his body and mind every day of his existence.

He keeps taking it away from me,
A little more each year,
And with my body and mind

So grows my fear.

Gio and I worked on lines. Though we both looked forward to our futures with great anticipation, we often talked about the "good old days" when our lives were less complicated. It was a time when our biggest worries were deciding when we would knock off playing stickball to have more time to watch science fiction movies. We both loved "our women" as we called them, but there was no doubt that our lives were infinitely more complicated. Although our contributions were nowhere near as life-shattering as the problems that faced Bracko, we felt that the song needed to speak to all of our issues. It needed to be about all of our lives.

> I sorely miss how it used to be,
> Before he took it all away,
> The time I looked not to the future,
> But lived day by day.

The next lines came from Jimmy Mac and were perhaps the most surprising to us. Our drummer's happy-go-lucky façade crashed. We saw the fragile side of his psyche. He was serious in his fear of being trapped in a life that he didn't want to live.

> Fear of things that have gone,
> And who I've always been,
> Fear of what I'll never be,
> Fear I'll never win.

As we tried desperately to blend each line into a cohesive pattern, we lay bare inner selves to each other. We tore down every barrier of privacy and self-importance and truly became as one person writing "The Thief of My Forever." Often when his original lines were recited, we saw Bracko touch the bruises on the left side of his face. He had paid the greatest price in this act of creation, and we all understood that.

When the day was done, there was no high-fiving or outward exuberance. We nodded at each other with a shared understanding that the fruits of our labor had been good. I remember a mental and physical exhaustion very seldom duplicated in my life.

I still have the words to that song on the same old piece of loose-leaf paper that Gio scribbled them on. They were tucked into a pocket of his guitar case that now stands in the corner of my room as a constant reminder of what the ultimate Thief took away from me . . . from us.

The Thief of My Forever
- Those Born Free
(Bracko Brackowski, Johnny Cipp, Gio DeAngelis,
"Jimmy Mac" McAvoy, &
Joey "Tinman" Tinley)

Suddenly I turn around,
And all of it is lost.
There is no going back now,
Once that line's been crossed.

I no longer look at the world
Huge eyes filled with wonder.
Now I have them closed,
My dreams torn asunder.

Sometimes I sit for hours,
Thinking of times that passed.
All those years of innocence,
That abandoned me so fast.

He keeps taking it away from me,
A little more each year.
With each part of mind and body,
So grows my fear.

Fear of things that have gone,
And who I've always been.
Fear of what I'll never be,
Fear I'll never win.

He pushes me too far, too fast,

Before I feel I'm ready,
Sometimes I walk a confident path,
Sometimes doubt leaves me unsteady.

I sorely miss how it used to be,
Before he took it all away.
When I looked not to the future,
But lived life day by day.

Standing here today, I condemn him,
For all that he has done.
I no longer laugh or smile,
In this, he has truly won.

In time, TIME takes everything,
As memories fade to never,
How long will he steal from me?
This thief of my forever.

Entry #63

"Who Are You"
- *The Who*

Yes, who were we? What was our identity as a group?

I remember long ago watching American Bandstand. As part of the show's format, Dick Clark asked various attendees to rate songs that were new to the scene. I still remember hearing a revolting amount of times, "I give it a ten because you can dance to it." Unfortunately, if we were going to be playing at dances, these were the audiences we needed to impress. This meant that we had to spend an inordinate amount of time learning to play songs we hated. It was not hard to learn these mind-numbing tunes, but we would so much rather be playing the more challenging songs that were turning up on late night FM radio. This was the late 60s, and we were still getting requests for the two-chord classic "Shout."

There were songs that we refused to play no matter who requested them. There was "Dirty Water" by those one-hit wonders, The Standells. I mean it did have a catchy tune, and the repetitive guitar and bass runs were fun to play, but . . . in a band of five New Yorkers, no one would ever be caught dead singing the lines, "Boston, you're my home." Then, of course, there was "Gloria," which we eliminated from our list as an act of exorcism, banished along with the memories it carried.

By mutual consent, all Beach Boys songs were taboo. If we had lived in California, we might have admired the melodic harmonies produced by these superstars. However, we had as much chance of going on an African Safari as we did a "Surfin' Safari." And that "Little Deuce Coupe," "409," and "I Get Around" crap meant nothing to city kids who not only couldn't drive until we were 18 years old but also lived a life that tended toward hoofing it or using public transportation. And all the talk of "woodies?" We never used that word to mean some form of transportation for people and surfboards. To kids from Queens, the word "woody" meant only one thing--an erection.

We were close-minded, and none of us had any conception of the outside world. I think I was twenty-five years old and thousands of miles from home before I stopped pronouncing "whore" as "whoo-a" (with two syllables).

One of the simple, one-hit wonder songs that did make it to our playlist was "Keep on Dancing" by The Gentrys. In a sense, that summed up what the public was coming to see, or rather do: hook-up with the opposite sex. We understood that we were just a vehicle to that end. The fast songs got them to introduce themselves to each other, and the slow songs allowed them to *really* introduce themselves to each other.

Thinking of those moments always brings a smile to my face. On a stage, playing a song, watching my best friends wield their instruments with greater skill each day, feeling my fingers glide over the bass strings with an increased ability (and less and less ice each day). Looking out into the crowd and watching the audience have fun because our music was a part of their lives.

Entry #64

"Hey Gyp"
- The Animals

Some of our performances remain in my memory more than others. This usually had more to do with the events that happened *off* the stage rather than on it. On a cold winter night in February of 1967, we were scheduled to play from 7 p.m. until 11 p.m. at the parish center at St. Clare's Church in Rosedale. My fascination with song lyrics almost led me to entitle this section "Crossroads' in deference to the Eric Clapton hit of that name. The Music Doctor doesn't always give me logical titles for my journal entries. The song lyrics, "going down to Rosedale with my rider by my side," would have made this an apt choice. However, the Rosedale that he refers to is in England, and the song's composer, blues great Robert Johnson had written the lyrics about Rosedale, Mississippi. *My* Rosedale was two towns over from my hometown of Cambria Heights. This was about as close to home as we'd ever play. Because of this, there were at least two familiar fans in the audience.

In the middle of a sea of nameless faces stood Maria, her large eyes peering at her superstar boyfriend. C'mon, it's my story. I'm allowed to embellish on the facts somewhat. She looked at me because I was me, not because I was a superstar. She loved our music and knew it held the hope for our future. However, if I gave up my guitar and my dream the next day, she would only be unhappy because of my disappointment.

Our eyes locked as I was about to begin our first set. She had used all of her considerable Daddy's-little-girl charm to convince him to let her and Diane be there. It wasn't the two-mile drive from their new residence in Valley Stream; it was that it was to see me. I still wasn't a big favorite of her father. The fact that my family hadn't chosen to flee the rising tide of integration had only proven to him that I was indeed "white trash." Being tolerant of other races in those days did have its drawbacks.

We opened that night with a very obscure song called "Hey Gyp." Gyp was Gio's father's name (short for Giuseppe.) After hearing the song, our exuberant rhythm guitarist ran out and bought the record. When he passed it on to us for a listen, it immediately became a band favorite. Before we had even started that night, one of the wanna-be groupies asked us what our most current cover song was. I'll never forget Gio laughing. He had gotten a pre-release copy from a friend at a store. The song didn't hit the public until that afternoon. "This song was released an hour ago," bragged Gio. Therefore, though we were extremely current in the song choice, very few others had ever heard the song besides us. In reality, it could have been a year later, and it still would have remained a mystery to most Americans.

Gio effectively captured the gravel-voiced pleas of Eric Burdon to his girl to "just give me some of your love." The crowd loved the song, especially Maria who stared at a certain bassist who mouthed (but didn't sing) the lines of plaintive love. Most of the night went well . . . until it didn't.

Entry #65

"Do You Want to Dance?"
- Mamas and Papas version

There is always one problem when a guy in a band asks his girl to come and see him play. He is locked onstage while his girl is at the mercy of all of the guys on the prowl.

That night tried my patience. By the time we had finished our first set of songs, one particular creep had circled Maria for close to an hour, like a shark looking to go in for the kill. He had even asked her to dance twice! Maria had had the sense to refuse.

During our break, my actions toward Maria made it abundantly clear she was taken. Our mutual affection strained the limits of the rules of behavior at religious institution dances. The jerk left the dance just as we were about to return to the stage for our second set of songs.

We didn't always include "Louie, Louie" in our set list, but I guess Gio figured I needed to take my mind off of the lecherous bastard and get down to business. I got my chance to sing in front of the crowd and can't deny I enjoyed my brief time in the limelight. I only wished I could do it more often. I enjoyed watching the admiration in Maria's eyes, though clearly it wasn't for my singing ability, which remained in fifth place in a five-man group. I was content to slink back off to the side of the stage when my moment of glory was over. I couldn't be happier. I had won the grand prize when it came to having Maria. It was then that our visitor gallery doubled in size.

We had often encouraged Tony to come and see us play a real gig as opposed to just sitting in at our practices. We all liked the guy almost as much as we had once feared him. Now he was just a big, friendly kid who would never grow up. He usually had a big smile when he was around us and just seemed to enjoy listening to our music. Tonight was the first time that he had shown up to one of our performances.

Of course, he didn't come alone. One of Mad Guy's gang, Greg Cincotta, had been given the job of driving and supervising Tony. Greg and I had grown up two doors away from each other, and though he was two years older than I was, there had been a time when we were good friends. Greg, however, grew up too fast when his father left his mother for another woman. By thirteen, he was on the streets hustling to help his mother make ends meet. By sixteen, he had dropped out of school and was employed by the one big business in the Heights, the Provenzano family. We had never officially ended our friendship. It had just drifted away and been reduced to a nod as we passed each other on the street.

Tonight was no different. As Greg entered the dance, with Tony by his side, he seemed happy to see me again and gave me a big smile and wave. I guess it would have been nice to catch up with him during our next break. However, that never happened. While nearing the end of our third set, I noticed Greg exiting the basement of the church. He gave me a quick smile and pantomimed his need to take care of his nicotine addiction. Implied in this was that Tony was safe with us for the five or ten minutes he would be gone. However, Tony underwent an almost immediate transformation into panic mode. Of course, he knew us well and was transfixed by our stage presence, but Greg had been his security blanket. He had never been out in a crowd of strangers before, at least, not since his "accident." The look of fear on his face made us all feel helpless.

Maria came to the rescue. Tony recognized her from their mutual attendance at our practices the previous summer. If he had any doubts, her warm and tender smile won him over. She softly touched his arm and told him that I was her boyfriend and, amazingly, Tony seemed to understand. He smiled at her, and they settled in to watch us perform.

Tony had never realized that kids danced to our music. He looked around in confusion and seemed to enjoy watching the movement of the gyrating teens. Maria noticed this cue and asked him if he wanted to dance. I had never seen such a broad smile on a human face before that moment. He looked lost at first until Maria deftly guided him to some basic moves. They both laughed and danced with wild abandonment. That was one of the many things I loved about Maria. She knew people, and she knew how to make them happy, and if they were happy, she was happy. Then it all went wrong.

Around this time, the asshole who had hit on Maria returned to the dance. He had been gone about an hour, and it was evident that during this period he had downed a significant amount of alcohol. He worked his way through the crowd, jostling dancers while angling his way toward the stage. From my raised vantage point, it became apparent that he was heading toward Maria. His courage bolstered by his hour binge, he seemed blindly focused on her. I knew that this time, I would have to act. Gio nodded his tacit consent, and I hurried to put down my bass and get to Maria's side. Maria was completely unaware of her erstwhile suitor's arrival and continued to dance and laugh with Tony. I tried to untangle myself from the wires on the stage and head off his advances before they gave Maria any discomfort. I knew I was too late when I heard his slurred voice scream at her.

"Hey, bitch, you're too good to dance with me, and you're dancing with a fucking retard." Those would be the last words that his mouth would utter for the next two months, and I didn't even get in a punch. My first move was to remove Maria from the equation. I pulled her aside and placed her by the footlights of the stage. But it wasn't necessary.

Greg Cincotta had returned and heard Tony being called a retard. His first right hook fractured the jerk's jaw in two locations, rendering months of wiring necessary to heal this initial blow. But, the beating didn't stop there. Greg liked Tony, perhaps more than the kid's own brother did. He continued to pummel the fallen victim as he lay helpless on the floor. Someone was going to have to stop his murderous rage, and it wasn't going to be me. I was enjoying the show.

The local parish priest attempted to intervene. He tried to get Greg's attention by placing his hand on the enraged man's shoulder. In his crazed state, Greg took this as an attack from the rear and turned swiftly to counter what he perceived as danger. He floored the priest with a left uppercut, only noticing the clerical collar as the priest staggered back, unconscious.

The realization that he had clocked a priest quickly brought Greg to his senses. He knew he was screwed. The sirens blared in the distance, and they were coming for him. Two bodies lay on the floor courtesy of his fists. The drunk had deserved what he had gotten, but there would be no explaining away the unconscious priest.

I rushed to Greg's side. "Go now. We've got Tony." He looked torn between his options. "No one knows who you are beside us and we're not talking. Go!"

He looked at Tony again who seemed to be comforted by the fact Maria put her arm around him. Bracko and Gio stood behind him, and Jimmy Mac and Joey approached to offer support. Greg turned to leave but didn't.

"Thanks, but no thanks." Then firmly took his place next to Tony and waited for the police to arrive.

———◆———

His trial was brief, and the judge's sentence was acceptable to the priest. No one cared what the other victim thought. Greg was placed on probation on the condition that he would volunteer to join the army. The judge stated, "He could find a positive outlet for his violent streak."

I never saw Greg Cincotta after that night. I found out later that he died in Vietnam in the summer of 1968.

Entry #66

"Love Hurts"
- Everly Brothers

The news of what had happened at the dance had spread almost instantaneously, and I mean that quite literally. Before we had even finished packing up our equipment from our abbreviated performance, parents were flooding the church basement to confirm that their precious children hadn't been harmed. Miraculously, the band itself was never connected to the violence. As soon as the police realized Greg had ties to the Provenzano family and who Tony was, they looked no further. As part of his plea agreement, Greg Cincotta had admitted to his actions. As a favor to us, he merely stated his motive as Tony being called a "retard."

While the band had escaped any repercussions, I can't say the same for me personally. One of the first people to arrive on the scene had been Maria's father. Upon seeing Tony and Greg at the center of the police action, and seeing the band, he immediately made the Cambria Heights connection. If he had been less than supportive of our relationship before that night, he now outright forbade Maria from seeing me.

Of course, that didn't split us up, but from that moment on, our meetings were secret and less frequent. Overnight, I found myself in almost the same situation as Gio. The only redeeming feature that I clung to was the fact that my parents still supported our love in spite of Maria's father, whom they referred to as a "racist lunatic."

I could never call Maria's house again unless we had prearranged a time she knew her father wouldn't be home. There was no way for them to know about our after school meetings. Even those were not as joyous as they had once been. Maria often cried in frustration over her parents' feelings toward me.

"Johnny, I can't believe this stuff is going on."

"Maria, do you still love me?"

"Yeah, how can you even ask?"

"Because I love you and nothing is going to stand in our way. We're gonna make it no matter what it takes. You've got to believe that." I swore I would find a way to do just that. I knew, or at least felt, it would be the band that would get us away from her parents. Was I sure? No, but I didn't want her to know I wasn't as confident as I acted. Maybe that's why I screwed up so badly.

Every action I took from that day on had new importance. As much as I always *wanted* the band to succeed, I now *needed* it to. I had to attain some financial success so that I could tear Maria away from her parents. Desperate times called for desperate measures. In the end, it was this desperation that destroyed everyone and everything I loved.

Entry #67

"Words of Doubt"
J. Cippitelli, D.J. Spinelli, J. Tinley

Words of doubt,
Because of lies,
Often come,
From tear stained eyes.

Understand,
Take my Hand,
Take a look,
Inside of me.

Sometime during the next week I talked with Gio. In his hand, he held Vinnie the Cat's business card. All we wanted to do was dial the number written on the card and tell him we were ready for whatever he could do for us. That would've been the wrong move. We knew we weren't prepared. We were confident we could already make a decent income performing as a cover band in any number of venues, but cover bands came and went. We were looking for something more permanent. Before we played the Cat card, we needed to have our own repertoire of songs.

Up until that point, we could count our quality songs on the one hand and still have a finger left over. We decided during the cold winter months of January and February of 1967 to step up our efforts to create. We would look anywhere and everywhere for inspiration. On one occasion, I found it at the back of physics class with my old friend DJ Spinelli. One day, I noticed him hard at work in his notebook, and he wasn't working on the number of foot-pounds needed to move an object a certain distance.

I snatched the whole book from his desk. It was there I first read the lyrics to "Words of Doubt." DJ had been going through a hard time with a girl, and he just didn't know where things stood. Those were *my* words to describe his situation. His words were a lyrically powerful tome to the universal frustration and doubt found in most relationships. As I took in the beauty of what he had written, I was already trying to compose musical tunes to correspond to the emotion evoked in his writing.

DJ liked the idea of putting his words to music, and we worked on it at lunch and after school the next few days. Joey got into the act on the third day, and his musical knowledge raised the project up to another level. By the end of the week, we were ready to bring the song to the whole group for its approval or rejection. I'd always admired DJ's writing. Why had I never thought to do this before? Perhaps, I was worried he might be jealous I had moved along with my musical career and had less time for him. He assured me this was not the fact. He enjoyed writing the same way I enjoyed playing, and he wished me luck. It then occurred to me that he was always writing (as witnessed by the D he received in physics). There must be more words that could be made into lyrics.

At lunch with DJ and Joey on Friday, I ripped the book from his possession (again) and started to probe through it for other material. I guess he had liked the results on "Words of Doubt" because he offered no resistance at all. Much of what was there was good but incomplete. There was a stanza here, a line there, and very often, they were disjointed lines about entirely different concepts. If I could only find a complete poem I could convert into a vehicle for our music.

It was then I turned the page and came upon "Enchanted Days." I have to admit I was excited by the fact that I had found a complete "song" hidden among all the flotsam and jetsam of DJ's notebook. However, any title with the word *enchanted* in it didn't seem cool. When I read that word, I envisioned fantasy castles from some fairy tale. Snow White was not rock and roll. If someone had attacked my work, as I had attacked his, I probably would have been extremely pissed off. Not DJ.

"I didn't write it as rock and roll," he calmly responded. "It was written as a poem . . . a story. Besides, what is wrong with wanting a little fantasy in your life? With wanting your life to be so much better that it doesn't seem real?"

He had me there. It was his poem. Who was I to criticize it for not fitting into the role I wanted it to play? Joey sat at his piano and quietly looked at the words, and he started to work on some piano arrangements complementary to the lyrics. I picked up a guitar (it's hard to write music on a bass!) and joined in. With DJ rearranging a phrase or two, and Joey and I tweaking the music, we soon had the outline of a ballad that could serve as one of the prerequisite grinders on our future album.

After we had finished, we asked DJ what the inspiration for this poem/song had been. His songs were always about his life and feelings. This song was about a relationship between two people who faced many obstacles in achieving their time together.

"Someday, in some place, they will find their enchanted days," DJ answered. He then looked me in my eyes and said, "I didn't write this song about me. It's about you, Johnny . . . and Maria." I then looked down at the last line of the lyrics and realized the truth of his statement.

> "So take my hand,
> And together we'll find,
> Enchanted days."

Entry #68

"The Piano"
- Joey "Tinman" Tinley and Those Born Free

When Joey and I brought "Enchanted Days" and "Words of Doubt" to the group that weekend, it seemed to open the flood-gates of creativity. DJ made the first of his many appearances at our practice to help us create more songs. Every song in some way was a part of us. As I've said before, our songs spoke for us and to us. That is why it seemed so strange Tinman didn't bring original material to the group. He had been generous with his contributions to what the rest of us had created, but had contributed no original ideas himself. In my more cynical moments, I wondered if Joey was saving all his ideas for some future time when he was a successful solo act. Or was it possible that someone so musical couldn't write lyrics at all?

During one of our breaks from playing, Joey handed two typed pages to DJ. He asked him to look at what he had written and make it sound better, more like a song. After reading and rereading the words carefully for fifteen minutes, DJ finally replied. "I wouldn't change a damn thing, Tinman. This is beautiful."

He then handed the sheet to me, and I understood. I asked Joey if he had music to go with the lyrics. He answered me by walking over to his keyboard and playing. Anyone who had ever known Joey understood the inspiration for this song. If they didn't know him as a person, they did after listening to this long and melodic piece. His words tore at our heartstrings. This would never be a dance song or played on AM radio. Yet, there was a place in the music of the late 1960's for something like this.

Would Joey's father understand and how would he take it? With elaborate piano riffs and lyrics that carried a powerful message, it ran over eight minutes long. Entitled simply "The Piano," it was a thinly veiled attack by Tinman on his father. I can't remember all the words, but I will never forget the story line.

The player (obviously Tinman) begins to play a piece for his taskmaster.

> As he sits down,
> And prepares to play,
> He begins to unleash,
> The pains of the day.

All is well as the classical piece is performed with correctness and strength.

> And all in the house stop to listen,
> He performs so well, so loud.
> They stop and pay attention,
> They smile, they are proud.

Yet, there is a part of the song that he cannot master and fear of failing causes him to panic. When he misplays a section, he is verbally attacked . . .

> The madman will shout,
> And make him feel small,
> He demands perfection,
> Not just giving your all.

Yet, he is true musician. He perseveres, finally playing the entire piece with skill and feeling. This assuages the judgment of the "Madman" (Mr. Tinley) who feels he has brought out the best in his pupil. He requests more and is rebuffed. The "pianist" explains why . . .

> "My overture is over now,
> The notes struck perfectly,
> Because, you stupid bastard,
> I played it just for me!"

There were approximately twenty verses to "The Piano," and I'm not even sure if I got the first three that I wrote in this journal exactly as he wrote them. However, I am positive of the final verse.

Tinman had a ritual he followed every time the band performed. He would lift the left sleeve of his shirt and write on his wrist. He told the four of us that when he turned eighteen he was going to get a tattoo to replace the temporary scribbling that needed to be hidden from his father. On the artery that led directly to his heart were written the words, "I played it just for me." He never got the tattoo.

Entry #69

"Enchanted Days"
- *DJ Spinelli and J. Cippitelli*

Maria and I had met here and there but not quite as often as we would have liked. Come summer, her parents would see I was worthy of their daughter. On the other hand, come the summer, we might be gone far away--together. Looking back, it seems absurd that two eighteen-year-olds could make such a commitment. As I write this, it seems to me that kids are waiting until they're into their late twenties to get married after a period of living together. I know that we hadn't discussed specific details of our future except that by September her parents would no longer keep us apart. We would do whatever it took to be together. However, that spring was hell for us, and I'll never forgive her parents for that.

June arrived and with it our last scheduled paying job. We hoped summer would be very busy, but had no guarantees. Maria had understood our forced separation would soon end. Though she never complained, I knew from Diane it had been even harder on her than it had been on me. We had only seen each other a handful of times since the night that Greg Cincotta had decked a priest. A large part of this was my lack of transportation and the amount of time I had spent practicing with the band. That is why that last dance job on June 3, 1967, was so significant to me.

We had landed the parish dance at Saints Joachim and Ann in Queens Village. As close as the St. Clare's dance had been to the Heights, this venue was nearer. The reason that this was important in the scheme of things was the secret assistance of Diane. She had arranged for Maria and her to be at the dance.

Without telling their parents who the band would be, they had prevailed in getting permission to go to this dance. If Diane's parents had entered the dance at any time, they would have seen I was there. Not only did the Romano family ban me, but also Diane's parents still had no use for "The Flamingo Kid." This didn't matter to us. It had been such a long time since we had seen each other that we were willing to take a chance.

We had invited Vinnie the Cat to see us play that night. We had prepared well and knew we could blow him away with our cover songs. But would he think our originals were good enough? We were already on the stage when Maria and Diane showed up. She gave me that beautiful smile of hers and all was right with the world. Interestingly enough, Vinnie had arrived before we even performed our first number and had remained (unknown to us) tucked away in the far recesses of the church basement. He would tell us later that he preferred to observe how we played and how the crowd reacted to us without the pressure of his presence influencing what he witnessed.

We were two sets into our show before we saw him. We had thought he had blown us off. Then, all of a sudden, he was there in front of us. We had done some of our best covers and even thrown in a few originals including "The Thief of My Forever." As we were shutting down our amps to take a break, he appeared at the foot of the stage. "I see big things happening for this band. I'll call in a few weeks with details."

Let the celebration begin. All the pressure of the previous year seemed to melt away in moments. The crowd, which hadn't been paying attention to the stage, now observed the five of us jumping around in wild jubilation. After a few moments of this, my eyes fixed on Maria. I motioned for her up to join me. She would have had to take the circuitous route up a side staircase. I intercepted her in a secluded backstage area. Before she could even say a word, I kissed her with all the joy and passion of the moment. When our lips parted, our eyes remained focused on each other. She spoke first.

"You made it."

"We made it." I corrected her. "You and I."

We lingered a bit longer in our little hideaway and stole a few more kisses. I brought Maria on to the stage, and we started to celebrate with the whole group. We both almost simultaneously noticed Diane standing alone on the dance floor and felt guilty for leaving her out. We waved her up, and she joined our happy little group. I couldn't help noticing that our resident playboy Jimmy Mac spent most of that break talking to Diane.

Entry #70

"Slow Dancing, Swaying to the Music"
- *Johnny Rivers*

We hadn't accomplished anything yet. All Vinnie had promised was a chance to be in the running for something big. Still, it seemed as if the weight of the world was lifted. We had been judged and found worthy of a chance – just a chance.

We played the rest of that evening with looseness and freedom befitting of our name. We played at least six of our originals to judge the audience's reaction and found it favorable. We took extended solos on some songs and stayed away from those tunes we found boring. As we neared the end of the evening, we knew our next performance would be for all the gold. We knew we would practice long and hard (again!) until we got the call from The Cat about an audition date. Tonight, however, it was time to enjoy and let loose.

As official timekeeper of the group, I told the rest of the guys that we were into the last fifteen minutes of the night. Usually, that meant that we would play one or two slow songs to allow the lonely young men in the audience to make their big final push to meet a girl. Anyone could slow dance. You merely held your partner tight and shuffled your feet a little bit. We wanted everyone to leave happy or at least hopeful so tonight we would repeat this ritual. When I looked over at Bracko to hit the first note, he gave me a strange look. Jimmy Mac and Tinman had shit-eating grins that told me something was up. Gio just walked from the middle of the stage in a direct path to me.

"Let me show you that anyone can play this damn thing." He took my bass right out of my arms. I was confused until Gio's eyes shifted to the dance floor and Maria. "Go ahead, lover boy, we got this one."

Dancing to Those Born Free was like an out of body experience. To do it with Maria was the best. I held her tight as the band broke into Johnny Rivers' "Slow Dancin'." What could be more fitting? As Jimmy Mac sang the first verse, I held Maria in my arms and thought how beautiful my life had become, mostly because of her. This was the peak. I remember thinking all through that dance, *Can it get any better than this?* We couldn't take our eyes off each other, and often she would give me that big wonderful smile and pull me closer to her.

Slow dancing, swaying to the music

The chorus of the song arrived, and the guys sang in three-part harmony, "Hold me. Hold me. Don't ever let me go." I was thinking exactly that sentiment.

With only one song left to play for the night, I gave Maria one last hug and started toward the stage. Gio merely rolled his eyes and waved me away, back to Maria's arms. The band never played original songs to close out the evening. However, tonight was different in so many ways that this seemed only logical to end with "Enchanted Days." Also, with all the Cmaj7 and Fmaj7 chords I had thrown in, the song fit the mold of a grinder. There were many profound and beautiful verses in this song. Try as I may I just can't remember them. I so wish that I could. Only the last two lines remain with me until this day.

Take my hand,
Together we'll find enchanted days.

As the song ended, I snuck one last kiss with Maria. The hell with the *Holy Ghost* police. We had overcome all the shit placed in our way. She had taken my hand long ago, and we were within reach of those enchanted days. Except they never happened. "Enchanted Days" would be our last dance.

Entry #70

"Wishin' and Hopin'"
- Dusty Springfield

The month of June flew by quickly. High school graduation would be upon us soon, and then a summer that we hoped would financially change our lives. There were finals taken, term papers written, and friends to bid farewell. All of this was happening as the backdrop of our upcoming audition. Vinnie hadn't been very clear about what he planned for us. All that we knew was that we had to be ready at a moment's notice to show someone what we could offer. At stake were guaranteed gigs and a record contract. Vinnie explained there were circumstances that were out of his control that kept him from giving us information about what was ahead. We were told to be patient and our time would come. And so, we waited.

Vinnie would call Mr. Tinley to talk business. Details need to be taken care of before we would ever perform. I learned too late that it's the details in life that define our futures. And when your manager is in over his head and refuses to admit it, details get forgotten.

Entry #71

"The Night Before"
- *The Beatles*

On June 18, we got the long awaited call from Vinnie the Cat. Our big try out was to be the next night. Mr. Tinley had to arrange transportation for the band and all of our equipment. We had to decide on a final list of songs to perform. There were innumerable other details we needed to take care in less than 24 hours. However, by eight o'clock that night, we had all arranged to be in Jimmy Mac's basement to have one final strategy meeting and short rehearsal.

We all seemed ready, except for Gio. He acted beyond nervous. He did his job well, and I don't think that the others noticed his mental state. But then again, they hadn't known him since he was an eight-year-old kid as I had. I wondered if it was a sudden fit of nerves caused by desperation. I knew that I needed this success to be with Maria and that the need was even greater for my best friend. If and when he went public with Riet, they could well be despised and cast out by not only two societies, but also two families.

As I write this now in late 1990, America is a much different place. Most people (but not all) are much more accepting of interracial couples. However, in 1967, only a living hell of prejudice awaited them. Was this what was bothering him? Or was it something else? Family problems? School? I took Gio aside and didn't get the question out before he said we'd talk later.

Entry #72

"Talk, Talk"
- *The Music Machine*

June 19, 1967
3:30 p.m.

I took my last test at McCarthy High that next day. The end of high school should have been a bigger deal in my life, but to be honest, I hardly even thought of it. My excitement about the coming night's events was all I cared about. By the time I took the long bus and train ride home and made my way to Gio's house, it was already late afternoon. I knocked on his door, and his mother met me with her usual welcoming smile and directed me to the basement. Gio sat on the old couch that had been down there molding since I had known him. He'd been awaiting my arrival.

He played his acoustic guitar with his usual active wrist motion, and I remember that I admired the sound created by the heavy beat of the A and G chord combination that he was playing with such ferocity. I knew that I had heard the song on the radio, but just couldn't place the name of the tune. But I wasn't there to play. Realizing that Gio was lost in the intensity of his strumming, I placed my hand on the strings of his guitar to make my presence known. "What's going on?" He looked surprised to see me and instead of putting down the guitar and having our planned conversation, he handed it to me.

"Play and just keep playing for about an hour. I have to run . . . "

"To Riet's?" I finished his sentence. It was June, and the sun would still be up for many hours. For him to attempt to meet her anywhere in broad daylight meant that it was very important.

"I'll explain it all when I get back. But I don't want to try and explain where I'm going to my parents, so I need you to play down here until I return." I didn't know why he just didn't say that he was coming to my house and then leave for his secret rendezvous. He then reminded me that our phone chain was set up so that Tinman would call Gio and Jimmy Mac with the last minute details for the night's schedule. They, in turn, would call Bracko and me. Someone had to be at Gio's phone or the whole plan broke down. I nodded my approval and started to play the same two chords that Gio had been playing when I had arrived. I watched as he tiptoed to the top of his basement stairs.

"We will talk. I swear. Tomorrow," Gio said as he left my sight and slipped out the side door.

14

The Other Side of Life:

"Time Has Come Today"
- *The Chambers Brothers*

4:00 p.m.

JIMMY MAC HAD THE HARDEST task when it came to pack-ing for a job. Unlike the others who merely had to unplug their guitars and put them in cases, he had to disassemble his entire drum set and pack each piece in its prearranged box or cover. This task was easily an hour or more ordeal, which left him the least amount of time that afternoon. This did not stop the love-smitten drummer from making a not too brief stop at his new girlfriend's house for a tension-relieving make-out session. Jimmy Mac had always been the love-them-and-leave-them playboy in the group. This time he was willing to give up his roaming. In the three weeks since meeting at the dance, Jimmy Mac and Diane had been inseparable.

4:33 p.m.

Joey accompanied his father to rent a panel van for the night's equipment transportation. He remained Joseph while in his father's company. Some things never changed. However, the involvement in the band had brought them a bit closer together. No longer master and slave, they could have conversations about the events they shared in common.

4:45 p.m.

"Well, don't ever fucking come back, asshole," screamed Vinnie into the phone. It was a big night for him too, and this prick had just bailed on him. Now besides listening to the final two bands that he had lined up for the club, he also had to work as the bartender. It was not as if there would be more than a dozen regulars at the Driftwood Club on a Monday night. However, The Cat was done with catering to these drunken slobs. He looked forward to being a full-time music promoter.

He had worked hard for the last year lining up some groups to be the foundation upon which the Provenzanos would build their network of clubs. Eventually, he would be rotating about ten bands through the five Queens-Nassau locations that the family would be opening. One of these groups would sign a recording contract. In turn, that band would rotate through all the clubs to attract new patrons with their "recording star" status. It had been planned to the last detail. There would be no more pouring drinks and listening to banal conversations.

All that was left to do now was to pick *the* group to be the foundation for his plans. One of these last two would be the lynchpin of the whole organizational setup. Both bands were informed about their auditions without ever realizing that the sole arbiter of their futures would be Vinnie alone. He just needed to hear his two favorites one last time before making up his mind.

One group was much more experienced and polished in their presentation. However, they might be *too* experienced and *too* polished. In their mid-twenties, they had been raised in the era of doo-wop music. Sometimes that tendency had shown through in their performances. The other group was young and current, and damned good to boot. But were they too young to handle the responsibility that would be thrust upon them if he chose them as the anchor in the whole plan?

As he thought this to himself, it reminded him of one final detail that he had to take care of before the competition. He picked up the phone and dialed the band's manager. No answer. *That's weird,* he thought to himself. The manager knew that he would be calling with last minute instructions, and he needed to check on something with him. After listening to the unanswered rings for what seemed like an eternity, he slammed down the phone. *More proof of their inexperience,* he thought.

Though the late afternoon crowd at the bar was light, Vinnie the Cat was the only one working. That meant being the bar back and the server all by himself. The patrons were growing impatient for their next round of Rheingold beers. These jerks would very soon have to find a new neighborhood bar to get soused in daily. The new dance club would not be a good home for these blue-collar workers.

Vinnie would take care of these drunks and then make a phone call to the other number on the band's business card. He hoped this was not a sign these people were undependable.

6:15 p.m.

Those Born Free waited patiently for the arrival of their final member. With their equipment loaded onto the rented van, all that was needed to be on their way was a guitar and the person who played it. His amp had stayed in the practice location since their last meeting, and all that was required to leave was Bracko himself.

The group by now knew too much about the guitarist's personal life to assume that his showing up was a given. Mr. Tinley had suggested that they drive to the boy's house, but the band had nixed that idea. Bracko only had a three-block walk once he made it out the door of his house. If he didn't make it out the door, there was nothing they would be able to do anyway. They never had, and never would knock on Bracko's front door. Doing so would risk the guitarist's father discovering what his son had been up to all this time. So they waited and hoped.

6:35 p.m.

"Where the hell do you think you're going on a school night?" In many houses in America, Stan's question would have been a legitimate topic. They both knew that school nights did not mean much to the younger Brackowski. If he could pass every subject this semester, he actually would graduate from high school. However, they both knew that Bracko had been trying to sneak out of the house when he had been confronted. Bracko did not respond because no answer would be the right one to fend off the beating. If he could just take that beating and get out the door, he would consider himself incredibly lucky.

"You little dumb shit, I'm speaking to you."

Still, Bracko did not respond. The only thing that the younger Brackowski did quickly was move his fingers over the well-worn frets of his guitar. Under pressure, he did not respond well. He struggled for the right words that would get him out the door to the waiting band. Nevertheless, nothing came to him . . . except for a left hook from his father's fist. It was a punch that should have collapsed the son to the floor. Under other circumstances, he probably would have taken a dive and put an end to the beating. However, tonight was different. Tonight his life was going to change. Tonight might hold the possibility of getting out of this house, out of this life. Tonight he stood his ground.

Stan's right fist caught the waiting boy in his mouth and blood immediately splattered the yellowing walls of the kitchen. Bracko just stared at his father. His left eye was already closed from the first blow, and his lip split open from the second. All of the anger of his seventeen years welled up in his eyes, trapped within the lids. *Men don't cry unless they're faggots.* The very same monster who was beating him had repeated this "golden rule" to him his entire life.

Staring blankly, he did the unconscionable: he spit the blood that had accumulated in his swollen mouth on to the linoleum floor. This act of defiance, as tiny as it may have been, drove his father to fury. He had consistently beaten his son for most of his life and Bracko had never displayed the slightest resistance to his onslaughts. He was blinded with anger by the insolence of this little bastard. His eyes turned to the guitar in his son's hands, and he knew beyond a shadow of a doubt how to hurt the boy.

As the son stared in bewilderment at the reddening face of his father, Stan reached for the wooden club that he always kept in the kitchen as a defense against any emergency. Bracko had never taken a blow from anything other than a human fist and started to retreat steadily in hopes of escape. The weapon was already in motion when Bracko realized its ultimate destination was not his head or his body, but rather his guitar. He had barely enough money to purchase the guitar. The recommended hard-molded case had not been an option. The soft, flexible canvas cover that Sam Ash music store had thrown into the deal was no match for the blow coming from the abusive maniac.

Though he attempted to move the instrument out of harm's way, he just could not move fast enough. The wooden club splintered as it crashed down on both the guitar and Bracko's upper thigh. The instrument and its owner fell to the ground with a sickening thud. Though he felt intense pain, Bracko's first and only thought was to see his guitar. His father stood over him in ominous silence, daring his son to disrespect him again. A numbness overwhelmed Bracko's thigh as he reached out for the encased Fender Stratocaster. The swelling was now evident on his face and leg, but he knew once again that he would survive it. He had to survive it. This was the night. The night that everything in his life would change.

His only concern was his guitar. Had *it* survived? While Stan Brackowski continued to stand over his wounded son, the boy slowly and defiantly unzipped the soft case from the top down. He didn't care that his father stood over him with remnants of the club in his hands. This guitar had been his only joy, his only love. He examined his precious possession much the way a parent would examine a young child who had fallen, carefully trying to assess the damage. The neck seemed fine, and the strings still seemed taut. Pulling back more of the canvass, he noticed that the frets closest to the top were undamaged, and body so far was intact. He quickly ripped off the rest of the bag to end the anguish of anticipation. He immediately saw the wound. The finish of his Fender had been obliterated on the lower body of the guitar, and the putrid pink prime coat was showing through in a spot roughly the size of a baseball. This was cosmetic damage, and Bracko could live with it if he had to.

Then he noticed that the mechanism for the vibrato stick was shattered and, indeed, the stick itself lay in the bottom of the bag, broken and misshapen. This was the part of the guitar that made it whine and sing with feeling. Holding down the bar with his pinky, he could extend the tones long enough to wring every last bit of emotion out of the notes he played. Johnny called it the soul of his guitar. This final act of violence had crushed that soul.

For the first time in his life, Bracko looked at his father in anger. In turn, for the first time in his son's life, the father looked at him with fear. Rocco Brackowski had long ago passed his father in size and strength and had submitted to the constant beatings out of misplaced respect and a touch of guilt. This would be no more.

In one motion, Bracko rose and slapped the pieces of the club from his father's hands. As the weapon spiraled into a kitchen cabinet, he pushed forward and drove Stan into the refrigerator. He held him pinned there with his two powerful arms. His face twisted into a grimace of pure hate as his overwhelming strength held his now terrified father motionlessly.

"No more! I'm fuckin' done with you. I'm going to play, and no matter how it turns out, I won't be back. I have paid for my crime for too long." He loosened the grip on his father and slowly bent to pick up his damaged, but usable guitar. He looked back, daring his father to try and stop him.

"What are you talking about?" asked the suddenly calm and subdued father.

"I'm sorry! I'm sorry that I killed my mother and made your life so miserable."

"But you didn't, you couldn't . . ." mumbled the father. However, the son never heard his father speak. He was done listening to him forever. With his guitar in hand, Bracko pushed by the quivering older man and walked out the door.

Stan Brackowski did what he did around this time every night. He ambled to kitchen cabinet that hung over the sink and opened the door. He reached in with his left hand to grab a bottle of Seagram's 7 whiskey. He placed the bottle on the counter as he surrounded a shot glass in the drain board. He screwed off the top of the bottle and poured himself a long stiff shooter. The glass and bottle never left his hands until he had repeated this procedure four more times. Stan Brackowski did this same ritual every single night of his life as a prelude to downing his six-pack of Rheingold. Tonight would be different. For the first time in seventeen years, he did it with tears in his eyes.

"What the fuck have I done?" He took another shot of whiskey.

15

Journal of Johnny Cipp

Entry #73

"Catch the Wind"
- Donovan, Blues Project, and Those Born Free

I CAN'T HELP BUT SEE THE irony in the fact that we would be playing music when the end came. I obsessed over music as my doctor, my comfort, and my soul throughout all the years of my life. I didn't call this obsession of mine anything until I heard a Doobie Brothers' song that had the line, "Music is the doctor, makes you feel like you want to." The fact that I didn't have the words to describe this feeling until that 1980's song came along doesn't diminish the fact that I indeed felt that music had some supernatural hold over me. This journal is living proof. There always seemed to be a song playing in my head that would describe that very moment in which I was living. I know I was, and am weird when it comes to this. And thus was born this mystical creature in my mind, "The Music Doctor."

Therefore, it seemed only right he would guide the band to play a fitting song when it all came crashing down. And so, it is with great sadness that I tell the story of the final demise of Those Born Free.

———————

Gio had returned to his house just in time for me to go home, eat, and get my stuff. There was no time for any conversation between us. I never found out what was going on with him. We were both late for the appointed meeting time at Jimmy Mac's house, but our lateness was the least of the band's problems. Bracko still had not arrived, and we all worried that perhaps he wouldn't make it at all. When he finally did make an entrance, we didn't have to ask what had happened to him. We saw the devastating new bruises on his face, and we knew.

Whether it was nerves or just the chaos of Bracko's late arrival, no one spoke during the short trip to the venue that held our future. We listened patiently as our competition played. We thought that they were good, but we were better. When they completed their turn, we set up our equipment quickly on the flat floor. An actual stage would be part of the future alterations.

We noticed that the sole arbiter of our fate would be Vinnie the Cat. Was this a good thing or not? Was it always meant to be this way, or had some twist of fate left our future in the hands of this one person? To be real, we didn't care. This was our moment, and to a man, we would make the most of it. We would play with every ounce of our hearts and our abilities. Each of us would hit our notes with skill and a touch of creativity. Each of us would do his part to make sure that we succeeded.

We had decided to finish with our interpretation of "Catch the Wind," a tune written by Donovan Leitch and covered by the Blues Project. We thought the creativity of our arrangement would seal the deal. Though we hadn't written its words, our final song eloquently told a tale that could have come from our inner thoughts.

It was as if the Music Doctor had looked down upon us and said, *oh, this is a good one! Play this one as your final tune! Because you see, you are never going to play again together. You tried to move up. You tried to move out. You decided that you wanted to reach for the stars, to catch the wind. I deem you unworthy.*

One moment we were on our way to stardom, and the next, Those Born Free was on its way to oblivion. Born of frustration and longing, we played with our hearts and our souls and every muscle in our bodies. We were five young men who had not been born free but rather had yearned to be free of the baggage that had held us down for all our lives. For love, for art, for sanity, we were trying to catch that wind. In my mind, the song stood for everything that we were striving for: the unreachable. I had told Maria to remember me when she felt the wind.

When Gio hit the first E chord and then followed it with a soft A, the house was silent. It was evident we had won The Cat over. It was ours. We knew that this had become a reality when we saw Mr. Tinley talking to Vinnie. A big smile had come across his face. They both gave us a thumbs-up. Our struggles had ended. Our style, talent, and hard work had guaranteed we would be performing at this venue for the foreseeable future. Our connections to the record company were set. We had done it. We were out from under the weights that had held each of us down for so long. We had grabbed the brass ring, and for that brief shining moment, all was good.

The Music Doctor had long ago inspired me to bring this song to the group. At the time, we were adding less and less of other people's music to our repertoire, but I convinced them that if we did it our way, it could be a crowd grabber. If it weren't, it would at least mean something to us. We had practiced it for many long hours to make it ours, and somehow it took on a life of its own. Not only did its theme speak to us, but also the style and arrangement of the song mimicked the history of the band.

The song *and the band* had started with Gio and Jimmy Mac singing quietly and softly together in that perfect harmony, their trademark. Gio with his patented wrist motion hit softly on the strings with alternating A and E chords. Jimmy Mac eventually eased into the vocal with his most aching voice. He sang how seeking goals could be as frustrating as . . . catching the wind.

At that point, I slid right in with a bass riff that flowed seamlessly into harmony with both the music and singing of Gio and Jimmy Mac, just as I had fit in as the third member of Those Born Free. After a few bars of this combination, it was Bracko's turn. As he had exploded on to the scene with a flurry of passion and anger, he entered into the presentation of the song with similar enthusiasm. Again, our singers repeated the frustration of trying to catch the wind.

Joey, our "Tinman," then entered with a whirling organ solo that made the song, just as it had made the group, whole. We were now in full mode. "The organ sounded like a carnival," to quote Billy Joel. The drums and bass kept rhythm, and both

Gio and Bracko dueled with alternating guitar riffs. Of course, Bracko had to teach Gio every note of the performance. Though Gio was still the voice and heart of the group, he still could only play mediocre guitar. Again, this just brought the group closer together.

As if I knew it would be the end, I remember taking one final glance at the band. I remember the looks on their faces only minutes before it was all over. They were so full of the joy of the moment.

Jimmy Mac, the happy-go-lucky free spirit was basking in the limelight that he had sought. He had an ear-to-ear grin as he sang and hit the skins of his drum kit. Life was beautiful. He wouldn't be selling egg creams and penny candy for the rest of his life. He felt it. He knew it. We had made it. He also had feelings for Diane he never knew he could have for anyone.

Tinman sat and played intensely on the keys of his instrument. He played his parts with a serious professionalism that belied the butterflies in his stomach. He could not believe how much he now enjoyed the music he played. I stared at him from my vantage point at the fringe of the performance area. Finally, he looked up and gave me a sly smile that told me everything. He had lost all the shyness and inhibitions that had made him always feel like he had been on the outside looking in. He held up his wrist. "I played it just for me."

Gio was out front, singing harmony with Jimmy Mac and loving it. The spotlight was on him as he had always wanted it to be. In between songs, he had bantered with the drunks who were the obsolete remnants of the Driftwood Club's life as a blue-collar corner bar. The club would soon reopen as a dance venue for the young. Gio interacted with the audience as if it were already filled with those youthful dancers. His personality was getting through to even these dog-tired workers. It was Gio at his best.

Bracko struggled to see out of one eye and even to stand correctly, yet he played brilliantly. I noticed that his vibrato stick was missing and his guitar had an ugly gash in it. Still, he somehow used his fingers to create the sounds that he would typically have used the stick to perform. As he sang his harmony parts, droplets of blood ran down his chin from a still open cut on his lip. As his guitar rang with a spirit that had been set free, his whole face twinkled with delight. As he turned to me, he smiled. It was the broadest smile I'd ever seen on my friend's face. All his troubles were in the past. He never had to face the maniac again. He now could deal with the world on his terms. It is how I will always remember him.

There I stood at the far right of the band, playing my heart out and thinking of just how far I had come. The nights with the broken hockey sticks. The failure of The Coming Generation. My broken hand. Buckets of ice. The frustration of trying to play the guitar. It was all over. With this success, I would be able to offer Maria a life free of her parents' disapproval. Nothing would stand in our way. The song went on building in volume and meaning. Nothing would stand in our way of catching the wind.

Then it was over. The sounds of our voices and instruments silenced . . . lost forever in the wind.

PART
3

"When the Music's Over"

-The Doors

16

The Other Side of Life:

"After the Gold Rush"
- Neil Young

HAVING COMPLETED THEIR SET OF songs, The Mello-tones felt confident they had secured the job. After all the years and all their musical transitions, they were going to have a good paying gig that would allow the four of them to quit their meaningless day jobs. They figured that they would listen for a few minutes to the punk kids play and then go outside and have that well-deserved smoke. However, the reaction of Vinnie the Cat had been immediate. The punks were not just punks, but talented musicians and singers with a style all their own. The Cat's exuber-ant smile after only two songs told The Mellotones everything. They had lost. It would be back to the oil pits and the grease kitchens for them. It just wasn't fair. Then *he* showed up.

"What the fuck do you want, old man?" yelled an annoyed Bob Carlotta in reaction to the drunken piece of shit that had walked up to the Mellotones at the peak of their melancholic mood. How this drunk had ever driven in his condition was both a miracle and a crime. They would not have believed it if they had not seen him exit his rust bucket of a car.

"Hi," was the only response from the drunk.

"Yes, you are." Tom Carson, the bassist, quickly elicited small smiles from his previously depressed bandmates.

"Do you know where the band is playing?"

"What band?" countered the now interested Carlotta.

"Those Born Free," replied the old man by merely reading the name on the front of a wrinkled card that he held in his out-stretched left hand. Without even looking at the card, Carson answered.

"Why we're all free here. Haven't you noticed you are in Nassau County, home of white Americans? No city coons allowed out here."

This comment solicited more laughs from his three friends. The old man continued to hold out the business card that he now turned over to the unprinted side that held a hand-written message.

Driftwood Club, 7 p.m., June 19, across the street from Great Eastern Mills store – Hempstead Turnpike, Elmont.

"This must be the place. I found the card where my son left it on the counter after . . ." His voice trailed off, and he stared down at his feet. Filled with remorse and Seagram's 7 whiskey, he seemed to have lost his train of thought. It was then that Bob Carlotta took the card from his hand.

"Those Born Free! So that's the name of those scumbags." With that, the old man's face regained its color and focus.

"Fuck you, you fuckin' asshole. That's my son's band. I came to see him play like I should have a long time ago!" He now openly dared the four Mellotones to argue with him. The anger and fire that had long burnt inside of Stan Brackowski now found an outlet in defense of the son he had so long abused.

"Whoa, old man, just having a little fun," said Tom Carson who had no interest in tangling with a possessed drunk.

"Who you calling an old man? I'm young enough to have a son who is only seventeen, and who can play the fuckin' shit out of a guitar." He hesitated as if pondering some deep remorse that should have occurred to him at some earlier point in time. He then continued in a voice that seemed meant for no one but himself to hear. "I heard him even though he didn't know that I was listening."

Stan Brackowski, now filled with pride, continued to ramble on to these strangers about all the nights that he sat with his ear against the basement door listening to the faint sounds coming through from his son's basement hideaway. Why had he never gone down there and told Rocco how good he was? He would make things better now. Give up drinking. Spend more time with the boy. It would start with finally coming to hear the band.

His rambling dialogue had degenerated into incoherent babble as he drifted away from the Mellotones and found a comfortable wall down a side ally. He passed into a deep drunken sleep.

This fact did not matter to Bob Carlotta. He had stopped listening when he heard the words "17-year-old son."

—————◆—————

The phone call had been anonymous. When the nicotine stained fingers of Bob Carlotta had dialed the fifth precinct of the Nassau County Police Department, he had used a pay phone more than a block away from the Driftwood Club. Bob reasoned that as a good citizen, it was his duty to report the presence of an under-aged band in a location that served alcohol.

The fact that he was the lead singer of The Mellotones, the band that had just lost out to those same kids in the audition, had absolutely nothing to do with his decision. At least, that was what he tried to tell himself in the days, weeks, months, and years to come. He was glad that the call had been anonymous when he realized that the owners of the Driftwood were "connected" and that they would not take kindly to informants, no matter what their motivations.

17

Journal of Johnny Cipp

Entry #74

"Season in Hell"
- John Cafferty and the Beaver Brown Band

I DON'T KNOW IF THIS PART of my story will be as descriptive or complete as it should be. I need to get through this quickly. I won't say painlessly because there is going to be a whole shitload of pain. I only hope to survive with my sobriety.

Everything went down only hours before what promised to be a glorious, exciting summer, a season that had always been my favorite. But that summer was different. That fateful summer was truly a season in hell. Need to stop for a while . . .

———◆———

It all happened so fast. One moment we were performing and basking in the glory of knowing we had won the job. Those Born Free had made it. And just as quickly, it was all over.

We didn't hear the sirens. We had no warning. The police charged into the club with all the force of a blitzkrieg army. They were quick to secure the scene of the crime and focused on their mission. Each officer latched onto one member of the band. However, what I perceived to be their inexperience allowed for the basic math of the situation to escape them. There were five musicians, but only four cops. That led them to ignore me as I stood on the fringes of the performance area. I was confused until I realized their narrow focus on the limelight had left me unnoticed. As each took responsibility for their own personal "criminal," I slowly drifted away and eventually found myself sitting at the bar pretending to be one of the patrons. Eventually, a supervisor arrived with reinforcements, and I overheard some of the conversations of the new arrivals.

"Captain Sederstrom wants to stick it to these city fuckers. He wants to cut off the balls of these Mafia types before they ever get started here," said one sergeant.

"Yeah, and it won't hurt his promotion chances either," said another. They both laughed.

"These poor fucking kids. They have no idea what a shit-storm they're in the middle of."

I sat cradling someone else's half-finished drink and was thankful that my five o'clock shadow and generally mature look did not give away my real age. Mafia? Shit-storm? What the hell was going on? I was feeling guilty about the fact that my friends were taking the fall, while I sat safely away from all that was happening. Would it help if I owned up to my involvement with the group? I soon got my answer.

"Can somebody answer a simple question for me? Just one simple fucking question?" bellowed a voice of authority. This had to the ambitious prick that they called Captain Sederstrom. He pointed at the four original officers who had entered the club.

"Yes. Sir," answered the bravest of the four.

"If there are five instruments on this stage, why do we only have four perps in custody?"

A good observant question. I could see the nervous looks on the original squad. A hush overtook the entire club. Then the silence was broken.

"Ah, sir," I heard the voice that I recognized as Gio's. "Haven't you cops, I mean officers, ever seen a live band? I alternate between these two." He pointed at his guitar and my bass. He spoke with such conviction that it re-enforced the belief that he was stating an undeniable fact. Even a person vaguely knowledgeable in rock performances would've realized Gio was not telling the truth. If he actually was alternating between the two then who was playing the bass while he played the guitar? Immediately after making that statement, he looked at me and winked.

Jimmy Mac and Tinman gave me barely noticeable thumbs-up, and Bracko rolled his eyes and gave me a half smile. They had all saved my ass.

I couldn't take my eyes off my friends even as I was then ushered out of the club by the police who never asked for the bar customers (including me) to give identification and pertinent information about themselves. Every person in the bar could and should have been called upon to testify to what they had seen that night. This testimony would include the fact that there were five underage performers in the club. I guess they thought that having caught four band members red-handed (along with Vinnie the Cat) was more than enough for their case. They let the crowd disperse.

Entry #75

"After Midnight"
- Eric Clapton

It was still early in the evening, perhaps 8:30 or so, when I found myself out on the street. I hadn't yet faced the reality of how serious this was going to be and thought only of how I would get home that night. I found a pay phone. Though I dreaded it, I called my parents to pick me up. I didn't mention what had happened and luckily, my father didn't press the issue. Unfortunately, he couldn't come and get me until after my mother came home from work with the car. That meant I had to hunker down in an alley across the street until her night shift was over. I found I wasn't alone. A passed-out drunk who looked vaguely familiar sat propped against the wall near me. He never regained consciousness while I patiently waited out the hours for my ride home.

I watched the club empty out of almost everyone who had been in there. This included my friends who were in custody of the police. Surprisingly, I hadn't seen The Cat leave. I tried to figure out a way to approach him about picking up my equipment.

Sometime after midnight, a black Cadillac Coupe de Ville pulled up in front of the Driftwood Club. Mad Guy Provenzano and two others exited the car and entered the club. *Oh, shit.* This just got a whole lot worse for the band and The Cat. I realized my equipment was the least of my problems. The band was in a great deal more trouble than I ever imagined.

Less than twenty minutes later, I saw the three thugs leave. My father pulled up shortly after the Cadillac left. I tried to think what to do and only drew blanks.

18

The Other Side of Life

"Psychotic Reaction"
- Count Five

June 19, 1967 – 10:53 p.m.

"YOU FUCKED UP, YOU FUCKING pieces of shit," railed Gus Travante into the faces of Dom and Guy Provenzano. He dared them to argue with his assessment. His prolonged stare forced the father to bow his head in submission, while the son defiantly stared back at the boss. Travante noted the disrespect. "I told you to take care of all the details. But did you? You fucking cocksuckers. We gave you a shot, but we told you to take care of the details. Did you?"

"No, Don Travante," whimpered the elder Provenzano. Dom Provenzano had been born and raised in a dirt-poor neighborhood in Sicily. He understood that all he had become had been the result of his lucky break connecting with the mob after coming to America.

Conversely, Guy had never wanted for anything in his life and therefore suffered from an overinflated view of his worth. He was a prince. *How dare this old man talk to me in such a manner?*

"Money . . . and resources . . . and power! That's what your screw-up is going to cost us. Oh, we'll take care of this situation legally, but you fuck-ups are going nowhere soon. Or ever!"

Guy's mind was racing. *It was that shithead Vinnie and those damn kids. I didn't screw up. The Cat was the one who was supposed to take care of those details. He was the one who had the connections to a record contract.*

"But it wasn't our fault," responded Guy as his father stood shocked that his son had dared to open his mouth. Dom knew that Guy had put too much faith in Vinnie. Worse than that he had never bothered to grease the palms of the police. His son had miscalculated much of the plan, and now they were both going down in flames.

"Who told you that you could speak, shithead?" Guy's eyes widened and his fists clenched. Unnoticed by Travante, Dom grabbed his son's sleeve in an attempt to calm him down. Outwardly it worked. Still, Guy seethed inside, his fury growing with each word from the boss's mouth. *No one speaks to me like that*, thought Guy. No one ever had before.

"You two assholes are going back to your little shithole in the Heights, and you are going to run your half-assed operation. And you better work on making sure that the cash keeps flowing up the line to us. Or else."

It's not my fault, thought Guy, but he had the sense not to speak. *That fuckin' prick, Vinnie, and those fuckin' punk asshole kids!* Rage exploded in Guy's whole being. *Fuck! Fuck! Fuck! They're going to pay.*

"I'm sorry that my son used such poor judgment, *Don* Travante," murmured Dom Provenzano using the term of respect.

Gus Travante continued his barrage of insults for another hour. He outlined the consequences to the organization and the Provenzano family in great detail as he harangued the two ceaselessly. Guy never heard any of it. Each moment of his embarrassment took him further away from any semblance of sanity. His father was now dead to him. The organization that he had once cherished now became a group of people that he would somehow use for his benefit. Hate became the only functioning emotion in his existence. It was on that night in June of 1967 that any speck of humanity that had ever occupied the body of Guy Provenzano left his being.

June 20, 1967 – 12:03 a.m.

Vinnie "The Cat" Catalano had no concept of how deep Guy's rage would be until he saw his boss coming through the door of the club. The Cat had wondered if Guy would allow him to keep his job after this royal screw up. He had asked the wrong question. He should have been asking whether Guy would allow him to keep *his life* after this royal screw up. It would have been a more pertinent question.

It was a little past midnight when Guy arrived at the Driftwood Club and calmly entered the venue. From now on, his actions would be thought out and done with an absence of emotion. This was how the bosses wanted it, and this was the way he would do it. Calmly and deliberately. Guy would live by those mantras. He swore that he would. His vow lasted about ten seconds after he entered the club and saw Vinnie the Cat for the first time since his humiliation at the hands of the bosses.

"You cocksucking shitbrain," were the only words that Vinnie would hear before Mad Guy vaulted over the bar and landed right next to him. Guy stopped for a brief moment as if to think about what do next. Vinnie could feel his breath on his face and prayed that his boss had gotten control of his emotions. His prayers were not answered.

Guy grabbed the first long-necked whiskey bottle on which his hand laid purchase and in one fluid motion brought it down on Vinnie's skull. As his victim was stumbling backward and already losing consciousness, Mad Guy reached for a second bottle to continue his assault. His two minions looked on in disbelief as their boss shattered a second and then a third bottle on the head of his bloody former friend and employee.

The madman then stepped away from the body and surveyed what he had done. He was very proud of the fact that he had not gotten a drop of blood on his new alligator skin shoes. He also complimented his forethought on having worn leather gloves throughout the entire encounter so that he left no fingerprints at the scene.

His anger vented, Guy instructed his two goons, Sammy Crespo and Sal Timpani, to empty the cash register and break the locks on the door. If any of those asswipe cops looked into this situation, they would write the whole incident off as a robbery gone wrong. As Guy left the bar and made himself comfortable in the back seat of his Cadillac, he waited until they had completely cleared the scene before addressing Crespo and Timpani.

"What do you know about the pricks who caused me all this trouble?"

"Not much. That was . . . uh . . . Vinnie's thing," replied Timpani.

"Well, how many of them were there? What are their names? Where are they from?"

"The police arrested four guys. The report will have their names. And get this. I think they're from the Heights."

"Why would you think that?"

"Well, uh, Vinnie told us one time that he was keeping an eye on a group that was from the Heights and that . . . well, uh . . . some of the guys in the band were the ones who saved your brother," reluctantly answered Crespo.

"What the fuck are you saying?" questioned Mad Guy.

"He knew the guys' names who saved Tony, and when he saw that they had a band, he made a point of going to see them," said Crespo.

"Why the hell would he do that?"

"He thought he was doing you a solid, Guy. He figured you would like to show them some gratitude, you know, give them a lift up."

"Are you two fuckin' kidding me?"

"Well, Vinnie thought . . ." said the reluctant Crespo.

"I don't give a shit what Vinnie thought. Saving Tony? That's just another good reason to kill those assholes. Those fuckin' kids didn't do me any favors by leaving me with a retard on my hands. And for Vinnie to think that . . . Well, now I'm *really* glad I crushed his damn skull."

"OK, Guy, we get where you're coming from," said Timpani meekly.

"So who were they?"

"We do know that they were damn good. After Vinnie heard them the first time at the Wollman Festival, he couldn't stop talking about them. The fact that they had saved Tony had gotten their foot in the door, but after that, he saw real talent."

"Crespo, I don't give a fuck. They'll be playing in motherfucking hell when I finish with them. Just tell me who they are."

"We don't know for sure."

"Why the fuck not? What do I pay you shitheads for, huh? Can't anyone do their job?"

———◆———

Vinnie "The Cat" Catalano sunk into a deep coma in the early morning hours of June 20, 1967. He died a few days later from complications incurred from his injuries. The Nassau police tried to salvage as much evidence as possible from the scene of the second crime. However, the sheer volume of blood on the floor obscured many relevant bits of evidence.

An overworked technician collecting evidence mistook a business card for just another scattered coaster lost in the commotion. To him, it was just more blood-soaked cardboard. He could not know that Vinnie had clutched it during the last minutes of his conscious life. He had intended to give the business card to Guy as soon as he saw him. The card would have answered at least one of the questions that his boss had asked that night. The card read listed the *five* names of the members of the band.

June 26, 1967

Sal Timpani showed Richie Shea into the living room of the Provenzano home. Though everyone knew they were first cousins, Guy and Richie tried to keep their dealings out of the public eye. It was better not to flaunt just how much control that the Provenzano family wielded with law enforcement.

"So, Richie, what have you got for me?"

"I got the four names of the kids that the police hauled in that night."

"What the hell took you so long?"

"It was Nassau County. I have no jurisdiction out there . . . and you . . . uh . . . we . . . have no connections to that force."

"Why not?"

"Uh," was all he could say? Richie Shea was not going to be the one to tell his boss that *Guy* had been warned by Gus Travante to take care of those kinds of details before ever venturing into this new territory.

"Being my cousin is only going to go so far, Richie. I want results. OK, so what do you have?"

"Those Born Free was the name of the group . . . "

"Fucking weenie name," interjected Timpani. Guy shot a glare. This was no joking matter.

"Four kids taken in. James McAvoy, Joseph Tinley, Rocco Brackowski, and Giovanni DeAngelis. All seventeen years of age."

"See I was right. Those last two were there in the Garden of Eden that night," screeched Crespo. Guy was not impressed by this interruption any more than he was by that of Timpani.

"OK, but what about Johnny Cipp? Was he there?" Guy knew exactly who had been in the Garden of Eden at his brother's tragedy. In his mind, Gio and Johnny were eternally linked together by that night. Would it be a stretch to think they played in a band together?

"There is no evidence of that," answered Richie Shea immediately. "However, there was an inconsistency in the report that a supervisor took note of."

"Yeah, what?"

"Well, there were five instruments on the stage."

"Logic would tell someone, any fuckin' one, that there was a fifth member of that group."

"Yeah, Guy, but there is no proof of that," countered Shea. "The police report noted the instrument, but didn't conclude that it meant that there was another member of the band."

"Do I look like a goddamned lawyer or judge to you? What the fuck do I care about proof?"

"I just thought that you would want the facts before you decide to do something."

"You fuckin' get me the facts, and I'll decide on doing something."

"I'll get to the bottom of it, Guy. You can count on me."

"You better, Richie! And don't forget I make the decisions *if* something is going to happen. I say when, where, and how things happen."

In reality, Mad Guy had already decided *if* something was going to happen. He would work out the details. The only question remaining was *how many*?

19

Journal of Johnny Cipp

Entry #75

"Time Won't Let Me"
-*The Outsiders*

I HAD THE COMMON SENSE TO realize that I shouldn't be seen in the vicinity of any of the band members. The police and Mad Guy's gang had overrun the area asking questions about a possible fifth member of the group. How come they didn't know about me? I mean Vinnie knew us well, and there was no way that he was going to hold out any information from his boss. Guy's brother Tony knew us each by name, perhaps better than he knew his own family. And Greg Cincotta sat in jail awaiting trial. He knew about me. Had my efforts to save him that night bought me his loyalty? What was going on?

I thanked God we had spent the last year playing everywhere but the Heights. That severely limited any eyewitnesses who would come forward and give accurate information about the group. Yes, there were people out there who had seen us, but they weren't in the places that the Provenzano gang would look.

I counted my blessings as often as I counted the days I assumed that I had left in my life. It seemed only a matter of time. When I heard about the break-in at the club and Vinnie's coma, I knew it was bullshit. I'd seen Guy enter the Driftwood. I didn't have to be a genius to figure out what happened. The stupid bastard had all the information right in his hands, and he had missed his chance. I wondered how long I would be safe before the facts came out.

I then heard of Vinnie's death. I felt guilty to be happy about his passing. He'd been good to us. He'd been a fan of ours. He was about to give us our big break. However, he could have fingered me to Guy if the thug hadn't killed him. My relief lasted only as long as it took me to realize that I was now in even more danger. What if Mad Guy figured out I had witnessed him enter the club the night he murdered Vinnie?

But who could I tell? I believed that any police officer I might confide in had a 50/50 chance of being in on the scam that deemed Vinnie's death the result of a break-in at the club. I was so confused that I kept my distance from everyone.

Entry # 76

"Dazed and Confused"
- *Led Zeppelin*

I needed to see Maria. I needed some sanity in my life. I knew I couldn't call her house. For that matter, I couldn't call anyone's home. Stupid me tried. After a week of sitting and meekly hiding at home, I reached out to Gio. It was a short phone call.

"Hello, Gio, it's me," I said cryptically, and he answered much the same.

"Sorry, I can't talk now. I've got to go to the *john*. Not that it's any of your business, stranger, but sometimes I hide out in there for extended periods of time. You don't want to be around when I come out . . . if you know what I mean."

"But I just . . ." I tried to get in a word which even under normal circumstances was hard to do with Gio.

"Listen, I have to hang up now. Don't call back unless you are the exterminator. If you are, then my father will want to talk about our insect problem. We need to do something about these bugs. They are all over."

Now I understood. To an outsider, Gio comments sounded idiotic. However, that was just the point he was making. There probably was an outsider listening to our conversation. Gio had many crude ways to describe taking a shit; "dropping a deuce," "squeezing one out," "laying a brick." What he never said was "going to the john." That was his way of telling me that he knew it was me on the phone. He was telling me to hide out and not to call because he believed that someone was tapping his phone. His final words were clear. "Don't call us, we'll call you." Stay away from all of them. He was warning me.

———◆———

"Johnny, you've got company," yelled my mother almost simultaneously with the sound of footsteps coming up my stairs. My curiosity lasted the seconds it took for her to climb to my attic hideaway.

"Wow, it's no wonder Maria told me you had some great make-out sessions up here. Your room is like a fortress."

"Good to see you too, Diane." I meant it. In reality, it was good to see anyone. Diane, as Maria's best friend, was particularly welcome.

"Johnny, you called Gio. That was a mistake. The guys are in deep shit, and they know it. You getting involved isn't going to help them."

"It's just not right that nothing happened to me, Diane."

"Johnny, you're an asshole, always have been. Do you think that joining them up shit's creek is going to help them?"

"I don't know? I've got to do something, Diane."

"No, you don't. To quote Gio, 'Tell that fuckin' idiot to stay away.' So stay away, dammit!"

"Alright, Alright, I get the message. Diane. What about Maria?"

"Well, Johnny, speaking of that . . ."

"Yeah."

"Maria and her family are coming to my house for a Fourth of July barbeque. I'm thinking that maybe about five-ish Maria and I are going to take a walk somewhere around, let's say, Sacred Heart schoolyard."

"Diane, I could kiss you."

"Hey, watch it."

"Yeah, I know. What would Maria say?"

"Screw Maria. What would Jimmy Mac say?"

"You? Jimmy Mac?"

"Yup."

"How is he? I mean besides having a lovely girl like you?"

"Cut the shit, Johnny. I'm not just here for Maria. You've got to take this seriously. Jimmy Mac and the guys want you to stay as far away as you can. They don't know what the hell is going down, but they don't want you anywhere near it."

"I've gotta know what's happening, Diane."

"They may just have to go to court to testify, but even that may be dropped on a technicality."

"What do you mean?"

"Well, the owner claims that Vinnie the Cat was entirely responsible for the violation and well . . . he's not around to defend himself."

"He's dead," I said. It was public knowledge that Vinnie had passed. However, I was the only one who knew how, why, and who did it.

"The police don't seem interested in pursuing it any further because . . ."

"Because they were paid off by the owner, Mad Guy Provenzano!"

"Right, Johnny, and what does that mean for Jimmy Mac and the rest of them?"

"I don't know, Diane. I just don't know."

I would soon find out.

Entry #77

"Piece of My Heart"
- Janis Joplin

On July 4th, I ventured out of the house, found my way to the Sacred Heart schoolyard by 4:30, and waited patiently to see Maria. A few minutes after five, the two of them arrived. Soon after meeting up, Diane bid us farewell to find her way to Jimmy Mac's house. As she was leaving, she made us promise we wouldn't go near them.

"That's the way Jimmy Mac wants it. He doesn't want to tie you or Maria to this mess."

"Diane, what about you? Aren't you scared?" asked Maria, always worrying about others.

"Who cares about little old me?" she said with a playful look on her face. "See you back here in an hour. That's about all the time we have before our drunken parents notice we are missing." Diane skipped all the way down the block and around the corner. She had a broad smile, and I heard her humming a happy tune.

Finally alone, Maria and I held each other tight and didn't say a word. We hadn't seen each other since the beginning of June and so much had happened since then. We both knew the story, and neither of us wanted to waste our precious time together discussing it. Suddenly, I had an idea.

"What are you doing Johnny?" she asked as I reached down and produced the silver band that had been on my pinkie.

"Please take this now," I said offering her the ring I had tried to put on her finger many months before.

"No, Johnny, no. Now more than ever you need to know that I don't need anything to prove your love to me or my love for you,"

"But we don't know what is going on . . . or what's going to happen."

"Johnny, that's all the more reason to trust our hearts. I will wait as long as you want for us to be together. No ring is going to change that. I've told you before that I want you to come to me when your journey is over. Whether it's music, or school, or something else. I'll take that ring when you have found your way in the world. Your way . . . get it? Only then, will I really know that you are OK. Only then can I join you."

I tried to answer her, but she shut my mouth with a tender kiss. I remember very little else of our hour together except that she placed the ring back on my pinkie.

20

The Other Side of Life:

"Paint It Black"
- *The Rolling Stones*

July 5, 1967

STAN BRACKOWSKI HAD CHANGED. HE had been sober ever since the night a few weeks before when he had faced what he had become. He would never beat his son again. The twelve-step program that he had sought out was in the slow process of reuniting the depressed father and his emotionally scarred son. Given time, everything might have worked out between the two. Unfortunately, despite Bracko's guitar riffs on a certain Rolling Stones' song, *time was not on their side.*

The events at the Driftwood Club had crushed Bracko's brief incursion into a life of music and friendship. He now had nothing. Stan also had an enormous void in his life now that he no longer spent the significant part of his days in a state of inebriation. Now they only had each other, and maybe, just maybe, a relationship would grow.

———◆———

The police concluded Stan had fallen asleep while smoking. This had happened quite often in the elder Brackowski's previous life. On many nights, sleep had been nothing more than an alcohol-induced stupor. But without the booze, Stan had found himself quite alert on most evenings. However, most evenings did not include a glass of plain orange juice tinged with a powerful sedative. The police never detected that drug in their post-mortem autopsy. This vital part of the investigation was skipped on the instructions of the supervising detective. With no evidence to the contrary, the investigators assumed that the drunken father was responsible for the tragedy. His cigarette had ignited the combustible liquid on the fabric of the couch (again not tested). The fire then proceeded to spread to the curtains and the rest of the house. Most of the important details had been overlooked by the lead investigator, Richie Shea.

According to Shea's report, the real mystery was the son. He wrote that his sources described the son as depressed about the failure of his musical career. In fact, if anything suspicious showed up in future investigations, detectives should consider the son as a suspect in a murder/suicide scenario. After all, there was no other explanation for the way *his* body had been found.

Despite being quickly overcome by smoke, Rocco "Bracko" Brackowski still should have had time to escape the inferno. At the very least, the police should have found his body sprawled in some unusual position that showed a valiant attempt to escape. Why had he not tried to exit his secluded location when the first whiff of smoke came to his attention? *Nothing* kept him in the basement. While the steel exterior basement door was bolted from the outside, there was no reason that Bracko could not have escaped up the interior stairs. That door was not locked.

The police report included glowing praise for a "good Samaritan," named Nicky Toto (whose mother's maiden name happened to be Provenzano). The report stated that *Toto had rushed into the building to save the occupants. Overcome by smoke, he had to retreat without being able to save either Brackowski.*

In truth, the rescue attempt had been the arsonist's third trip in the Brackowski home. In the early afternoon, he had spiked every liquid in the refrigerator with a massive dose of a tasteless barbiturate. When a significant period had passed after both father and son had arrived home, he made his way into the house with the same flammable substance that he had used to torch the Men at Arms hobby shop. After spreading the liquid and igniting it, Toto began to make a hasty retreat. Only then did he hear the powerful notes of Bracko's guitar. It became evident that the boy had not touched any of the tainted liquids in his refrigerator. Panic overwhelmed Toto as he heard the music come to an abrupt halt and Bracko's footsteps climbing the stairs from the basement. He rushed to lock the door with the deadbolt that Stan Brackowski had installed during one of his crueler phases of parenting. There was now no way for Bracko to escape his fate.

Toto found that the suffocating smoke was affecting him. He had to find air. He would return later to unlock the door and therefore ease any suspicion of foul play. As he found cover outside, he could not believe his ears. Through the crackling of the flames and screeching of fire engine sirens, he heard the faint sounds of a guitar.

At first, they were loud and vibrant with all the strength that dying hands could muster. Soon, however, they started to fade into weak, unintelligible notes. Finally, there was total silence. As Toto watched the first rescuers approach the scene, he knew that he had to rush in to unlock the door. He never expected that the rescuers would hail him as a hero.

Knowing that his fate was sealed, Bracko had chosen to spend his last moments with his guitar. In defiance of all the shit that had been thrown at him in his life, he was going out his way, playing his Fender Strat. As he inhaled the smothering fumes, he grew weak and was forced to sit. As his eyes closed for the last time, his fingers never stopped moving over the frets of his guitar.

The police found Bracko's body sitting in a chair with no outward sign of distress or panic. Even in death, he still had his fingers wrapped around his guitar in the position to play one last chord . . . and he was smiling. Bracko's hard life had finally come to an end.

August 15, 1967

Jimmy Mac had been under house arrest since the incident at the Driftwood Club. No judicial system had imposed any such restrictions on him. He was bound by what he referred to as the "McAvoy Laws." He spent almost every waking moment under the watchful eye of either his father, Noel, or his mother, Adele.

A more accurate term for what Jimmy Mac was experiencing was *store arrest*. The family business had become the former drummer's place of residence for almost every waking hour since that fateful night in June. Because school was out for the summer and band practice nonexistent, Jimmy Mac had nowhere else to be. He missed the band and the music, but the members of his family were good people.

Jimmy Mac never realized his father had not been teaching him a life lesson. The elder McAvoy had been around Cambria Heights and the world long enough to know that there would always be consequences for screwing with powerful men. Better to keep his son where he could guard him. *Hadn't one of the guys from the band just died in a fire last month? Accident my ass.* Noel McAvoy knew vengeance when he saw it. Though his son had begged to go to Bracko's funeral, Neil decided to err on the side of safety and keep Jimmy safe and secure.

———◆———

Timpani and Crespo were excited about their first hit, but not too excited to forget that they had been instructed to make sure that no civilians were in the store when it happened. Guy wanted it clear that all who died were tied to the band. The two young assassins waited until the last customers of the night had left the store. It seemed as if the lovey-dovey teenage couple would never finish sharing a milkshake and doe-eyed looks at each other.

At 9:05 on the night of August 15, the two novice hit men entered the store. The out of season sock hats pulled down over their faces were the first hint to Noel McAvoy that this was not a good situation. However, the hastily cut out eye slots limited the intruders' vision, and they did not see Jimmy Mac approaching from the side candy counter. While they stood with guns drawn and aimed at the elder McAvoy, the son had quietly taken hold of an old Little League bat. Jimmy Mac acted quickly, crushing a home run swing across the nose and eyes of Sammy Crespo. Blood immediately began to spurt from the thug's head and soaked the sock hat with a coating of red liquid.

"Shit," was all Timpani could say as he looked at his partner and then quickly turned in anger and put two shots into Jimmy Mac's chest. As the former drummer fell to the floor, the dazed

Crespo ripped his disguise from his face to allow more air into his broken nose. Simultaneously, Noel vaulted the counter in a futile attempt to save his son and exact some vengeance on the now recognizable assassin. Shaken by his first murder, the shooter did not react quickly enough to prevent the onslaught of punches from the outraged father. Timpani's only thought was that they would be lucky if they escaped with their lives, as Neil McAvoy tore off Timpani's mask and pummeled the shooter into submission.

It was then that a shot rang out. Crespo, barely able to see through his swollen eyes, had taken point blank aim at the back of Noel McAvoy's head. As blood and brain splattered the penny candies that only moments before Jimmy Mac had been restocking, Noel breathed his last breath.

The now unmasked duo looked down at the two dying McAvoys and discussed whether or not they should put their masks back on. It was then that they heard the muffled sound of weeping. Slowly, Timpani moved toward the back of the store. He used his hands to motion Crespo to keep the conversation going. There in the bathroom, he found Diane where her boyfriend Jimmy Mac had hidden her. Timpani realized that his face was showing. The distinctive port wine birthmark on his face would leave him easy to identify to the police. He had no choice. He put two bullets in the left temple of the weeping girl.

Sammy Crespo and Sal Timpani somehow found their way back to a Provenzano safe house. When Guy viewed his two employees, he briefly contemplated ending the two young assassins' lives right there and then. It was only the fear of a rising body count that preserved the further existence of his two inept hit men.

All was now quiet in the store, as Jimmy Mac opened his eyes. As he choked on the blood accumulating in his throat, he knew it was bad. He crawled towards his father and saw no hope. The damage to his father's head was devastating and fatal.

"Oh, Dad, no," he cried, and as the tears flowed down his cheeks, they mixed with the blood that continued to erupt from his mouth. He had to tell someone what had happened. He had to get to the phone in the back office. Slowly he crawled past the stools and counters that had been so much a part of his family's life. A few more feet and just past the restroom and he would be there.

He saw Diane's motionless body curled in a fetal position on the floor and tried to call to her. However, blood now choked his throat to the point that he could not speak or breathe. He knew he was not going to make it to the phone. Suffocating on his own blood, he crawled the last feet that separated him from the girl who had finally won his playboy heart. He held her breathless body tightly . . . and died.

September 6, 1967

It is very hard to die from alcohol poisoning. The drinker usually loses consciousness before reaching lethal levels of alcohol in the bloodstream. Passing out acts as a safeguard. The drinker must swallow an excessive volume so rapidly that the body does not have the time to shut down. In reality, the amount in the throat sliding down the esophagus races the body's reaction to the amount already in the stomach, initiating the pass out or gag reflex in the brain.

This kind of poisoning occurs most commonly at college parties. At least once a year, the wire news services tell the story of some young student who dies while pledging a fraternity. Usually, that fraternity is punished with the suspension of its charter. Lawsuits against the group and the college are lodged and quietly settled out of court so that the college does not incur any serious negative publicity. The college issues a strong state-ment of policy against such activities and institutes an alcohol awareness program. Soon, all is forgotten.

"Yeah, that's the way I'll do it," said Jerry Marchant to no one but himself. He put down the magazine article that he was read-ing, satisfied with his research. He had been given a job to do, and now he knew how exactly how to do it.

———◆———

With the demise of Those Born Free, Joey Tinley had conceded that perhaps his father had been right all along. The deaths of two of his friends had been life-altering events he would never forget. Joey knew he would never be the Tinman again. He needed to get as far away as possible from the memories that followed him every day he lived in the Heights. Going away would be a good thing. A fresh start was just what he needed to refocus. But he would never forget Bracko and Jimmy Mac. Never.

Joey agreed to follow the path his father had mapped out for him from the first moment he touched a piano at the age of five. His dalliance with rock music had robbed him of just enough practice time so that Julliard proved out of reach for his abilities. He would make up for the time lost while at his second choice, the Berklee College of Music. In a sense, it was a win-win situation for Joey. He often had to ask himself if he had not sandbagged the Julliard audition. In reality, Berklee had been *his* first choice. The up-and-coming school specialized in jazz and contemporary music as opposed to the elite classical preparation of Julliard. He might still be following the right path after all.

Much to Joey's surprise, his father was thrilled to see him leave for Boston. The naïve Joey had not realized his friends' deaths had not been accidents. His father had accompanied him to court only to see the whole situation dropped before trial. That did not happen unless somebody knew somebody or somebody paid off somebody. Mr. Tinley knew what kind of people had that kind of power, and it scared the hell out of him. Perhaps if his son was in Boston, he could remain under the radar of the Provenzanos. He was wrong.

Though life at Berklee was not like most other colleges in the Boston area with their historic parties and activities, the students were still college students, and as such, liked their alcohol as much as anyone. As the fall semester of 1967 commenced, it was at one such party that Joey died. His body had been found in the back room of a house rented by a group of upperclassmen who had thrown the party as a way of welcoming fellow New York students. Because the school session had only been a week old, the upperclassmen had only met Joey once. They could shed no light on what had happened that fateful night. A few remembered Joey had been talking to another freshman at the party before he disappeared.

Upon further investigation, the police could not match this other student to any name that had been invited to the party. Indeed, they could not match the mystery student to any list of incoming freshmen or upperclassmen in the entire school. In reality, they could have cross-referenced every college list for the whole city of Boston and its surrounding areas, and they would not have found a match.

Jerry Marchant could never have made it into Berklee College of Music. No college in America would accept him unless it had an admissions policy based on having a heartbeat. Getting through 10th grade had been a challenge for the street-wise, book-dumb Marchant. However, what he did have was an ability to be a chameleon. A rare WASP in ethnic Queens, he quickly learned to adapt his speech and mannerism to those around him, therefore making him able to fit into any social situation. For that reason, Guy Provenzano had chosen him for the task. That reason, and the fact that Marchant knew how to hit just the right pressure point on the human body to make it lose consciousness long enough to be withdrawn to a secluded area for further actions.

Looking so much like a clean-cut college freshman, no one imagined he was a cold, calculating killer. Therefore, when he told Joey Tinley of his collection of rare jazz records in a back room, the new student had no idea he was being lured to his death. Once behind the closed door, Marchant used a pressure point on the neck to render his unsuspecting victim unconscious. When Joey awoke, he found himself bound hand and foot to a chair with his mouth tightly gagged.

"I'm going to take the scarf from your mouth. If you say a word, the first thing to go will be your tongue. Am I clear?" said Marchant, holding an extremely sharp stiletto knife next to Joey's throat. Joey nodded in the affirmative and his mouth gag was removed.

"Why?" was Joey's only query.

"Let's just say we have a mutual friend. However, if you do everything I say, you will get out of this alive." Marchant was lying.

"Why should I believe you?" responded the terrified former Tinman.

"Well, you don't have much choice. Do you?" He brandished the knife and stuck the blade into Joey's mouth. He was careful not to nick the skin of his lips. It was not that he cared in the slightest, but a body free of injury suited his plans for how the post-mortem would go.

"Please, I didn't do anything wrong."

"Joey, Joey, Joey, . . . or should I have said Joseph. Isn't that all a matter of point of view? I've got a boss who would disagree." He produced a full quart bottle of vodka from a cabinet where he had hidden it earlier in the night.

"What the heck?" responded the confused Tinley, but Jerry Marchant said nothing as he produced a black marker from his pocket. He held Joey's bound hands and put a black line at the meeting point of Joey's right pinkie and the back of his hand. He then proceeded to duplicate this line on the pianist's ring finger, index finger, and thumb. Marchant then took Joey's left hand and reproduced the four lines on that side. He then stuck the gag back in Tinley's mouth.

"You are going to drink that entire bottle of vodka in three minutes. Yeah, I know, you've never had a drink, and you promised the old man that you wouldn't until you were twenty-one. Apparently, your father likes to brag."

"Argh." Joey tried to yell 'No way.'" Marchant laughed in his face.

"That's what I thought you would say or try to say. Let me tell you my second option before I take the gag off and you drink heartily. Once I tell you what it is, you might scream. I wouldn't want that, so I would have to knock you out for option B. You would miss all the fun."

"Waaaa?"

"What? Oh, I thought it was obvious, but maybe you aren't as smart as they say. Option B is that I'm going to cut off one of your fingers for every minute extra that it takes you to drink that whole bottle. Right there, where I drew the lines. Notice I'm going to leave you your two middle fingers. I think that's perfect punishment for the perfect boy who never cursed. Think about it for a second. Forever and ever, your two remaining fingers would be saying to the world, "Fuck you!"

"Argh, Argh." Joey's eyes filled with terror.

"Hey, at least you'll be able to play 'Chopsticks,' right?" Marchant waited a few seconds for the thought of what he was going to do to sink in. "So, what did you decide? Option A or option B?"

He held the full quarter of vodka in one hand and the knife in the other. He then held the knife down on the pinkie of Joey's right hand and applied just enough pressure to break the skin. Blood started to flow down the sides of his fingers as Joey resigned himself to his fate with a slight nod of acceptance toward the bottle.

"Remember, if you renege on our deal and scream, I cut out your tongue . . . and then we go back to option A or B."

Jerry Marchant knew that he would never have to use his knife. He had calculated that Joey's height, weight, and inexperience with alcohol would ensure that the amount in the bottle would do the job.

Joey had a feeling that drinking an entire quart of Vodka in three minutes could be dangerous, maybe even fatal. It didn't matter to him. He would rather die than live life without his fingers, and more importantly, without his music.

Within thirty minutes, most of Joey's body functions shut down. He lost consciousness even as he choked on his own vomit.

———◆———

"TWICE THE TRAGEDY"
Headline - New York Daily News

September 8, 1967

Tragedy struck the same family twice within two days. Faced with the devastating loss of their son Joseph, Jr. (17) to an alcohol-related death, the rest of the Tinley family also met its demise under tragic conditions. While traveling from their Cambria Heights home to the Boston site of their son's untimely end, the family perished in a violent single-car accident.

Joseph Tinley, Sr. and his wife Margaret died when their car veered off the road and crashed not far from their home. Police are ruling the deaths accidental. However, they are still investigating whether it was a mechanical failure or driver error that initiated the tragic string of events that led to Joseph Tinley's losing control of his vehicle and veering into the side of a stone overpass on the Cross Island Parkway.

The couple's son had been found dead only the day before.

Investigators believe that the younger Tinley died after ingesting massive amounts of alcohol while attending a college party. Only the day before his death, a reporter interviewed the senior Tinley about his tragic loss. He vehemently denied the police conclusion and said that he would do his own investigation once he arrived at the scene.

"My son would never have one drink, let alone enough to kill himself," said the grieving father to reporters. However, John Hanratty, spokesman for the Boston Police, verified that their investigation had shown very little chance of an alternative scenario. When faced with this comment Joseph Tinley responded, "We'll see."

———————————

The Tinley family would never get a chance to see what the actual account of events had been. Guy Provenzano had seen to that. Those following his orders had acted quickly. A pinhole in the brake fluid line had allowed the liquid to drain at a rate that ensured that the victims' car would gain enough speed to put them in harm's way. The Provenzano connection to a larger organization provided them with access to an expert in "accidental" events.

Even Guy Provenzano's closest associates could not be sure of his motivation. Was the accident to keep the Tinley family from investigating their son's death on their own? On the other hand, was this just another part of his reign of terror upon the band that had caused him so much grief? Had he arranged for not only the deaths of three band members, but also the demise of many of their loved ones?

September 9, 1967 – 7:05 p.m.

Gio and Johnny had not talked in two months. But now Gio had called Johnny's house, and his mother had told him he could find her son at the schoolyard. Johnny spotted his friend and followed his hand signal directing him toward the Garden of Eden. They both squeezed through the hidden entrance and found a secluded corner. Gio was sweating profusely, and Johnny knew why. They had just gotten the news about Tinman. Up until then they had tried to convince themselves that the deaths of Bracko and Jimmy Mac had been coincidences – strange overwhelming coincidences, but nothing more. Acknowleding reality meant their own lives were in peril.

Tinman's death had hit them over the head with the truth. Three members of Those Born Free had been executed. All this and the police suspected nothing, or at least pretended to suspect nothing. Gio and Johnny's fear was further fed by the fact that no one but them seemed to care.

How could they understand the anger that dwelled in the aptly named Mad Guy? How could they know the intricate web of planning needed to commit the murders and then make them appear accidental? The police wrote reports but did not make connections. No one *wanted* to connect all the dots. Too many men were being paid to ignore the obvious.

"Fuck it, Johnny, we're the only ones left. Bracko, Jimmy Mac, and now Tinman! What's going on?" Gio seemed ready to break. He seemed ready to cry and just let himself go. He then summoned inner strength and calmly spoke again, "And the families?"

"It's Mad Guy. We know it. There's just nothing we can do about it."

"I'm not waiting around for my turn, Johnny. I'm leaving and you should too."

"But where will you go? What will you do?"

"I don't know, and I don't give a shit. Maybe, just maybe, if I leave, I can save my family and myself. You know, out of sight, out of mind."

"Guy will still be out of his mind, even if you are out of sight."

"But maybe he wants to do it while my family is there. You know, like Bracko and Jimmy. And I think that he especially wants to hurt me because I was, you know . . . the leader of the band."

Johnny shrugged off his friend's assumption. Perhaps in a different place or a different time, he might have argued the point. "Yeah, you were the leader." However, even as he said the words, the powerful guilt he had held in since that night surfaced. Because he had never spoken to anyone, what he had done had never come up. The guilt that festered in Johnny's heart and soul ate away at him with an intensity that would never end. Johnny had killed Jimmy Mac, Tinman, and Bracko as much as if he himself had put a knife in each of their hearts. He had destroyed families, and Gio was next. He deserved the truth.

"Gio, it's my fault. The deaths, all of it."

"Yeah, right, it was not the crazy man. It's freakin' Johnny Cipp."

"No, listen!" Johnny knew he had to get it all out soon before his courage deserted him.

"Go ahead," said the skeptical Gio.

"That last afternoon when I was in your basement, and you left to go see Riet, your mother called down to the basement. She said you had a call from the Driftwood Club. I was so sure they were going to give directions, or times or something, that I picked up the phone. I was just so excited."

"Yeah, so?"

"The Cat assumed that I was you and immediately started talking. I just listened. He asked me if we were all over eighteen. Gio, I saw the whole thing slipping away . . . the job playing . . . the money . . . our way out. Gio, I did it. I told him we were all eighteen."

"What the fuck?"

"I justified it because I thought that Joey's father said it was just a formality. He said he would dig us up some phony proof if anyone asked. Well someone was asking, and they were asking me! I wasn't going to be the one to end the dream."

Gio stared blankly but said nothing.

"The Cat had called the Tinley's house, but no one had answered. Your name was the other number that we gave him. I was caught by surprise. Gio, I screwed up, and I'm the only one who *isn't* paying for it."

"Hell, I probably would have done the same thing if I had answered the phone." Johnny didn't know if that was true, but he did know that his best friend was being just that, a friend.

"Gio, they're dead because of me. I can never forget that."

"Johnny, you're a good person. You were doing it for all of us. It just didn't turn out right."

"Can you ever forgive me?"

"Yeah, say three Hail Marys. Shithead, this isn't confession and

I'm not a goddamn priest. But as your friend, I'm telling you don't worry about it. You'll make up for it someday. You'll do something great for someone."

It was then that Gio pulled a duffel bag and his guitar out of a hidden section of undergrowth behind him.

"I'm leaving the Heights tonight. I only have one more thing to take care of." The look of disbelief on Johnny's face said it all.

"And that's it? That's all you're taking?"

"Yeah, I couldn't get a moving van on such short notice. You asshole, I'm hitching a ride somewhere. How much do you think I can take?"

"So, when will I hear from you?".

"Maybe never. Johnny, you still don't get it. I'm only still alive because even Mad Guy couldn't kill everyone at once and not raise suspicion. I just lucked out to be last and to see it coming."

"And I . . ."

"Johnny, I don't know if he knows about you. If he does, then I'm not the last one − I'm second to last. We're both targets. Come with me!"

"But, there's Maria."

"And you don't think I feel the same about Riet? But if I stay around it might not just be me. It might be her . . . and my parents. If you stay around and Guy knows about you . . . and then finds out about Maria?"

"Are you saying that she could be in danger too?"

"Whether she's with you at the wrong time. . .or just out of sheer meanness, Guy wouldn't hesitate. . ."

"To kill her?" Johnny and Gio had not lost the ability to finish each other's sentences.

"Tell me, Johnny, have you ever seen Mad Guy show mercy?" Changing the subject abruptly, Gio started for the hole in the fence. "I have to go. Riet has no idea what's happening. I have kept the whole situation from her. In fact, I have kept away from her completely so that . . . well, like I said about Maria."

"You haven't seen her since before the Driftwood?"

"No. We were in the middle of some heavy shit that day, and I just left her hanging. I have to risk going there now to tell her . . ."

"That you're leaving?"

"That . . . and that I love her and will be back for her when I think that it's safe. She's got to know that!"

Johnny was speechless. He had no idea that it was this serious. Gio had shared much with his best friend, but Johnny had never considered it might be a life-long commitment. Gio's face told him the whole story.

"I can only imagine what she's thinking of me now. Not knowing that I was avoiding her for her own good. Especially at . . ." It seemed that Gio wanted to say more and Johnny waited, but all that came out was, "Gotta go."

"But your parents?"

"I left them a note. Not much detail about why. Just told them I needed to sort some things out so I was leaving for a while."

"That's how you left it with Gyp and Rosalie? You bastard."

"That's Mr. and Mrs. De Angelis to you, asshole." For their entire friendship, Gio's parents had tried to get Johnny to call them by their first names, as everyone in the Heights seemed to do. However, Johnny couldn't bring himself to be that informal. The fact that he had chosen this time to comply to their wishes caught them both by surprise. After a few moments of silence, they both smiled. Gio got up to leave and turned one last time to his friend.

"Gio, don't go," but even as he said the words, he knew it was futile.

"Johnny, I'll be back in an hour to pick up my stuff. I really think that you need to come with me. Think about it." With those words, Gio was up and walking along the inner edge of the garden until he reached the hidden cutout in the fence. He looked both ways before exiting and quickly was on the sidewalk. He now walked along the exterior length of the fence, the same ten feet he had traveled inside. He was soon at the location exactly where Johnny sat covered by the bushes and fence. Without breaking stride or even looking in the direction of the garden, Gio said just loud enough for his friend to hear, "See you in an hour, asshole, and remember to do something good, make us proud, and we'll all forgive you."

Both outside and inside of the garden they shared one last smile. The moment was interrupted by the screeching of car tires and voice yelling, "Get him!"

September 9, 1967 – 7:26 p.m.

They had been waiting for him. Mad Guy had instructed his followers to establish 24-hour surveillance of the DeAngelis home. Once Gio had emerged from his self-imposed isolation, a messenger had been sent to the boss telling him that their prey was on the move. Guy had arrived on the scene with his new favorite henchmen, Crespo and Timpani, and waited for Gio to emerge from the overgrown garden. Wishing to limit witnesses, he sent away everyone except his two favorites. Quickly subdued, Gio now found that Mad Guy held a knife to his throat.

"Go see if anyone else was in there with him," ordered the boss, nodding at Sammy Crespo.

"Holy shit, I would never have known there was an entrance here if I didn't see him come out with my own two eyes," offered the amazed Crespo.

"Well, take your own two eyes and your own two balls and check the place."

Crespo crawled through the hidden fence opening and searched for clues as to what Gio had been doing in there. Hearing the conversation and knowing that if he were caught, it would not go well for him, Johnny slid into the darker recesses of the undergrowth. He heard Crespo's footsteps grow closer. Now safely tucked away in a secluded location, Johnny realized that he had left the guitar in the open. If the searcher found it, he would know exactly where Gio had been. It was then that he heard Mad Guy bellow, "Get your ass in there." Such was the volume of the order that Johnny used the noise to pull Gio's guitar into the hiding place with him. His breathing grew heavy. His perspiration became so intense he feared his overpowering body odor would lead even the idiot Sammy Crespo to his hiding place. *Give him something else to find. He'll use any excuse to get out of here and appease his overbearing boss. But what?*

He heard the outside voice of the inquisitor and knew that Gio would need to explain why he had stopped in the garden. "Why did you make this little pit stop here? Meeting your friend, Johnny Cipp?" Johnny's mind raced. Why else would Gio be in here? Why would anyone be in here? It was too late and dark to track down a home run ball from a stickball game, so what other reason would drive someone in here. *Of course,* thought Johnny, and looked around for the item he needed to perpetrate a ruse. Once he found it, he pushed the paper bag filled with a used glue tube into the opening where only moments before Johnny and Gio had sat talking. He puffed out the bag by blowing into it and laid it upright thus giving the impression of recent use. Old bags were usually crushed and discarded by huffers, but when Johnny had finished working on his prop, its presentation was perfect.

"Look what I found. Our little faggot was doing some glue to boost his nerves," spoke Crespo as he emerged from the garden holding the proof. Noticing the telltale bag and the fact that Guy momentarily looked over at his henchman, Gio poked his two index fingers into his eyes. Though painful, his actions did produce the glassy, bloodshot appearance. The deception was successful as Guy, Crespo, and Timpani now looked at their "high" victim and understood why he had left the safety of his home and ventured out to his unfortunate fate. Johnny would be safe for now.

21

Journal of Johnny Cipp

Entry #78

I CAN'T EXPLAIN WHAT'S GOING ON in my mind. I couldn't write any more for a while. This time I fought the urge to fall back on the crutch of drugs or alcohol. I will make it. I owe it to them. But I can't write the words.

Entry #79

Ten days later, here we go again. I've made it this far by telling the story like I wasn't there. But I was. I've started every entry into this journal with a song title I thought meant something. But I can't do that here. The Music Doctor wants to accompany me on this final leg of my journey. I think I need to do it alone. There will be no song titles. What would I write? "Another One Bites the Dust." Oh, it would've fit perfectly with the theme of what I was about to write. But, oh, how it would have trivialized the lives of Bracko, Jimmy Mac, and then the Tinman. Is that what I have become in the ensuing years?

I think of those days after the deaths of my three friends. I am back there. I'm feeling the pain all over. Right now, I find myself desperately wanting to walk down the short flight of stairs to the ground floor . . . just a few more blocks and I can wipe all these tremors away in the sweet companionship of my friend Johnny Walker. But even the act of writing that sentence has woken me up to the reality.

Yeah, I owe the guys more than tacky song titles for this part of my journal. They are all gone now, and that is my fault. I'm the only one left to tell the story, and they are the heroes of that story. As I have said before, we weren't born free but rather yearned to be free. If there is freedom in death, they have made it. I'm still chained to a world that I don't have a place in. Will I ever know joy? Probably not, but maybe if I finish this story, I will find peace.

All I know for sure is that by the second week of September of 1967, Gio and I were the only survivors of the band. The official explanation of the series of events that had taken place never tied all of these deaths together. Reports never vaguely resembled anything close to the truth. Indeed, no one ever mentioned the name Those Born Free. It was as if we'd never existed.

I have relived my final night in the Heights a thousand times in my nightmares and my waking hours alike. After two months of silence, Gio and I met in the Garden of Eden. He was leaving. He knew he didn't have long before the vengeance of Mad Guy would turn to him. He begged me to come with him, and I should've said yes right there and then. I shouldn't have let him out of my sight. He made enough good points that I thought about it seriously. I could picture us on the road together starting a new life, a new band.

And then I thought of Maria. I couldn't leave. I loved her and was going to spend the rest of my life with her. And so, I let Gio go out of the yard. Before he left, I told him the secret that I had held inside me since that day. I had told the Driftwood Club, specifically Vinnie the Cat, that we were all legal age. I had gotten them all killed. Gio forgave me. However, he didn't have the power to forgive me for Bracko, Jimmy Mac, and Tinman. In my mind, any chance of forgiveness had ended with their deaths. And more importantly, could I ever forgive myself?

"Do something good. Make us all proud, and we'll forgive you," were Gio's final words to me as he exited the Garden of Eden. His voice was calm and serious. It didn't have his usual sarcastic tone. His face had lost its perpetual smile. It was as if Gio knew that this was goodbye forever. And yet, did I heed his final advice? I guess that this journal is undeniable proof that I did not.

It was only seconds later that I heard the screech of tires and the

unmistakable voice of Mad Guy calling for his capture. Though
only about six or seven feet apart, Gio and I remained separated by
bushes and a chain link fence. This vegetation obscured me from
the vision of Guy and his gang. However, it didn't keep me from
hearing every moment of Gio's last breaths. I was frozen in time
and space with nowhere to go and nothing I could do. Trapped
in the Garden of Eden, I couldn't get help. I sat, and I listened,
hoping against hope that we'd been wrong about what had been
going on. Every word of the conversation remains emblazoned in
my memory. It haunts me with never-ending guilt. I will forever
have blood on my hands.

Though I only could hear what occurred, I knew Gio so well
that I could picture his every movement and facial expression. At
first, he tried to reason with the madman. He explained that he
was leaving town and that he'd already left a note for his parents.
If Guy would just let him go, he would disappear forever, and
that would be punishment enough. It was a long shot that had
no chance of succeeding. How could you reason with a lunatic?
I will never forget the brief but violent exchange that followed.

"So tell me, Gio, who was the fifth asshole in your little group?"

"There was no fifth. Tell me you actually believed that rumor?"

I knew now that Guy hadn't found a stray business card. I knew
that Vinnie the Cat hadn't regained consciousness enough to tell
his boss about me. I knew that no unknown witness had come
forward to confirm the suspicions aroused by the extra instrument. More than that, I knew that his brother Tony hadn't given
away anything about us. Whether because of his limited capacity
or his heartfelt loyalty, I will never know. And still, Mad Guy
pressed Gio.

"C'mon, it had to be that punk Johnny Cipp."

"Who?" answered Gio in feigned confusion. With that, I heard
the unmistakable sound of a fist pounding raw flesh. Gio had just
taken his first blow.

"Gio, that's your first lie. You would've been more believable
if you hadn't pretended you didn't even know him. Why would
you do that if you weren't protecting him?"

"Oh, you mean *that* Johnny Cipp . . . the guy I threw out of my
band over a year ago."

I tried to make out the next sound, and when I couldn't, I was tempted to move closer for a peek. Any movement would have been a mistake. But how could I let Gio take this beating for me? It was Gio who answered that question *for me.*

"You're going to kill me no matter what I say or do. So even if there were someone I was protecting, *I would tell him to hide the best he could . . . no matter what.*"

"Well, yeah, you're going to die," Guy said with an evil laugh. He'd dropped any pretense of letting Gio survive. I heard the noise again. I wondered what was happening. Then Guy spoke and made it clear, "Pull that rope around his neck a bit tighter every time he doesn't answer me."

Goddammit, they were strangling him. They were doing something called a "schoolyard lynching." A rope had been placed around his neck and then through the chain link fence openings. The line was then pulled out from the fence by two helpers. The more the rope was pulled out by them, the tighter the noose pulled on the victim's neck. Guy was the inventor and reigning expert in the use of this crude form of torture. I couldn't take it anymore and tried to work my way out of the bushes to perhaps escape the distant fence.

"What was that? Are you idiots sure you checked everywhere in there?" I heard Guy bellow. I didn't dare move again.

"Oh, the big bad men are afraid of a few squirrels. *Hey, squirrels, maybe you should hide from them so they don't come and get you?*" Gio gasped for breath as he spoke. He was talking to me by talking to them. Meanwhile, I stayed hidden as they continued to take Gio's life away. His voice grew more strained as the rope around his neck grew tighter.

"You know it's not just you. We can take out your loved ones too. We've done it before."

"Someday, someone is going to put all the pieces together and nail you," said Gio as his voice faltered under the tightening rope's pressure.

"Not during your lifetime." Guy laughed as he looked at his watch. "Which by my calculation, has about thirty seconds left in it."

"My parents have the note that I'm running away. Let me go, and I'm gone. It won't be as suspicious as if I turn up dead."

"I had the same idea. Only in my version you die *and* disappear." It sounded as if they had tightened the rope more. I dared to move just close enough to take a peek at the scene. I could make out the dim shadows of Crespo and Timpani who held the rope in place. I could hear Gio struggling to breathe. Each attempt to take in air grew more difficult.

"One more time. Who was the fifth guy?" I then heard Mad Guy say to his two henchmen, "Does he have a girlfriend?" If they found out about Riet, Gio might give way to their questions. Luckily, before Gio could respond, I heard Timpani answer.

"We couldn't find no fucking skank. Maybe he's fucking queer. You a queer boy?"

I didn't hear Gio respond, but again Mad Guy spoke, "What the fuck are you smiling at?" I knew the answer to that question. Drawing his last breaths, Gio knew that Riet was safe. They knew nothing about her. He then started to hum softly. Again, I concentrated to hear. It was a game we often played in better times. One of us would hum a song, and the other would guess what tune it was. I usually won because my humming barely carried a tune to recognize. In this case, his humming was a message, "Tell Laura I Love Her" was the song. He knew no one named Laura. He was making one final request to me – *Tell Riet that he loved her.*

Guy's temper began to boil at Gio's seemingly flippant attitude toward his torture. Thinking they were doing his wishes, Timpani and Crespo pulled on the rope one last time.

"You fuckoffs, I wasn't done grilling him."

I would never hear Gio's voice again. In this last attempt to get info out of him, both Crespo and Timpani had pulled the ropes too tight. Gio was gone.

"Now what?"

"Take his body and dump it in Jamaica Bay."

With Gio's last act of bravery, he hadn't only saved me, but his entire family. Even the madman saw the logic in leaving his family free to tell everyone that their son had run away. Sheer genius.

I lay in the bushes for hours. Gio was dead. They were all dead. I alone remained alive to tell the tale. But who could I tell it to? And it was my name that Guy had tied to the band as the fifth member. He wouldn't rest until he had me. I lay in the Garden of Eden shaking, overcome by an overwhelming sadness. For the first time since I was a little child, I cried . . . I cried for those I had lost.

PART
4

"Eternity Road"

- The Moody Blues

22

Journal of Johnny Cipp

Entry #80

"Hit the Road, Jack"
- Ray Charles

I NEVER TOLD RIET THAT GIO loved her. I never contacted her at all. In the many years following that night, I justified my inaction in many ways. Would I lead them to her? *Fat chance. They wanted me now, not her.* Would it be safe for me to go to *that* part of town? *Yeah, because it was so safe for me in this part of town now.* Would she believe me? *Really?* I justified my inaction by claiming confusion. In later years, it was so much easier to justify my cowardice by merely being in a constant state of drug and alcohol-induced indifference. *That* night there had been no chemical crutch to explain away my actions. I was so damn fucking afraid of Mad Guy!

And so I left. The message was clear . . . wasn't it? Those Born Free, my friends, were all gone. Somehow in the shuffle and the chaos of that night in June, I'd been left out. No one had picked up on the fact that there were five of us, not four. And now there was one. I should have told someone . . . anyone. A hard, cold fact now dawned on me and punctuated my guilt. If I had told the Nassau police that I had witnessed Guy enter the Driftwood that night, perhaps they could have acted. Vinnie was murdered, and I'd been there. If I had said something would my four friends still be alive?

And so, I ran . . . I ran to save my own ass. However, I always questioned whether I didn't tell anyone that I was leaving because I was trying to protect them or because I was too chickenshit to face the ones I loved with my fears and problems. Whatever the reason, I told no one where I was going, or even that I was leaving. Someday I'll figure out who to give this damn book to and who to seek forgiveness from. But those things weren't on my mind at the time. Pure unadulterated fear was all I felt.

In those days, you could still hitch on the highways. In a time before perverts drove thumbing-a-ride out of American culture, I needed to put some distance between the Heights and me. I had no destination in mind besides far away. I took Gio's bag he had left in my safekeeping. We were approximately the same size so all his possessions would become all that I owned in this world. For some reason, I stuffed my beat up old baseball glove into Gio's bag and started for the exit of the Garden. I'd been playing around with the glove and ball at the stickball courts when Gio had arrived. I realize now that all I had taken with me that was mine was that old glove, the clothes on my back, and the wallet in my pocket . . . and a silver ring on my pinkie. I looked at Gio's guitar as it lay in the bushes and made the decision to take that with me too. It more than doubled my load, but I couldn't bear to disregard our musical past. Gio would live on in me every time I strummed the strings of that instrument. I tell this part of the story now as only a vague memory. In reality, I remember being rendered numb and incoherent by a combination of sadness and terror.

I moved with the stealth of a secret agent, at least that is what my memory tells me. It was probably more like a snake slithering through the grass. I needed to walk some distance before I even tried to bum a ride. It would be just my luck to stick out my thumb and have the first passing car belong to a Provenzano lackey. I spent much of that night walking toward safety. When I reached the location where the Sunrise Highway and Belt Parkway merged, I started the long journey that would take me away from the Heights forever.

It's all a blur. I remember my thumb aching from being stuck out so much. I imagined that each passing driver gave me a look of scorn. I could imagine they were thinking things like, "punk kid," "drug addict," and "hippie freak." In reality, I would've accepted those names over the one I had given myself . . . coward.

The first ride took me across Queens into Brooklyn. I then hooked up with someone who took me over the Verrazano Bridge to Staten Island and then onto the Jersey Turnpike. "Don't know much about geography," to quote the Sam Cooke song, but I did know that once on that section of the I-95 corridor, I could end up anywhere on the east coast. The police weren't too cooperative about actually letting people walk on the shoulder of the road there, so I was forced to stay at the Molly Pitcher rest stop and look for a southbound trucker who was sympathetic.

Carolina Charlie, as he called himself, was heading as far as North Carolina. We talked a bit. I don't remember about what. I was an 18-year kid whose two-month hair growth had started to make me almost border on a hippie appearance. He was a middle age trucker who was proud to say of himself that his neck was red, his hair was white, and his collar was blue. I'm sure if I'd stayed on the path that I thought my life was going to take we would have been on opposite sides of the approaching generational conflict that would tear America apart in the late sixties and early seventies. As it was, we were just two travelers passing the time.

I guess somewhere south of Baltimore I started to doze off. The adrenaline had finally stopped flowing as all the emotions of the previous night gave way to profound and deep exhaustion. I stayed up as long as I could out of gratitude to Charlie for the ride. The least I could do was be good company. As I started to fade in and out of consciousness, I remember reverting to my habit of singing to myself in an almost inaudible tone. As usual, I picked a tune that seemed to fit the moment. The Music Doctor was traveling with me.

"What's your name, kid?" Charlie asked. The question woke me from my stupor. I struggled to come up with an answer. Johnny Cipp was gone. I could never use that name again. And then it came to me what I would call myself. I'd been singing it for a while. With a little all-knowing smile, I answered him, "Jack's my name." As in: "Hit the Road, Jack."

At first, I thought that I would eventually go back to be with Maria and my family. However, the long hours on the road allowed me time to think, and I realized that I couldn't go home anytime soon, if ever.

Carolina Charlie ended his run at a large cotton farm. There was lots of labor involved in getting the white stuff to market, and I soon got hired as a laborer in Enfield, North Carolina. I made a stunning dollar an hour for some back-breaking mindless work. I emphasize the word *mindless* because this allowed me to spend every working and waking hour thinking about my past, present, and future. I thought of all the people I'd hurt.

First, there were my parents. I haven't mentioned them very much in this ongoing missive of my life. That isn't an oversight. They were good, no change that, they were great parents. They taught me to love and laugh often and to enjoy whatever I had. They sacrificed so that little Johnny could live a better life than they had. I've done them a disservice by not talking about them more. I have to look deep into my heart to figure out why that is. Why do they not fill the pages of this beat up old book? Perhaps because they were always there for me. Probably they were so steady in their support that I no more noticed them than the walls of my house. Or maybe it is too painful to think about how I repaid that support by running away and never telling them.

Right or wrong, I justified my actions (as usual) with excuses. If I called them, they would know what had happened. It would have given them an understanding of what had transpired, and more importantly, let them know I was alive. I hoped they would assume that like Gio I had run away. What other conclusion could they have drawn from the fact that two best friends had gone missing the very same day? And Gio had left a note!

However, calling them would mean telling the truth, including Gio's death. My parents and Gio's parents wouldn't just sit back and take my exile and his murder lightly. They would notify the police and anyone else who would listen. And how would Mad Guy react to that? No, I couldn't do it. Perhaps in a year or two, I would make that phone call home. Again, I satisfied myself with this solution. I could never have foreseen that I was only months away from slipping into a depression and lifestyle that would destroy the next two decades of my life.

And then there was Maria. Because of her geographic distance from the Heights, she had remained out of the view of anyone who might be looking for me. If I called her, she too would have somehow tried to right the wrongs that had befallen the group and me. Any action would have shined the spotlight upon her existence that up until that point had remained below the radar. If Guy were to know about her wouldn't he use her as some form of hostage to draw me back? I just really believed that if she knew about me, they would know about her.

And so, I made no phone calls. I sent no letters.

Entry #81

"Strange Brew"
- *Cream*

Life in Carolina was surreal to me. I lived in a barracks type situation. For company, I had two friends named Jim-Bob and Bucky. I don't say this in the usual condescending way that Northerners usually make fun of Southern folk. Named after his father James and his grandfather Robert, Jim-Bob could trace his lineage back to the Civil War. Excuse me, down here it was always referred to as the "War of Northern Aggression."

Bucky got his name because almost every male relative in his family was named after the same famous ancestor (you guessed it – a Civil War hero!). Rather than be the fifth Joshua Wilson in the county, he learned early on to answer to Bucky. I liked these two guys though I knew we'd really never have much in common. I also knew that at some point I had to be on the road again. Yet, for about six weeks these were my friends.

It almost felt like I was betraying Gio and the guys by even thinking of friendship while they lay dead. However, I kept telling myself that I had to start my life over. I will never forget the time that I met those two. I believe it was Jim-Bob who caught me by surprise by asking me my name. I should've anticipated the question, but I didn't. I had decided in the truck with Carolina Charlie that I would use Jack. It wasn't a stretch. Jack is a nickname for John anyway. But I hadn't yet considered the fact that I would need a surname.

"Jack Paradiso," I remember responding quickly to the question. It had been my mother's maiden name, and I thought it had a nice ring to it. It was no Johnny Cipp, but it would do.

"You must be one of those *I*-tal-yuns," was the almost synchronized answer of both of my new friends. I immediately realized I had a problem. If — or when — Mad Guy sent someone looking for me, I had just narrowed his search by using a name that gave away my ethnicity. It was already too late to make a change here in North Carolina, but the next time, I would be "Jack Paradise." Not that different, but *paradise* is a word in the *English* language. Later, its hedonistic implications would make it a fitting stage name.

Bucky, Jim-Bob, and I got our notice that the seasonal work was coming to an end. Our last night together we sat around a campfire outside our lodgings. I remember that it was Bucky who produced the moonshine that appeared in our midst. Though I'd finally reached the legal age to drink, I'd yet to have my first try at alcohol. A clear liquid filled a glass bottle that had once been used for cider.

At first, I was hesitant to try it. I knew its taste would be abominable and that even the smell of alcohol brought back memories of the Heights. The first whiff of the homemade concoction reminded me of the abuse of Bracko's father, the death of Joey, and the half-finished drink that was my cover in the Driftwood Club deception. Alcohol was all of those triggers to my emotions. The more these thoughts tore at my insides, the more that I needed an escape. That escape became obvious when Bucky again forwarded the moonshine.

"That there is white lightning," said Bucky. "It's the most powerful stuff known to man. My cousin Josh puts it through the still six times to get out the impurities."

"And by impurities, he means anything that isn't pure alcohol," added Jim-Bob with a chuckle as he again passed the liquid to me.

I took it . . . and I've never stopped taking it. I'd found my way out. I *would* never go home again. I *could* never go home again. My life would become lost in the sweet release of being high. I believed that I had found a way to forget my parents . . . and Those Born Free . . . and Riet . . . and Maria. When I was high, all those thoughts disappeared, at least temporarily. They always seemed to return with a vengeance as my system suffered the hangover pains of a steady stream of morning afters. The bad memories would return until I drove them away again in a never-ending string of lost days and nights.

My hell had begun.

23

Journal of Johnny Cipp

Entry #82

"The End of the Line"
-The Traveling Wilburys

AFTER LEAVING ENFIELD, NORTH CAROLINA, I didn't stop running until I was as far away as I could go ... Key West, Florida. Because this is the southernmost point in the country, continuing any further south at this point would involve getting wet. It seemed a logical place to stop running.

It's a place where the laws treat chickens much like the sacred cows of India. It's a place where eyebrow windows are left open so that the passage of the wind through them will help to ensure survival from the all too frequent hurricanes. It has been the home of pirates, lunatics, and gambling entrepreneurs. Ernest Hemingway once lived here, and he might have been a bit of all three.

When I arrived, Key West wasn't the isolated little fishing village and drinking town that had been made famous by Hemingway. However, it hadn't yet become the tourist trap of today. If you found anyone awake during the day, there was a good chance that person was going to smell like fish. He was going to catch a fish, transport a fish, gut a fish, sell a fish, cook a fish, serve a fish, or at the very least, eat a fish. However, considering all that, fishing was still only a daytime activity.

At night, the action moved inland to Duval Street and the side streets adjacent to it. With the beautiful weather and abundance of fishing and drinking opportunities, many people who visited never left. They dropped out of their prior lives once they had become entranced by its lifestyle and climate. The primary activity of many remained the *Duval Crawl*. This tradition required its participants to accomplish the incredible feat of hitting every bar along the main thoroughfare and still be conscious enough *not* to fall off the pier at Mallory Square. Many residents weren't even that energetic. They simply settled in at Sloppy Joe's or Captain Tony's. These diehards never moved a muscle besides their drink-hoisting elbow. In a town that boasted an *8 a.m.* happy hour, locating yourself on a particular bar stool was often considered a full-time job.

Years of living this idyllic lifestyle often exacted a price. Fishing all day and drinking all night didn't provide much of a future to those who believed they had found paradise. This kind of life took its toll on the minds and bodies of the many vagrants who spent their lives living from day to day or drink to drink. They could be found sleeping outside the bars or behind dumpsters. Those who could get up in the morning and function were often referred to as being *Key-wasted*. It was a club in which I'd soon claim proud membership.

———◆———

At first, I settled into a little one-room apartment and paid for it with the only skill I had, playing the guitar and singing. I hadn't mysteriously gained any great talent by merely changing latitudes. But it was Key West, and this meant there were more bars than there were passable singers who could accompany themselves on a guitar. Besides, the customers were mostly too drunk to notice how off key I was. Paranoia was a factor, and I was glad I had already started to use my new Jack Paradise moniker. It was a fitting stage name.

Time passed, and to my surprise, no one came to kill me. Had they ever found out about me? Or couldn't they find me? I didn't dare contact anyone. Not my parents. Not Maria. Nor Riet. I always thought about it, but my answer was always much like Scarlett O'Hara in *Gone with the Wind*, "Tomorrow's another day." But those tomorrows turned into weeks, and the weeks into months and then years. I can't say I loved my life, but I was alive. It ate at me what had happened to my friends. It tore at my heart how I had left everyone without a word. I spent endless nights wondering what happened to DJ Spinelli, Brother Christian, and even Tony – all the people I had left behind. But most of all I thought about how I had abandoned Maria to live her life in doubt.

Gradually, I did more than play in the bars. I spent many a night doing the *Duval Crawl* to wipe away the memories and the guilt. I had come to admire the stories about Ernest Hemingway and his drinking exploits during his time down here. Already reasonably well off from his writing career, he bought a house next to the Key West Lighthouse, which interestingly is in the heart of town. His strategy was sound. Every night when he staggered drunk out of Sloppy Joe's in the wee hours, he could always find his way. Just look up in the sky, locate the lighthouse, and follow it to home sweet home. I didn't have the money to follow his lead, and therefore many nights ended for me in some back alley, knee deep in my own piss and puke. Somewhere in this fog of existence, my nineteenth birthday passed by and so did my twentieth. In fact, I know that most of my twenties went by, but I don't remember them.

———◆———

Long ago sailors coming into port in Key West thought that manatees were mythical mermaids. By 1982, I had been in Key West for fifteen years, and the massive influx of drugs made sailors and everyone else hallucinate on a more grandiose scale. It seemed only natural that the Overseas Highway to the American mainland would become a major entry point for drugs to be transported into the United States. This became such a serious problem that the United States Border Patrol blockaded Route 1, the only road into Key West. In response, the town declared its independence from America and established the Conch Republic. By then, I was so far gone on drugs that I took this issue seriously. I was right there as a founding father of the Conch Republic. If they were going to take away my freedom of drugs, just call me John Cippy Adams. Though the government in Washington never took this threat to its sovereignty seriously, the blockade was lifted, and the drugs continued to flow liberally along the highway.

To supplement my meager income and pay for those drugs, I started to pick up some scattered work on the local fishing boats. Nothing much. Help the charter fishermen do their lines and ice their fish. Get a beer for them (and myself) when they asked. No skill involved. I thought I was having fun at the time. I was fishing my days away and singing, drinking, and drugging my nights away. There was music and way too many forgettable groupies. There were sunsets on Mallory Square and quite a few beers at Sloppy Joe's. But in the end, I remembered less and less of it the next day. I was slowly doing to myself what Mad Guy had not been able to.

Entry #83

"Captain Jack"
- *Billy Joel*

It's getting hard to write about these events. This isn't because of the sadness or the embarrassment of how low I'd fallen. My memories and emotions were insulated from my real world by layers of dead brain cells. Now there was no more sadness, no embarrassment, no feelings at all. No, the real reason that I can't write descriptively of these days (years) is that I just don't remember much of what happened. The blackouts and lost moments far outstrip any fragments of lucid thought. What little I do remember comes back to me in disconnected segments of insanity. I know I didn't stop at alcohol. I remember this well because I carried a name to prove it. At some point, I started to take into my body all kinds of chemicals that could be snorted or taken in convenient pill form. I'm trying hard, but I just can't remember.

One night I went outside to get something a little stronger than the Jack Daniels that the bartender had given me. I scored something from a stranger. I couldn't figure out why he was so generous to me. As we got high, or should I say higher, he looked at me and started laughing. When I asked him what was so funny, he told me he already knew me. I'd been on the boat he'd been fishing on all afternoon and had served him the beers that acted as his appetizers for the evening's main course. Then he had been in the audience for my performance. I still didn't get the joke.

"Captain Jack," he said and started to laugh so hard I thought that he was going to choke."It works on so many levels." When he started singing the song, I finally got it. The Music Doctor had found a Billy Joel song that fit into my lifestyle. His quintessential song about getting high had been called "Captain Jack" and featured lines like, "Captain Jack will get you high tonight." From that day on, I performed under the name of Captain Jack Paradise, a great stage name with a lousy lifestyle to back it up. It did sound like I was a pirate. In reality, I was a strung out, dying alcoholic and addict who had long since passed the level of being "Key-wasted." What was my drug of choice that night? Hmm, I'll have to work on that . . .

Entry #84

"Cocaine"
- *Eric Clapton/JJ Cale*

I remembered what I used that night. Enough said.

Entry #85

"Eight Miles High"
- *The Byrds*

It seemed like always. Is this what passes for descriptive journal writing about that period of my life?

Entry #86

"One Bourbon, One Scotch, One Beer"
- *George Thorogood*

And that was a slow night for me! The Music Doctor is on a roll.

Entry #87

"Fear the Reaper"
-Blue Oyster Cult

If I'd been braver and this song had been released earlier in my downward spiral, it would've been my anthem. It would've been my guide to what to do with my life. If I could've gotten up the nerve, I would've ended it all. I knew I couldn't go on like that forever. It had already gone on way too long. What had my life become? I owned a used guitar. My wallet contained a fake driver's license, about twenty bucks, and pictures of a girl I'd loved but not seen in two decades. My jewelry consisted of a silver ring on my pinky. The fact that I hadn't lost or hocked it was bordering on the miraculous. Somewhere in my duffel bag of possessions was an old baseball glove. And I had my name, Captain Jack Paradise.

Thrown out of my apartment months before for failing to pay the rent, I now lived full time on a boat. The boss allowed me to sleep on the deck because this gave him a cheap form of security. He even put up with the fact that I occasionally (ok, more than occasionally) heaved up the previous night's intake all over the deck. He accepted this on the condition that I cleaned it up before the paying customers arrived. Yeah, I was truly earning my title of "captain."

Though Paradise had started as a play on my family history; it soon came to stand for the "paradise" I had found. The audiences loved the name during their brief visits to this vacation escape. It *was* a paradise for them for a day, a week, or a month. To me, it had become a prison.

The name Jack now seemed like an anchor around my neck. I'd adopted it because it was the first thing that had come to my mind decades before when Carolina Charlie put me on the spot. After all this time, it now only served to remind me that I had hit the road instead of facing my problems. If I'd continued to follow the path I'd chosen, I would've died. Maybe, I should've died. That was my realization. And when I said this to myself, I knew that one way or another, the end was near.

Entry #88

"Here Comes the Sun"
- *The Beatles*

It was a Sunday morning when I started to turn my life around. To be more exact, it was Easter Sunday morning in 1989. The only reason I recall this exact date was that the tourists in town for the holiday weekend were particularly generous with their drink buying. I know that I was far-gone, even for me. At the end of the previous evening's performance, I remembered leaving my guitar and most of my other possessions at the bar and going out into the street (in theory) to get fresh air. In fact, I was looking for a hookup to score some cocaine or pills. I wasn't particular. I remember little else of that night. I endlessly rambled on Duval Street with no specific destination or goal. This was what my whole life had become, no destination, no goal.

I eventually found myself hanging on the big buoy at the easternmost tip of the main drag. The sign in front of that landmark reads "Southernmost Point in the USA." This only reminded me I was a long way from home. There was, and still is, a sign next to the buoy that reads "Cuba, 90 miles." I know I was out of it because as I read this sign and looked at the arrow pointing out into the water, I started to slip off my shoes. A voice in my head (or one of the many mind-altering additives floating there) said, "Go ahead, and swim for it." Why this thought came to me, I've no idea. I had no desire to be a communist, I didn't speak a word of Spanish, and I wasn't even a decent swimmer.

The next morning found me sprawled on the beach outside of Fort Zachary Taylor. Often, when I was mentally lost, I found my way to this beach. I awakened that morning to find sand in my eyes, my nose, my mouth, and a few other locations that I'd rather not mention.

As I looked into the rising sun, I noticed a figure coming toward me. At first, he was only silhouetted against the rising eastern sun. It wasn't long before I decided God was finally coming to get me. At least, that was what I thought at the time. As I remained immobile in the sand, his flowing robes and sandaled feet were the first details I could make out as I strained my eyes at this Easter morning vision. When he grew closer, I gasped as I focused on his face with its flowing brown beard and long hair. It was a picture right out of my second-grade Baltimore Catechism. It was Easter Sunday, and God was walking toward me. I was finally being made to account for my many transgressions. Boy, had I screwed up my life. Was this real or the product of permanent brain damage? Soon he (He?) was standing over me and looking down.

"Somebody had a rough night," spoke the vision to me.

"Oh, my God," was my panicked reply. I wasn't ready to be taken yet. *Somebody help. Please . . .*

"No, just one of his employees," he responded and just laughed. He could see the look of bewilderment, and soon explained he was there to do Easter Sunday mass on the beach. I had heard of Padre as most locals called him, but I had never met him. He wasn't your usual priest. His outward appearance was known to most around Key West, and if I had pressed my brain, I would've remembered what I'd been told about him. This probably would have kept me from imagining that God had come to take me away as a part of his "Clean Up the Sinners on Easter Program."

He was an institution. He fed the poor, helped teenagers in need of guidance, and, yes, ministered to the alcoholics of the area. So that was it. Someone had called about a drunk on the beach. He could've had a full-time job taking care of just that one problem in Key West. That was it. He was here to save me. I waited for his sermon, knowing I wasn't in the mood to hear whatever he was going to say.

However, he delivered no words of wisdom. He said nothing. He went into a beat up old brown leather bag, took out a glass bottle of orange juice and handed it to me. Next from his bag of tricks came a shirt and shorts, his civilian clothes. He laid them next to me. It soon became evident why he had given me his extra clothes. Apparently, my desire to swim to Cuba must have happened at some other beach because my clothes weren't on this one! I was totally naked. He smiled and continued down the beach. While still in my line of sight, he was joined by many others who were there for the sunrise mass on the beach. He hadn't judged me or put me down. He didn't need to. Through his eyes, I could see what I had become.

I thought at first I could do it on my own. Sometimes my attempts at being clean lasted a few days. However, it soon became evident I needed help to get the courage to do so, I stopped at Sloppy Joe's. A bit ridiculous. I stopped for a drink to get the nerve to get sober! I dragged myself out of the bar that night wallowing in failure. I turned up Truman Street and headed away from Duval. It wasn't long before I found myself in front of St. Mary's. I passed out.

It was about 6 a.m. when I woke up under a bush that landscaped the church's exterior. A few chickens nibbled at the ground around me. Chickens do that in Key West. While I sat there with my head throbbing in pain from a hangover, the door to the church opened. Out came Padre with a glass of orange juice in his hand. OK, here is where I get a lecture, right? No, he merely gave me the juice and turned to go back inside.

"Well?" I yelled out.

"Well, what?" he replied.

"Well, aren't you going to say anything?"

He kept walking through the doorway and said almost as an afterthought, "You certainly are a slow learner," and promptly closed the door behind him. What did he mean? Was I slow to recognize that he wouldn't say anything judgmental? Was I slow to learn I needed help? Or that others could give me that help?

I realize now he'd read me perfectly. I judged myself harsher than he ever could. Given time, I would either use that feeling to ask for help or to destroy myself. If I were going to destroy myself, any comment by him would only hasten the process. If I were going to straighten myself out, he would have plenty to say when I requested it. Time had come that day to make a decision. I rose and knocked on the church door.

I began to meet regularly with Padre and was ready for my first AA meeting later that summer. I won't go into all the progress I made in the twelve-step program, or how I dealt with it. The journal that you are reading is *Step 8*. That is the step where you make a list of the wrongs you have committed and all those you have hurt. I understand that I ran away because of the fear, and I compounded my problems with substance abuse to hide my guilt. Admitting these facts doesn't ease the feelings that I hold inside me. I know now, twenty years too late, that there were other paths I could have taken. And so, here I am at *Step 8,* hoping to move on.

Life isn't easy. It is now February 1990, and I have been working on this journal since last August. My primary source of income brings me to bars every night, and I have slipped more than once. I keep saying to myself I have to do it; I have to get better, "for the guys." Gio's final words to me haunt me. I have to accomplish something in life to make my survival mean something. Padre and my sponsor Cal keep telling me I need to do it *for myself.* The debate remains open.

Entry #89

"Sitting by a Window"
-Moby Grape

I have found that this book is the only way I can deal with all the ghosts that haunt me every day and night. And so, I laid my life bare in its pages, willingly allowing my failure to be apparent. At first, I couldn't see the purpose. Then the act of writing became the ultimate test of my memory. It later evolved into the painful and compulsive task of getting facts (and yes, feelings) down on paper before the long-term effects of my self-destructive existence made that task impossible. I have reached *Step 8* in my *12-Step Program.* I understand what I have done wrong and to whom. However, *Step 9* requires I contact those people and make amends. Can I do that?

———◆———

Today I made a phone call. It's a call I should have made years ago. I had to know what state my parents were in before I spoke to them directly. I called my Aunt Terry, my mother's sister. I pretended to be an insurance agent who needed to talk to them about a claim. I lied and told her the number I had listed for them was probably a wrong number.

"You sure got something wrong," she said to me.

"I don't understand," I answered in a voice that didn't need to be disguised. I was now forty years old. I wasn't the 17-year old who had sat next to her at Easter dinner in 1967. I loved her, especially that day. She had kept me supplied with cannoli and pizzelle and told me that Maria was a keeper.

"My sister is dead," she said with a deep sadness in her voice. "They said it was her heart and I agree. Only they talked about valves and arteries. Me, I thought of it as a broken heart. First, Johnny, then her husband. So, no, you won't be able to contact them unless you have a direct line to heaven."

I didn't answer. I couldn't answer. My throat closed with suffocation caused by deep emotion.

"Hello . . . you there?" my aunt questioned when I couldn't respond. "It was a long time ago, but I think about her every day."

"My records don't mention a 'Johnny.' Who was that?" I had summoned some inner strength to ask. I had to know what she thought had happened to me.

"Johnny was their son, but he disappeared in the fall of 1967. Anna believed he'd run away and would come back someday. She spent hours sitting by the window waiting. When her husband developed cancer, she dedicated her life to making him comfortable. Yet, she still used her free time to sit by that window."

"Did he ever come back?" I asked knowing full well that the bastard never did.

"Me, I think he's dead and has been dead all along. I knew Johnny, and he was a sweetheart. He could never have been alive and not told his parents. Well, it doesn't matter now."

"Thanks," I said unconsciously to her kind words about me. "Thanks, for the information," I added to cover my feelings. No, Johnny wasn't dead, but he certainly wasn't the sweetheart she thought he was. I was a selfish prick who had left my mother watching and waiting for me to return.

Entry #90

"I Love You More Than You'll Ever Know"
- *Blood, Sweat, and Tears*

I'm sitting in my room, and the Music Doctor is haunting me with tunes of love. As I twirl the silver band on my pinkie, I settle on the title I wrote above. I do love her more than she'll ever know. Of course, she'll never know because I screwed up.

I was trying to get up the courage to send this ring back to her. She had told me to give her the little silver band when I had *finished my journey*. Could this be any more ironic? I am fifteen hundred miles and twenty-three years removed from our love and *now* my journey is over. *Step 9* required that I make amends. I thought I would try to find her and send the ring. I listened to old tapes, and each song spoke to me in fantasies of love.

I imagined she'd get the ring and track me down and pledge her undying love for me from a distance. I would then drive to her along the crystal blue seas of the Keys. I don't have a convertible, but I do in my fantasy. The wind is blowing in my hair and The Moody Blues' "I Know You're Out There Somewhere," is playing on the radio. We will live happily ever after. It is the ending that Hollywood would want. But it's not real. Yesterday, I found out the truth.

It had all started last year during the peak of snowbird season. I was playing at Reilly's three times a week. During one of my breaks, this guy offered to buy me drinks, and I willingly accepted. In the course of our conversation, he claimed to be a skilled private investigator. He told me he could find information about anyone. As we continued to talk, the germ of an idea took hold in my mind. First, I played the cynic to the man's ramblings. This caused the man to embellish further on his tales of greatness in the field of "information assessment." Eventually, I offered my drunken companion a challenge whose results could be verified.

"If you can find anyone, let's see you find her!" I then handed the braggart a simple cocktail napkin with drunken scribbling covering much of its surface. I wrote, *Maria Romano, born 1949 in Queens, NY, lived in Cambria Heights from 1949 to 1966 and graduated Dominican Commercial HS 1967.*

"Go ahead, genius. Do your magic." The snowbird tucked the napkin away in his pants, and I assumed it would find its way to the nearest trash receptacle. Of all the goddamn irony, the man returned yesterday. He now found me as a sober human being who remembered very little of our previous meeting. When he approached me with a broad smile and an opening comment about being owed a drink, I was at a loss.

"Johnny Black on the rocks and make it a double. It's the least you can do for all my work." I just looked at him dumbfounded and continued to do so even while the stranger handed me a slim manila envelope. "Last year, you doubted me. Well, stick this where the sun don't shine and pay the bartender please." I was still in a state of confusion as I carelessly ripped open the envelope and slipped out a single sheet of paper. At first, I said nothing as I read the hand-typed sheet. I soon found my fingers caressing the printed page.

Subject: Maria Carlson (nee Romano)
Education: Graduated Queens College 1977
Occupation: English Teacher - New Hyde Park High School
Marital Status: Married Jason Carlson 1980
Family: son - William Carlson (aged 7), daughter - Samantha
Carlson (age 5)
Current Location: 1 Chestnut Street, Floral Park, New York

"You made it, girl. You made it. Good for you," I mumbled to myself as I turned away from the stranger. As I folded the paper carefully and tucked it into the front right pocket of my jeans, I suddenly wished I had not recently given up drinking. *I Love You More Than You'll Ever Know.*

Entry #91 – Feb 14, 1990

"Dancing on the Other Side of the Wind"
We listened to our hearts,
Never thinking we had sinned.
We went down together,
Throwing caution to the wind.
- *Chris Delaney and the Brotherhood Blues Band*

It is Valentine's Day 1990. Young lovers (and old lovers for that matter) are celebrating in front of me. They are holding each other tightly just as I did when Maria and I had our last dance to a Johnny Rivers' song. There have been no valentines for me since 1967. It was one of the many nights that I tried to give Maria the ring that has caressed my pinkie ever since. Could either of us have imagined my journey would end here Key-wasted and alone?

Still, I'm paid to play here at Reilly's, and so I picked up my guitar and ran through my sets of songs as if on automatic pilot. I am thinking of my parents, and Maria, and even Riet. As always, I have been offered drinks by the bartender and my fans. I turned them down, but it wasn't that easy.

I often thought of playing "Catch the Wind" in one of my sets, but its memory and feeling hurt too much to get the words out no matter how many times I tried. Therefore, I substituted a Kansas song from the 1970's entitled "Dust in the Wind." I had convinced myself that the finger-picking required of this song would be therapy for my arthritis damaged hand.

Sobriety has returned, and so has my power to think. "Dust in the Wind?" "Catch the Wind?" I even recently worked Chris Delaney's "Dancing on the Other Side of the Wind" into my song list. How come I didn't realize these symbolic songs followed a theme? Where the hell was the Music Doctor hiding while I was making these choices? Couldn't he have given me a heads up about the "wind" theme that was so prevalent in my mind? The wind? It now occurs to me what I've been thinking . . . what I've been feeling.

My friends had died sudden and violent deaths. That had only been the end of their physical existence. The *memory* of them had suffered a different fate. Almost every person who had known them had gradually been eliminated from this world, except me. And what had I done? I had let their memory drift away. Much like a gentle breeze blows away the petals of a flower and robs it of its beauty, I had let them drift away. Later, I had tried to push them away by destroying myself. But they wouldn't leave me as I'd tried to leave them. They stayed around, waiting for me to remember them. Waiting for me to catch their spirit as it lay in the wind.

With this journal, they returned, ever in my conscious and unconscious mind. They are always around now as much as the air that I breathe every moment of my life. Now they will never leave.

As I sing, "Dust in the Wind," I wonder if the crowd will notice I have changed one word in my presentation. It's a simple but meaningful change. Just one pronoun. Instead of "we" I sing the words "all *they* are is dust in the wind."

When I completed my last set of songs, I took a walk down to Zachary Taylor Beach . . . me, my guitar . . . and this book. As I sit here, I contemplate hurling this worn black book into the crashing surf. Perhaps, I should follow my journal into the waves. What do I have left? I can't make amends. Mom and Dad are gone. I don't know whatever happened to Riet. In fact, I don't even know her full name. And Maria . . . dear Maria . . . gone from my dreams forever. Contacting her would not help either one of us.

Ironically the book is opened to my entry about Gio's last night. Even my own writing is taunting me, a reminder of what I had done to my friends. I can never get their forgiveness. I can never make things right . . .

A gentle wind blows across my face.

I rise from the sand and take a few steps into the chilly waters of the Zachary Taylor Beach. I can almost see their faces in the moonlit clouds. I can hear their voices in the wind. They are waiting for me. I hear them calling my name.

The coolness of the saltwater tickles my toes.

I can hear Gio and Jimmy Mac singing in harmony. My drummer is still wearing that eternal grin that so enthralled the ladies, and Gio gives me thumbs up and starts laughing.

The water now surrounds my calves and splashes on my knees.

I won't throw the book out into the waves. Instead, I will send it back to the waiting sand. Perhaps someone will find it?

My thighs feel the tingle of the salt water as I start to approach the crashing waves.

And Tinman is wailing on the organ. He looks up and takes time to wink at me. He is playing our music and loving it. He puts his head down to concentrate on a solo part. Next to him is Bracko and he too is smiling. No! He is laughing with wild abandon as I had never seen him do before. There are no bruises on him. He nods at me and returns to bending the strings of his Strat. I can hear them. "Johnny, Johnny!"

The water now straddles my waist and starts to caress my shoulders.

They beckon me. The band needs a bass player to give them a backbeat . . . and a friend to share their joy. I will join them, and again we will be complete. We will make music . . . and we will laugh . . . and the band will again be together . . . in the wind . . . forever.

Epilogue

"Strangers When We Meet"
-*The Smithereens*

Three months later
June 7, 1990

THEY SHOULD HAVE KNOWN EACH other. They had grown from infancy to late adolescence only a casual five-minute walk apart. In a perfect world, they might even have developed a long abiding friendship. The links between them might have carried them through adulthood into the golden years of their lives. Yet, in the real world, twenty-three years had passed, and they were still strangers. That world had conspired to prevent even their slightest acquaintance with each other.

When the visitor knocked on the door of the pre-war clapboard home, only confusion emanated from the face of the home's owner. Moments before opening the door, the resident had been in the midst of a great moment of happiness. Recent events had meant that many years of hardship would soon be ending and a brighter future was assured. Not wanting anything to interfere with this change of fortune, there was trepidation to entertain any visitor, especially one whose face exhibited a mournful look and recently dried tears.

Silently, the visitor extended a right arm. Both sets of eyes followed the path of an extremely worn black composition note-book as it changed possession from one to the other. Some of the white portions of the amoebic design on the hardcover had been filled in with black ink as the author had doodled in his free time. There were also signs of water damage from some unknown event in the book's history. Other than that, the only writing on the outer section of the book was its simple title, "Journal of Johnny Cipp."

Recognition of these words brought on heart palpitations that only a moment before had seemed impossible. Both strangers knew the name. However, he was of another time and another life. He had disappeared over two decades ago.

"You'll want to . . . no. . . you *need* to read this journal," said Maria as she handed the book to Riet.

Author's Note – In My Real World

"Just A Song Before I Go"
- Crosby, Stills, and Nash

IN EARLY JUNE 1967, FIVE young musicians auditioned for a steady paying job that would have financially and professionally raised their lives to a new level. The house band position at the Driftwood Club in Elmont, New York would have freed them from financial worries for their foreseeable futures. Their competition, older and more polished in their presentation, lacked the creativity and musicianship of their younger counterparts. Faced with the embarrassing loss of the position to these young upstarts, they resorted to their only remaining option. They called the police to report the underage presence of this band in the club.

Because of a kindly bartender and the loyalty of a friend, I was the one never booked that night. It was my bass guitar that lay there unattended. It would be five years before I would ever see any members of the band again. Through either cowardice or instinct, I laid low for five days after the incident. And then on the following Saturday night, I assumed the outward cloak of a normal existence.

While walking in a park on a date, I observed in the dark far reaches of my vision a sight that seemed surreal. Under a dim fading light, I could make out that a group of teens had attacked and thrown another teen to the ground. After a few moments of securing the safety of my date, I hurled myself into the situation. I realize now that it was probably a very foolish action to take, as I am not usually the hero type. The ensuing decades have helped me understand why I acted as uncharacteristically insane as I did. The guilt and depression of not sharing in the fall of my friends and band mates had filled me with a great deal of anger and self-loathing. I needed to do something to justify my singular survival of the incident. And so, I chose to run head long into a life-threatening situation.

Due in large part to the damage suffered to my head, the events that followed remain a blur in my memory. I know that I did confront the gang and I did somehow stop the beating that I soon realized was at the hands of drug-fueled fists. From the glazed expression on their faces, the assailants probably have as little memory as I do of that night. If they are still alive, the difference between us is that my brain cells were not encased in drugs and alcohol but rather almost distributed among the blades of grass in Brookville Park, Rosedale, New York. I do know that I dragged the stranger to safety before myself passing out from the injuries sustained in my ill-advised rescue.

My next memories were of being able to walk down the aisle at my high school graduation three weeks afterward. I wasn't pretty, and many of the signees of my high school yearbook referred to my new look. By the time I knowingly walked the streets of Cambria Heights almost five weeks had passed. My calls to my friends' houses were met with dead silence from their parents. Not knowing if they were protecting their sons or me, I decided to let a short period pass before I pursued the issue any further. That short time period became an extended time period.

In his song "American Pie," Don McLean sang of "the day the music died." For those who don't remember the song or never picked up the nuance of its meaning, that day was real to the singer-songwriter. It was the day that Buddy Holly, who many consider one of the first and best rock and rollers, died in a tragic plane crash. I was too young to remember that event. To me, the music died on a night in June 1967. After spending three years bringing the band together from all different parts of my life, my heart was torn out by the events of that evening. I had neither the will nor the ability to go on with music. Therefore, my life took another direction.

I never saw or heard from any of the band members for five years. I went on with my life, but I continued to be perplexed by the lack of any knowledge of what the hell had happened. And then in 1972, an ironic turn of events led me to run into one of them. The character Gio was actually an intertwining three of my childhood friends with a strong emphasis on one of them. Artie had been the one to claim the two instruments that night thus saving me any chance of being caught in the web of their problems. We talked long into the evening, but every time the subject of the Driftwood came up there was an evasive attitude that permeated the conversation.

He moved to Florida only days later, and it would be nine years before we again reconnected. I had gone on to live my life as a teacher and not thought much about it. When I saw him again in Fort Lauderdale, I was on a family vacation with my wife and two children. (Sorry, Brittany you hadn't been born yet.). We talked about many things but not that night. We did take out the guitars and played and sang our old playlist. OK, reality check, we both played, but only he sang. My voice is even worse than I wrote about in the story. For the next seventeen years, we continued to write letters to each other about once a year and see each other every time I went to see my grandparents who at the time lived very close to Artie's location.

By the mid 1990s email came along and the contact was more often and informal. And then on November 3, 1998, more than three decades later, he told me what happened. "I will never forget my father had me so scared the Mafia was going to rub me out for having the bar closed down. I had to testify before the New York State Liquor Authority, and the bar *was* closed down."

Neither one of us knows what happened to the other three. They truly are in the wind. I would like to complete the tale with an accounting of what really happened to the drummer, lead guitar, and keyboardist of the group that had once been Those Born Free, but I simply do not know! Artie and I live 1200 miles apart but remain close and dear friends. When we meet once or twice a year, we rehash the good times and skim very loosely over the bad. In the end, the more than three decades of searching have produced absolutely no leads to the others. I do not think in my wildest dreams that any events vaguely resembling those depicted in this story befell them. However, the fact that I did not know what happened led my imagination to run wild for those thirty years that followed the event. And that is what resulted in this book.

Many of the chapters leading up to that night in June are based on real events. I exaggerated some events and twisted and molded many of the characters (especially the villains) to make the story flow. All of the band members are composites of three or four different people (some musicians and some not). Not all of these distortions are on purpose. While writing my story, my vision is influenced by seeing events through the eyes of child, but with the memory of an old man.

All of the chapters occurring *after* that night in 1967 happened only in my mind. The reality is that after that night and my subsequent hospital stay, I followed Johnny's promise to go Queens College with Maria if events did not work out as planned with the band. Yes, there actually is a Maria (real name: Marilyn Daniele). Some of the events dealing with her in this story occurred as written (even the Pretty Flamingos). She was even the one there in the park that night and had indeed called the ambulance. We now have been married over forty-five years and have children and grandchildren. She has been there for the entire story from the time I was fourteen years old. In the real world, there is a happy ending to my tale.

However, as if fate was telling me that my story would never truly be over, two final ironic events occurred as I was putting the finishing touches on this book. Through the wonders of the internet, I have been in contact for decades with the friend on whom I strongly based the character of DJ Spinelli. I had already decided that my ten-year ordeal of writing this book was merely for self-gratification and that I was going to place the finished product in the same imaginary drawer where Johnny placed his journal. However, when Jimmy (that is James J. Spina to the rest of the world) became aware of my secret writing, he encouraged me to send him a copy. Now a writer and editor, he became the first person to read this book. Full circle . . . from the back of physics class at Archbishop Molloy in the 1960's, he had now become my supporter and muse. What a long, strange trip it has been. You would not be reading this if it were not for him.

The second instance falls under the category of "what a small world we live in." An ex-student contacted me a few years ago and said he would like to meet with me. I had been his sixth-grade trade teacher a quarter of a century before, and he wanted to talk to me about the good old days when I used to let him play guitar during recess in my class. He is now a famous musician who can be seen nightly on a late night show playing with the same enthusiasm I saw in that twelve-year-old.

He came out to my house, which is located 60 miles east of New York City, and we talked long into one Sunday night. He had taken out his guitar and played for me, and I was duly impressed with how far he had come since he had exhibited raw but untrained talent oh so long ago. Still struggling to regain some stability in my life after nearly six months of surgery and radiation treatment for a very aggressive form of cancer, his visit cheered me up in ways I can't explain. In this case, *music really was the doctor.* I thought back to all the students whose lives I had affected in over three decades of teaching and realized I had left an impression upon the world that went beyond my loving family and friends. No, I have not become a musical superstar, but I have a good life. No, make that a great life, and there is hopefully much more to come.

As he went to leave that night to go home to his wife and kids in Brooklyn, I asked him how he had happened to be on Long Island. Though raised in Holbrook, NY, Kirk now spends most of his time on tours or playing nightly with The Roots on the Tonight Show. He replied that he had just come back from taking his mother to a family function in Queens where most of his relatives lived. I asked him where in Queens he had been? His reply was simple.

"Oh, it's a place you probably never heard of . . . Cambria Heights."

Acknowledgments

"A Little Help from My Friends"
- *The Beatles*

<u>*The Music*</u> – I have been told it would be logical to limit the song titles to the sections of the book that are Johnny's journal. I agree. However, your humble author also believes he has a Music Doctor in *his* life so the titles just slipped in there on their own, and now they refuse to leave. The truth is that music inspired much of the writing in this story. During its creation, I would walk a few miles each morning while listening to my iPod. The music would speak to me, and I would return home and write pages to the plot based on a song title. The truth is that I was emotionally inspired by each note and word of the music that I heard . . . and always will be.

<u>*The Musicians*</u> – Every musician in this book is based on two or more real people. However, it must be understood that no one I ever played with was as evil as Frank or beaten down like Bracko. My mind created these scenarios even back when I was playing. If someone was late, I imagined a dramatic reason why. Most of this story is fiction tinged with perceptions of real life. If you ever meet me, ask what was real and what was not. I *might* remember, or not. My first band was indeed *The Ravens* and later *The Coming Generation*. I still have fond memories of my first venture into music with Charlie, Bob O., and Rick O. Later, with *Those Born Free,* I got to experience the glory of the performances at the Wollman Concert (complete with the "Gloria" fiasco) and the Café Wha. The harmonies of Cliff and Artie made us something special, and there was a guy named Frank in the band who was a good musician and good a person. The incarnation of that band that was crushed by the events at the Driftwood was named The Styx. For obvious reasons, I didn't use that name for the book (though we did have it first). The basis of that band was again Artie and Cliff's exceptional vocals (and Cliff was the

professional drummer that I described Jimmy Mac as being). I was on bass, but for reasons lost to time and memory, a variety of musicians manned the lead guitar and keyboard positions. Special thanks to Bill (PJ), Ricky B., Bob (Rocco), and Carl for sharing their talents with me.

The Stanners – What's a Stanner? The fictitious Bishop McCarthy High was based on the real Archbishop Molloy High School in Briarwood, Queens. Students who attend are called Stanners (long story). Over the course of the five-year edit of this book, five people were consistently there to help me with endless suggestions for changes and corrections. Two of these were family (see below), and three were "Stanners," but more importantly friends. James J. Spina (Jimmy) encouraged me to get this book out there. He endured the long process with ideas, opinions, and encouragement. Additionally, Jimmy *is* DJ Spinelli in both the real and imaginary senses of the character. Dennis Spina (Jimmy's brother) also contributed with edits and suggestions even though he has not seen me since he was fourteen years old and listening to me play the guitar in his basement. Robert (Bob, Rocco) Cappuccio has put in numerous hours not only encouraging me but also editing and fact-checking my story. His knowledge of music is boundless and kept me from including many inaccuracies in my book. (There are still some there that I excused with "poetic license" because they were vital to the story. In two cases, songs are sung that were not released prior to the date Those Born Free sang them–Go ahead find them!) Additionally, Bob, Robert, Rocco (he has many aliases) played briefly with Those Born Free and is the musical inspiration for Bracko (not the personal side of the fictional guitarist). The only time I ever picked up my bass after the Driftwood was to jam with him in his basement while we were in college. "Mr. Downchild," "Train Kept a-Rollin'," . . .

The Places - *Cambria Heights* – I was born and raised in Cambria Heights, and when my parents finally moved away in 1970, I stayed in the area for one more year to finish college. To get free tuition, I had to be a resident of New York City. I slept on quite a few couches of friends and relatives that year before finally relocating to Suffolk County for a teaching job. *"The Garden of Eden"* – There really was a garden in the schoolyard of P.S.147. However, I made up the name. I also fabricated the layout. Homeruns never went into the garden but instead away from it. *Key West, Sugarloaf Key, and Cudjoe Key* are my home away from home. However, as I am writing these final acknowledgments, Cudjoe and Sugarloaf have just been decimated by Hurricane Irma. Much of what I described is no longer there. (Though Mangrove Mama's survived).

The Family – No man is an island, and no writer exists in a bubble. Every moment of my existence is made enjoyable by the constant presence of my family. So, thanks for keeping me smiling through the good times and bad; Justin, Heather, Samantha, Jarrod, Erin, William, Bella, Mike, Ava, and especially my daughter Brittany who was so integral in creating this book. She was not only an editor but my harshest critic, pushing me hard to make changes that I too often resisted. The original forms of "Thief of My Forever" and "The Piano" were written by Brittany many years ago and remained so ingrained in my mind that they helped form many of the concepts in this book. And last but certainly not least, I would like to thank my wife Marilyn, my Maria. From the days in the Heights to our cross-country adventures in retirement, she has been there since 1964. Johnny and Maria's feelings are merely a mirror of our own. All that I am as a writer and a person comes from our life-long love. Love Ya!

Pat Dilandro - Friend and coworker, who left us way too soon. Besides my wife, Pat was the only person who has read every word that I have ever written, including this book and its sequel. Unfortunately, never again will I get to hear her words of wisdom.

Visible Ink – This arm of Memorial Sloan-Kettering offers a program for patients that encourages them to write. Founded by author Judith Kelman, *Visible Ink* publishes an anthology every year. A mentor is provided to each patient/writer to enhance his/her written work. A special thanks to my mentor, Keyan Kaplan who helped me in so many ways as a writer. A dozen pieces from the anthology were chosen for a live reading and performance at the Kaye Theater in NYC. "Pretty Flamingo," an excerpt from this book, was staged on April 18, 2018 (*Google* - Youtube-Visible Ink- Pretty Flamingo). Thanks to Greg Kachejian, artistic director for the event. He not only directed the entire production but also stayed in contact with me to offer valuable advice for all my endeavors. The Visible Ink organization of Memorial Sloan Kettering should be supported in its efforts to help patient/writers in their quest for creative outlets.

Killion Group – to Kim, Sara, and Jenn who helped finally put this book on paper.

The Past – Over one hundred agents rejected this book. I guess I would have been discouraged if it had not been for the fact that not a single one of them ever read a word I had written. Those that had the courtesy to even reply to my queries stated that the topic of the book held no interest for them. If you have gotten this far, you obviously disagree.

The Future -

SOUND OF REDEMPTION

Band in the Wind – Book 2

Now Available
in eBook and Paperback

———◆———

BandintheWind@gmail.com